My Alpha's Retribution

RISING FROM THE ASHES OF HIS VENGEANCE

BOOK 2

MOONLIGHT MUSE

My Alpha's Retribution

CONTENTS

A Fact to Hide

YILEYNA

NUMB… THAT WAS HOW I felt.

I was bound in silver with some sort of spell upon me down in the cells. My eyes were covered with a piece of cloth whilst my mouth and neck were bound with rope. I could barely breathe with how tight the rope was wrapped around my neck.

It was somehow… over. The future looked dark, but despite the agony within me, I refused to give up.

Theon was my mate. My fated mate… how had the goddess paired us? What was I being punished for?

The moment I had realised it, something had struck the back of my head. I remembered the white-hot pain erupting in my head, then I woke up, and I was here. How things had changed overnight…

The mind link, no one knew I had it, and even the silver didn't stop the voices pouring into my head, but I kept silent. For now, I didn't want anyone to know I had the link, and I could hear some of the pack members through it. They were mostly of women or those who weren't warriors.

The Silver Storm warriors were all in the cells around me. I had heard them earlier when I first came to. My sense of smell and hearing was far more sensitive than before as well. I don't know how I acquired the mind link without shifting… did this mean I had no wolf?

No… that couldn't be true.

I felt a faint presence within my mind, like an extra set of emotions… but it made no sense that I was able to feel the mate bond or get the link before a shift. Was it because I was a hybrid? Either way, I wouldn't complain. I would use the mind link to my benefit.

I needed to think of a way to protect our pack. The pack was my responsibility now. Who had we lost already? Was Charlene okay? Fear enveloped me at the very thought of something happening to my queen. The guards seemed to have signalled they had gotten away, and I hadn't seen them being brought back or even smelt them, so I hoped they had gotten far away.

Wait! What if Raiden and the others were in range of the mind link? My heart skipped a beat when the thought crossed my mind.

Raiden… Charlene? I tried calling through the bond.

What the… Yileyna? Raiden's voice answered. It sounded weak and hoarse. My stomach did a somersault in relief.

Thank the goddess…

You shifted? He asked softly.

No, but I broke the seal on my abilities. How are Charlene, Ryan, Gamma Grayson, and Rhys? I asked quickly.

Charlene and Ryan are still unconscious, Gamma Grayson is fine, and Rhys is okay, too, but how are you? My heart squeezed at the concern in his voice, but I was extremely happy to hear they were okay. I didn't want to worry them… I needed to make a plan.

I'm fine, just in the cells, but completely fine. They won't hurt me… when Charlene awakens, tell her to link me. She will fill you all in on everything. Are you all safe?

Yes, we are at -

Don't tell me, it's not safe, just take care of yourselves. The Obsidian Shadow Pack killed the Alpha and Luna… let Charlene know. Silence followed before Raiden spoke once more.

I will… Theon… he betrayed us. A flare of anger and pain rushed through me.

Yes, he did. This is all wrong. He may have thought the Obsidian Shadow Pack is innocent in all this, but that's far from true. He saw what his father did out there… Theoden Hale is a monster. I shuddered, remembering how he devoured the king's heart…

Yes, he is…

Theon asked me to join him the night of our engagement... I began before I quickly filled Raiden in on everything Theon had told me.

That's... he fucking pushed you. I could feel the anger in his voice. *The fact he was Theoden's son, how did the king not realise?*

Before Theoden killed the king, he said a simple charm was used on Theon... this man has access to some powerful magic, Raiden. Theon's aura... you should have felt it... the power that he's suppressed...

We need to get you out of there. You and our pack members.

No, Raiden, we cannot let Astalion fall into the hands of that monster. We need to derive - The sound of footsteps echoing reached my ears, and the delicious, intoxicating scent that belonged to Theon approaching filled my nose. *I got to go.* I cut the link, not waiting for a reply as I tried to calm my thundering heartbeat.

I heard the scrape of metal against metal before the door was opened, the hinges screeching before he walked in. I could feel the heat from his body as he stopped in front of me. Was it just me, or was his heart beating faster than it should? I felt him reach behind me and undo the rope that had been shoved into my mouth and wrapped around my neck. I gasped for air despite not wanting to show any sign of weakness in his presence.

I could feel his anger radiating off him, but I remained silent. If he was angry at me, I didn't care. If he was here to speak, he could, but it didn't mean I'd reply. I felt his fingers ghost along my stinging skin where the ropes had cut into my cheeks and the corners of my mouth, letting off intense sparks in his wake.

"Yileyna..."

I didn't respond. The pain in my chest was too much. The agony, the bitterness, and the despair I was beginning to feel were overwhelming. I didn't want him anywhere near me.

"Yileyna."

It hurt... the fact that he was also my mate... I didn't respond, and he exhaled in frustration.

"Dad wants to speak to you. I'm advising you to stay silent." His voice was so quiet I just about heard him. I smirked bitterly, glad he hadn't removed the blindfold. I don't know how I'd cope looking into those eyes.

"Why? Not like you care if he kills me, right?" I scoffed, feeling the sting in my eyes.

"He will make your life worse than death, don't push him, Yileyna." His voice was cold and hard.

"Yet you still see him as the innocent party in all of this. If he was a good person, why would you need to warn me to behave?" I cocked a brow.

"I already told you the truth, yet you didn't care to listen," he said coldly, yanking the blindfold from my eyes. My eyes met his cold amber ones, and I wondered how such a warm colour even managed to look so cold.

"I listened. I just refused to become a traitor. I asked the king for his version, too. Did your father ever tell you that Andres protected your mother in battle against the Dark Ones? I'm not saying the king was right, but there's always more than one version of a story, but it doesn't matter, right? Anyway, congratulations, Theon Hale. I hope you're proud of your accomplishment," I replied bitterly. His eyes flashed, but he simply looked away.

"Andres is dead. His word doesn't really count anymore, now, does it?"

We simply stared at each other. I hoped he saw the anger and hatred for him in my eyes. He unhooked me from the wall, my wrists still bound in silver chains. I almost fell forward, but he caught me around the waist, and I gasped, jerking away from his touch at the sparks that coursed through me. If I thought touching Theon before was mind-blowing... these sparks...

I looked up at him, but there was no change in him at all. How could he feel this yet not even react? He took hold of my wrist, looking at the marks the silver was making.

"Silver doesn't affect you as badly as it does werewolves..." he muttered. I pulled free, giving him a contemptuous glare. Whatever they had done to me was weighing down on me, even if silver didn't have the effect they wanted.

"Are my powers sealed?" I asked coldly as he took me by my arm, leading me from the cell.

"No, we don't have magic that strong."

Hmm, so if I tried, I could break whatever this was? He held on to me as we made our way through the dungeons. I almost laughed at the fact the ice still coated the walls and floor.

"Nice castle. Don't feel too cold, do you?" I asked, making him glare at me.

"You spared nothing."

"Neither did you," I replied coldly. "What did you do with Andrea, Zoe, and Gamma Henry?"

"You don't need to worry about them."

I clenched my jaw but said nothing. I'd try to mind-link them later... but I had a feeling they would be bound in silver if they were alive. I hoped they were...

"Dad does not have patience, Yileyna... for your own sake, don't anger him," he warned me again before he pushed open the doors to the courtroom. *Like you care anyway.*

There he was, Theoden Hale sitting upon the king's throne, one leg draped over the arm, a cigar in hand, and a young woman leaning at his feet, holding a bowl of fruit. His amber eyes turned upon us as we entered, and he watched like a predator would watch its prey. His eyes didn't move until we stopped before him.

"So, this is the heart of our world," he said, motioning for the Omega woman to move aside. Our eyes met, but I refused to look down in respect, glaring coldly at him. "She's a feisty one, and clearly, she doesn't know how to submit. I can feel her aura, but you said she has not shifted yet?"

"Yeah," Theon said emotionlessly.

"Make sure she doesn't shift. Keep her filled with wolfsbane. I wouldn't trust it. Even with her being a hybrid, there's still a chance she could shift," Theoden said, his deep, cold voice echoing in the silent room. "And we don't know what type of hybrid she is either, do we?" Theoden stood up, and my heart thudded as he closed the gap between us.

"No, Andres never mentioned it," Theon replied curtly.

It took my all not to look at him in surprise. Why didn't he tell his father I was part Siren? Despite the confusion that settled within me, I remained indifferent, keeping my gaze on the approaching man. He grabbed hold of my face, turning it sharply to the left and then to the right.

"Maybe Fae... she'll need training before we put her to use. You know it's never said anywhere how the heart will benefit us, but she needs to learn to control her powers, regardless. Arabella will know how to keep her under control." For the first time, he looked down and spoke directly at me. "Listen here, you may be the heart of Kaeladia, but you are still the bastard's child. One wrong move, and I will kill you and the rest of the Silver Storm Pack, one by one. Remember that."

"You said Alpha Andres was a bad person... but can you guarantee you will be a better king and leader?" I asked challengingly. "You are already threatening the lives of innocent people."

I was suddenly backhanded across the face so hard I fell to the floor, my head bursting with pain and my vision blackening at the force behind that swing. I could feel blood trickle down my forehead where his ring had split open my skin.

I took a deep breath, trying to let the pain ease up, when I felt a flutter of electrifying sparks go through my back. I turned to Theon, who was looking up at his father. Despite the emotionless expression on his face, his eyes were hard.

"I'll take her if you're done," he said tersely. Theoden's eyes flashed, and he raised an eyebrow.

"I will initiate you back into the Pack tomorrow," he said dangerously. I don't know what that was about, but Theoden was angry.

"Get up," Theon commanded me emotionlessly, and I got to my feet.

"Take her to the room prepared for her," he hissed.

We left the hall, and I saw groups of werewolves walking, carrying large barrels and chests. So, the Obsidian Shadow Pack were moving in already. Neither Theon nor I spoke as he held me by my arm and guided me down the hall.

I frowned, realising we were walking towards the old Beta quarters, a place I once called home... *Oh, how times have changed...*

To my dismay, Theon stopped outside the very door to those quarters and unlocked it. Instantly, I could feel the magic in here. Whatever they had done was powerful, and it was weaved through every inch of this place.

"Why here?" I asked icily as memories flooded me. He didn't reply, stepping inside and shutting the door behind him. I saw him lock it and noticed how his aura seemed to lessen drastically.

"Does it matter?"

I just gave him a cold glare in reply as I turned away from him. I gasped when he took hold of my arm once again, letting a storm of electrifying sparks rush through me. I needed to learn to get used to those...

I saw him frown slightly at my reaction. How was it he didn't even seem bothered? I guess he really didn't have any emotions left...

I looked away from him as he brushed my hair up and examined what I knew was a bruise forming from Theoden's hit.

"I told you not to piss him off," he said quietly, his voice devoid of emotions.

"I said one sentence. If the monster can't take the truth, that is not my problem." His eyes narrowed at my words, but I raised an eyebrow.

"You don't want him catching you saying that."

"Tell me, Theon, am I not right? What happened out there... was that not enough to show that he is a monster? Oh, and one more question..." I stepped closer, despite not wanting to touch him again. "If you truly think I'm wrong... then why didn't you tell him I'm part Siren?"

He tensed, clearly not expecting me to ask him that. His cold eyes met mine before he stepped closer so we were only inches apart. But it was his words that truly shocked me...

"Because my mother and sister were killed by a Siren... he won't care if you are the heart or not. So, unless you want to lose your head, you might want to keep that little piece of information a secret."

A Broken Promise

YILEYNA

KILLED BY A SIREN… I was unable to ignore the pang of pain that washed through me. No matter what he had done, his mother and sister were not a part of it, and my heart broke for them. So, that was why Theon held so much hatred towards the sirens. This war between our species had gone on for far too long. How long would the two species carry on like this? What started it? Was there a way to end it all?

I didn't let my emotions show, and instead, I raised my eyebrow challengingly, trying not to be drowned by his scent.

"Well, I'm sure you will at least be pleased when I lose my head," I replied icily, turning away from him.

Deep down, I was unable to shake off the fact that he had warned me about his father and was telling me to keep my heritage a secret from him. Was there a part of Theon that knew his father was wrong? Was there anything in him that I could justify?

"I'm warning you. From tomorrow, I will take you to train as Dad wishes. Be on your best behaviour, Yileyna, because no one is here to play."

"No promises," I muttered, wanting him to just leave. I could no longer feel my abilities in here, almost as if whatever was in the air was sucking it away. I heard him walk towards the door, and he paused.

"You could have tried to run when I took you to Dad… why didn't you?" He asked quietly. I frowned, confusion hitting me at his question, and I turned to look at him.

I hadn't even considered it. After all, how could I when there were so many of our people here? This wasn't just about me.

"I won't abandon my people. I'm Alpha, now, remember?" I replied coldly.

"You are no use as an Alpha if you don't take the hard path and make sacrifices. Sometimes you have to let those beneath you suffer the consequences of an action that would ultimately favour the rest…. Dad assumed the same. He didn't think you would risk running away when he has those you care for hidden away. One wrong move, and he will kill them. Remember that…" I frowned, hating how he was talking as if this was just a light conversation. "Oh, and one more thing… it's funny that not once did you ask about Charlene. How did you know she's not here?" My heart skipped a beat, but I simply glared coldly at him.

"Because I made sure they were taken away," I shot back.

"Yet they didn't take you."

"As I said, I'm the Alpha," I replied, clenching my jaw.

That may have seemed like a distant statement at one point, but now the meaning of it was embedded into me, weighing down on me with the sheer truth that I was indeed in charge of the Silver Storm Pack and that it was my duty to protect them. To find a solution for all of this.

"You're crazy," he said before he opened the door and stepped out, leaving me alone.

I sighed heavily, looking around the empty place. It was stripped of everything. It had been cleaned up, but there was no furnishing left here. At least I wasn't bound to one spot.

If Theoden thought I would be this meek, obedient doll for him to use, then he had another thing coming. But for now, I needed to think of a plan properly. This didn't just involve me but everyone…

Was I enough? Was I doing the right thing? Will I manage to do something? *Okay, breathe…*

I took a deep breath, slumping down against the wall and staring at the ice-covered floors. A plan…

Raiden? Charlene? Ryan? I called through the link.

Nothing. So this room blocked my mind link.

Fine, I'll think of a plan and then when I'm out of this room, I'll contact them. If they were still close enough to mind-link... it was risky for them to be so close as well, but I did need to communicate. We needed to think it over.

What do I do... What do I do...

Should I try to kill Theoden Hale? Was this endless cycle of killing for revenge and victory the right thing? No, it wasn't.

I needed to get through to Theon. Something told me that I needed him on my side to stop this cycle, for him to realise that his father may not be who he portrayed to be. I rested my head against the wall, trying to think over everything that had happened. My heart squeezed at Theon's words on the balcony.

"Please..."

Theon never said please. I wanted to say he cared somewhat, even if everything he had done was unforgivable.

This wasn't about him and me. That was long over, even if he was my mate.

I sat forward, crossing my legs as I tapped the icy floor with my nails, wondering why no one had de-iced the castle, or at least some of the rooms. I shook my head, pushing the unnecessary thought away.

Theon was behind everything that happened to my parents... and I could never forgive him for it. However, I needed to follow my instincts and prove to him that Theoden was a monster, otherwise, this cycle of hatred would never end. I had to put an end to this game of power over a title and throne, and I would do it the right way, even if it was going to be extremely difficult. For that, I needed to try to get through to Theon, something that was going to be almost impossible, as well as extremely painful for me, knowing that he was my mate who had ruined everything. I never thought I'd ever find my mate, but the moon goddess had other plans...

I stood up, pacing the room as I pondered over everything I had learned, from what Andres said to Theoden's version... someone was in the wrong, or there was a misunderstanding.

One thing was clear – Theon was vital in this plan. He was the Alpha of the Obsidian Shadow Pack after his father. I refused to believe that there was no part of Theon that didn't care. In his own way, he had looked out for me, and I had no choice but to hold on to that. I needed to show him the truth of his father's wrongs, but the most important question was, how do I do that?

I ran my hand through my hair, glancing around the room as if it would give me the answers.

Something told me if I wanted, I'd be able to break out of here as well. Didn't Theoden tell Theon to keep me full of wolfsbane and silver? Theon wasn't careless, I just wished I knew what exactly was going through his mind…

Do I pretend to be on his side? Or was it too late to do so? Or more importantly, would I be able to pretend to when my heart had been crushed by him?

Goddess, what do I do?

THEON

Nothing went the way I had wanted it to… nothing.

As I walked through the iced halls, ice that no mage or fae had been able to get rid of, I sighed inwardly. Seeing her bound so roughly in the cells had angered me, but how do I tell her without making it obvious that she needed to leave from here?

Things weren't as I thought… Dad was hell-bent on his revenge, and it was justified, but seeing the way Yileyna, who was innocent in all of this, was treated, didn't sit right with me. It fucking hurt, and I wished I had managed to get her away, but there had been no way for me to do that.

Seeing Hunter in Westerwell had thrown me; although I had been raised in secrecy since our Pack was already considered a rogue or criminal pack, there were still a few who knew who I was. Not even the enchantment on me would blind those who knew who I truly was. Hunter and I weren't exactly on good terms… but he hadn't said anything.

After I had knocked Yileyna unconscious and the party had come to an end due to the staged attack, I had met up with him. His words still niggled at the back of my mind, and I knew Dad wouldn't approve, but I needed to see him again.

"Theon."

Fuck, I didn't hear him again.

"Dad," I said indifferently, turning.

"You seem far more distracted than you once used to be… tell me, has being under Andres's command lessened your sense of vigilance? Moments of distraction can cause you to lose your head or heart," he said, his hard eyes on me.

"I was thinking about the ice," I lied, not wanting him to push me further. He seemed to have bought it.

"Powerful magic," he said, knocking against the ice wall. Even with his strength, it didn't crack or chip. "Imagine shields or armour of such calibre…"

"Yeah," I responded. "What is your plan from here? We have Westerwell, the city and the kingdom have been notified that we have taken over. Now what?"

"You seem in a rush. You know it's not that easy. We need the other packs to accept me as the king, and for that, we need the heart."

"Do we really need her? We are strong enough without her."

"The marriage still needs to take place. You need to mark her, train her, and then we will reveal the prophecy to the world. When people know that we have the prophesied one by our side, they will bow to us." I wouldn't mark her. Ever.

I nodded.

"I see, so you want me to train and mark her so we can use her… efficiently?"

"Yes, exactly."

"She's the heart, I don't think she's made to be controlled."

Our eyes met, but I didn't look away. I hated how he was observing me as if he was looking into my soul. He looked away after a moment and nodded, once again examining the iced-over walls.

"You are right. We need her to obey. Arabella has already said her powers are far too strong to contain… if she wanted to, she could break out of those quarters, but she seems naïve. Otherwise, I don't think she'd still be here." *Maybe, but in this case, she's too fucking concerned for others.*

"Hmm, most likely."

"But we can't have her chained… it may just trigger her… we need to do this wisely. As long as you keep her heavily dosed on silver and wolfsbane, she will be weakened to an extent. You seem to care for her anyway. Perhaps you can use that to seduce her to our side?" He suggested so nonchalantly, as if we were discussing the weather, but I didn't miss the subtle remark about caring for her.

"I did as you said, however, the attack that took place took away the chance for me to mark her… and then, of course, everything went down," I reminded him emotionlessly.

"Ah yes, that… attack…" He turned to me, running his fingers through his beard. "It was a rather interesting one, wouldn't you agree? I wonder what the assailant's attempt was… knocking the Alpha princess out instead of killing her."

I nodded, not giving away anything. I wasn't stupid. I knew Dad wasn't the type to buy just any story. I frowned, placing a slightly thoughtful expression on my face.

"Hunter was there," I said, making Dad freeze. His heart skipped a beat, and he turned to me sharply.

Perfect.

"Hunter…" His eyes blazed and he punched the wall, yet despite the cracking sound of his knuckles, the ice didn't move or break.

"I'm not certain if it was him, but it could have been. He knows of the prophecy after all."

"That bastard…" Dad thundered with rage. "He has done nothing but thwart my plans!"

"He's never liked Andres either. I think he's neutral," I reminded him.

"No, but it does not mean he isn't a bastard! No matter what I attempt, he doesn't fucking die."

Attempt? My head snapped towards him, my eyes flashing with surprise.

"Have you tried to get rid of him?" I asked sharply.

"Of course, he knows far too much," he spat. It took my all to contain the emotions that wreaked havoc inside of me. Gold eyes met orange, and I was unable to stop the burning anger that accompanied the statement that left my lips.

"You promised Mom you would never touch him."

CRASPING ONTO HOPE

THEON

*H*IS ANGER WAS OBVIOUS as he glared at me with complete rage.

"So now you care what happens to him?" He hissed.

"No, I don't. But he is still her son," I shot back coldly.

"She's dead. She doesn't know what's happening here," his cold reply came, his chest heaving as he fought his anger.

"It's about being loyal to her and honouring your word. You know when it comes to Mom I won't let it slide. You are not to touch him. No matter how much he becomes a thorn in our side, he will not be touched. Understood?" His features began morphing as he fought himself from shifting, lunging to grab hold of me, but I raised my arm, my own eyes flashing in warning. "I told you; I will obey you, and I am… but when it comes to an oath given to Mom… I won't tolerate it."

I had mentioned Hunter to divert the conversation for me, but I hadn't expected him to want him out of the picture.

"Then you better obey me properly, because I'm beginning to see a change in the man that I sent on this mission… you drugging so many of Andres's closest as if you did not want them to lose their lives…"

I didn't react, but I knew why I kept them alive… because Yileyna needed someone. That bastard Raiden…. Ryan… and, of course, Charlene, who was like a part of her soul. Annoying. I couldn't deny that I had fallen for the one woman I shouldn't have… but I had, and no matter what I did, I couldn't stop myself from worrying about her. Even the poison I was giving her was such a low dose. I wanted her to break away, to get far away from here, but she was far too stupid and stubborn to do that.

"You confuse me. You said you need this city and the packs to accept us. By killing everyone, how would that win you points? Care to explain? I thought it was a smart move to keep those who were once in power alive. However, if you want me to go behead Henry and the two Gamma females, I will willingly do so," I said, ready to walk off when Dad raised his hand.

"No. You are correct. I'm sorry, son, but we have spent a lot of time apart. You seem to have more… emotion than you did two years ago when Iyara died -"

"Was killed," I corrected, remembering it was an attack by Andres… seeing her body lying there… her heart ripped from it. She had been missing her leg, and her neck had had a chunk bitten right out. The stinging pain when I remembered it was still there…

"Yes, by Andres. However, you didn't seem to care, only wanting revenge… I fear this woman may change you -"

"How? I was ready to burn her, how exactly did I show compassion?" I asked, my eyes flashing.

I hated how it fucking got to me that he seemed to see right through me. I was fucking hiding how I felt. The urge to knock some sense into her dumb blonde head and drag her from here was so fucking compelling… and the way she reacted since everything went down, she would jerk and pull away from me as if my touch burnt her.

I guess I should have expected it. I betrayed her, was the reason her parents were dead, and more… I had tried to burn her… I threw that match knowing I had to prove to him that I didn't care, and I hoped that it was enough to be the final trigger to break her seal. I had relied on the power of her love for me and broke her faith entirely to unleash her powers. Those moments had been some of the hardest moments of my life.

"True… true… perhaps I am just on edge. We may have this city, but we are not acknowledged yet. If the packs rally upon us, we are in the centre -"

"And we can be cornered from all sides, but you killed Andres and there were witnesses to show you are the new Alpha. As long as everyone learns the truth of what Andres did years ago, people will see we weren't in the wrong."

He didn't reply and I frowned slightly, turning my head as I watched him. Was it just me, or did I sense a flicker of unease from him?

"Of course. But still, we need to be careful. Win her over and make sure she is ours," he commanded before he turned and walked away.

There was no chance for that anymore… no matter how much I may want it. I chose vengeance and justice for my pack and family, and the price… the price was the most fucking precious thing of all; Yileyna's heart.

Deep down, a selfish question arose, but I refused to acknowledge it. This is the path that I have walked for over a decade, and no matter if I strayed, I was now back on it. All who caused my family and pack injustice would pay.

YILEYNA

"Get up."

My heart thundered, and my eyes flew open to realise I had fallen asleep on the floor. I looked around as Theon pulled me upright, his touch bringing me back to reality.

The fire I had been dreaming about was fresh in my mind. I looked around, realising it was still dark outside, before I turned my attention to Theon, who was looking at me intensely, his heart seemingly thudding loudly.

"What are you staring at?" I asked coldly, pulling free from his hold that was making my mind go blank.

"Nothing." It was something, but he looked away, standing up from where he had been crouched by my side. "Come. I brought you food, clothes, and toiletries. You can bathe, change, and then we'll go train." He turned the light on, and I looked at him.

My heart skipped a beat when I realised he had just showered. His skin still glistened with water which meant he had come here straight after. His white T-shirt with a V-neck showed his toned, defined collar bones, and when he swallowed, his Adam's apple bopped.

"Yileyna," he growled.

I blinked, realising I was staring. I turned away, grabbing the bag that was on the floor. Without another word, I walked into the bathroom. Looking in the mirror, I stared at the grime on my face and the stains in my hair. He said we were to train. I had a list to relay to Raiden and the others when I was out of these quarters.

I showered swiftly, organising my thoughts before I brushed my teeth and stepped out of the shower, towelling myself dry. I rummaged in the bag and realised Theon had gotten my clothes... so he had gone down to the inn?

I pulled on the red lingerie and put on the black pants, tunic, and a black corset before I ran a comb through my wet hair and stepped out into the living area. Theon was staring out the window but turned when I approached. He motioned to the brown bag that sat on one of the empty boxes to the side with a jerk of his head.

"Eat, then we'll go."

I wanted to deny him, but I was ravenous. I sat down on the icy floor, intrigued as to why it was not melting. Was it the intense cold outside? It must be...

I opened the bag and took out a wrapped toasty, and bit into it. Chicken from Madam Marigold's. Did that mean everyone was allowed to get back to work?

"Is the city carrying on as normal?" I asked coldly.

"They have been given the command to. Aside from the warriors who are imprisoned, the city will carry on under a new Alpha." Some Alpha Theoden was.

"Then... why not simply remove everyone from the Silver Storm Pack from the city? Let them relocate?"

"After Andres forced the Obsidian Shadow Pack into hiding? Why should we be merciful?" He replied coldly, not even looking at me.

"So by acting just like him, how are you any better? Let them go." He turned to me, crossing his arms as his eyes bore into mine.

"Stand by my side, and we can combine the packs under one law, one pack."

There was a time, long ago, where perhaps a younger Yileyna would have become giddy at the thought of running a pack by Theon's side. A dream of a happily ever after, but there was no happily ever after in reality.

"I'm afraid it's too late for that... because this isn't about you and me. It's about your betrayal, and the one who is using you as his puppet." I turned away, only for him to grab me by the arm, yanking me back around. His eyes flashed as he glared at me.

"I am not a puppet."

"Aren't you?" I replied coldly, ignoring the delicious currents that rippled through me. He clenched his jaw, and I pulled free. "And… don't touch me without my consent."

Our eyes met, his anger rising before he brushed past, picking up some chains of silver that I had not noticed before and shackling me before opening the door.

"Let's go," he hissed, his voice dripping murderously, but it didn't affect me.

The moment I stepped out into the hall, I felt the link open. I closed myself off, focusing on Raiden, Charlene, Gamma Grayson, and Ryan.

Hello?

Yileyna! Gamma Grayson's voice came.

Yileyna! Oh, my goddess! I almost smiled at Charlene's voice, trying to hide the emotions from my face as I kept my gaze on the ground and followed Theon.

Hey… Ryan's voice.

Yileyna, you vanished yesterday.

I'm okay. I was kept in a secluded room that cuts off my mind link. They don't realise silver isn't working on me. I don't have long; from what I know, Gamma Henry, Andrea and Zoe are safe, but they are held and bound by silver. Thank the gods, Grayson murmured. **Charlene filled us in on how you are the heart. I knew of that prophecy, well, parts of it. Yileyna, you can do this. You are the heart, and this is your duty.**

Well, good luck. While you're at it, kick your ex-boyfriend's fucking dick. Hard, Ryan growled, clearly not happy with the turn of events. Charlene and Raiden chuckled, and I suppressed my smile.

I'll try if I get the chance. They want to train me to use my powers. I'm going to try to pretend that I'm giving in, but we need to gather our allies… Gamma Grayson, will you be able to go to our most trusted allies? Also, I know it's risky, but is there a chance any of you can get in touch with Zarian?

Your wish is my command, Alpha. I will reach out to them. We will travel carefully. As for Zarian… we can try. Can he be trusted?

I think he can. It's worth a try... I will try to ask Theon if I can get in touch with him, but I'm not sure they will allow me.

Fear not, we will try our best. After turning to our allies, what do you wish to do?

First, I need to know the numbers. I will be honest, Andres was not a good king, but Theoden gives me a darker vibe... he seems far more dangerous. Tell our allies about the heart of Kaeladia, I want them to know of the prophecy that has been hidden for so long. If they know there's hope, they will willingly help us. Or our true allies will, at least.

Yileyna... if we leave from here... it means we won't get to mind-link... Raiden's concerned voice came. My stomach sank, but there was no other choice...

I know. But I'll be okay. Just... stay safe.

A silence fell before Ryan spoke once more.

Well, we'll try to get in touch with the Fae first, get in touch with you either way, and then move on to finding our allies.

Perfect. Raiden, from this day forth, you are my Beta... Ryan and Gamma Grayson, you are both Gammas.

You need to stop saying Gamma, Grayson's voice came.

We were already leaving the palace grounds, walking through the snow, but every step I took I realised the snow was spreading away, letting my feet touch the stone ground beneath.

I can't change old habits. Charlene... my queen, you will always be my queen. Stay safe, okay?

I will, my angel, you take care, too. You are in the lion's den right now.

I'll manage, I replied before I blocked everyone off, hoping I was focusing only on Charlene. Who can hear me?

I can, Charlene replied. Yileyna, no one else can.

Good... I wasn't sure if I was doing this right. It comes pretty easily, doesn't it?

Yeah, it does.

Tell him the truth, Charlene... Gamma Grayson is a good man... and although it might trouble him a little, he deserves to know, and you deserve to talk about this. Silence followed as Theon watched me, frowning. I simply ignored him, following emotionlessly.

I... I'll think about it. Thank you, Yileyna, she replied quietly.

Take care. Theon's watching.

We ended the link, and Theon's gaze bore into me.

"For a moment there, it was almost like you were mind-linking." His calm sinister words made my heart skip a beat as our eyes met...

Breaking My Limits

YILEYNA

I RAISED AN EYEBROW.

"I wish I could. If you forgot, I don't have a wolf, nor is it possible when I'm bound in silver." I raised my shackled wrists, giving him a dirty look.

"But silver hasn't brought you to your knees as it should now, has it?" He remarked. I couldn't let him know the truth, and I simply shrugged.

"Think whatever you want."

He didn't respond as he watched me calculatingly, clenching his jaw. I knew Theon, and sadly he knew me. He had been around us for so long, and he often knew what I would be up to. For the first time, I wished he didn't know me as well as he did. To my surprise, he didn't bother me any further, glancing to the left fleetingly before we continued on.

"Don't you think it's foolish to have me only bound by a little silver and a few suppression spells?" I asked instead, hoping to divert the conversation from any suspicion he may have.

"No, because the moment you try to escape, I will give the signal and they will kill the Gamma females." My blood ran cold at his words, and I frowned.

"So then, why were you surprised that I didn't run?" I spat angrily.

"Because you didn't know of the consequences, so I expected you to," he said, and I saw him glance to the left once again. Was someone there?

"Fear not, I know I won't get far. I know Theoden has enchanters on his side." I wanted to say a lot more, but I wasn't going to risk anyone becoming an example to teach me a lesson.

"Good," he replied before we finally reached a large area within the walls of Westerwell. So, he was not going to take me out beyond the walls. That made sense, they had only secured this city…

"Zarian was a good teacher; can you not summon him?"

"No. I'm teaching you," he said curtly. "Come at me… let's see what you are capable of."

"So, I can attack without anyone getting killed because of my actions, correct?" I asked.

"Yeah, do your worst."

Oh, I will…

He unchained me and stepped back, his eyes on me. I jumped forward, feeling the blazing power rippling through me, but deep down, something told me not to show the true extent of my abilities. I kept it pulled back as I sent a wave of ice shards at him. He ducked before he lunged. In a flash, he was in front of me.

All those emotions that I felt were raging inside of me, and I wanted to hurt him… I wanted him to feel what I felt.

I threw a punch at him, a blast of wind throwing him back. His eyes flashed as he grabbed the metal cuffs and chain, using it as a weapon as he swung it at me. I blocked with a wall of ice before I broke through it, kicking him straight in the stomach. The impact felt satisfying as he was thrown to the ground, the snow beneath him cushioning his fall. He was up in a flash, his aura raging around him, and I could see the faint glow around him. What was that?

"Nice kick. Let's see how many more you get in."

With those words, he grabbed me by the arm, flipping me over and tossing me over his shoulder. Twisting, I landed on my feet, the snow erupting in a cloud around me, and our eyes met before we both ran at one another at the same time.

Years of fighting and trying my best were ingrained into me, but with the speed, strength, and agility that I now possessed, I felt far more powerful than I ever had before. At the last moment, I flipped, sending a blinding flash of lightning at him, forcing him to step back, but he didn't back down. To my surprise, he raised his forearm, that amber glow weaving around him like fire as the lightning struck the fire-like shield that encased his arm. What the....

"Surprised?"

"No," I lied as I backed away, watching him. He smirked as he lowered his arm.

"You don't know me as well as you thought," he said as I felt a wave of energy roll off him.

"No, I don't know you at all," I said quietly, the stinging pain of his betrayal returning with full force. "Let's train."

I felt the dark power in the shadows, and I knew it was strong magic. Was it the one behind these spells that helped Theoden?

Not another word was spoken between us as we began exchanging blow after blow…

I had held back, knowing that Theon and those who were watching from the shadows had their eyes on me. For the next two weeks, Theon pushed me to my limits. The training would continue in three steps, and the first part was always in the open ground at the edge of Westerwell before we would return to the training barracks of the warriors, a place that now teemed with Obsidian Shadow Pack warriors. However, the moment Theon and I would enter, they would clear out. This was the only place I never felt eyes upon me.

The ice castle remained covered in ice, and I heard whispers of the unrest that was passing through the kingdom. Questions of the magic that enveloped the castle arose, and although Theon didn't know, the ice became my sense.

I was slowly able to sense where everyone was. Only when I was in our old Beta quarters did it diminish. I often wondered if there was a way to break those warriors free, but I didn't because, until now, Gamma Henry, Andrea, and Zoe were not accounted for.

I had heard fleetingly from Raiden and the others saying Zarian was nowhere in sight, and they had not managed to locate him, so they had left. They would gather whatever help they could. With the Obsidian Shadow

Pack not really venturing from the city, I knew they would be okay. With their departure, I lost the last remaining contact I had with anyone who truly cared. I did reach out to a few of the pack members I recognised through the link, but so far, they were under full lockdown as well.

I saw Theoden thrice, and each time my anger only rose. The first time he was beating a man, and I had felt the bond snap, realising it was one of my men that he had killed, but Theon had dragged me away before I could even speak. The second time, he had lit ablaze a small clothing store, but I had no idea why, and Theon refused to tell me. The third time, he had been walking through the city of Westerwell with a crown upon his head as if he was king.

Theon remained cold, indifferent, and passive. Every day he pushed me to my limits, and it was a struggle knowing I had to hold back. At times I felt like he knew that I was doing that, but he didn't question it, simply criticising my weaker points. Every day doing as he asked became easier, and although we were enemies, he was an impressive teacher, even though it was painful to see him daily. Every time we'd touch, that bond tugged at my heart, and I was unable to stop the pain from tearing me up inside.

After the first part of our hand-to-hand combat, combined with our abilities, we would come to the indoor training areas. That's where we were today, and as usual, it was eerily empty. Like usual, we spent thirty minutes of weapon training before Theon tossed his sword to the ground. My top had several slashes, and his shirt was half hanging off him from the intense session. He pinned my wrists to the ground, straddling me. Our hearts thundered at the proximity we were in.

Our eyes met, and the moment his eyes flickered gold, I pushed him off, moving away quickly. He backed away, his gaze as cold as ever, yet his breathing was heavy. We were both sweating, and I was exhausted.

"Not too shabby," he said emotionlessly before reaching for the hem of his shirt and pulling it up and over his head, making my heart thunder. His inked skin was glistening with sweat, and every breath he took made his muscles ripple. I forced my gaze away, frowning deeply as he tossed the shirt aside.

He had lied and betrayed me. Every time I saw him, it was all I could think of. I hated how the mate bond pulled us together, and the urge to reject him was niggling at me… it wasn't like the bond mattered to him. Not once had he acknowledged it.

He walked to the far end of the training hall, returning with two bottles of water. He held one out to me before taking the lid off the other and chugging it down.

"Now for the main training... your abilities." I took a few thirsty gulps of the cold water before looking up at him icily.

"I still think someone with elemental power will be better," I remarked, remembering that hot, flame-like energy that had surrounded him whenever we sparred. "What is that ability you have?" I couldn't help but ask. He seemed to hesitate as if considering whether he should answer me or not.

"It's none of your concern," he remarked coldly. "Get up. How about we start with you melting the layer of ice you have coated the entire castle in?"

"I like the ice," I remarked, "and besides, I told you, I don't know how."

"Well, right now, it's not about what you like. It's been long enough, remove the ice." I frowned.

Theon was in his father's pack once again, and I hated the fact that all conversations between him and others when I was around were through the link.

"Ask nicely," I almost spat.

"I don't do nice," he replied with equal venom.

The moment back on the balcony when he had said 'please' returned to me, and our eyes met. Do I try to get close to him, get answers, and try to show him the truth? The risk of getting hurt tore me up inside, but I needed to make allies from within... I needed to remove the mask from his eyes, but how do I do it without getting hurt in the process?

UNLEASHING IT ALL

YILEYNA

"Then... if I manage to remove the ice, will that count as a lesson taught and accomplished?" I asked, standing up. He narrowed his eyes at my softer tone.

"Maybe." He tossed the empty bottle aside.

"Can I ask a question regarding something you mentioned?" I asked, stepping closer despite the pain that threatened to suffocate me.

"What is it?" He asked quietly, his voice deeper as he looked down at me.

"Will you tell me everything? From how you were forced into hiding to how your mother and sister died?" I pushed gently.

Put aside your own pain, Yileyna, try to reach the man deep inside, a man who showed he did care...

"It's a little late for that, don't you think?" He replied coldly, turning his back on me. I stared at his broad chiselled back, ignoring the pull of the mate bond, and placed a hand on his back. Was it wrong that I wanted to use the mate bond to get him to listen?

"Please?" He tensed, and I could feel the anger radiating off him.

"Double standards, don't you think?" He spat, stepping away from my touch and glaring coldly at me over his shoulder. "I don't need to tell you anything. It changes nothing. We're done for the day."

I guess I was the only one who seemed to be affected by the mate bond. He strode toward the doors before pausing mid-way and turning his head slightly.

"There is something I do want to tell you…" My heart skipped a beat, and I wondered what it could be.

"What is it?"

"That night of the rogue attack that the Obsidian Shadow Pack staged, it was pre-planned. Every little detail of it right down to the specific target…"

"Target?" I asked hoarsely, remembering the massacre of that night and the bloodied bodies that littered the ground. "So many died that night." The pain of that night would never leave me… now accompanied by another similar one. I was beginning to hate fire. Every time I saw it, it brought those painful memories to the forefront of my mind.

"Yeah, they did, but there were only two main targets. The rest were just caught in the attack… I made sure these two targets would be there at the forefront."

Two…

My stomach churned sickeningly as a dreaded thought came to me. My heart clenched as his words echoed in my mind. *Guaranteed to be there…*

What was he telling me? What did it have to do with me?

"Who were they?" I asked quietly.

"Who else? None other than William and Hana De'Lacor." I closed my eyes, refusing to allow the emotions to show as a single tear escaped down my cheek. "I knew where you and Charlene would be… I knew of your visits to the White Dove. I knew you'd investigate, and the love your parents had for you… I knew they'd follow you, and when they did, they would be the first in the line of fire. With their deaths, I removed Andres' closest confidant from his side and instead stepped into the place that William De'Lacor left empty."

My chest was heaving as I stared at his back. That storm of emotions inside of me was screaming to come out. How could he? How could he speak as if it was no big deal? How many more secrets and lies was he going to kill me with?

I couldn't hold back.

"Not only did you frame them and plan that attack… *you murdered them!*" I screamed as the pulsing in my head heightened.

Theon turned as the entire ground erupted, the soil moving in waves as a violent wind whipped around me. My aura surged and blasted the roof above us right off. The weather was chaos. Bolts of lightning flashed in the darkening sky, striking down on Theon, who was forced back, a shield of that amber glow energy shielding him, but nothing could stop me. I wanted him dead.

"Yileyna…"

His eyes met mine, and I saw a flash of an emotion I couldn't place as I advanced on him. Long, thin shards of ice rained down on him as I felt the darkness of Theoden's enchanter approaching, but I didn't care. All I could think of was how Theon should die.

"I hate you!" I hissed, seeing the long claw nails on my hands. They were not the thick claws of a werewolf, but the long, thin claws of a siren…

My skin seemed to have changed, a faint hue of silvery blue covering it. I lunged at him, digging my claws into his chest. He grabbed my wrist, but I refused to remove my hand from his chest, not caring as blood spilt down my hand and his body. He was looking at me as if it was the first time he had seen me.

The sharp, scissor-like teeth in my mouth were cutting into my lips. My heart was thumping too loudly. The sky was almost pitch black, and the hurricane was only growing far more powerful. The thunder roared deafeningly as I fought against Theon's grip on me, dragging my nails down his chest painstakingly slowly as he held me at arm's length. One hand was around my throat, but for some reason, it didn't hurt at all. His other hand still gripped my wrist.

"*I hate you!*" I screamed, punching him with my other hand.

I felt that same darkness, a darkness that I knew belonged to Theoden's enchantress, approach. I could feel her touching the earth I now controlled, and I sent a blast of stone and earth her way. Whatever she had begun to mutter was cut off. I felt the stone and earth encase her in a tomb, then felt her anguish and anger, but I didn't need her to interfere.

More wolves were approaching, but I didn't care. They wouldn't get close enough. Blood filled the air as they were cut to pieces by the violent winds, but that was on them. My only aim was to kill the man before me.

"You were right! Revenge! I want revenge, too! For my parents!" I cried. My hot tears stung my cheeks as they streamed down my face. No longer was I able to hold those painful tears back.

Locks of purple and blue hair whipped around me, but all I could think of was their dead bodies lying on the ground in the aftermath of that attack...

Lies... all lies!

"How could you? How could you think you could ever have a relationship with me after what you did?" I screamed as we both went tumbling to the ground. "How dare you even touch me after killing my parents!"

"It was never meant to be more than one night." His words were faint and distant, and his grip was growing weaker.

With a burst of energy, I dug my claws deep into him and down his chest to the side of his waist, feeling a flare of satisfaction at the three long wounds that painted his chest. He fell back, his face ashy.

I was suddenly violently pulled back, feeling something being stabbed into the back of my neck. The heavy darkness of the spells in the air was weighing down upon me as I fought against the four wolves that were shackling me in silver and the power of the enchantress.

"I hate you, Theon!" I screamed, staring at the man who was half sitting, half lying propped on one elbow, one hand trying to stem the blood that was flowing out of him faster than normal.

I hated this. These sparks, this attraction, and above all, his betrayal. I knew what I needed to do. Despite the heaviness and the pain that was slowly spreading through my body, I glared at the man with all the hatred that I felt for him and took a deep, shuddering breath. Rage was overwhelming me as I channelled every ounce of my emotions into my words.

"I, Yileyna De'Lacor, Alpha of the Silver Storm Pack, reject you, Theon Alexander Hale, as my mate!" I shrieked, feeling the violent ripping in my chest as Theon stared at me in shock, pain and confusion, his heart thundering loudly. "Go to hell, Theon," I spat before I finally succumbed to the darkness...

A New Perspective

THEON

*M*Y MATE?

I could hear my heart beating violently in my ears. Her words and the pain that ripped me apart internally shocked me to the core. She was mine…

But with the mate bond sealed, I had never realised. Now the jerking away and the struggle I often saw her in made sense. It wasn't her hatred, although I knew that was there; it was the bond.

The night when she released her powers, she must have realised. I remember the look of pure shock in her eyes before she had been knocked out. *What kind of game are you playing, Selene?*

I saw Arabella approach her. Knowing she was about to do something to her limp body, I forced myself to sit up. Although I was in enough agony to pass out, there was something about these cuts that were burning me up. The pain spread through me and up my neck. They made my head squeeze in agony.

"Don't do anything! Bring her to me," I growled, unable to move with the intense pain.

Arabella paused. With her long black hair, dark eyes, and ashy skin, she gave me the same unnerving feeling that I always felt around her. The men obeyed me, bringing her body to me. I pulled her into my arms, feeling her heart thudding faster than it should be.

Her hair was its usual blonde once more. She had transformed, even if not fully, but her teeth… her hair… her claws….

I'm sure they had seen it, but I knew, even if no one else saw it properly, Arabella would have, and she would make the link knowing she was a siren.

The warmth of her body made me want to hold her tightly, but I was unable to, not with so many watching. My own body was becoming heavier.

Her rejection still rang in my mind. The pain that had been on her face and in her voice pulled viciously at my heart. I did this. I broke her in ways worse than I could have ever imagined.

"Alpha Theon, you are injured," Arabella murmured.

"Remove the seal upon me. Now," I growled, ignoring her statement.

"Alpha Theoden has not given me the -" My eyes blazed as I looked up at her, my gaze full of hatred.

"I'm the one who agreed for him to have those seals placed on me, and if I say I fucking want them gone, I mean gone!" I growled murderously.

The mate bond seal was one I did not hold the key to. Just as Dad had given me the tool to remove the one on my powers a week before the attack on Westerwell, this was one I hadn't bothered about. But now I wanted to feel it.

The storm was still raging, the rain and hail beating down on us through the roof that she had blown off. I looked down at her… wishing I didn't know just how we had come to this point. She was meant for me….

Even though she severed the bond from her side, these feelings didn't stop, feelings I had to hide, even if Yileyna was mine…

They were talking to me, but I was no longer able to hear; the pain, these emotions, the guilt… I had told her the truth about her parents because I had been unable to keep it from her. It was something I had carried for far too long, and she had the right to know.

They were calling me, saying something, but I was losing consciousness. Arabella stepped forward, murmuring a spell before she let a few drops of her own blood join the stream of blood that was running from my body. I felt the final seal on me snap, and then the sudden sparks and her scent fill my senses. Goddess, if it was gorgeous before, this was fucking heaven…

Even if she had weakened it by rejection, she was still bound to me…

"…eon…"

They were saying something, but everything was getting dark.

"…blood… faster!"

"… son!"

"…on… hold on…"

I couldn't…

For the first time in my life, I wanted it all gone, everything that I kept inside of me. I was far too tired…

Voices. I could hear them faintly, but I felt too tired to open my eyes.

"…won't heal, no matter what we try."

"Why not?" Dad's growl. They weren't in the same room, but they were close.

What happened? Was Yileyna okay? Surely Dad wouldn't hurt her. She was the heart, after all… right? *I need to get up…*

"I'm afraid it was the touch of death, Master," Arabella's whispery voice came. Master? Why was she calling Dad master?

"Are you certain that's what she is?"

"Certain… these wounds, her appearance before she fell unconscious. She is a siren," Arabella's quiet reply held no hesitation. I couldn't even move or react. My heart was beating slowly, and my body was far too heavy to even lift a finger.

"So, Andres even copulated with a siren. Disgusting. Do not tell Theon of this. We will make sure he doesn't find out."

"Yes, Master… but what about them being mated?"

"He knows…"

"Yes, he commanded me -"

A thud and a gasp followed. Although I couldn't see, I knew he had hit her. That was the second time he'd hit a woman for simply speaking…

"You only obey my command, no one else's," he hissed.

I frowned, trying to open my eyes, but I couldn't, almost as if my body was no longer mine to control. The seal on my mate bond was encouraged by Dad, but I had agreed. If I wanted it removed, that was my fucking choice.

Once again, Hunter's words from the night of my engagement returned to me.

"*When word went around that Andres had a Theon who was found on the coast as his closest man, I found it intriguing, but not once did I think it would be you until I stopped at a little Island called Bellmead...*" My eyes flashed, and he raised an eyebrow.

"*I heard some pretty interesting stories, stories that told me this Theon of Westerwell may just be someone more. What are you doing here, Theon? The man is a bastard and a liar, yet, despite your engagement to the pretty blonde, I know that you are not here for romantic reasons alone. That attack earlier was proof of that. Or staged attack anyway...*"

"*Why I'm here is none of your concern, Hunter, so leave without causing an issue.*" He smirked as he took a drag on his cigar.

"*Leave? Oh, I'm leaving... but I wanted to warn you, Theon, I've heard and seen things... dark things. Whilst you've been here undercover, your father has been moving around -*"

"*He is only working on overtaking what is rightfully his, nothing more. Those are simply rumours going around. You are a fool if you believe them.*" He looked at me, sighing slightly as he shook his head.

"*I fear they are far more than rumours, brother.*"

"*Don't call me that,*" I growled. A smirk curled the end of his lips, and he nodded.

"*Of course, we are simply born from the same mother...*" His smirk faded, and he frowned. "*Then, for her, and you know I loved her, take heed of my words. Your father is dealing his hands in a pool of darkness that should never be touched. Do not follow him blindly, or you will regret it. Keep your eyes open, Theon. I know the saying goes, 'keep your friends close and enemies closer...' but right now, I'm uncertain who the real enemy is.*" I knew he meant Dad.

"*He isn't like that. He's doing what's necessary. Andres sent people after us to kill us all, not just me and Dad. He even attacked our women and children, who were defenceless, years ago. I've lost far too many at the hands of Andres.*"

"*I heard... but I also heard that it may not have been Andres' doing.*" I glared at him, feeling my anger rising.

"*You weren't there,*" I growled.

"*Nay, I wasn't... but my mother was, and I dug deep for answers. Why else do you think I've been scouring the fucking seas? I'm trying to find the ones*

who killed her, including the ones who forced her aboard that ship. What I've
discovered is questionable."

We both fell silent, hearing faint voices approaching.

"I should go, but if ever you want the truth, you know where to find me…
and remember… the heart of Kaeladia belongs to all. She's the true Alpha Queen,
Theon. Not you, not Andres, and not Theoden."

With those words, he walked away, casting one final glance back at me.

Hunter…

I never really knew him since he was raised by his father, a man Mom
was mated to before she and Dad discovered they were fated mates and
Dad claimed her. He was three years older than me, and although Mom
was unable to keep him with her, she always missed him. The bond of fated
mates was powerful, and she was unable to refuse Dad when he wanted her
to come with him. With the situation of the Obsidian Shadow Pack being
forced into hiding, she couldn't visit him as much, but she loved him as
much as my sisters and me.

His words didn't leave me. What had he discovered? I wish I had found
out…

The sound of footsteps approached, and I knew it was Dad by his scent.
He exhaled with obvious irritation, and I could feel the anger radiating off
him.

"Fool," he muttered before he retreated.

I finally managed to force my eyes open, staring at the ceiling, the word
'fool' echoing in my mind. Fool. No one could call me that, even if it was
Dad. I think it's time I found my own answers and stopped listening blindly
like a fucking fool.

I forced myself to sit up. I needed to go find out where Yileyna was. Was
she safe, or had they done something to her?

Dad's temper was not something I could ignore, and deep down, if I
really believed he was good, then why was I so worried?

Hard Choices

YILEYNA

The three-headed whip with spikes dragged on the floor as I did my best not to lash out in anger. The man wielding it looked at me coldly, his eyes hard and devoid of emotion or compassion. Right in front of me, Andrea and Zoe were kneeling on the floor, beaten and bloody because I had hurt Theon. They were being punished to hurt me. They had both lost so much weight since the last time I had seen them. Both were covered in burns from the silver they had been bound in.

I had awoken to find myself tied in this empty room, drugged and poisoned. The spells and chains that shackled me were powerful, yet the moment I had created a barrier around me, they had brought Andrea and Zoe, forcing me to lower it.

I had been whipped and beaten for hours. There were moments I would black out and others when it was taking my all not to unleash hell upon them all. But even though I was remaining calm for the two women before me, my anger was rising.

I needed to get out of here. The only person who I didn't know the location of was Gamma Henry. The urge to break free and get my pack out of there was tempting. As he lashed me continuously, my mind was working on a plan, refusing to give in to the pain.

"I told you not to shield yourself!" He hissed, bringing the whip down on my back with a violent lash.

"I'm not," I hissed back, but the pain wasn't as severe as it was moments ago.

"Then tell me, why you aren't bleeding?" He growled, yanking me back by my hair. I didn't scream, even when he snapped my head far back and I heard something crack.

"Monsters don't bleed," I spat resentfully.

"Yes, and we both know you are nothing more than a filthy monster." He slapped me across the face, and I clenched my jaw.

I didn't regret what I did to Theon, even if it hurt me too, because he deserved it... but the look of confusion on his face when I rejected him niggled at my mind. What did he expect? That I would forgive him and join sides with them?

"Fine, then I'll teach these women a lesson instead." He moved away from me, his dirty blonde hair sticky with sweat and his pale eyes full of hatred. He grabbed Zoe by the hair, yanking her to her feet before running his hands down her waist. She tried to pull free, but she was too weak to even put up a fight. "I think this will be better if you strip," he said, his eyes raking over her before he tore her shirt from her body, leaving her in her bra. My eyes flashed at the fear in Zoe's eyes. All three of us knew his intentions were far worse than a beating.

"Don't touch her," I warned quietly, trying to remain calm, despite the heaving in my chest. My anger was increasing, and the pain in my back was fading with each passing minute, despite the fact I had been bound and beaten all day.

"Why not? She is a beauty..." His gaze went to her breasts as Zoe covered her chest, only for him to slam her into the wall and yank her arms away. "Do not disobey me!"

Andrea looked at me, her eyes calculating, as if trying to devise a plan herself. I had tried to mind-link them all throughout the time they were here, but the silver in their bodies was stopping me.

Andrea! I tried again, but once more, I hit a wall.

Andrea stumbled to her feet, trying to pull the man who was trailing his filthy hands up Zoe's leg, but she was far too weak, and he kicked her to the floor. My anger was pulsing within me, and my eyes flashed.

"I said, do not touch her," I growled, feeling my alpha command ripple through me and into my voice. The man instantly turned, his hands pausing from the band of her pants where he had been trying to one-handedly remove her belt.

"You bitch!" He growled, angry at my interruption, but it was obvious I had an effect on him.

I could hear it all; the blood rushing through our veins, our erratic heartbeats. The temptation to free myself and punish him rose. I could feel the presence of my wolf come to the forefront of my mind, as if wanting to break free. It was different, this feeling… it wasn't like when I was screaming at Theon. It was so intense, full of light and strength with the urge to protect.

"Yiley…" Andrea trailed off, but my eyes were on the man whose hands remained on Zoe.

"You will lose the hands that commit sin," I whispered. My voice was deeper and more eloquent. Then I felt it, the shift within me as I almost felt like I was pushed into the back of my own mind.

A true growl left my lips as I used all my power to break free from the bindings that held me, feeling the intense pain as my bones snapped and reformed. It was a feeling I had never experienced before, and I realised what was happening. Shimmering, pearly white fur now covered me.

I launched myself at the man. Without a second thought, I bit a chunk out of him, crushing one of his hands at the same time as he fell to the floor unconscious. My eyes blazed as I tossed the chunk I had taken out of him aside, breathing heavily.

Any pain I had felt was gone. I looked at Zoe and Andrea, both of whom were staring at me in awe. I knew I was larger than most wolves.

"You are an Alpha," Zoe said hoarsely, clearly in awe, as if my wolf was the proof of that, which I guess it was. I looked down at my body. Aside from the pale lilac in my tail, which looked a lot fluffier than the usual wolf tail, the rest of me was a pearlescent white.

Thank you, I said in my mind to my wolf as I felt her step back and return control to me once more.

It took me a few moments to force myself to shift back. I turned to the body on the floor. He was bleeding out fast. Before he died and Theoden realised the bond broke, we needed to get out of there. That's if he hadn't managed to warn him already. I was done. We needed to get out of here.

"We don't have much time. Where is Henry kept?" I asked, pulling the shirt off the man and slipping it on. Although I didn't want to touch anything of his, I had no other choice.

"He is not in the palace, but there's a room under the stables. That's where we were kept," Andrea said quickly.

"We'll get him. It's time to get out of here," I replied quietly. "We can get the women and children to make their way to the western side -" Andrea placed a hand on my arm and shook her head.

"We can't. If we take them, they will be caught. The Obsidian Shadow Pack is huge, and the majority of its people are warriors. If we leave them here, they will get to carry on as usual, but if we take them -"

"They may get killed..." My heart crumpled at the thought that I was about to abandon my people.

"She's right, Alpha. You need to get out of here so we can fight against them, to gather an army. There's also no place where we can hide them all. We'd be caught instantly," Zoe added, squeezing my hand. I pressed my lips together. The thought of leaving them here, would they really be safe?

"What if he kills them in anger?" I asked fearfully.

"If he wanted to kill us, we would have been dead by now. Let's have faith in Selene. It would only make him look worse if he does so."

"Then what of the warriors? If we took them, they would kill their women..."

"Then... you are the only one who needs to get out of here," Zoe said quietly.

"I'm not leaving you two, and Gamma Henry -"

"Listen to me Yiley- no, Alpha Yileyna. You can only truly help us if you go out there and seek the help that only you can gather," Andrea said firmly.

"It's wrong." I could hear shouting coming closer.

"No, it's a sacrifice you need to make for your people."

"Theon said that Theoden would kill you all."

"Then we will die martyrs," Zoe said firmly.

What was the right thing to do? I ran my hand through my hair, looking at the two women, it was obvious their minds were made up.

"Okay, what about the three of us? We can at least go together?" I asked, glancing towards the door.

"Then we will all be caught and killed. You need to go alone, Alpha, now," Andrea refused firmly. I looked at them, torn between the choice before me.

"Gamma Grayson, Raiden, Rhys, and Ryan are all alright. I've been in touch," I added quickly, wanting to give them something to hold onto, taking their hands before giving them a quick hug. The relief was clear in their eyes, and pulling away, I closed my eyes, sensing the presence of every being that was touching the ice that encased the entire castle through it.

My heart skipped a beat feeling Theoden and Arabella not too far. If he gave Arabella the command to find me, we might have some trouble. She was disturbingly powerful, and, for a fleeting moment, I wondered how she had come to be on Theoden's side.

"May Selene be with you," Zoe said.

I looked at them, they were weak, and despite not wanting to leave them… I had no choice. If we stayed here, we would die.

"Take care," Andrea added.

I nodded before taking a deep breath. Pushing open the door, I glanced back at the two brave women, giving them a smile of promise. *I will be back.*

I ran out of the room and through the dark halls.

"Get her! She's gone that way!"

"There's nowhere for her to run to!"

I could feel several heavy footsteps closing in on me as I ran up the only stairs ahead. My heart thundered when I realised I was in a simple circular room. I looked around, spotting the small window right ahead. This room was in one of the towers of the castle, and that was the only way out. My heart was pumping, I knew this was a risky idea, but it was the only one I had…

Taking a deep breath, I ran to the tight window, slamming my fist into it and shattering the glass just as several men came through the door behind me.

"There she is!"

One foot on the windowsill, I turned quickly, creating a huge wall of ice to stop them in their tracks before I turned and looked down at the ground far, far below.

Here goes nothing.

Closing my eyes, I jumped, willing myself to shift. I felt the power roll through me, using the wind to slow my fall. I landed on my paws and broke into a run. *Get to the wall and get out of Westerwell…* Once I was out, I would be safe.

The wind and snow were swirling around me as many wolves followed me, yet I was faster, using the wind to slow them down greatly.

To everyone, if you can hear me, then I just want to say that I promise I will fix everything. I don't know how, but I will. Stay strong and protect each other. I will return for you all.

Murmurs of good luck and 'we will await your return' followed me, but I was unable to reply, feeling the deadly darkness of Arabella approaching. I wasn't strong enough to fight her and an army of wolves right now. The beating and poisoning had still weakened me to an extent. I changed direction, heading towards the White Dove. The narrow path that only someone small could fit through would be my way out.

I had left the blizzard behind, and I hoped Arabella became confused. I squeezed between the fence, trying to calm my beating heart as I squeezed my way behind it right to the end, ignoring the way my chest and behind were being scraped. It was too tight here...

I finally reached the end and climbed out, remembering that night I had tried to alert everyone about the attack.

I kept running, my paws barely hitting the ground. My wolf was confident and headstrong, and she didn't stop even when I felt pained at the thought of the people I was leaving behind. While staying there, I had not been able to do anything.

A sudden sharp pain wrapped around my left leg, and I went crashing into the snow. I growled looking down to see the silver that was wrapped around my leg. So in wolf form, silver hurt me...

"Congratulations on your shift."

My heart thumped as I looked up at the one who had stopped me. He stood there, with the wind wreaking havoc behind him. The entire city was covered with a blinding hurricane that loomed above the city walls behind him, yet he stood unmoving despite how pale he was. Bandages that were already staining red covered his torso, and I was forced to shift when the silver became too much.

"What do you want from me?" I asked icily, moving away from him and the silver, inching towards the raging waters behind me. He closed the gap between us, and I looked into his pale amber eyes that were half lifeless.

"This wasn't how things were meant to be," he said quietly, his eyes skimming my body. I saw the slight frown on his forehead, and was that anger in his eyes?, before he looked away, almost as if trying to stop himself from looking at my naked body.

Why hadn't Arabella come by now? She would be here soon. I had to go.

"You did this when you betrayed us. If there is an ounce of compassion within you, at least keep the people of Westerwell safe."

"Until you return?" He asked emotionlessly, looking back into my eyes.

I didn't respond, and he advanced closer. I stepped back, not wanting him near me. Until he accepted the rejection, this bond would continue to sizzle between us. He stopped in front of me, and the water was already lapping at my ankles.

"Go away, Theon," I said, not hiding the hatred in my voice.

"Is that your final wish?" He asked quietly. I frowned.

Final wish? I raised an eyebrow.

"Do you really think you can defeat me? Right now, I'm a lot strong than you. Go run to your precious father," I spat, turning away. I had no idea where I was going, but it was anywhere away from him. I didn't have much time, I needed to leave.

He grabbed my arm, stopping me from leaving. The tingles were still there, stronger than before the bond but weaker since my rejection.

"Tell me, is that what you want from me?"

"Yes! What else did you expect? I rejected you! I hate you, and I want you far away! I want you to accept this rejection and just let me go!" I snapped in exasperation, the pain of my parent's death killing me. He had hurt me far too many times.

He nodded slowly, before he let go of my arm and I let out a breath of relief, turning my back on him. But to my surprise and irritation, he wrapped his arms around me from behind, making my eyes widen in shock, my breasts resting against his arms. My stomach fluttered, and my body disobeyed me, reacting to his touch. What was he doing?

Our hearts thundered as one and I felt the sting of agony within me, accompanied by the prickling of tears wanting to fall. Why was this love so painful? Why didn't it just go away?

His arms squeezed around me, and, for a moment, it felt like it was just him and me. Every sound from the crashing waves, the roaring wind and the howls of the wolves faded away. He buried his face in my neck, and I suddenly tensed, thinking he was about to mark me, ready to jerk away. Instead, he spoke, his voice low and thick.

"I, Theon Alexander Hale, accept your rejection. Goodbye, little storm."

THE AETHIRIAN OCEAN

YILEYNA

MY HEART THUNDERED AS I felt the final severing of the bond, and the pain that came with it, unable to stop the tears from falling. This was it…

Thank the gods for the rain… the whimper of my wolf and the ache in my chest only grew as Theon stepped away from me.

"You should go, I managed to direct them the other way to give you some time, but it won't be long before they realise -"

"I don't need your help. I was doing fine… without…" I managed to say, still thrown by his acceptance.

For the first time, it was as if he did something to make me happy… and not for his own selfish gains…

Suddenly, a huge wave reached the sky. Theon pulled me on instinct away from the sea, but to my horror, there within the wave were not one, but three Sirens. Three terrifyingly beautiful Sirens and their eyes were on me.

"That's…" I heard Theon murmur.

"Tempest…"

With cold realisation, I looked at the blonde in the middle. With her deep red eyes and black and red tail, I recognised her.

"The Siren from the Abyss…" I whispered, my eyes falling to her body. Sure enough, the long scars that covered her confirmed it.

"Fuck, run!" Theon growled as he yanked at my arm, just as I felt the darkness approaching. Arabella was near!

The Sirens began singing, and I felt Theon's hold loosen, although he was still trying to fight it.

"Run, Yileyna," he growled.

"We found you," the pale blonde whispered.

"Kill the man," I heard one of them command.

"No! Do not kill him!" I shouted.

I don't know why, but I couldn't see him dead. We may not be for one another… but I couldn't let him die.

I tried to fight against them, but I couldn't. Suddenly the water began swirling beneath me, and it made me lose my balance. Theon grabbed my arm just as I sensed Arabella and an army of wolves approaching through the blazing storm.

"We cannot delay. We are on your side," the dark-haired Siren said, looking at me. I looked around, seeing Theon's blood spreading as he refused to let go of me.

I had no choice… if they wanted me dead, I'd be dead by now. This may just be the start of my answers.

"Let me go," I said quietly, looking into his eyes.

His eyes were a turmoil, and when the blonde Siren raised her hand, ready to strike, the anger and hatred in her eyes already clear, I used all my energy to send a surge of waves at him, throwing him onto the shore.

"Yileyna!" He shouted, and then I was pulled under.

Goodbye.

I closed my eyes, trying to reserve the oxygen I had.

"Sleep, little one… you are home," the ethereal voice of the red-headed siren came, and I felt a heaviness begin to spread from between my shoulder blades, and then darkness welcomed me into its folds…

I awoke with a gasp, to find myself lying on what appeared to be some sort of bed. What on Kaeladia…

I sat up, my eyes widening as my hair flowed around me. I was in the water! I was in -

I froze, realising I could breathe. My heart was thumping as I looked around the odd room I was in. It was bathed in a deep aqua-blue glow. There were stunning flowers and coral lining the side of the room, which seemed to be carved from some sort of sparkling stone. From the glowing purple vines that ran down one wall and the shimmering water-like veils that covered the windows, I knew I was in a place far from Westerwell, and I knew exactly where I was...

In the Siren Kingdom...

I tried to walk before I gave up and swam to one of the windows. I pulled the delicate iridescent cloth from it and wrapped it around myself before swimming to the archway, which was the only entrance into the room. The moment I swam out of it, I stopped, seeing that it was a huge room. It was equally magical and mesmerising, but what terrified me was the five Sirens that lounged there, and to my horror, there were eight mermen as well.

These men were rumoured to be the slaves to the sirens, there for their protection and desire, yet they were just as dangerous as Sirens... or so the old stories told. The only difference was they did not venture to the surface. They were all as beautiful as the next, with long hair, pale skin and long, strong tails. My gaze dipped to the deadly weapons that each male held. I'm dead, or I will be soon. Wait, what if I was dead already?

"She's awakened," came the ethereal, powerful and beautiful voice of the eldest siren there, making my attention go to her.

Her hair was pure white, braided into a long plait, her tail a deep steel grey which bled into a rich plum purple. She wore a thin, sheer fabric wrapped around her breasts. Several necklaces hung around her neck, and her hands were adorned in bracelets and rings, but what caught my attention was the huge crown adorned with jewels of several colours that sat upon her head. This woman was powerful and of importance...

My heart pounded as I looked into her eyes. They looked almost black. She stared at me, and I wondered if I should bow. Doing what I thought was best, I lowered my head politely.

"Raise your head," she commanded.

I did as I was told, looking at the other sirens. The three who had brought me were here, as well as one other that I didn't recognise.

"She looks a lot like her. She is hers without a doubt," the blonde with the scars down her chest said as she swam towards me and grabbed my chin. The older woman frowned as she rose from her seat and came toward me. She didn't respond to the blonde as she examined my face.

"Your father must not know, not until she arrives. Shall I lift the last of the spells from her? By Oshera, if anyone else finds out she is here, they will come for her." The elder siren turned, and I couldn't help but wonder what they were talking about.

"How am I breathing underwater?" I asked, finding it weird that I was even able to talk without gargling bubbles.

"A spell. I am a sea witch, and we have been waiting for this day since the day you were given away. My name is Lavina." Given away? What was she going on about?

"Nice to meet you… I'm Yileyna," I replied warily. Sirens were monsters… right? The women looked at each other.

Shouldn't we hide her before she sees her? The redhead asked.

We must explain to her that we have brought her here before she loses her temper, the fifth siren said, her voice now in my mind.

You are correct, Cailena, but there is not a chance that she does not know. She would have known the moment she touched the ocean water, Lavina replied firmly.

My heart thudded as I remembered the young siren who had asked for help. A wave of guilt washed over me, and I realised how I had heard her, she had somehow felt or known what I was…

Oh, I want her to come, because it's high time she realised that this is a fact we can't hide any longer, the blonde with the scars replied. Did they not realise I could hear? And who were they talking about?

Calm down, Ariella, let her come.

I didn't say anything as Lavina motioned for me to take a seat and I obeyed. Right now, these women may look effortlessly beautiful, and I could admire them all day… but I knew what they were capable of, and I wasn't sure me being a hybrid would guarantee me my safety.

I felt the intense stare of one of the guards, turning and staring at him. With his angled jaw, slightly silvery skin, plump lips, and sharp eyes, he was handsome, but unlike the sirens, he looked more like a predator. I gave a hesitant smile, and he returned it with one of his own. My stomach sank at the sharp piranha-like teeth in his mouth, and I quickly turned away, my heart pounding.

Focus, Yileyna.

Ariella chuckled as she came over.

"Don't be too scared. If we wanted you dead, you'd be dead back on that insulting ship. We let you pass without incidence," she said, her tail swishing as she swam around me. She seemed to be telling the truth, but... was that why our journey had gone rather smoothly after that initial attack?

I looked around, realising I had no idea where I was. The worst thing was, what if they didn't let me go from here? What if I'm held captive forever? What will happen about the Obsidian Shadow Pack?

"She's here," the redhead announced, and I felt the sudden tension that spread from them. Who was here?

Stay calm. I will handle her, Lavina's voice came in my mind. The other four sirens nodded, and my heart pounded.

Who had they called? Was she their leader? Did she hate werewolves? Well, all sirens did, what am I thinking. It was taking everything in me not to run from here. The cloth I was wearing was ballooned with water, making it float around me. I pushed it down, trying to look presentable for whoever was coming.

I turned to the entrance to see two males enter, each one carrying a spear. They had their dark hair in ponytails and a silver band around their foreheads. Both had tails of completely black glittering scales, and for a moment I wondered where their male parts were. Did they magically grow? Or were they hidden behind those scales? I shook my head, annoyed at my own random train of thoughts.

If the men in this room looked dangerous, then the two in front were absolutely lethal. They flanked the door before a beautiful siren entered. Power oozed off her. Her long, pale blonde hair, that was the same shade as mine, was pinned back from her face with an extravagant crown that put Lavina's to shame. Her breasts were barely covered with a small armour-like silver metal piece that came from behind, cupping them. Several chains of diamonds and pearls wrapped around her slender toned waist and stomach. Her wrists held jewelled cuffs, her upper arms had bands of silver around them, and her ears glinted with jewels. Her silver and blue tail sparkled magnificently, and it was clearly longer than the ones in this room.

I didn't need a statement to tell me this woman was far more important than any of the ones I had met so far. Everyone in the room bowed to her. I was about to lower my head to her when her deep blue eyes met mine, my heart thudding as I held her gaze. Nervousness filled me as I watched her. She glanced at my legs before she frowned and her eyes snapped back to mine, a glimmer of recognition in them. Her heart began racing, and my own emotions were a mess. Not once did I ever think this would be possible... but it was...

Goddess...

I didn't need anyone to tell me who this was... how could I when her face reminded me so much of my own?

"Ah, Queen Deliana, thank you for gracing us with your presence."

Of Land & Sea

YILEYNA

*D*ELIANA…

She didn't respond as she watched me, her eyes growing darker, and I felt the anger spreading from her.

What is the meaning of this, Lavina? Her voice rang in my head. It held power and suppressed anger.

Forgive me, but we had no other choice… Lavina replied, her head still bowed to the queen.

My birth mother was a queen. It felt strange to see her before me, it just… I would do anything to have my mom back. My real mom who raised and held me… but instead, I was finding royal parents who I didn't want or need.

Do explain.

She was in danger. We've been watching the shore, they were ready to kill her! Lavina exclaimed.

She is not a child; she can look after herself. Bringing her here is a death wish… she trailed off before glaring at all the guards and the other sirens.

"Leave us." They all listened, aside from Ariella, who raised an eyebrow.

"May I stay, sister?" Sister? Deliana pursed her lips before giving a small

"Of course, since you were clearly a part of this. It seemed your last rendezvous with animal shifters wasn't a reminder enough," she said, looking at her sister's scars. Ariella smirked.

"No, but fear not, the males tend to find them very sexy."

Deliana didn't seem impressed, her gaze turning back to me once it was just the four of us in the room. She waved her hand, and a shimmering veil-like cloak covered the entrance.

"Explain," she said to Lavina before her gaze turned to me.

"It's the prophecy, Deliana," she began. Prophecy? "The heart of this world resides within the child born of the land and sea, she *is* the child born from land and sea," Lavina whispered. "We need to unlock the final seal. Your father -"

"I do apologise, but can you please include me in this conversation instead of acting like I'm not even here?" I asked, looking between the two women.

Deep down, I wanted to ask Deliana why she abandoned me, but I couldn't complain because I had found the best parents.

"She has your spark," Ariella added amused. She was an entirely different person than the monster who had attacked our ship...

"Then let us start at the beginning," Deliana said, going to the seat Lavina had sat in previously and sat down, her tail flicking as she did so. We all sat down and Lavina smiled at Deliana.

"Tell her the truth."

"I know the king's version, I mean, Andres Apelion's version," I said.

Deliana's anger sent a wave through the room, her heart thundering. When she turned to me, I could see her long nails and the sheer hatred on her face, her eyes shimmering with hues of purples, blues, and silver.

"Never mention that liar's name in front of me ever again," she hissed. I nodded.

"Understood... he's dead anyway," I said quietly.

"Good. He was too much of a coward to ever approach the sea... and Father forbade me from ever setting foot on land again, or I would turn to sea foam," she scoffed, clenching her fist. A silence fell, and Lavina looked at her.

"Go on, My Queen. She deserves the truth."

Deliana closed her eyes and began telling her story. How she had saved Andres, spent the night watching him, and had been greatly attracted to him. She sensed the bond was of a true mate. Andres seemed not to notice it, but he was drawn to her. They began spending time together. Weeks became months, and they got closer until one day, he told her they had to end it. She had pleaded and begged for him to accept her, and he had given in.

"But I was fool… when I fell asleep that night, he tried to take my life." She opened her eyes, and I could see the pain in them. My heart clenched at the story she was telling me. The pain in her eyes somehow told me she was telling the truth. "He said I was a monster, but I had done nothing to be called one. He forced me to the ocean, knowing full well my father would kill me. He didn't care, and from that day forth, he had the sea and coasts scoured for Sirens, killing them mercilessly in fear that his truth of having a relationship with a Siren would come to light. Yes, we have killed men at sea, but not as often as they killed us, stealing even our young."

I felt… stunned, it was all too much to take in. A true mate bond… Andres had lied. Deep down, I had a strong feeling that perhaps they had been mates, but Soleil had enchanted the king. If she hadn't, so much could have been prevented.

"But I, too, promised revenge, and I followed up on it, taking an oath that I would kill every alpha-blooded male that set foot upon our seas, something that father approved of, despite my sins. When I found out about my pregnancy, Lavina helped me hide it, and when you were born, we realised you were a hybrid. If you were a full Siren, I would have kept you here, but your lungs weren't made to live underwater constantly," Deliana continued, "It had been one of the more difficult decisions I had to make, but your health was vital. I commanded Ariella to go on land to find a couple who could take care of you, and at the same time make sure you were close to that scum father of yours, knowing he held power at least on land."

I could see she was trying to act indifferently, but this topic was still painful for her. Her eyes were boring into mine, as if she wanted to ask me something, but her pride refused her from doing so.

"I saw this couple, who I overheard discussing how they were unable to conceive, and so I decided to do a little more research upon them. It turned out they were close to the king, too," Ariella added smugly. "Then I snuck you out of the water and left you there since Deliana couldn't step foot on land. Our father is the ruler of the seven seas, and although he sees all, we managed to hide this pregnancy."

"Before Ariella took you, Deliana and I placed the barriers upon you so no one ever found out what you were. Without realising, we suppressed all your abilities. It was only after you were given away that we realised what you truly were, but we couldn't let the power-hungry wolves use you, and so we approached you once again to strengthen those spells. We decided the barrier would weaken upon your eighteenth birthday and slowly, slowly you would come into power," Lavina said quietly. So did my parents know what I was? My heart was thundering as I struggled to process it all.

"But still, whenever you touched the water, the Sirens sensed it," Ariella remarked, running her fingers through her hair.

"When you began playing in the water, Sirens were drawn to you for who you are, and knowledge of your existence reached him, of the legged siren who lived on land. Our Emperor, my father: Queseidon," Deliana continued. My heart skipped a beat as I took in everything they said.

"Does he know about me?"

"Yes, he does, and he knows you are the child of prophecy. However, he does not know you are mine, but if he sees you, he will," Deliana sighed with a tilt of her head. Every move they made was full of grace and beauty, and I found myself enchanted by them. "Which means you need to leave the waters soon. Once we remove your final seal, you must fulfil your destiny," Deliana added.

"My destiny?"

"Reunite the people of Kaeladia before we kill one another to the point of extinction," Lavina added quietly. "For if this continues, Kaeladia will not last long…"

Despite her soft melodious tone, her words held a sinister warning, and it was one that I knew held true.

"The Emperor has been building the imperial army for decades, and the time has come for us to destroy the surface dwellers, or more specifically, the werewolves," Ariella added.

"And as much as I hate them, especially those of Alpha blood… killing them all will cause havoc," Deliana added darkly. I looked at her in surprise, trying to ignore the sliver of fear within me.

"But only the imperial sirens can walk upon land…" I said quietly. "There's not much they can do from just the coast." Deliana scoffed lightly, as if what I had said was ignorant.

"Indeed we know that, but Father has over two thousand children and each one can walk the land with ease." My heart sank at just the thought of that happening. Didn't they say the imperial sirens were far and few?

"Many many years ago the werewolves drove another species to the brink of extinction, and now it's time that we dealt them the hand of fate," Ariella added, examining her nails.

"But it will not end well. That is why you are here. You must protect our people from being sent to war and from those who seek us out. You are the heart of Kaeladia and the future queen of the Aethirian Ocean," Lavina claimed, now taking my hand in hers. For a moment I forgot that she was a dangerous siren, she reminded me of a wise grandmother.

"Queen?" I asked, realising what she said a moment later.

"Yes. Queen. I am the most-pure blooded of my siblings, and one of the rulers of the seven seas beneath our supreme ruler, my father. However, I only have one child. You." Deliana said quietly, "When I die, my title as Queen of the Aethirian Ocean will pass to you." Confusion and panic hit me. Yes, I loved the sea, but live as a siren? I couldn't do that!

"But you said I can't live underwater! That my lungs aren't built for it. Plus, I shifted into a wolf! I can't shift into a siren!" I tried not to argue, not wanting to anger her either, but I was unable to keep the panic from my voice. She raised a perfect brow.

"Yes, as a child you were not fit for the sea, because you were born from land. We realised we may have to wait until you were older to become one of us, and Lavina discovered that you may be... let's just say you are not a hybrid, Yileyna. You may have a wolf form, but you will certainly get your tail," Deliana said it with such conviction that somehow I felt she was telling the truth.

"I don't think -" I was cut off by Deliana, her eyes darkening.

"You will, because you are a triform shifter, a miracle among species, and in your hand, you will hold the power of both earth and sea. You are the light of this world, and it's high time you understood that."

THE IRON CLAW PACK

CHARLENE

I WAS TERRIFIED FOR YILEYNA. With every passing day I wondered if she was okay. She was alone, and although I knew Theon loved her, after his deceit, I didn't know what to think. I was trying to tell myself he wouldn't let anything happen to her, but I was terrified, too.

She was brave, but she was all alone. It was hard for Gamma Grayson, too, knowing that his mate was left behind, but there was no other choice. I hadn't told him about who I was because I didn't want it to become an extra burden for him. I was okay with him not knowing.

Knowing that Mom and Dad were killed felt painful. Even if they weren't fully good people, I still loved them. Dad's death had hit me harder; I just wished I could have told him goodbye and that I loved him. Even if he wasn't my biological father, he was the one who raised me, and had always treated me better than Mom.

We had travelled to two packs, however Obsidian Shadow Pack guards stood at the entrances, and we were not even able to meet those Alphas. It was obvious they were either looking for us or keeping an eye on everyone.

Would no one stand up to Theoden? It seemed not. He was known for his ruthless ways. It was Raiden who had suddenly decided we should go to the one pack that was powerful and neutral to all. The Iron Claw Pack, home to the infamous Alpha Hunter Slade Carson.

"This is going to be hard. Hunter doesn't deal his hands in political matters," Gamma Grayson said as we stared at the huge iron walls that surrounded the pack. Foot-long blades crowned the wall, and every two metres apart, I saw there were guards on watch duty. But as suspected by Gamma Grayson, there was not one Obsidian Shadow Pack wolf here.

"What are those..." I murmured, seeing something move from around the walls.

"His moat, a moat full of serpents," Ryan added with a low whistle. "I thought it was a damn joke..."

"Oh, it's very real. Hunter became an Alpha at the age of eleven, two years before he shifted. He is currently the youngest recorded shifter alive, having gotten his wolf at the age of thirteen," Gamma Grayson commented. "He's powerful."

"That is so cool!" Rhys exclaimed. It had been hard for him, having to travel like this, and often he spent his time with me when the men were more restless and angrier.

"Well, we have nothing to lose. Hunter is one Alpha who didn't bend to Andres, unlike many who yielded to him due to him being a king," Gamma Grayson replied.

"Well then, let's go ask for this badass, shady-as-fuck Alpha's help. Oi, Charlene, maybe you can use some charms on him?"

"Do not be disrespectful to the princess," Gamma Grayson warned him. Ryan shrugged.

"She wasn't the king's real daughter." That did hurt, but I simply smiled as Gamma Grayson's irritation rose.

"It's okay, and I don't want to be called Princess either, Gamma Grayson."

"Also, if you continue to be childish, Ryan, I'm sure our Alpha will remove you from the position of Gamma," Raiden added with a smirk.

"Well, let's go meet Alpha Hunter who will help us!" Rhys said confidently. I hoped, at least not to break his heart, he would agree to help us.

We left our hiding spot in human form, and I held Rhys's hand tightly. Immediately we were spotted, and several bows and arrows were turned upon us.

"We wish for an audience with Alpha Hunter Slade Carson," Raiden said loudly, raising his hand in surrender as he stepped forward.

I looked into the dark moat of water. Although we were still very far, I could see something move beneath the surface. My grip on Rhys tightened, and I moved him behind me. Although I knew we were a good few metres away, those things were huge, and I knew they could come out of the water.

"State your business!" The man shouted, scanning us all.

"We are here on behalf of the Silver Storm Pack," Gamma Grayson said, placing a hand on his chest.

The man frowned, exchanging a look with one of the other guards before he gave a curt nod. He seemed to be mind-linking as we all waited nervously. Raiden glanced over at Gamma Grayson, frowning slightly, and I knew they were mind-linking.

Do you think he'll agree to see us? I asked nervously.

I hope so, Raiden replied.

"Names!" The man called.

"Beta Raiden Bolton, Princess Charlene Aphelion, Gamma Grayson Sanchez, with his son Gamma Ryan and my younger brother, Rhys," Raiden answered clearly. "As you must have heard, Alpha King Andres is dead. Yileyna De'Lacor is our new Alpha and is currently in the hold of Theoden Hale."

The man nodded before we heard the grinding of the drawbridge being lowered. My heart lurched as I saw the crossing. Goddess, it was so narrow, and there were no supports on the sides. I swallowed hard before giving Rhys a brave smile.

"Don't worry, Princess, I'll hold on to you tight," he whispered. I nodded, giving him a cute smile. What a brave boy he was without his parents, yet he was still acting so strong.

"Cross!" A man shouted.

"Thank you," I replied softly to Rhys before Raiden led the way.

It wasn't big enough for more than two people to walk side by side. Rhys followed Raiden, whilst Ryan stepped up behind me with Gamma Grayson at the back. *It's just a few metres… you got this, Charlene.*

I kept my gaze on the other side, which was at least twenty metres away. Goddess, this man had planned this. How dangerous to have such a moat! I heard the hissing of a serpent at one point, seeing its long body under the moat.

"Keep going. If you scream, they will react!" The man shouted.

I nodded, although my heart was ringing in my ears. The moment we reached the other side, I let out a shaky breath, and Raiden smiled at me.

"You did well," he said as we waited for the huge gates to be opened.

Goddess, their security was better than that of Westerwell. We stepped inside to see the area was huge. It was a full village in here, yet there were only warriors in sight. Most were well-built with scars that spoke of many battles fought.

I heard footsteps, and that familiar, seductive smell of none other than Alpha Hunter approached. I suddenly felt very self-conscious, knowing I was covered in dirt and all I was wearing were worn-out leather pants and an oversized shirt. I don't know why it mattered, but I was unable to stop myself from trying to smooth my shirt and tilt my chin up.

"Well, well, who would have thought anyone from the Silver Storm Pack would be so kind as to visit a simple Alpha like me?" He said mockingly, clasping his hands in front of him as he tilted his head. He looked as handsome, if not more, than the day I saw him at the ceremony in a fitted shirt, pants, and boots. A few strands of his hair fell across his forehead, although most were messily tied back.

"You are no simple Alpha, Alpha Hunter. However, we had no choice," Raiden said quietly, glancing at the guards.

"My men are loyal. Speak," he commanded before his gaze fell on me. Our eyes met, and my heart skipped a beat as a small smirk crossed his lips. "On second thought, I don't think it's fitting to make such a pretty lady stand and wait when she looks… exhausted. Come, I will give you a place to rest."

We were led through the village. The houses were humble, but they were strong and rigid. Shops and food stores were aplenty, and although I knew Alpha Hunter owned the lands around the fortress, it was obvious everyone stayed within the safety of these walls. We stopped at what looked like barracks or a pack house, and he entered, leading the way to the left. After a flight of stairs, he stopped at a door and took the key that hung on a hook.

"I'm afraid we don't have many rooms. If the Beta is okay to share with his brother?" Hunter asked.

"Of course, thank you, Alpha," Raiden said with a nod, yet he didn't go in. Hunter smirked as he continued down the hall. He gave the next room to Gamma Grayson and Ryan before he stopped at a third door further down.

"And the room for the lady," he smirked as Raiden opened the door, stepping inside. "I'll have one of my Omegas bring you clean clothes. Rest, you are safe here," he added to me, his tone dropping an octave, making me nervous.

"Perfect. Thank you, Alpha Hunter. I do apologise for the quick check, but she is important to our kingdom and our Alpha."

"Ah, of course, she is."

Our eyes met before I mumbled an 'excuse me'. I took the key from Raiden and entered the room quickly. Goddess, he was such an intense man. I closed the door and looked around. It was modest yet clean. There was a wardrobe on the left side with a high chest of drawers, a mirror, and a vanity table. When I saw the bed, I had an intense urge to run and jump onto it, but I needed to bathe first. I looked at the door across the room, hoping it was a bathroom…

Half an hour later, I stepped out of the bath, wrapping a towel around myself whilst I used another on my long hair, which was once again vibrant and clean. That had been the best bath I had ever had. Never had I ever appreciated clean water as I did today. I stepped into the bedroom and almost jumped to see a middle-aged woman placing clothes into the wardrobe. She instantly stopped and bowed her head to me.

"I apologise for alarming you, my lady," she said politely.

"Not at all." I waved my hand, spotting the basket that sat on the bed.

"The Alpha sent clothing and some items for you," she said, gesturing to the basket.

"Thank you…" I said, not expecting this kind of hospitality from an Alpha rumoured to be so dangerous. But did he have other motives? My heart sank, remembering the way his eyes had raked over me at the ball.

"Thank the Alpha, my lady, not me. Would you like any assistance?"

"Not at all, thank you," I answered. She nodded, closing the top drawer.

"Once you are dressed, please come and join us for dinner," she replied before taking her leave.

I quickly locked the door and walked to the chest of drawers, taking out some panties. I slipped them on and walked over to the wardrobe to look at the clothes. To my dismay, they were all dresses.

I took out a dark green one which had long sleeves with a boat neck and a flared skirt that reached below my knees. Slipping it on, I added a black corset belt before I quickly got to work on my knotty hair…

Ten minutes later, I left my room to see Ryan and Raiden, both already dressed and standing there waiting for me.

"Well, let's get this over with," Ryan remarked as Rhys and Gamma Grayson joined us. We were then led by two guards. I hoped he agreed to help us because we truly needed his help…

Thirty minutes had passed, and I was a mess of nerves. We had entered the hall only for the Alpha to motion for me to take the seat to his right, complimenting me that I looked beautiful, but it was how his gaze kept finding mine that made me nervous. To make up for it, the food was warm and tasty. We had not had a hot meal in days!

We had explained our full situation to him, including how Yileyna is the heart of our world. Although we weren't sure if he would believe us, he didn't argue about it, simply listening, and let us speak as we put everything on the table. It was mostly Raiden and Gamma Grayson who did the talking, with Ryan and me inputting a little.

He seemed to have frowned at certain points, but he said nothing, not until we were done, having no idea what he was thinking as his face remained emotionless.

"So… you are not even able to get in contact with your allies because of the Obsidian Shadow Pack guards… Andres was killed, and his daughter is held captive. Theon betrayed you all…" He ran his fingers through his short beard thoughtfully.

"Yes. We are being sought out, and, on our way here, we heard Theoden has commanded for us to be brought back to him, dead or alive didn't matter," Ryan added. Hunter nodded before he sat back, placing his knife and fork down.

"Tell me, was your king any better than Theoden?" He asked. "Why do you think you should get Westerwell back?" I frowned at his question as Gamma Grayson spoke up defensively.

"Of course, Alpha Andres was hardworking, fair-"

"We cannot answer that, but what we can say is that right now, there are innocent people being held captive, and this is not about Father, but Yileyna, the heir to that throne, not because she was the king's real daughter, but because she is the heart, and therefore the rightful ruler. She is a person who stood up to the king countless times. Please, don't do this for Father, but for the new Alpha, for Alpha Yileyna of the Silver Storm Pack, " I said softly yet clearly. Hunter tilted his head, smirking slightly.

"Smart answer… however, why should I risk my men? What do I get in return?"

"What does the Alpha wish for? I am sure Alpha Yileyna would agree to your demands, within reason," I replied.

"A hand in marriage," he replied, picking up his knife, shocking us all.

"We can't promise you that she'll agree," Raiden said sharply. I saw his eyes flash, possessiveness clear in them.

"How do you expect us to give our word to something that is not in our control to agree to?" Gamma Grayson asked. Despite staying calm, he was clearly worried. We needed his help, and the situation was tricky. Hunter himself simply raised an eyebrow, that same tiny smirk playing on his lips.

"Then why don't I ask her myself?" He suggested before turning to me. "Tell me, Princess Charlene, is my army and support an offer fair enough for your hand in marriage?" Rhys and I both gasped as I stared at him.

"M-Me?" I asked, confused. He leaned over, forcing me back in my seat, my heart thumping as that tantalising smirk crossed his lips.

"If I'm going to choose a woman, it will be one who is equally ravishing in looks as she is in character. I'm certain that you will make a fine Luna. So, what will it be? My help is in your hands, Princess," he asked huskily.

My heart thudded as his words rang in my mind. I had always been told that I should choose a man who would benefit the kingdom… agreeing to an arranged marriage was not something so foreign, and if Alpha Hunter was willing to have me, then I would do this. For my people, my kingdom, and my sister.

You don't need to agree, Raiden's quiet voice came into my head, but I looked into the eyes of Alpha Hunter, my mind made up.

"I accept your offer."

My Decision

CHARLENE

I HADN'T BEEN ABLE TO sleep all night. Alpha Hunter seemed to have been satisfied with my response and had ordered wine to be brought in celebration of my agreement. I ran my fingers through my hair, watching the men train far below, lost in thought. I hadn't gone to breakfast this morning, unable to face him.

I had gotten dressed in a black dress with a plunging neckline and a flared umbrella skirt, but all I wanted to do was get into bed and hide from the world, so I could have some time to comprehend and digest everything that had happened. Raiden and Gamma Grayson had mind-linked to ask if I was okay, which I had cheerily told them I was.

Living in this place so far from everything I was used to was going to be different. I had always thought Westerwell would always be my home…

I sighed heavily. Hunter wasn't a bad person, and he was handsome. I blushed at the realisation that getting married also meant…. My heart thumped, my cheeks burning even more at the idea of being intimate with him. My stomach felt funny, and when there was a knock on the door, I jumped in alarm. I exhaled. Walking over to it and smoothing my skirt, I opened the door.

My heart skipped a beat at the sight of the tall, muscular man before me. His hair was sleeked back and tied; it was obvious he had just showered from the smell of the woody shampoo that mixed with his own scent. He was dressed in a black shirt and brown pants, and he was smirking slightly. Did he always have that look on his face?

"Alpha Hunter..." I said, smiling politely.

"Princess Charlene," he replied, almost sounding mocking. Was he teasing me?

"Can I help you?" I asked, tucking my hair behind my ear and looking down to avoid his intense gaze. To my utter dismay, my gaze fell on the front of his pants to the very noticeable bulge that was packed away. My cheeks burned as I looked up at him, only to see that small smirk had become a full-blown grin. Oh, my Goddess, he had seen where my attention had fallen! "Uhh, I didn't mean help like that! Can, can I ask why you are here?" I asked, knowing my entire face was flushed. He stepped closer, and I jumped back, my heart thumping as I pressed my lips together. He bent down slightly until his lips were close to my ear.

"I would tease... but I don't think your fellow pack members will appreciate me having an unconscious princess in my hold," he growled huskily, his fingers running through my hair. He chuckled, moving back, and I let out the breath I was holding. My heart thundered extremely loudly. "Fear not, Princess, I'm only here to ask how you are since you did not come for breakfast. Are you nervous?"

Nervous? Of course I was nervous! I was going to get married! I had made the decision myself... it felt strange. Usually, someone or other always made decisions for me.

"A little," I replied bravely, smiling slightly. His smirk vanished, and my stomach sank. Did I upset him? "It, it's nothing to be worried about, I'm perfectly fine, and it is an honour to be chosen by the Alpha. Please don't think that I'm backing out or -" He placed a finger to my lips, cutting me off before he cupped my face in his large, calloused hands.

"You ramble when you're nervous." If my face wasn't red already, it must now be a terrifyingly plum colour! Oh, how he must think I look awful! "Look, I'm not one to charm women, but my mother always told me to be faithful and respectful to the one whom I choose to keep by my side. I will treat you well, Princess, and give you anything that you wish for. The only man I will ever challenge will be if your fated mate shows up," he said, his eyes flashing possessively. I didn't think that would happen. Mated women usually didn't venture out on full moons once they had taken a chosen mate. That wouldn't happen.

"Forgive me if I'm out of line, but the Alpha doesn't really know me, and marrying me does not get you any assets. I am not the king's biological daughter, so why would you choose me?"

"The first time I saw you, you caught my eye, and with you walking right into my pack… it was such an opportunity, why wouldn't I take advantage of it?" He had already marked his claim, and it was clear, for some crazy reason, he wanted me. "You might not see it, but a woman with a good heart is far more valuable than jewels or assets. I have that already. All I need is my Luna by my side." I couldn't argue with him, he seemed to really want this, and I couldn't deny it made me feel all warm inside.

"Then, I hope I can be the Luna you deserve. If I'm out of line, please guide me. I am willing to learn and become better," I replied. "I sometimes speak up when I think something is not right, and I apologise in advance, but I never mean to offend anyone."

"I need a woman who does. A Luna is meant to stand by her Alpha's side as an equal. I can be pretty hot-headed. I need a woman who is confident and just, yet, at the same time, willing to be submissive when the time calls for it…"

His gaze dipped to my breasts, my heart hammering loudly, and I knew what he meant; in bed. My cheeks burned once again, but what more was I expecting? He was an Alpha, and their sexual energy was even more than a normal werewolf.

"I will aim to please," I found myself whispering as I nibbled on my lips.

"Goddess, you're a tease," he growled, surprising me before he pulled me against him.

My hand instantly went to his chest, very aware of every single ridge and curve of his body. My pussy clenched, and I bit my lip to stop the sigh that threatened to escape. His arms tightened around my waist before he leaned down, his lips brushing my ear, making my breath hitch.

"I think we will get along perfectly… the wedding will be held at the end of this week." He turned away from me, and I looked at his back, concerned at the way he had suddenly turned.

"Of course," I replied.

A week… Goddess, that was soon, but we didn't have time to waste.

"I've already sent out my men to secretly pass messages to some of Andres' most loyal allies and those who are my own. We will gather the army we need, have no doubt."

"Thank you, Alpha Hunter," I replied politely.

"Hunter," he corrected.

"Then please call me Charlene. I'm not really a princess anyway."

"You're still one in my eyes," he replied. "Excuse me."

"W-wait…" He turned to look at me from over his shoulder, and I looked down, ready to brave the question I had in my mind. "Will you mark me at our wedding?" I asked nervously. Obviously, it was to be expected, but the thought scared me.

"I intend to take you as mine and to show the world that. My pack will expect a marking."

"Of course. Sorry for my ignorance," I replied, feeling foolish.

Naturally, there would be a marking. How else could we guarantee that I wouldn't break the marriage after we got what we wanted? He turned back to me and closed the gap between us.

"Do not apologise to me for voicing your thoughts. My people need a marking. You can mark me, and I will mark you when you are ready. How about that?" He suggested, raising an eyebrow. I looked up at him in surprise. Was an Alpha really allowing me to claim him first?

He smirked at my amusement and placed his hands on my hips, pulling me against him. My cheeks burned up again as I felt something rather big and long against my lower stomach. I dared not look down, realising why he had jerked away from me before. The Alpha desired me. Just the thought made me feel even more nervous and somewhat excited.

"But, as an Alpha, you should claim me first. It's fine, you may -"

"Hush. An Alpha is said to have to claim his mate because he's an Alpha to show his position, dominance, and power, correct?" I nodded, and he smirked confidently. "I already am all those things, and allowing my chosen mate to mark me first is not an issue. Does an Alpha not submit to his Luna?" He replied.

I couldn't do anything but stare at him in awe. If he had not had an effect on me before, he did now. I don't know if he was simply good with words or if he actually meant those things… but he had made a warmth settle within my chest. I couldn't help but smile, a faint blush coating my cheeks.

"Thank you," I whispered softly.

He didn't reply. Instead, he leaned down, his lips grazing my cheek in a soft kiss that made me gasp. My head felt light before he stepped back and left the room, leaving me lightheaded and oddly happy. I shook my head, touching the spot on my cheek that he had kissed. His touch remained, and I did a twirl, trying to contain the happiness that had filled me.

"Smiling like that, and I was worried for no reason," Raiden's voice came, making me look up, startled, as he knocked lightly on the open door. He sniffed the air and raised an eyebrow. "I thought I saw Alpha Hunter leaving." I blushed and shook my head.

"He just came to say the wedding is in a week!" I said quickly, making Raiden chuckle.

He had taken good care of me, and I knew although he was a wonderful person, it was also because of the fact that I meant a lot to Yileyna. Deep down, I wished she took Raiden as her mate; he would be good for her. He'd treat her like the queen she deserves to be treated as, and he would always cherish her.

"So soon. Clearly, he seems impatient," he smirked as he came over to me, crossing his arms, a look of concern on his face. "Are you sure, Charlene? I don't want Yileyna coming for my head."

"Don't worry. I'll make sure when I see her again that she knows it was my decision," I reassured softly. I really missed her.

"I miss her too," he murmured, looking down at his hands, knowing what I was thinking.

"We'll see her soon enough," I replied with confidence, looking out of the window.

The weather was still freezing, but it wasn't as bad as it was in Westerfell. I knew I was doing the right thing. This marriage would promise me an army and the support that Yileyna needed.

"He's a good person," Raiden said quietly. I nodded, remembering what Hunter had said about his mother.

"Gamma Grayson said Alpha Hunter became an Alpha at an extremely young age. What happened to his parents?" I asked Raiden suddenly. He frowned, tilting his head.

"No one really knows. This pack and Alpha Hunter have always been very private."

I nodded, yet I couldn't help but be curious. After all, it was clear that Alpha Hunter held his mom in high praise. Perhaps I'll ask him if I get the chance.

DISTRUST

THEON

"How could you lose her?" Dad roared at Arabella, who had her head bowed, almost as if wanting to flinch, but she remained in her position, her head down. "Both of you!" His orange eyes turned to me, but I remained indifferent.

I had been dragged back from the coast, but even now, the panic that was consuming me was outweighing the fact that I had rejected her. I felt empty, but it was okay. I had been emotionless, simply a shell for vengeance, until she had made a place inside of me. Maybe I was just not meant for anything more than this.

I just hoped she was safe.

I wish I had dived into the water, but I was fucking useless, unable to even swim because a Siren's injury was far more dangerous and powerful than an ordinary injury, and my little storm had fucking dug deep. I deserved it, though; I had hurt her far more than these mere injuries. She could do this ten times over, and it would never be enough…

The bruises that covered her body, the lashes on her back… Anger blistered within me, and only when Dad shouted did I snap out of my dark thoughts.

"Get out!" Dad thundered at Arabella. She bowed her head before she left the room. "Fucking useless!" He slammed his fist into the ice that was finally melting away, creating large cracks through it.

I remembered the question between him and Arabella, the way she had addressed him as Master and the way he had called me a fool. Things like that were not something that I was just going to forget.

"Calm down, I'll bring her back," I replied coldly, knowing I needed to keep up the façade as if I didn't know what he had called me. He looked at me keenly.

"How did she escape? Where did she go?" He asked. Was he hinting at the ocean?

"Into the water, but I'll find her... I saw what she partially became before she attacked me," I said, forcing as much disgust into my voice as possible. He tensed before nodding.

"Ah yes, of course, I wanted to discuss this with you."

Oh really? I heard you say to keep it from me.

"I know how much you hate Sirens, as do I. After all, it's because of them that we lost your sister and Nathalia," he growled. I nodded.

"Then let's find her and kill her as we promised. All Sirens must die," I said, crossing my arms despite the agony in my chest at the simple move. I heard the faint change in his heartbeat before he calmed it almost instantly.

"You learned she was your mate... are you willing to kill her?" He asked me sharply.

"Of course. She's nothing to me," I scoffed resentfully. She was fucking everything to me, but I didn't have the right to be possessive of her anymore.

Dad frowned, watching me for a moment, but I remained indifferent, and he came over, sighing in relief.

"I'm glad... for a moment, I thought you would bend because she was your mate." He patted my shoulder, and I resisted the urge to speak my mind.

He was right, I had changed in two years. All my adolescent years, I had trained to hide my emotions so when the time came, I would be able to deal with Andres. It was something I had mastered skilfully. Now, I would use the same on him.

"No. It changes nothing. Mom was killed by one, do you really think I'd have any consideration for her?"

"The bond does things to us. It can blind us and deter us from our goals," Dad replied, frowning deeply.

But you loved Mom, right? I didn't say it out loud. It was crazy, but I was beginning to question even the things I had witnessed and known as a child.

"You need not worry. I am going to find her and bring her back. We need her, right?"

"Yes… but I'm uncertain if sending you is the right thing to do. You aren't healed, and you are my son, I don't want anything to happen to you."

You didn't have an issue sending me to Andres.

"I can handle myself. Besides, we've worked too hard to get to where we are today. We need the heart under our control." His eyes sparked with a fire of approval, and he nodded.

"It seems knowing her truth has changed your view of her. I was beginning to worry that you were far too madly in love with her." I looked at him sharply. My heart skipped a beat at his statement, but I simply scoffed.

"Her being a Siren changes all of that. I will never forgive their kind," I growled. But she wasn't a monster… even when she rejected me and she took on the partial form of a siren, I couldn't hate her. She had remained forgiving for far too long.

"Good, good, but we need her for the power she possesses." He was still so hell-bent on having her when I thought he hated Sirens more than me and would rather want him dead.

"You hate them as much as I do, isn't killing her better? Do we really need her? After all, you vowed that we would kill them all," I questioned. I wasn't sure, but there was a flicker of unease there in his eyes…

"Of course I do! Those things are the reasons I lost my daughter and my mate! I have a plan, Theon, a plan that will kill them all," he hissed, gripping my shoulders painfully. "But I need her powers, hers and Arabella's combined. Just imagine it, I will be the most powerful Alpha alive. If the packs of this kingdom wish to live, they will have to rely on and submit to me."

"What do you mean combined?" I asked, trying to keep any trace of accusation from my voice. "What plans do you have, Dad? Don't you think I should have been told? I feel there's a lot that you are not telling me, and if we are meant to work together, then I should at least know."

"You are right, but we haven't really had the time, now, have we? But do you remember you asked me why I wasn't scouring the seas to find the Siren responsible for your mother's death? Well, it's because I have been working on a better way to kill them all." I frowned, looking at him sharply. I had begun to think that he really didn't care, but he had a plan?

"What other way is there?" A cold smirk crossed his face.

"Nathalia was mine, and she was taken from me far faster than she ever should have. I don't just want to kill the one who did it, but all of them. They all need to die." His words were full of venom. Strange... he hadn't seemed so bothered the last time we talked. Was he messing with my mind? "Tell me, Theon, how are the Sirens safe from us?"

"Because they reside in the oceans and seas that they control?"

"Exactly, and what if we poison those seas with something that affects only Sirens?" I looked at him sharply, my heart thundering. Yileyna was down there right now.

"How is it possible?" He smirked.

"I haven't completed it. There are certain elements we still need, but don't you see, Theon? I have been working extremely hard on this. To get revenge for your mother," he said quietly.

I frowned, trying to get my head around it. Something wasn't right. I just couldn't believe that he had kept this all from me and was now suddenly telling me. Why?

"What are the elements we are missing? If this is your plan and you can execute it, then I want to make sure we succeed."

"The heart. It possesses the ability of the land and sea. She is the only one who will be able to drive the poison deep into the farthest depths of the oceans."

And with it, make Yileyna claim the lives of thousands... I remembered her sadness for the Siren girl in Bellmead. There is no way Yileyna would be able to do it. Back then, she hated Sirens and still felt sorry for her; how would she feel killing them all, children and adults alike? She would never be able to live with the blood of that many on her hands.

"We will get her back, but how do you plan to get her to obey?" I asked emotionlessly.

"Perhaps it's a blessing in disguise that she is your mate. Although I know just the thought repulses you, this is for the greater good. When you mark her, your bond will strengthen, and she will succumb to your will. You can manipulate her to our bidding," he responded, smirking coldly. "We were meant for this. That was why you were mated to her, and with your hatred, there is no risk for you to lose your way!"

Lose my way? Or find my way? I loved Mom, and I always would, but me seeking revenge and manipulating someone else to do so on my behalf were two very different things…

My initial plan was to find that Siren, kill her, and then I would have let it go… killing the entire race was never the plan. Perhaps I was losing my way, but I needed to find Yileyna, and I wanted to find out what Hunter had discovered. I had to find the answers on my own accord and fast.

"That is the perfect plan," I said to Dad, placing a confident smirk on my face. "I'll search for her."

"You don't need to go, Theon, I have sent my men already."

"We cannot afford to waste time. I will go too."

He seemed to hesitate, obviously not happy with my stubbornness, but I knew he could tell my mind was made up. Besides, no one knew that she had been taken by Sirens. When Arabella had shown up, the storm had been far too violent. I had said she escaped. It was no mystery she controlled water, and Arabella had bought it.

"Fine then… but be careful. We have many enemies out there, Theon. I can get Arabella to put a spell on you, those who do not know you won't be able to recognise you." There was no way I was going to let that woman put another fucking spell on me.

"No thanks, I'll be fine. You don't need to worry about me. I will bring her back immediately." He gave a nod, slapping my shoulder and sending a violent flare of pain through me.

"That's my son. I'm glad that her true form and reality have made you see how very right we are in doing this."

"Of course." No, I'm just agreeing with you so I can find my own answers… "I do have a question. Where is Thea?" He looked at me, raising an eyebrow at my question.

"Oh, she's safe in Lochfox. She is residing in the city with a few of our older wolves. No one knows she is mine. She will be safe there until we can bring her here. She is a bit of a daredevil, and having her here would only have gotten her in trouble."

I almost smiled. She would be seventeen now. She had gotten her wolf shortly after I had left. She was fierce and feisty, and I had a feeling that wouldn't have changed. Dad's words proved that.

"That's good, she'll be safe." I nodded.

"Yes," he agreed.

"I will plan to leave immediately. I will start on getting supplies together for my journey," I replied, turning away, but he stopped me.

"No, Theon, there is no rush. You need to at least heal. I am as restless as you to get her back here, but I also need you to heal first. You are no use to me dead." Our eyes met, and I shook my head.

"I will gather supplies and set out. I won't fail you."

We both knew the wounds were far too deep for me to heal from. An injury made by a Siren was not one that would heal overnight. After I returned to the castle, the healer who had rebandaged my wounds had warned me. His words still rang in my mind.

"The chances of healing from these wounds are minimum… They are far too deep… I'm sorry, there is nothing more to do…"

Would I ever heal fully? Only time would tell.

Dad frowned, staring at my chest. Concern flickered on his face before he exhaled.

"That's my son. Stay resilient," he said simply. I gave a curt nod before taking my leave.

Yileyna was on my mind once more. Fated and rejected… was this our fate? The paths we walked were so different that I don't know why I had been so stupid to let myself get caught up in my emotions… I had destroyed not only my own resolution but, above all, her. I had lost the only thing that made me feel alive in the process too.

She told me to make sure the people of Westerwell were safe, but I needed to make sure she was okay before anything else. Call me selfish, but knowing the Sirens took her was fucking worrying me, and she was the only fucking thing I cared about.

It was high time I did a bit of snooping around here, and no matter how fucking angry I was at the bruises that littered her body, there was no way I could ask Dad without giving away my concern for her. I would find out who did it, and I would kill them, but before I left… there were two bastards that I was going to fucking castrate.

First, I needed to get in touch with the captain of the Siren Killer and its crew.

A Transformation

YILEYNA

*I*T HAD BEEN so much to take in, and although I was told to rest on it, I was unable to. Being underwater was daunting in itself, despite the fact that I was getting used to it.

Not to mention the dark-haired distraction that stood in my room. His dangerously handsome looks did not help my nerves. He was staring at me with intrigue and something more. Aquarius, that was his name, one of Deliana's guards. I had been mortified when she had said he would take care of me and how our guards were meant to satisfy us if we wanted. I had gotten embarrassed, however, none of the other Sirens had even batted an eyelid.

I was given some clothing, if you could call it that… it simply consisted of sheer fabrics or tiny jewelled pieces of metal for my breasts and a sheer piece of cloth to wrap around my waist. I sat on the bed, swinging my legs as I watched the ripples in the water.

I felt frustrated. There was so much to take in. I first thought being the heart was stressful enough, now, throw in the seven seas! I sighed, lying down on the bed, and stared at the glowing light around the edge of the ceiling, only for Aquarius to come over.

"Are you restless?" He asked.

"Umm, not entirely," I replied, feeling very naked right then. He nodded, his eyes raking over me as they lingered on my legs.

"You are beautiful... if you want to relax, I can help," he whispered seductively, his dark navy shimmery tail whipping as he closed the gap between us. Despite the coldness of the water, I was certain my cheeks burned at his words.

"I-I think I'm okay!" I mumbled, embarrassed as his fingers grazed up my inner thigh, making me gasp. I quickly pulled away and tucked my legs under me, but my curiosity had piqued.

Sex with a merman... imagine telling Charlene about that!

Theon's face came to mind, and my spirits were dampened. I did not want to let him get in the way. All he brought was pain, but I couldn't deny my heart still belonged to him. Or whatever was left of it.

"Well, I actually have a question," I said, staring at Aquarius's perfect abs. He crossed his arms, raising one of those dark, arched eyebrows.

"Ask away."

Well, I have always been a curious girl...

"Where is your... penis?" I asked confidently, ready for him to get embarrassed or think I was crazy, but hey, I am a weird-legged thing anyway. He smirked instead.

"You are a strange one. Isn't that obvious, or is it that you wish to see what I have to offer first?" I pouted and gave him a look.

"No, I'm just curious." I think I did want to see it... "I want to see if it's like those above water." I shrugged haughtily. Was I really asking a male to show me his manhood? Yes. Yes, I was.

He smirked. Then I saw where there was a slight curve to the front of his tail. The scales rippled before they moved aside, and out sprang a long hard dick.

I couldn't help but giggle, making him frown slightly, but I didn't care. I was far too intrigued to bother. I crawled closer, looking at the smooth cock. It was a bit darker in colour compared to his abdomen, with the scales blending around it. There was not one hair in sight. The tip was sharper, and it was rather long too, maybe twelve or eleven inches... although it got thinner towards the tip.

"What do you find so funny?" He asked as I smirked and moved back.

"Nothing, I just never thought I'd ever see a merman's cock," I said bluntly. He raised an eyebrow, smirking slightly.

"So, how is it?" He asked in a lower, huskier voice. I looked down at the merman's penis, blushing once more.

"It's nice and big," I complimented. "You can put it away now."

He seemed satisfied with my compliment before slowly letting the sheath of his scales hide it away once more. He didn't seem too impressed that I didn't want more as he backed away and took his place by the door.

Yes, I actually asked a merman to see his dick, I think I am losing my mind.

The moment's distraction vanished, and I became lost in my thoughts once more. It had been a while since Deliana and Lavina had begun to prepare the spell to remove the final seal. I was getting impatient. Deep down, I was scared… would I become a monster? Would I start killing people?

A light knock came, and the veil on the door lifted. Aquarius bowed his head to Deliana, and I wondered if he had slept with her, too, since he was her guard. Goddess, that would have been gross if I had accepted!

I looked up at Deliana once he had left the room. Her powerful gaze was on me, I tried to act normal, but it was obvious she could see right through me.

"What troubles you?" She asked. I looked down at my legs before I mustered the courage to speak the rather insulting question.

"I know Sirens hate our kind… but when I shift, when the seal is lifted, will I too get the urge to enchant and kill men mercilessly?" I asked, flinching internally at how that sounded. She raised a perfect eyebrow.

"If you hate them, yes, just as a werewolf would kill those they hate. I don't think you realise the damage your kind has done to us. We are sworn enemies, and the death of the other pleases us. Do you know the only men that died at sea long ago were the ones who we fell in love with? Without realising the risk of our desires upon man, they drowned in our arms… so, to answer your question; no, your desire to kill will not be stronger…" she replied, crossing her arms, "However, your sexual desire may be far stronger."

Great… that was all I needed. Now it made sense why they said to use Aquarius…

She smiled at my obvious worry and, coming over, ran her fingers through my hair. For a moment, I tensed at the intimate move of tender care, seeing her eyes soften.

"You are so young and innocent. I feared you would become a monster, just like him," she mused quietly. I looked away, trying not to stare at her magnificent tail as she sat beside me. It was interesting how both sides saw the other as the monsters…

"He didn't raise me. When my parents were killed and framed, he cast me aside… he only acknowledged me when he realised I was the heart," I found myself telling her. She frowned.

"Good. You didn't need him in your life. I am glad he didn't get to spend that time as a father with you," she spat, her eyes flashing angrily. It was obvious the hurt she felt was still extremely painful, far more than she would ever let on.

"I don't know if it helps, but the woman he thought was his fated mate had a spell put upon him to make him think she was his true fated mate," I said quietly. I saw the flash of anguish in her eyes before she tilted her head haughtily.

"I care not," she said with a coldness to her voice, despite the fact that I could hear the denial in it. "Yileyna… when I chose your name, I chose it for its uniqueness and strength. In the old language of the oceans, your name stands for light. In my darkest hours, you were the one keeping me from losing my mind. The temptation to end myself had grown stronger, but I was unable to, knowing I had you within me." She ran her fingers through my hair once more. I furrowed my brows and looked at her curiously.

"If you chose my name… does that mean Ariella told my parents or did you leave a note?"

"We left a note," she said, smiling slightly. "They are the only two werewolves that I may actually like. Ariella made the right choice."

"Did they know what I was?" I asked, my heart skipping a beat with worry at what the answer may be. She tilted her head once more, looking up at the glowing ceiling of the room.

"The note told them that you were the illegitimate daughter of the king and to keep you safe. However, when we needed to strengthen the spells, we sent Ariella to get you. We managed to take you; however, when she was on the way to return you, your father saw Ariella as she stepped out of the ocean. Although she was in her legged form, he would have surely known what you were, but he simply took you and told her that if she wanted to see you, she needed to be more careful, that if anyone was to find out, it would put you in danger. You were still so young at that time…" She sighed, but I couldn't stop the smile that graced my lips. My parents knew who I was, and they loved me.

Goddess, they loved me for me.

The fear that perhaps, if they had found out, they may have hated me had been something I dared not face, but now, hearing that they most likely knew… remembering how Mom told me my voice was just for her, to sing only for her… I covered my face as tears of relief and sorrow flooded my eyes. Could you even cry in water?

"What's wrong, my little tempest?" She asked, placing a hand on my back.

I don't know why, but I leaned into her, allowing her to hug me tightly. I couldn't explain it; yes, she was a Siren, and yes, it was the first time I was meeting her, but somehow there was something about her gentle, loving touch that reminded me of my mom, Hana.

"Hush, all will be well. You can see them soon," she whispered soothingly.

I pulled away, my eyes full of pain. I realised she didn't know that they were gone. I shook my head.

"No… they were killed a while ago," I whispered. Her eyes saddened as she stroked my hair.

"I am sorry. I owe them a lot for taking care of you. Every time I sent Ariella to shore to observe, she said you were loved and well taken care of. I often thought she was lying to make me feel better, but they raised you well."

"They did." Then Theon took them from me. "Why do you call me Tempest? Even Ariella did when we were travelling by ship." A small smile crossed her lips, and she stroked my hair.

"It was my name for you. My little tempest."

Little Tempest…

Little storm…

I smiled softly.

"I like it."

A knock at the entrance made us both turn, to see Lavina standing there.

"The preparations are done," she announced, motioning for us to come. Deliana stood, taking my hand as she swam to the door, pulling me along with her.

The fact that the king had tried to kill her in her sleep… just imagine the person you love the most doing that. My heart squeezed painfully at the thought. I had been betrayed by my beloved too...

Stepping out into the room, there were several things set up on the ground, along with some colouring on the floor. I wondered how they got it to stay rather than wash away... probably magic.

"Swim into the centre, Yileyna. This may hurt a little, but remember to stay calm."

I had been in enough pain. I was sure I could handle this. I nodded before swimming into the centre of the spell markings. I glanced at Deliana, who was watching sharply before she raised her hand, and a trident appeared in it.

"One of the seven tridents of the sea. They hold immense power and can only be yielded by the rulers of the seven seas," Deliana explained. I nodded in understanding.

Taking a deep breath, Lavina began chanting something in a hissing voice, whilst Deliana simply raised her trident and pointed it towards the circle around me. Her eyes turned darker as I felt the surge of power that enveloped me. I closed my eyes, feeling a sudden intense coldness encase me. It got tighter and tighter, until I felt like I wouldn't be able to breathe anymore.

Stay calm, Deliana's voice came into my head.

Calm...

I remembered the fields that Dad took me to as a child, the buttercups and daisies I used to pick... the calmness I felt... his embrace, his laughs... Mom's kisses and cuddles... her stories as she made me go to sleep...

Tears streamed down my cheeks as a sudden surge of emotions filled me. A wracking sob left my lips at the intensity of the emotions I was feeling. I missed them, I missed them so, so much.

She is in a lot of internal pain, yet she hid it so well... Lavina's murmur came. There was no way I was able to stop the sorrow that enveloped me.

Theon tickling me playfully... him making me coffee... him leaving me in the snow as I tried to give him the key to the cabin... oh, how naïve I was...

Suddenly the crushing pain of the cold that seemed to encase me vanished, and I gasped as I felt an odd heaviness wash over my lower limbs. Then to my surprise, right before my eyes, I saw a beautiful tail in the place where my legs were moments ago.

Lavina gasped in awe, and I had to admit my tail truly was a sight. It began low on my hips in a dangerous V that dipped right to my pelvis, and blended into a shimmering pearlescent silvery blue that dazzled and glittered like a thousand crystals, was a darker stunning blue where my knees would be, and then it went into shades of stunning purples, blues, and silvers, spreading across the pair of magnificent fins at the end. Instantly, I realised my tail was longer than even Deliana's. I could breathe perfectly, too. Before, it felt a bit stuffy, but now, it was like fresh air was surrounding me.

"A true royal," Deliana murmured with pride as she motioned to the mirror that hung on the wall. "She has the three fins at the back... Father will not be able to deny her..."

"And her eyes," Lavina added with awe.

I approached the mirror, the swimming coming a little easier than I thought it would, and stared into it. My waist looked narrower, and my breasts were slightly larger. My skin shimmered with a pearlescent sheen. I turned and saw the three little frilly fins at the back of my butt. My hair was much longer and was blonde from the top, which bled into an icy blue, with the tips a stunning purple that matched the purple in my tail. I looked into my eyes, framed by long, lush lashes, and saw the magical iridescent irises that stared back at me.

"I... I can't believe that's me," I whispered in a voice far more alluring and melodious than it used to be. I turned back towards Lavina and Deliana.

"With your final seal broken, you will now be able to shift at will, control the elements as you please, and become the queen you were born to be," Deliana said with approval and confidence.

Somehow, those words no longer worried me. They didn't scare me... because I was ready to be the queen I was destined to be.

A Challenging Condition

YILEYNA

Two days had passed, and when Deliana had said I'd feel far more desires, she had not been wrong. When I slept, I dreamt of Theon fucking me, and when I awoke, the thought irritated me, but I couldn't deny that I often had the most explicit images in my head of him. I just felt so horny to the point that I was often tempted to invite Aquarius over for some fun, but I refrained.

I tried to focus on other things instead, learning more about the sea and the issues here. Deliana, Lavina, and Ariella trained me a little, giving me tips on how to use my abilities. The way it rippled through me was so natural and felt so right. Swimming with my tail had become easy, and it was almost as if I had been born with a tail. Deliana told me that once I went ashore, I would be able to shift into any form I wished by simply thinking it.

We were travelling towards the Obsidian Ocean, where the sea emperor resided, the supreme ruler of the seven seas. It blew my mind how fast one could travel in Siren form, our strong tails never tiring. A few days ago, I never would have thought that I would be at the bottom of the ocean, swimming with the Sirens. A tale to tell one day…

From my time with Deliana and Lavina, it was obvious they did not want this war, and they had hopes I would be the one to be able to change the sea emperor's mind. The closer we got, the snappier and more restless Deliana got. I knew it was because she wasn't looking forward to seeing Queseidon, knowing the truth that I was her daughter was going to be revealed and his wrath would follow.

It was several hours later when we finally reached the magnificent golden undersea castle of the imperial ruler. It was breathtaking, with several turrets, towers and jewel-encrusted doors, and it oozed wealth and elegance. We were led inside, where hundreds of guards armed with spears flanked the glittering magical halls as we swam through them towards the emperor's throne room.

King Andres… a man who had been unfair, selfish, and thoughtless… then we have Theoden, the man who overtook us and took the position as king but was a true tyrant… and now, I was to meet a third king… one who is also hell-bent on power and revenge. Was this why a female was chosen? I didn't know, but I hoped the ruler of the oceans was different.

"Her Royal Majesty, Queen Deliana of the Aethirian Ocean, the Sea Witch Lavina, Princess Ariella, and…" The merman looked at us, and Deliana stepped into the grand hall.

"Allow me," she stated haughtily as we all entered behind her, my eyes falling upon the emperor.

He looked far younger than I had imagined he would, with a muscular upper body and a big, thick tail, which was in hues of shimmering greens and copper. His shoulder-length hair was a few shades darker than mine, with a beard. He wore a necklace and gold arm cuffs, and in his hand, he held a trident far bigger than Deliana's. It dazzled brightly with a silvery staff, and the three-speared head was of a pearlescent silver that seemed to glow. Upon his head was a gold band. It may not be the most extravagant, but he didn't need a huge headpiece to let all know he held immense power. That trident alone was enough proof of that.

They all bowed their heads to him, and I followed suit. The door slammed shut behind us, and I could feel Queseidon's gaze upon me.

"To what do I owe the pleasure of this meeting?" His voice was as cold as his pale grey eyes as he looked upon us from his magnificent dais, where he had sat upon his huge throne.

"Father, we all ask for your forgiveness, but there is someone I wish for you to meet," Deliana announced gracefully.

"And you brought her," he said with contempt, glaring at Lavina. She smiled gracefully at the Emperor.

"It is always a pleasure to accompany my granddaughters," she replied, taking me by surprise.

So that meant... her daughter was the mother of Deliana. Lavina was my great-grandmother! And it meant that Deliana and Ariella were not half-sisters as I had begun to assume. I had learned that the king had all his children from countless Sirens, the most powerful being given titles and oceans to call their own. The emperor didn't reply, turning his gaze upon me.

"Your majesty, allow me to introduce to you the heir to the Aethirian Ocean, the Alpha of the Silver Storm Pack, and Queen of the Kingdom of Astalion by right. This is Yileyna, the Heart of Kaeladia itself, and the first ever triform shifter as mentioned in the prophecy of the ancient Sea Witch Olaphena," Deliana said clearly.

His frown deepened as he stared at me. It felt like his eyes were going to burn two holes into me, but I steadily held his gaze, my face calm and with no hint of challenge or disrespect in my eyes. My only aim was to show him I wasn't afraid of him.

A light seemed to radiate from around him. It became blinding, but I refused to look away. The heaviness in the air was growing, and I saw Lavina, Deliana, and Ariella lower their heads, shielding their faces from the sheer brightness of the glow.

"The goddess Oshera's trident itself will show you who you are facing." His voice seemed to echo from every corner of the hall. The sea was becoming darker, too.

He raised his silver trident, and I saw the four pale blue jewels that were decorating the trident, only adding to its beauty. When he swung it towards me, sending a huge wave of power at me. I raised my hand in a flash, creating a barrier of ice. A glimmer of amusement was all I saw before the blinding wave of power hit the ice, just as Deliana summoned her own trident, but then the light vanished at the same time the ice shattered.

Queseidon's face seemed to pale as the sea water became lighter once more, his trident shook in his hold, and I felt an odd pull to it.

"She holds immense power," he remarked quietly, now clearly intrigued. His knuckles turned white, his hold incredibly tight.

"She does," Deliana responded. He looked between us, and I knew he had made the connection.

"So back then, you birthed a child." It was a statement, one that held a menacing undertone.

"Because of the prophecy, you were not told," Lavina intervened, but the emperor's rage was not going to be quelled. He looked at her murderously.

"I am the ruler of the seven seas. Do you think that I want anything of land down here?" He seethed.

"She is of us, too," Deliana reminded him of the obvious that he seemed to be forgetting.

"Then she must prove it by swimming with our army to land! Let's see how she is ready to kill them all," he hissed.

"I don't wish to kill anyone. What I want, and what I'm sure is the reason I am on Kaeladia, is to end this war between our kinds. Why must the innocent suffer for the crimes of a few?" I asked. He shook his head, slamming the bottom of his trident into the ground, making it tremble.

"There is no talk of negotiations here! You are not the one sitting on the throne of Astalion to be making talks of peace! You are a mere speck in a much bigger picture. Do you know how many of our kind are killed daily? Do you know how many poachers take my people for their scales and blood? Tell me, how many werewolves die per season?" He thundered. I didn't know... "I'll tell you! Not even a tenth in comparison to those Sirens!" He raged, his eyes darkening as he rose from his seat.

"Then allow me to fix this," I countered defiantly. Deliana stepped forward.

"Father, the prophecy was made for a reason... one born from land and sea, to unite us."

"Do not disobey me, Deliana! You committed sin by copulating with a werewolf! You should be imprisoned for your crime."

"Please consider this, Your Majesty. Will you sacrifice your children for something that can be prevented?" Deliana asked icily, her gaze steady as she stared at her father. He frowned, slamming his trident on the floor once more. Goddess, this emperor had such a temper...

"We may manage to kill many of them, but we will also lose many in the process, Your Majesty," Lavina said quietly. "Shaylena would not have wanted this." The emperor tensely looked down at the ground, as if suddenly remembering something, making him hesitate.

"Father, Mother always wished for peace... I know she is no longer here, but she would want us to, at least. Is her tail not proof of her royal blood?"

Deliana said quietly, taking my hand and making me do a full turn. I didn't understand what exactly they were looking at, but I remained silent.

"You will still be punished." He glared at her.

"Then punish her, but can you not trust in the one sent to us? We can try to make amends. I'm tired of not being able to sit on the shore and enjoy the attention of the pretty legged men," Ariella added, twisting a strand of her hair around her finger. That sounded rather fun…

"Please, at least give me a chance. When I regain the city of Westerwell, I will put new laws in place and make sure they are enforced. It's time that we do not live in fear of one another but cohabit in peace and without the constant threat that we may be killed. I promise I will make things better for your people and those upon land as well," I added with determination, and I planned to.

"Very well then. I will challenge you, the triform shifter. If you fulfil the quest I bestow upon you, we will hold off our attack and give you a chance to fix things. Do you accept?"

"What is the challenge?" I asked keenly.

"Do you accept or not?" He asked dangerously, clearly wanting me to agree blindly. Deliana frowned, giving me the slightest shake of her head. A warning not to.

"I accept." I knew that he wasn't going to trust me easily. Let's see what he wants from me. He smirked in victory.

"Then so be it. Retrieve the Pearl of the Enchanted Waves, and I will give you a chance to prove your control over those animals. Fail, and we attack two moons from now." My heart thudded at the thought that he was only giving us two months. Only two months before an army of Imperial Sirens stepped ashore with the aim to kill us all…

"The pearl?" Deliana looked shocked. "Father, that pearl is lost…" He shook his head.

"No, centuries ago, the Naga King of the Naran Empire stole it from us, and it is said to be in his possession until this day, passing it down to his successors. I can feel it. It hasn't been moved in years. Retrieve it, and I will give you the chance you want."

The Naran Empire was a dry area with little to no sea or ocean in it, with dense forestry. Was it hard for the Sirens to retain human form for long? Why did he want me to retrieve it? Aside from the dangers of course.

"Only a Siren can hold that pearl… if anyone else tries, they will die. What if her being a triform risks her -" Ariella was cut off when Queseidon's burning gaze turned upon her.

"Then she is not worthy to even be an heir to the Aethirian Ocean! If she is truly a Siren, then this will be the proof I need," he replied. "Remember, Deliana, if your child is not strong enough, I can give the title to someone else.

"She is far more powerful than us all!" Deliana hissed, her eyes flashing.

"What is this pearl?" I asked quietly, trying to calm the tension between the daughter and father.

"You need not know," Queseidon responded coldly.

"She must know to understand," Deliana retorted. Silence fell upon the room, and the emperor sat down once more before Deliana sighed and pointed towards Queseidon's trident.

"The trident of our goddess Oshera… can you see where the head joins the staff? The pearl is meant to stay there. It had the power of healing… a power that if we had had it in our possession, my mother and the first queen of His Majesty would still be alive…" she said quietly, "a pearl that can heal the deadliest of injuries and illnesses."

"The pearl is in the driest place in Kaeladia, a place that Sirens cannot venture," Lavina explained, confirming my thoughts.

"I'm sorry about her loss… I will do this, and I will retrieve it," I promised, making up my mind despite the fact that it was spinning with the high risk of this quest and the time limit I had.

"Then may Oshera be with you," the emperor said with a cold smile before he looked at me with a challenge in his eyes. "Time's ticking. You should really be going. I don't trust you, no matter how much power you hold… this will prove if all you want is power or if you truly wish to help." His grip tightened on his trident.

I realised that he didn't trust me, and if I wanted to win him over, then I needed to hurry up and retrieve the pearl to prove that I could do this.

A UNION

CHARLENE

THE DAY OF THE wedding had arrived, and I had never felt so alone. Hunter had been nothing but pleasant whenever I saw him, but it hadn't been as often as I had wanted. Being the Alpha, he was extremely busy. He had already begun to work on the team that would travel with us, sending scouts and messengers out in secrecy to our allies.

Although I had only attended one or two meetings, I realised Hunter was a man who was admirable. He was a little arrogant at times, a little teasing, quite handsome, and undeniably sexy... I had seen him with his shirt open two days ago and my stomach did not settle. Of course, I wasn't ready to be intimate with him yet, but I couldn't deny that the idea was beginning to entertain my mind quite often.

I was dressed in the lace dress that Hunter had asked the pack dress-maker to create for me, with my taste in mind. It had turned out far more beautiful than I had ever imagined it would. My hair was left open, styled in loose waves with a braid around the crown. A few strands framed my face on either side, and my make-up was soft and elegant. I looked pretty, but I was missing Yileyna. I always imagined her being by my side at my wedding, as I would be at hers.

Oh, how innocent we were. Back then, we would giggle and talk of marrying a handsome man, of having a magical wedding with dancing and many glasses of wine and ale. I smiled sadly, wishing she was here. I could just picture her, bubbling with excitement and naughty words, with her arms around my shoulder, telling me I looked amazing. She would whisper and tell me she wanted all the details of the wedding night and how she was happy for me…

"Luna, are you alright?" The Beta's mate, Polly, asked in concern. I blinked, realising I had tears in my eyes. I smiled and nodded reassuringly.

"I was missing my sister," I explained gently, giving her hands a comforting squeeze.

From the moment everyone realised that I was to marry Hunter, they were already addressing me as Luna. I did notice that there were a few who seemed irritated with this engagement, but I couldn't really blame them. Alpha Hunter was an ideal man to have by your side, not only because I know many women would love an Alpha, but because he was handsome, strong, and charming.

And he chose me.

"I'm sure when things are calm once more, we could perhaps throw an additional party," Polly suggested comfortingly.

"Thank you, Polly," I said, smiling at the woman who was only slightly shorter than me. Her stunning brown hair was in an elegant bun, and she wore a light mint dress.

A gentle knock on the door made me turn, and I saw Gamma Grayson standing there, dressed in a smart tunic and pants. My heart skipped a beat when I realised that I would be walked out by none other than my biological father.

"You look beautiful, Charlene."

"Thank you, Gramma Grayson," I replied. For a moment, I wanted to tell him that he was my father, but I knew I couldn't do that.

I had always imagined a wedding in the castle of Westerwell… full of high officials and nobles. A wedding where Dad would lead me to a groom that was chosen by him. I was nervous, yet I wasn't doubting my decision, something told me that it was all going to be perfect.

"It's time," he said, and I nodded as he held his hand out to me. I took it, allowing him to lead me from my room.

My strapless ivory lace gown flowed around me. The flower motifs covered the entire bodice, stopping at my hips before scattered lace flowers covered the tulle skirts. A row of button fastenings was on the back, and the train spread on the ground behind me as I allowed Gamma Grayson to lead me down the hall towards the backyard.

"I know your father would have been proud of you. You've made a decision that will not only benefit this kingdom but one chosen wisely. Alpha Hunter will also make a good partner. However, rest assured we will always be there for you if you ever need us," he said, making me smile. I looked into his brown eyes and nodded.

"Thank you," I whispered before I turned to the front, ready to do this...

We stepped into the open grounds, which had been decorated with garlands of flowers with a sprinkle of lanterns. The setting sun cast a radiant red glow upon the entire area. Everyone from the pack was there, sitting upon the rows of chairs. Soft music played, and a bed of rose petals ran down the centre, leading to the archway where none other than Hunter stood, looking like a god. My heart thudded seeing him in a white shirt tucked into black pants, his hair was sleeked back, and although he was dressed smartly, it was still casual, only adding to how extremely handsome he looked.

I watched as his eyes trailed up my form and noticed them flash silver. My chest was heaving, and when our eyes met, I almost stopped moving at the look in his. I didn't understand it... I didn't know why he chose me when there were so many beautiful women in his pack. I was forced to look away from his gaze the moment that small teasing smirk crossed his lips. I knew everyone could hear my pounding heart. As we passed Ryan, Rhys, and Raiden, the Bolton brothers gave me the thumbs up whilst Raiden gave me a smile.

You look beautiful, and it's obvious the Alpha is head over heels for our princess, he said through the link. I smiled slightly, and then we were stopping before Hunter.

"Please take care of the light of our pack," Gamma Grayson said to Hunter, who was staring at me intensely, holding his hand out to me. Was it my hair? I know in the sunlight, it always looked like it was on fire. Yileyna said it was beautiful, but I wasn't sure. It was Hunter who had chosen the time for the wedding to take place.

"I'm afraid she is no longer the light of yours but the light of mine," he replied the moment I placed my hand in his, making my stomach flutter nervously as he tugged me away from Gamma Grayson. I looked into his eyes, trying to calm the storm of emotions within me. "You even make the sunset fade in comparison to how beautiful you look, my Luna," he said, making a few of his men whistle and hoot. I blushed.

"Thank you… you look very handsome, too," I managed to reply.

His response was that teasing smirk of his before he kissed my hand softly, making my core knot at the way his lips grazed my hand, sending a ripple of pleasure through me. Every time he saw me over the last few days, he would bid me farewell with a kiss on the cheek, and each time it left me a hot mess.

"I was right… sunset was the perfect time," he murmured, taking my other hand and placing both against his chest. He forced his attention away from me and looked at the huge gathering. "As everyone knows, I have chosen for myself a woman to become my Luna, my mate, and my wife. Today we bear witness to this. Elder Lorenzo, proceed."

The Elder stepped forward, holding a velvet-encased plate that held two small knives. It was time.

"Do you, Charlene Aphelion, daughter of the late king of Astalion, take Alpha Hunter Slade Carson as your husband?"

"I do," I replied softly as Hunter placed another kiss on my knuckles.

"And do you, Alpha Hunter Slade Carson, take Charlene Aphelion as your bride?"

"Of course. Yes, I do," his confident reply came.

"Then, by the gods, we witness this moment. Alpha, please proceed with the pack oath," Elder Lorenzo advised.

"Do you, Charlene Aphelion, vow to love and cherish the Iron Claw Pack and take me, Alpha Hunter Slade Carson, as your mate and Alpha?"

"I, Charlene Aphelion, vow to love and cherish the Iron Claw Pack as my own. I vow to take Alpha Hunter Slade Carson as my mate and Alpha."

We both reached for the knives and sliced our hands before we shook hands, binding our oath. I felt the jolt of the pack link being created, and with it, I felt the bond to my old pack break away, a bittersweet moment. I'm sure Yileyna had felt it too.

"You may mark the bride," Elder Lorenzo said, making my heart skip a beat. The marking. Hunter's eyes met mine and I forced a small smile, but he simply glanced toward the pack.

"Due to the upcoming war, I've decided that my Luna will not be marked by me in case of my unexpected death," he proclaimed clearly with a small smirk on his face. A murmur spread through the crowd, and even Gamma

Grayson looked shocked too. My stomach plummeted as I stared at him. The thought of him dying at war...

"Don't say that," I said quietly. He raised an eyebrow.

"We are barely married, and you are already going to command me?" He teased, making me blush.

"N-no, I just meant don't talk about dying at war," I murmured softly. He cupped my face, giving me a wink.

"I will try not to. No man with a woman as beautiful as you would wish to die." Goddess, he was so flirty now. I tried not to pay attention to the awes and compliments that ran through the crowd. "Mark me, My Luna," he commanded quietly, serious once more. He was giving me the time I had asked for, but to mark him...

I glanced at the crowds, knowing that many were going to disapprove. He was the Alpha, and an Alpha always marked his mate first...

"Alpha..." someone began, but one dangerously cold look from Hunter cut him off, and to my surprise, he grabbed me by my waist and lifted me up. I gasped, holding onto his shoulders as he smirked, slowly tilting his head to the side. He wrapped one arm around the back of my thighs, and my heart thumped as I looked into those taupe-coloured eyes.

"Mark me."

"Are you sure?" I whispered.

"From the moment I laid eyes on you." I heard a few chuckles, but his words gave me confidence.

"The Alpha is head over heels," someone teased. I ignored them all, bending down slightly. I brought my canines out before I bit into his neck, hearing his heart race as I felt the bond strengthening. I slowly extracted my teeth from his skin, licking the wound slowly. My core clenched at the intimate move, and I softly placed a kiss on his neck, hearing him suck in a breath.

Thank you, I whispered through our newly formed bond. His hand gripped the back of my head before he pulled me down, placing a peck on my cheek and lowering me to my feet.

"Applaud your Luna," he commanded, making the crowds burst into cheers and howls.

I had never thought that I would ever be the Luna of the pack on the borders of the Naran Empire, but here I was, and I was excited about the future. I looked at Hunter and smiled softly. Something told me he was going to be the perfect mate...

"Congratulations, Alpha Hunter, Luna Charlene," Elder Lorenzo said as we finished our vows.

"Thank you," I responded. Hunter turned to the people and, taking my hand, raised it.

"Tonight, we celebrate our Luna, we drink, and we feast, and tomorrow... tomorrow, we prepare for a battle."

Everyone cheered, and although his words held the ominous reminder of what was to come, everyone was still very happy.

I stared into the eyes of the man who had made a bond with me, the pleasant sparks of that bond which was now partially formed. They may not be as strong as those of a fated mate, but it was a bond that had been made. His scent was slightly stronger, and I had the urge to lean into him and take a long whiff. He smelled very good.

He placed his hand on my waist as several people came to congratulate us, starting with Gamma Grayson and the boys.

"Congratulations," Ryan said, giving me a hug before Raiden and Rhys hugged me too.

"Drinks for the bride and groom!" Someone shouted.

"Do you drink, My Luna?" Hunter asked as I was about to reach out to take a glass from the tray.

"A little, yes," I replied, pausing. Hunter smirked, taking two glasses.

"Then let's keep it to a little..." he said quietly.

Because I want My Luna to be in her right mind tonight, he added through the mind link. My heart thudded, and my eyes widened as I looked at him. He simply smirked. Don't worry, I won't touch you. Not unless you want me to, his husky voice assured me through the link as his eyes skimmed over my heaving chest, leaving me a giddy mess...

TRUSTING HER

HUNTER

THE WEDDING HAD GONE well. We all dined on plenty of meat and wine, and we had finally retreated for the night.

My bedroom had an extra wardrobe and a chest of drawers in it now, stocked with clothes in her size beforehand. Polly, or someone, had scattered my dark brown bedding with red and white petals. A platter of chocolates and wine stood on the table beside the bed, and lanterns had been lit, casting a warm dim light around the room.

I removed my shoes the moment we entered, wanting to pull my shirt off, but I wasn't sure she was ready for that. Her heart was already beating louder than the drums of war. My pretty little cherry-faced princess.

"Do you wish to undress?" I asked, jerking my head towards the bathroom and locking the bedroom door. She shook her head quickly, and I nodded.

"Will you tell me a little about your family? I have wanted to ask you about your mother. It was clear from our short conversations that you respected her highly." She asked, taking a seat on the bed. It was obvious she was trying to make conversation.

Did she not realise how beautiful she looked? Not to mention enticing. Seeing her bathed in the glowing rays of the sunset was a moment I'd never forget… she looked absolutely breathtaking tonight. I pushed the thoughts of how she would look naked out of my head and focused on her question.

I needed to tell her the truth about who Theon was to me…

"My parents are dead. My mother found her fated mate when I was almost two years old. She was unable to deny the bond between them and left my father to be with him." It always stung, knowing that she left me… that part always did, no matter how many times I tried not to think of it. I didn't look at my new bride, not wanting to see the sadness or pity on her face.

"She kept in touch, or at least tried to. She first wanted to take me with her, but my father refused. He was already angry at the fact that she had left him, but he didn't really blame her either. The bond of true mates… it's strong." I clenched my jaw, remembering seeing her with a baby Theon, then Thalia and Thea. It hurt to see them having a happy family whilst I was just alone…

"I'm sorry."

"Don't be. It hurts a little, that won't go away, mostly because I felt like I was just cast aside. Dad was mortally wounded by a Naga when I was ten and he forbade me from telling anyone. However, he didn't get better, and when I was eleven, he passed away, leaving me alone. I hadn't seen my mother for nearly nine months at that time. They were on the run, so I only got the occasional letter. Sometimes they'd come in bulk, sometimes single. She always wrote them, every Friday… even if she couldn't send them, but she'd send them in bulk when she could… telling me how she was, how my siblings were doing." I walked to the window, looking out at the moon, lost in my own thoughts.

"Then… what happened?" I heard the rustle of her dress.

"I was never able to write back because her location was always a secret. I was never given the chance to tell her I was scared when things got hard." I don't even know why I was telling her; I didn't tell anyone this crap. I should just skip to the main part. Her hand rested on my back, sending off the rippling sparks that we had formed, and I tensed, turning slightly to look at the woman before me.

"I heard you became Alpha at the age of eleven… that must have been hard," she said softly.

"It was fine. Mom came from a special race of werewolves who held a sort of elemental ability, so even if I hadn't shifted, I have my powers," I mused, raising my hand and watching the silver glow wrap around my hand. She gasped in awe, and I smirked.

"It's not as strong as my brother's but it worked well, and I was recognised as Alpha."

"You are an incredible Alpha," she added, giving me that gorgeous smile of hers. I turned to face her, crossing my arms as I leaned against the wall.

"Oh yeah? How so?" She blushed before pouting.

"We are deviating from the conversation, Alpha Hunter. Tell me more about your siblings. Did you keep in touch?" My smile faded and I nodded.

"Yeah. She used to tell me that I was their brother, and she had told them about me too. She made me promise that I would look out for them and take care of them. I have a brother and two sisters. I never really thought much of it until I found out she died at sea. Killed by a Siren... her and my baby sister." She placed a hand on her chest, and although she didn't speak, I could see the pain on her face.

"I'm sorry... what of your brother and your other sister?"

"My sister... I don't really know. I've tried to find her, but I'm not getting far... I'm assuming she's hidden, by magic, maybe. As for my brother... he is currently in Westerwell, following his tyrant of a father blindly. He has been raised by a man who is nothing more than an evil killer," I confessed, shaking my head.

"Westerwell?" She asked confused. I looked at her, the chance to tell her right before me.

"Theon. Theon is my younger brother," I replied quietly, making her eyes widen as she stared at me.

"By the Goddess! I see it!" She exclaimed, staring at my face.

"I really don't think you did," I replied, amused, raising an eyebrow. Her sudden surprise vanished, and the weight of my revelation finally seemed to dawn upon her.

"So... going against... by helping us, you may have to face your brother," she whispered, concern clear on her face.

"Perhaps I just needed an incentive to do what's right." She looked at me thoughtfully before she smiled, stepping closer and placing her slender hand on my arm.

"Thank you. Not only for your help but for sharing this with me. As for Theon... I think he just needs the truth to be shown to him. Before the attack, when he drugged me, I saw the conflict in his eyes. I think his father has poisoned his mind. He does care for Yileyna... maybe you and Yileyna both can help him see the truth."

"Yeah, he is blinded by Theoden, but Theon needs to realise the truth soon or he will never be able to forgive himself. Let's hope that we can reach out to him." She nodded, her hand still on my arm as she gazed up at me with those gorgeous green eyes that were far too mesmerising for me to ignore.

"We will." The conviction in her voice made me smile slightly, despite the fact that I wasn't sure if she was right. Was Theon reachable? Or had he gone past the point of redemption?

"With those alluring eyes staring at me, there is nothing that can make me disagree with you," I replied, reaching up and brushing her hair back. My knuckles caressed her forehead before I twirled a strand of her hair around my finger, and for a second, her eyelids fluttered shut. The urge to see how far she'd let me go consumed me, and I pushed myself away from the wall, cupping her face.

Her eyes fluttered open, her breasts heaving, but she didn't move away from my touch, instead placing her hands on my chest. Her touch made my dick throb, and I wouldn't deny I wanted her. I had touched no one since she had set foot on this pack, and I craved far more than she was ready to give me. Her gaze dipped to my lips, and she licked her own, not even realising what she was doing.

Fuck this, I wanted her, and unless she told me to stop, I wasn't going to. I tilted her face up, staring into her eyes for a moment before I claimed her lips in a kiss.

Fuck, her plump lips were far softer than I had imagined. A low growl escaped me as I kissed her with passion and hunger. She slowly began kissing me back, and I slowed down, letting her lead and experiment. Her heart was pounding, the sweet taste of her mouth making me want to plunge my tongue in until she begged for air. We kissed for a few moments, her soft whimpers and moans turning me on, but when she finally gasped for air, I moved back. The dangerously intoxicating scent of her arousal hit me, awakening the beast within.

I was going to make her mine.

Her heart was pounding, but her eyes were full of desire, and I ran my thumb over her lips.

"If you want me to stop, tell me," I whispered huskily.

She nodded before she wrapped her arms around my neck, pressing her lips against mine with a burst of confidence. I almost smirked. Seems like I'm not the only one who wants a taste of the other. I wrapped my arms around her, kissing her harder while my hands roamed her waist and back. Our lips were moving against one another's, and she was far more confident in herself now. The pleasure that was consuming me was driving me crazy.

I had never wanted a woman more. I fiddled with the buttons of her dress, pulling them open as she whimpered against my lips. Her hand ran down my chest, and as much as I wanted to feel her hands on my skin, I wanted her naked first.

"I may not mark you yet… but I will make you mine," I promised, letting her dress slip to the floor, leaving her standing there in a tiny ivory lace lingerie and garter set. Her body was perfect; tall, slender, and lean. Her creamy skin was a perfect contrast to her fiery hair. Her cheeks flushed a pretty pink as she looked down and covered her breasts with her hands, pressing her knees together.

Just the way she stood there made me throb hard, my hard-on straining against my pants. I stepped back, pulling my shirt off as she coyly looked up at me. I gave her a smirk, pulling her into my arms and lifting her bridal style, making her yelp before I carried her to the bed. Her heart was thumping as she clutched my shoulder. I placed her on the bed, climbing on top of her before kissing her lips.

I wasn't certain, but the way she was acting made me wonder if she was a virgin. I wanted to make sure I took it slow, even if I wanted to fuck her senseless. Besides, virgin or not, it was our wedding night, and I wanted to make her feel like the queen she was. I needed to keep my beast under control, at least for tonight. I kissed down her neck, sucking and licking it sensually. She whimpered in pleasure. Her eyes shut as she lay there, her hand caressing my arms and chest.

I went lower, kissing her over her plump breasts and reaching behind her. I unclasped her bra, slowly pulling it off her. I stared at her creamy white skin and those soft pink nipples, pleasure rushing south as my eyes flashed with desire. I straddled her before caressing her hair gently as I looked into her eyes.

"You are indeed the epitome of beauty, My Luna," I whispered huskily, kissing her plump lips softly before I licked her stiff nipple. She moaned hornily, clamping a hand over her mouth, and I almost smirked.

You need not hide how you feel. Don't hold back. You belong to me, and so do your moans.

She whimpered, nodding her head as I played with her breasts for a few moments longer before I trailed kisses down her waist.

"Goddess," she moaned when my lips touched her lower stomach, just above the band of her tiny panties. As much as I wanted to eat this pussy out, I wasn't done. She parted her legs ever so slightly, although she struggled internally before her body won, and she relaxed, baring her pantie-clad pussy to me. Oh, I couldn't fucking wait to fuck this...

I simply placed a kiss there, making her gasp as I inhaled deeply, throbbing hard.

"Not yet, Princess... not yet," I whispered huskily before I parted her legs and kissed her inner thighs, making my way lower. She writhed under me, her chest heaving, her nipples standing to attention as I kissed her ankles teasingly.

"Hunter..." she moaned, making my eyes flash. Fuck, did that sound good coming from her. I pulled her panties down and raised them to my nose, taking a whiff, my eyes on her. She blushed, pressing her legs together as she stared at me.

"You smell incredible," I murmured, fisting up a handful of petals and sprinkling them over her. A true work of art...

She sat up, her heart pounding as she pulled me gently towards her.

"Take me," she whispered softly.

"I plan to... but not so fast, My Luna. Patience..."

She almost pouted as I pushed her back onto the bed and pressed open her thighs, then went down on her. She gasped, crying out in pleasure the moment my tongue touched her hot, dripping pussy. I would show her heaven.

"Oh, Alpha..." she whimpered, her back arching off the bed as I devoured her.

Fuck... I wasn't showing her heaven, this right here was fucking heaven.

Her entire body writhed with pleasure, her erotic moans only breaking the bindings on my self-control. I could eat her out all night, but she was near, and I needed her. I moved back just as she was on the edge, making her whimper as she looked at me with a confused disappointed look, and I almost chuckled. Ah, she was so innocent.

I removed my pants, and she slowly sat up, helping me yank my boxers down with trembling hands. Her flushed cheeks darkened when she saw my cock. She ran her hand under my hardened balls, her heart thumping as she leaned up for a kiss. I kissed her back hungrily, thrusting into her hand as she wrapped it around my cock.

"I need you now," I growled, pulling away.

Her heart thumped, but she nodded, and I lay her back gently before I climbed on top of her. Our eyes met, and she locked her arms around my neck. No words needed to be spoken. She knew I'd be gentle, and I knew she trusted me…

I reached between us, guiding my cock as I rubbed the tip against her clit. She whimpered, her eyes closing as she gripped my shoulders tightly. Oh, fuck.

I pressed into her, feeling her tightness. I kissed her softly, trying to distract her, and she relaxed slowly as I began thrusting into her, little by little. Her heart was racing, but her body craved more, locking her legs around my waist as she pulled me closer.

"You're perfect," I murmured as I thrust into her in one slow, deep move, making her gasp. I felt the trickle of her hymen breaking, the smell of blood mixing with the smell of sex and sweat, a smell that was my new addiction.

"Don't stop," she whispered as our eyes met once more. A small smirk crossed my lips, and I kissed her hard as I slowly began making love to her.

Oh, my beautiful Luna, I don't plan to…

Their Punishment

THEON

THREE DAYS HAD PASSED since Yileyna had vanished beneath the surface. Despite the worry I felt, I knew she was alive. She was out there, and I would find her.

I had gone to Ailema to tell her to get in touch with Flynn and that I needed to travel once more, but she had told me it would take a bit of time. As much as I hated to wait, I had no other option.

I unwrapped my bandages, staring at the wounds that were simply not healing at all. They had been stitched as well, but they were still raw and bloody. The stinging pain was a welcoming reminder of the invisible internal wounds I had inflicted on her…

A Siren's attack in anger was far more deadly than those in a normal attack. The head healer had explained that their anger and rage created a poison that was excreted through their nails and lips, hence how the name 'the touch of death' came about. I cleaned the wounds, hissing at the stinging pain, pain that was beginning to spread to the rest of my body slowly. I grabbed fresh bandages, wrapping them around before I glanced at my watch.

It was past ten at night, and there were a few things I planned to do… something that had been on my mind for far too long, and I would do it before I left, just in case I didn't make it back. I wasn't the type of person who forgot or forgave those who had crossed me...

I got dressed quickly, pulling on black pants and a black t-shirt, then put on my coat and slipped one of my daggers into my pockets. The one blade would be enough to get the job done. I left the castle after applying a scent-disguising charm, trying to hold back my aura as much as possible and keeping my head down as I made my way out into the city of Westerwell. The snow had melted, and the ice was quite dangerous now, but it wouldn't remain for much longer, and once these paths were cleared, Dad would launch his plan... a plan that I had discovered yesterday when I did some prying of my own.

A plan that involved him making sure every pack saw him as the king. There would be legions marching out to each pack and making them take an oath. That was the part that made no sense. People would swear their allegiance to their kind, but what kind of oath was he planning to enforce? It angered me that Dad had a lot more fucking planned that he hadn't even bothered to share with me. I wasn't treated like his fucking son but just a tool for him to use.

Fuck that shit.

My eyes blazed as I stuck to the shadows of the streets that were far quieter than they used to be under the rule of Andres. Dad's men were everywhere... pack members who I didn't recognise from two years ago. That was another thing... none of Dad's closest were there. They were all new, or people I had never really been close to. Where exactly did he get all the manpower he held? The Obsidian Shadow Pack wasn't as big as it is now. There was a lack of women and children, and although that could be because many were still not here, the question still stood. Where were these men from, that seemed to be strangers to me?

Walking through the crowds, I felt detached. This place was never home until Yileyna and I spent that short period together at the cabin. Back then, I used to look forward to the time I'd return home to her, seeing her waiting for me and holding her whilst I tried to get some sleep. Those were things I would always miss the most.

I had hurt her to the point that I broke her repeatedly. The most I could do was punish those who had tried to hurt her. But what about me? I deserved to be punished for hurting her as well, but being apart from her was a punishment far more painful than any physical form of attack.

I walked down the side of the White Dove, slipping past the guards with ease. I knew he would come here; once a week on his day off, he would be here. Every single time he'd take the same room. I silently made my way around the building before I stopped outside the window to the room I knew he would be in. The curtains were drawn, yet a small gap allowed me to see in.

He was there, fucking one of the Omega whores. I moved back, frowning; I'd give him time to have one last woman in his life…

I crouched down, looking at the flimsy lock on the window that I had tampered with earlier in the day. I glanced inside once more, just in time to see him push the woman off of him as he stood up and walked towards the window. I smirked, pulling away as he opened it and lit a cigar. Well, this made things easier. It seemed even Selene wanted me to deal this punishment.

I reached for my dagger, pulling it out. I turned in a flash, slicing off his testicles and penis without even casting him a look. Blood sprayed everywhere, and I swiftly walked away as Kyson's scream of agony filled the air, taking him a few moments to realise what had happened. If he survived, he would live his life as a eunuch. If he even for one moment thought he'd get away with what he tried to do with Nikolai, then he had been sorely mistaken.

As for Nikolai, he was ten times worse than Kyson, and his punishment would be that much worse too.

"You wanted to see me?" Nikolai asked, crossing his arms as he glanced around the training area, the very same one where he had tried to assault her. I looked up at him as I leaned against the tree she had been practising on.

"If it comes down to what I want, I'd rather never see your fucking face again." He scoffed, crossing his arms.

"Yet you called me here… what do you want?" He replied. I didn't miss the irritation in his voice, but he was trying to control himself, knowing who I was. Wise move.

"Do you recognise this place?" I asked, looking around as if to prove my point.

He looked around before a flicker of understanding settled onto his face, along with unease. He didn't reply, and I continued.

"The very place where you tried to rape her. What made you think you'd get away with it?" I asked, raising my eyebrow. He clenched his jaw but didn't speak, so I walked toward him. "I'll tell you why... because she had no status or protection, right?" I asked, dangerously quiet as I circled him slowly.

"She was a whore who enjoyed the attention. Was that not obvious from the way she dressed?" He replied with a cold sneer. Anger flared through me, but I kept it in.

"Hmm, so her dressing how she wants makes her a whore? I'm tired of hearing it and putting up with it..." I replied quietly.

"What did you want? Surely you didn't call me here to lecture me about a woman who ran away," he replied.

"You mean your Alpha," I reminded him. He scoffed but shook his head.

"She can never be an Alpha."

Wrong. She had the fucking fire to become one from day one.

"We both can't stand one another, so I will get to the point. What you did that day was something that I don't plan to forgive. You tried to take away her choice. She was fighting you, yet you refused to let her go..." Remembering that day, I felt the burning pain of rage in my chest.

"What do you plan to do?" He asked, and for the first time, I saw fear in his eyes. I smirked coldly. Yileyna had had fear in her eyes that day, too, but he didn't care.

"I'm going to make you feel pain," I whispered, menacingly grabbing hold of his skull.

My aura surged around me, and he screamed in agony as the amber flames enveloped his head. With my other hand, I grabbed his wrist, crushing it in my hold. A scream left his lips and in a flash, I had my claws out, slicing his neck. His eyes flashed as he fell to his knees, clutching it. It wasn't deep enough to kill.

I kicked him back, grabbing his other hand and squeezing it in my hold until I heard the cracking of bones. I did the same to the other again, making sure it was broken to the point of no return. I would make sure they were so damaged that no healing would be able to fix them. I looked into his eyes and saw my own blazing gold.

"These hands tried to hurt her," I replied quietly before shoving him back onto the ground and taking out my dagger.

His eyes were filled with fear as he looked at me, trying to crawl away, but I was faster, plunging the dagger into his crotch. Blood began staining his dark grey pants instantly. His eyes flew open in agony, but there was nothing he could do; his hands, broken beyond repair, lay uselessly by his side. I stood up and tilted my head.

"If you do end up surviving… which I highly doubt, let this be a reminder to think before you act." I bent down, twisting my knife, knowing I had torn up his cock before I yanked my dagger free roughly.

He let out a choked scream, his eyes rolling. He wasn't going to survive because I had made sure the blade had been coated in poison, but it would be a slow death. Strangled noises left him as he tried to say something to me, but he wasn't able to. I turned and walked away, leaving him out there alone.

The rain was falling steadily, and I welcomed it. It reminded me of her… the storm that I had pushed away…

Dad would know I did this, but I didn't care. I never bent to anyone, and Dad was no exception.

I let the darkness welcome me, making my way towards our cabin… a place that held memories that I needed to help clear the havoc from within me…

FACE TO FACE

YILEYNA

"Ah, I could look at you all day," Ariella swooned, smiling as she looked at my tail. "And it seems like none of the males could stop staring either."

I know. Deliana had given me several more mermen, which didn't help the temptation they offered. Once I was on land, we wouldn't need them, but when I had come face to face with a deadly shark or two and a sea monster, I had felt relieved to have them handle it.

We were currently in Deliana's kingdom. It was my final night there. I had seen the emperor this morning, and tomorrow we would set out for the surface. I would go back on land and then I would get in touch with Raiden if I could, but more so I needed to head to the Iron Claw Pack. It was the only way into Naran, from their territory or unless, of course, I went around to the deadly marshes. Then there was the Fae Kingdom on the other end which would take far too long.

I was worried too. I had felt some pack links break and it terrified me. What was happening? Who had died?

I looked at Deliana in the mirror. I was dressed in a silver breastplate like Deliana's, encrusted with blue and purple jewels, and she was busy creating small plaits in my hair, adding in jewels and pearls. I had told her she didn't need to do all this, but it was obvious she had wanted to.

"Oh, how could I have forgotten? I will go get it," Deliana murmured before she swam off to get something. Ariella looked at me as she combed her own hair.

"Let her. She is only taking care of her child for the one day she has, something she has yearned to do for years. Deliana holds a lot of anger and pain. She might come off as haughty and reserved, but she loves you," she remarked, giving me a pointed look.

I nodded. I had figured as much. For the last few days, she had taken good care of me, and even Lavina and Ariella didn't think she'd forgive them for bringing me into the ocean. However, she seemed far happier to get to spend some time with me than any of us had thought possible.

"Here, look," Deliana's voice made us turn to see her carrying a large, light blue, glittering box.

"That's…" Realisation struck Ariella, and she trailed off.

"Yes, the eighteen gifts I had purchased for her for the last eighteen years," Deliana confirmed, placing the box in front of me. My heart skipped a beat, accompanied with a pang of pain remembering my mother, Hana.

The Siren before me opened the box and I realised that although Deliana could never replace Hana, she may find her own place in my heart. Her love was obvious in her own way, and she wasn't afraid to express it.

I turned my attention to the box just as she took out a multi-coloured jewelled necklace first, then she took out a coral pink jewelled one, followed by three necklaces with drop pendants.

"For your first five birthdays, I purchased these," she said, fastening them around my neck. "I apologise that they are not in the shades of your tail, I never knew what colour you would take."

"They are beautiful, thank you," I said quietly, admiring the pendants around my neck. I was surely wearing more jewels than I ever had in my entire life, but I didn't complain, allowing her to show me the bracelets, arm bands, and body chains. Seventeen items later, I was decked out in earrings, rings, and hand chains as well.

"Now… the final piece was the headpiece. Let me finish your hair…"

She went back to finishing the intricate plaits she was creating on the top layer of my hair, leaving most of it open. She then took out a stunning silver halo headpiece set with pale blue jewels.

"The final gift, with some of the most precious jewels in the seven seas," she said proudly, placing the headpiece on my head. I stared in the mirror.

"You look beautiful, and why wouldn't you? You are my daughter, and I'm certain no one will be able to resist your charm." She looked at me proudly. I knew Sirens were vain but it was obvious they took greater pride in their appearance than I thought.

"Well, I will leave you two to have some time together. I will sleep since tomorrow we will be heading to the surface," Ariella said, swimming out of the room. I looked at Deliana, who was preening a few strands of my hair again.

"Do you… live here alone?" I asked. She looked up at the silver roof of the room, casting a glance around it before she nodded.

"Yes. Ariella prefers to travel, and I do not have a mate. My harem is in a separate cove, away from the castle," she declared. I nodded, feeling sad for her.

"When things are sorted… I will come to visit you," I found myself mumbling. Her heart thudded as she stared into the mirror, our eyes meeting.

"You will?" She asked quietly.

Yes, she already told me I'd be the future ruler of the Aethirian after she passed away. Although I had no idea how that would work, I wouldn't think of it now, but I was talking of the present.

"Yes. When we don't have the threat of war upon our heads, perhaps you can come to the surface too? If the emperor lifts the punishment. Westerwell is near the coast. I would like to do your hair and makeup in the style of our kingdom," I offered. A smile crossed her face, and she nodded, wrapping her arms around my shoulders.

"I would love that," she replied, giving me a squeeze. She didn't move, resting her head against mine. We remained like that for a while, before she tilted her head. "Do you have a lover?" She asked suddenly.

My heart thudded, and the suffocating pain in my chest returned with vengeance. Theon…

"He isn't my lover anymore, but there is a man that I love…" I said quietly. "He turned out to be my mate, too, but he betrayed me. He betrayed our pack. He was the one who set up the attack and targeted my parents, the reason they are dead." My eyes filled with tears, and I looked down, the agony in my chest growing. "How can I still love someone who has caused me so much pain?" I whispered without looking at her, unable to hold her gaze any longer.

She sat beside me, placing her arms around me and resting my head against her chest.

"We can't control our hearts. I still loved him, even after he tried to kill me… even after he commanded the death of us all… and I still love him." Her heart was pounding, her voice extremely low. I closed my eyes, simply letting my tears flow. In a way, we were similar; both having been betrayed by our beloveds, yet neither of us could stop loving them.

In his own way, Theon showed some care towards me by accepting my rejection. The way he kept protecting me in front of his father. I needed to make him wake up and see the truth. Somehow, not for the sake of my feelings, but for his sake.

"What is he like?" She asked.

"He's… very closed off, but he cares in his own way. He's protected me several times since my parents died… I wonder if he felt like he owed me that," I mused, hoping it wasn't so. I stared at my hands. The ring he had given me was missing, along with my mother's ring. When I had awoken in the cells after the takeover, all of my jewels had been removed.

"Then it is his loss. Perhaps you should kill him and eat his heart? It will take away some of the heartache," she suggested, so casually and seriously that I stared at her. Her words made my stomach churn.

"Uhh, that's a thing?"

"Yes, of course, it really helps too."

I think the only reason it would help is because you would feel guilt for murdering them – win-win.

"I don't think I can do that. I don't want him dead." Her small smile faded, and she ran her fingers through my hair, careful not to tug at the braids or jewels.

"Then perhaps there is hope."

My heart clenched at her words, which held some confidence, but I highly doubted it. How do you forgive someone who killed your parents?

It was the following day, and we were headed to the surface. After I had bid Lavina farewell, she had given me a necklace which would help me keep in touch with them. It was me, Deliana, and Ariella. The mermen had come with us, but they were staying far below from the surface. Only the three of us were venturing upwards. Aquarius had bid me farewell, hoping I returned soon and saying it was an honour to serve me.

Ariella had heard some disturbances, and she had swum ahead. We needed to be careful; Lavina had told us something dark had been heading closer recently. When I had asked what she meant, Deliana had responded with,

Just the usual sea monsters who attack.

I'm to the west, we may just be in luck. Yileyna, that ship, the Siren Killer, isn't far from me. That handsome Alpha is aboard it, too. The Siren Killer?

Alpha? I asked confused.

The copper-headed wolf who was with you at the coast. Aww, it seems he came looking for you. What a cutie, I wonder how his heart would taste?

Ariella, Deliana warned.

"It's Theon…" My heart pounded as I looked at Deliana. What was he doing here?

We are coming, it's highly likely he is here for her, Deliana deduced, before we began swimming faster up towards the surface.

It was a good five minutes later before we finally saw Ariella circling the bottom of the ship. My heart pounded as I saw the looming base of the ship from underneath. It looked even scarier from down here.

"We won't go any further. Perhaps you should shift," Deliana suggested. Her eyes were darker, and I could tell she was fighting herself.

"What's wrong?" I asked.

"There's an Alpha on board," she hissed. No matter how much she didn't want this war, her hatred remained.

"It's Theon, the one I told you about," I whispered quietly, taking her hand.

"Still, it's better that I do not surface," she said, turning her gaze away from the ship and towards me. "Use the necklace if you ever need us. It will help you get in touch with us. When you find the pearl, call us; we will come for it." I nodded as our eyes met. I was the first one to swim forward and slowly wrap my arms around her shoulders.

"I will miss you," I said quietly, as she hugged me back tightly.

"I will miss -"

I gasped when something was shot into the water as the huge bullet went zooming down into the depths.

"I'm getting one," Theon's faint growl came. He had spotted us and he was about to jump in. Was he crazy? He knew there were Sirens down here!

"No one attack him," I warned Deliana and Ariella just as Theon jumped into the water, his eyes blazing gold.

His aura surged around us as he looked at Ariella, and then his eyes flicked to me. He was about to look away when he frowned, his eyes widening slightly, and realisation hit him. His gaze dipped to my tail. My heart thumped with fear. Would he want me dead? Would he turn his back on me quickly? His eyes slowly raked over it, his heart thundering to match mine.

"How handsome..." Ariella hummed, about to swim closer to him when his eyes snapped away from me, and I saw that look in his eyes.

"Theon! They mean no harm! They helped me!" I wasn't sure if it was any use, so I swam towards him before he could attack her. His eyes snapped to me; he couldn't speak underwater, but I saw the distrust in his eyes as he grabbed hold of my elbows.

Our eyes met, and he was about to say something when he caught sight of Deliana behind me. I felt the change in him and the urge to calm him came over me.

"She's my mother," I explained quietly, but Theon was no longer listening.

His chest was heaving, his face pale, but what caught my attention was the look of recognition and hatred in his eyes. He let go of me, his amber aura wrapping around him as my gaze snapped to Deliana as well. She had her brows furrowed as she watched him edgily.

"Go," I ordered, and just when Theon sent a surge of amber flames spiralling towards her, I raised a shield between them both. "Theon! She's not an enemy!" I shouted, my eyes blazing as I used the water to push us upwards, breaking the surface.

Goodbye, Tempest, Deliana's voice came in my head before I sensed them swimming away. Theon's heart was raging.

"Let go of me! I can't let her get away!" He growled, trying to pull free, but I was strong enough to slow him down, much to my surprise.

"Theon! I said she isn't here to fight!" I shouted.

"I said let me go, Yileyna!" He growled, ripping free. The faint smell of blood reached my nose. Was he injured somewhere?

"Theon, listen to me!" I cried, refusing to allow him to dive into the water. The look of anguish on his handsome face was worrying me. My own heart was thumping with fear.

"I can't let her go. It's been too long," he replied hoarsely, trying to dive under. I grabbed hold of his arm, wrapping my tail around him.

"Theon. She's gone," I said, grabbing his face in my hands and staring into those amber eyes that were full of anger.

"I need to kill her, Yileyna, she's the one who killed my mother!" He shouted. My eyes flew open, shocked at his revelation, followed by the icy rush of devastation, my heart crumbling a little more.

My mother had killed his mother and sister... he killed my mother and father... how cruel life was... I had never seen Theon so emotional as he was at that moment.

"Shush... calm down," I hummed. He tensed, about to pull away, when I pressed my forehead to his. "I know how it feels, seeing the one who killed your parents before you."

He froze, as if suddenly realising what was happening. We stayed there in the water, the rocky waves throwing us around. Pain that would never leave us...

My words seemed to get to him, and he stared into my eyes, his chest still heaving. I could sense the storm of emotions as he seemed to take in everything. I created an extremely heavy fog around us and manipulated the water to push us out and overboard onto the deck. Theon instantly caught me before we hit the deck. A big dose of water splashed over us both. I landed on top of him, gasping at the impact. I was still shaken by the revelation. I closed my eyes, focusing on my legs. The same odd heavy feeling overcame my lower body, and then I felt my legs appear.

Theon sat up, but I could tell his mind wasn't there. Directly and indirectly, we had hurt one another far too many times. He looked up at me, and I looked back into his empty eyes. I was unable to decipher what he was thinking...

My heart squeezed as we stared into one another's eyes, and I realised how true the fact that we were just not meant to be was...

TURMOILED THOUGHTS

THEON

YILEYNA'S MOTHER WAS THE one who killed mine… the conflict I felt inside of me had shaken me to my core. I paced around my cabin; it had been an hour since we had found her, but I had been unable to stay in her presence. My head was about to burst.

I looked around the room. It was too fucking small, the sway of the ship was making me sick, and it almost felt like I couldn't fucking breathe. What do I do? What the fuck do I do?

I stared at the ceiling that was only a few inches above my head. It was too fucking claustrophobic in here. I threaded my hands together, placing them behind my head as I took deep breaths.

I had killed Hana and William De'Lacor, something I regretted every single fucking day… I know, I fucking know I no longer can take away her birth mother from her. I know what I fucking need to do…

But everything I had worked my entire fucking life for was unravelling. First from the image of reality that Dad had portrayed, one that was beginning to hold a lot of questions and holes, to the revenge I craved… I had spent the last decade waiting for the day I'd see that monster and kill her…

She had been before me, but Yileyna had protected her, and I had

My chest was burning up from the wounds. I needed to change my bandages before anyone saw them but I just… I couldn't fucking focus…

I exhaled sharply, pulling my shirt off and unwrapping the bandages that were a disgusting mess, making my wounds itch. I looked down, seeing the injuries were looking as bad as they did days ago. I dropped down to the ground by the door, staring at the wall across from me as the ship swayed.

What do I do? I felt fucking lost. Every fucking thing I had worked my life for was… gone. I closed my eyes, squeezing my head, rocking slightly as I took deep breaths. When everything you have worked your entire fucking life for is just… gone, what do you do?

A knock on the door made my head snap up, but I didn't move. I didn't want to see anyone. Not when I felt like I was going to fucking spiral. Another knock followed but I didn't reply until I heard the footsteps retreating. I stood up, grabbed the bloody bandages along with my dirty shirt, and walked to the bathroom, ready to wash off.

Night had fallen, and I had gone out briefly to tell Flynn we were to head to Eastcourt, but I had avoided Yileyna. I just needed to make sure Thea was okay. From there, I would see what I could find out, and then head to Hunter's pack. I needed fucking answers, or I was going to lose my fucking mind.

Yileyna… I needed to find out what she planned to do… but as relieved as I was that she was alive and near, no matter how much I wanted to pull her into my arms and never fucking let go, I couldn't. The rejection was still painful in my mind… everything that had happened… it all was fucking too much… and on top of that, her Siren mother… her identity… fuck, why couldn't it be anyone else but her?

My mind was still reeling. I dropped onto the bed, shirtless. The stinging had eased a little, but the wounds were still fucking hurting. Sleep didn't come and I sat up. Maybe I'd pop down to the hold and get some ale or wine…?

I stood up, picking up a shirt, and pulled it on, before leaving my room. Her scent lingered in the halls, and I frowned. What was she doing out here? She had changed slightly, looking even more beautiful, although I had no fucking idea how that was possible. Yileyna… I was unable to get how fucking appealing she looked out of my mind…

The urge to strip her naked and admire her was a temptation that would never be a reality. There was something different about her Siren form, she had looked different than others. Her tail was far more extravagant, with her scales hanging low on her hips and dipping in a V. That had been a turn-on in itself… but no matter how fucking good she looked, I couldn't face her…

It didn't take long to pick the lock on the door to the hold, and I walked down the steps. I remembered the time Yileyna and I had been down here after I had that nightmare. I opened a crate and took out a bottle of wine. It would do nothing to ease the pain but… why not. I bit the cork off and dropped to the floor, resting my head against the hard wall of the ship behind me.

Does it get any easier? Was I going to feel like this for the rest of my fucking life? Fighting against everything to a point where I no longer knew what was right and wrong. It was hard, even harder when there was no reprieve from anything. If anything Dad has told me turns out to be a lie… I will fucking lose it.

The door creaked open, and I opened my eyes as her familiar scent invaded my nose, a scent that I fucking desired. What did she want?

Her feet padded down the steps and her creamy legs came into view, clad in just an oversized shirt. She paused at the bottom of the steps and looked towards me. Her aura radiated off her and it was far more powerful than was when she had been pulled into the waters. Whatever happened down there had given her more powers. Perhaps it was her shifting into her Siren form.

"I hope you don't mind if I join. I need to talk to you," she spoke. Her voice held a sexier edge, a little more dangerous and a little more exotic. I wondered how it would sound if she was under me moaning in fucking pleasure. I could use the distraction right about now.

"What do you want?" I asked as she came over and sat down next to me, stretching out her legs and crossing her ankles gracefully. I tried not to look at her flawless thighs, taking a swig from my bottle instead.

"So…" she began softly. I knew she wanted to talk about it, but was there any point? I remained silent, letting her carry on if she so wished. "Deliana was the one who killed your mother and sister… I'm sorry… and I'm not trying to justify her actions, but it's because of the king. He tried to kill her in her sleep."

I froze, looking at her sharply. Her cheekbones were more prominent, and she looked a little older, as if she had shed the last remnants of the girl she once used to be...

"What do you mean tried to kill her?" I asked for the sake of entertaining her, or maybe because I needed a reason to justify not killing her. Something other than her being Yileyna's mother.

She took a deep shaky breath and began telling me the version that Andres had not told me. A few minutes later we sat in silence as I pondered over everything. So he literally used the Siren, who had obviously been his fated mate considering they made the Heart of Kaeladia, and then when he was done, he tried to kill her...? Her anger was justified... wasn't it what we all did?

"Say something, please," she said quietly.

"There's nothing to say. She's no different than me, Dad... or Andres. We are all hurting so many others in the name of revenge, to justify our own fucking actions," I murmured quietly, looking at her. Her iridescent eyes seemed to be fixed and they drew my attention; purple, pink, blue, yellow, and green blended together, more vibrant than I had ever seen them before. Concern was clear on her face and her rejection came back to mind. She was made for me, but I was far too fucked to keep her.

Her chest heaved as she licked her lips, her gaze flickering to mine before she looked away. But I didn't miss the look in her eyes.

"I want that to change. We can't keep going on like this, Theon... it's a vicious cycle. The king apparently betrayed your father, I'm saying apparently because he, too, seems like a monster, whether you agree or not. The king also betrayed Deliana, forcing her to want vengeance on all Alpha males, and in the process, she killed your mother and sister, which was so wrong... and now you want to kill -"

"What?" I asked sharply, something she said making my heart thud. She frowned before her face paled, and I knew I was right.

"What is it?" She asked, trying to brush it off. My eyes flashed as I grabbed her neck, pulling her close.

"What did you just say about the Siren?" I whispered menacingly. "Repeat it."

"She... she attacked the ship because she smelled an Alpha male on board," she whispered, her eyes looking pained.

There. She said it. She came for me. If I hadn't been there, they wouldn't have died. Fuck, it was my fucking fault.

"Theon. Stop it," she said, gripping my wrist and pulling my hand away from her throat. "Theon, look at me." Her alpha aura unknowingly rolled into her command, but it didn't work on me. I was an Alpha too.

I looked at my hand, staring at my palm. Maybe I was the one behind it all, with enough fucking bad luck that I constantly hurt those around me... everyone. Mom.... Thalia... Yileyna... even the Beta couple who had done no fucking wrong, yet I-

"Theon!" She placed a hand on my shoulder, and I turned to look at her, doing my best to contain my emotions.

"I killed your parents. You should stay away from me," I warned her quietly as I stood up, downing the last drops in the bottle. She stood up, blocking my path.

"And that's something I won't forget... but this isn't about me and you. Theon, there's so much more going than you think, and I need you by my side, the side of truth and what's right." I frowned, looking down at her.

"News flash, the Obsidian Shadow Pack is looking for you."

"But I know you tried to protect me. You led them away so I could get away. Theon, your father... he's stuck in his ways, just like the king, but, Theon... you are the heir to the Obsidian Shadow Pack, and despite everything you have done, I have seen the good in you. Can we not put aside everything and work together as allies?" That wasn't what I was expecting her to say. I frowned, stepping closer and tossing the bottle to the ground.

"Do you really think there's good in me? Or have you forgotten that I betrayed you all? I murdered your parents. I'm no fucking angel, Yileyna."

"I know you aren't. I said there's good in you. Whether you believe me or not, I don't believe we have the full story of what really happened between Theoden and King Andres," she replied, staring back at me squarely.

We wanted the same fucking thing... But how do I fucking survive around you when all I want is to fuck you into damnation? Being around her was painful, far more than the wounds she had inflicted upon me...

I tilted my head, taking hold of her chin as I leaned down.

"But the question is, can you be around the man who killed your parents without it causing you pain?" I asked coldly. Her eyes filled with grief, and she wrapped her hand around my wrist as she stared back at me.

"It will always hurt… but like I said, it's not about you and me… Theon, we are in far more danger than we imagined. It's not just about Westerwell and the throne of Astalion. The Imperial Emperor of the Sea is ready to march onto land and destroy us all. He's given me two full moons to find something and return it to him, and if I don't, then he will attack with two thousand Imperial Sirens who can walk the land. If that happens, we will be ruined," she confessed, her words weighted with the consequences of what the future may hold. Her words echoed in my head, and as much as I didn't think that could be a possibility, the conviction in her eyes said otherwise.

"Time is running out Theon. I need to get to the Naran Empire and find this pearl the emperor wants, but if you're here to take me back to Westerwell then you have another thing coming. I won't go. This isn't just about being the ruler of the middle kingdom, there is so much more at stake. If you don't want to help me, will you let me go without a fight?" She whispered.

Her breasts brushed against my forearm as I still held on to her. Even when we were talking about such a serious matter, I couldn't stop the desire and hunger I felt for her consuming my body and mind. I wanted to throw her up against the wall and fuck her right here.

"Venturing to a Naga empire is equal to suicide. You won't get far," I replied frowning. "You may be a goddess in all other aspects, but you are not fucking immortal. Do you really have a death wish?" I wouldn't let her go to Naran, not alone.

"I don't have anyone that I can turn to. I'll be fine," she replied icily, her eyes changing to that beautiful iridescent mix of colours as she glared at me. I was not going to let her go alone… did that mean I was willing to go with her?

"Fine. I'll go with you. I need to go towards that side anyway… but if I help you, what do I get in return?" I asked huskily.

"What do you want?"

You. To kiss you. To fuck you. To call you mine… for one fucking chance… The world could go to hell, as long as I had her, I didn't care… but above all, I wanted her forgiveness… forgiveness for killing her loved ones. To turn back time and change that plan… but I couldn't force her to forgive me, and as much as I wanted to ask for so much, I didn't.

This would be my silent redemption. Even though nothing could change the past, I would help her because I owed her, and right now, she was the only one being entirely honest with me. She didn't need to tell me about this pearl, or Naran, but she did…

"What do you want in return, Theon?" She persisted softly, her heart pounding as she stared into my eyes with a glimmer of fear and uncertainty. Did she think I'd blackmail her into something?

I wanted her happy… I wanted to see her smile, I wanted that innocence she had held before I broke her to return.

I leaned into her ear, her scent washing over me, and it took my fucking all not to yank her close. My voice dropped to a whisper as I gave her my answer,

"Nothing."

BETWEEN TWO ALPHAS

YILEYNA

"NOTHING."

His words made my stomach somersault. He had offered to help me, and I was sure he would ask for something in return, but he didn't. Once again, in his own way he was showing that there was some good in him, only making me more determined to remove the veil from his eyes, to show him that his father may not be what he thinks.

"Nothing?" I asked, looking into his amber eyes. They were as gorgeous as ever, but they didn't seem to be as vibrant as usual. I guess he must be exhausted.

"One would assume your hearing would be impeccable… what's wrong? Do you need me to get closer and whisper it in your ear again? Or perhaps you secretly wanted me to ask for something else?" My core clenched at his tone. That urge to advance on him tempted me. I was certain that he wouldn't refuse, but where my body craved him, my heart still bled with the pain of his betrayal.

"I heard… but it's…" I shook my head, clearing my mind the best I could. "What is your plan? Why are you out here? Did your father simply send you to bring me back?" I tugged out of his hold and stepped back, waiting for him to answer as the ship lurched a little.

"Yeah, he wants you back, but I'm not the only one looking for you. He has sent out others."

"That's surprising. Doesn't he think you alone are capable of the job?" I asked, crossing my arms. He tilted his head, looking away.

"I don't think he trusts me entirely." He turned away from me, but I wasn't done with this conversation.

"Why? Because you have some morals?" I asked. He didn't reply for a moment before he looked at me over his shoulder.

"I have a question. How are you doing it? How are you able to stand and talk to me after everything?"

How? I shook my head, shrugging as our eyes met.

"I don't know… it hurts. It hurts so much. I can forgive everything but my parents' deaths… it wasn't your dad who did that, it was you. You used me as the bait to let them rush to their deaths," I whispered, refusing to allow the pain in my chest to overwhelm me. I took a deep breath and looked him square in the eye. "But, like I said, this isn't about me, but the people of the kingdom. We need the fighting to stop. Enough is enough." He nodded, looking away.

"Makes sense… then for the greater good, I guess we do this together."

"Mm." I nodded.

Surely there was a reason that Selene chose us to be mates. Perhaps this was what it was, to unite the kingdoms, to bring peace between the packs, as well as with the Sirens. As for this visit to the Naga empire… maybe me going beyond the borders of Astalion into Naran is all part of a bigger plan. Perhaps they, too, are misunderstood. I know they are dangerous and deadly, but didn't we think the same of the Sirens? Sure, they kill, but we do too and are seen as monsters to someone else.

"It's time we didn't let what we are taught be our only verdict. We need to look beyond that and find our own answers," I said quietly.

"It's not going to be easy…" he replied. I shrugged.

"The most precious things in life are never easy to attain, but we do our best until we succeed in achieving them."

"What if it's impossible?"

I frowned slightly as the ship lurched, and he automatically grabbed my arm, steadying me. My heart skipped a beat. I had my balance…

He looked down at where he was holding my arm, those faint sparkles dancing through us, and he let go.

"Nothing is impossible. If we truly want something, we can achieve it," I replied with confidence.

Our eyes met, and he nodded. For a moment, I felt as if the question he was asking wasn't about all of this... I would be a fool to deny that I didn't know what he may be insinuating. Me. I didn't know what I was to him... he had confessed his feelings to me, but then that was right before throwing me from a building...

Stop. Stop, Yileyna.

I wouldn't think of this, I needed to focus on the truth. Theon and I were broken beyond any chance of fixing. I once thought love was something different, but it was darker and more painful than I had ever thought possible...

"You should head to bed, it's late," he remarked.

"Yes. So, we head towards Naran?" I asked as I brushed past him. Again I thought I smelt the faint smell of blood.

"I need to make a stop first, then we will head that way. We will need to pass the Iron Claw Pack. Luckily, it is a neutral pack, and he will let us pass. Besides, I have my own business with him," he replied. I nodded.

"Okay, that sounds perfect. Time is short."

"I know... I just need to see if my sister is okay." His reply surprised me, and I looked at him, shocked.

"Sister?"

"I have another sister who survived the attack on that ship a decade ago," he replied. "Night." He was about to walk off, but I grabbed onto his arm, my heart thumping. I knew the topic was still hurting him, but I wanted to know.

"Can you tell me exactly what happened?" I pushed gently. He turned back to me and crossed his arms.

"We were being chased by the Silver Storm Pack apparently, forcing us to take to the sea. Dad stayed behind to hold off the attack, and we were simply given a crystal that was embedded with powerful magic. It would work only once. It was a teleportation spell, which Dad said only to use if we really needed to as there was a chance we could die mid-way..."

"Yet he gave you that?" I asked, appalled. He frowned and nodded.

"It was meant to be a last resort. We had our men with us, but then we were attacked by her..." I knew exactly who he meant as hatred flashed in his eyes. "She killed Thalia, who was only five at the time, and then Mom...

when she came towards me, I unlocked the enchantment with the spell we were given and grabbed Thea. I didn't know if we'd make it to safety, but if we remained on that ship, we would have died anyway. It was the hardest decision I had to make... I hesitated, not knowing if Thalia or Thea would make it, and I couldn't leave Mom either... but then it was the only option left..."

"I'm sorry... I can only imagine the pain you were going through. Will you still seek vengeance upon her?" I asked softly. He looked into my eyes, a frown creasing his handsome face.

"For now... no. Maybe the day you decide to seek vengeance against me will be the day I might do the same," he smirked slightly, despite no humour in his eyes. He knew I never would...

My heart skipped a beat as I realised what he meant. He was letting it go. In his own way, he was letting it go, despite the pain he felt from that incident. I would get Deliana to talk to him. It wouldn't change the past, but it might give him some closure.

"One day, I hope letting it go makes it easier for us both... I can't wait to meet your sister." Maybe she would have some insight on Theon before he became a weapon for revenge. "Will you bring her with us to travel?" I wasn't sure how old she was, but the mission would be dangerous.

"Yes. I plan to take her to the Iron Claw Pack... she'll be safe there." Without another word, he turned and left, leaving me alone in the hold. I know the topic wasn't easy for him...

There were many answers we needed, and I hoped that we would find them soon because these differences needed to be set aside.

Thank you for sharing your pain with me.

The following day, the weather was slightly warmer; well, I wouldn't call it warm, but it was not as cold as the day before. The wind was rather strong, and the ship was rocked back and forth, the masts withstanding the violent wind.

I had awoken from an irritating dream about fucking Theon. I had woken up before I had come, leaving me feeling horny and irritated. Deliana had not been wrong; sex was often on my mind, more so than before.

I had just showered, donning clothes given to me by Cleo. It was a cropped maroon bralette and black pants that sat low upon my hips. I stepped onto the deck, wrapping my wet hair in a bun. The necklace that Lavina gave me hung around my neck on a silver chain. At the end was a plain white seashell, simple yet useful.

The team had been happy to see me, and although I had caused a mist around my disguising my tail, the fact that I had come from the water had made most of the crew rather wary, but after a few hours, they had all started acting normally with me, and I had ended up telling them about the truth of my heritage. To my surprise, they had all sworn allegiance to me, with Fynn saying I had to promise him safe passage in the sea from the Sirens. I said I would try my best as long as he changed the name of his ship. Not all werewolves were monsters, and not all Sirens were killers…

I felt Theon's eyes on me as I used a few pins to pin my hair into place. I turned, spotting him against the far wall. He instantly looked away, and I almost smiled. He looked handsome as ever. My gaze dipped to his sexy ass, and I sighed inwardly. I needed to get over my morning disappointment.

Did he not realise I always knew when his eyes were on me? I walked over to him and leaned against the side of the ship, looking up at his face.

"How long until we reach the location your sister is currently at?" I asked. He raised an eyebrow.

"You could have asked anyone here where we were headed. Or did you just need a reason to talk to me?" He asked, surprising me. My heart skipped a beat as I realised he had a point…

"Well, I don't know where we are headed. Am I allowed to mention your sister?" I asked quietly. He gave me a pointed look before his gaze dipped down to my breasts, which were almost spilling out of the bralette.

"Isn't your top a few sizes too small for you, or is that your bra and you forgot your top?" He remarked, not even pretending to hide the fact he had just stared at me openly. I raised my eyebrow.

"It's not that small, and besides, I like it. I think it's the perfect size, actually, or are you getting distracted?" I taunted mockingly. I was expecting a cocky reply, but instead, he ignored me, turning back towards the water.

"There's something down there. What is it?" He asked, making me frown and turn to the water.

"What do you mean?" I asked, my heart thudding.

"It's big, and it's been getting closer… we haven't managed to figure it out yet." I frowned, realising the tension that was amongst the crew, all of them looking out at the sea and being on alert. I turned, staring at the water intently.

"Shall I go swim and check it out?" I asked, stepping back. He frowned.

"No. Don't you have any other way to find out?"

"Not really. I'm a Siren, not a sea god," I said sceptically.

"Part Siren," he corrected.

"No, I'm not a hybrid. I'm a triform shifter, which means I am Siren and wolf," I explained, making him look at me with a look I couldn't decipher. Before he could reply, I saw something dark in the water and turned sharply towards it.

"Not all beasts of the sea are good. Let it come. I'll destroy it," I murmured, closing my eyes as I called on the water, letting my senses flow into it. I wasn't sure I could do the same with the water as I could with ice…

I closed my eyes, breathing deeply, and that's when I felt it. Something dark, big and wicked…

Lust for blood.

Hunger.

Rage.

I opened my eyes, staring at the water. I knew what it was, and my stomach sank.

An Ancient Monster

YILEYNA

"WHAT IS IT?" THEON asked me sharply.

"Theon, that's a -"

When the spear-tipped tentacle burst from the sea, I raised my hand, pushing the water that splashed high above the ship back.

"A Leviathan," I finished as the beast rose into the air from the sea, his speared tentacles longer than the ship itself. His tongue whipped in the air as the crew stared at the creature before us.

"A harbinger of death…" Leto muttered.

"Well, we are not lingering!" Flynn shouted as he barked orders.

Theon and I stood there looking at the beast that was said to remain deep within the waters of the ocean.

"I'm going to fucking kill it," Theon growled, about to draw his sword.

"Those who kill a Leviathan are doomed to death. We can't kill it," I reminded him quietly, placing my hand on his wrist and stopping him.

The curse on the Leviathan was known to all. Long ago, Oshera cursed those who tried to kill the Leviathan so that they would end up dying soon after, a creation she had made to protect the seven seas.

"Who cares? Death is inevitable in the long run. I'll do it," he muttered, making me frown.

I stared at the creature, who was trying to get closer. I used the wind to push the ship away from him, using the full force of my powers to put distance between us, but it simply loomed above the ship, ten times the size of it. His eyes darted around the ship as if searching for something. The moment his putrid yellow eyes landed on me, he let out a ground-shattering shriek that made me flinch before he brought one of his spear-ended tentacles down towards the ship.

"Move!" Theon shouted.

His arm wrapped around my waist just as I created a shield of ice that rose from the water. His tentacle crashed into it, shattering the barrier upon impact. Slabs of ice flew in the air just as both Theon and I were knocked to the ground. The ship tilted, sending us rolling violently. His arms wrapped around me, and we hit the side harshly as another tentacle came crashing down. This time, I raised my hand, trying to force it back. Maybe I couldn't kill it... but I could encase it in ice.

The smell of blood reached me now, and I looked at Theon worriedly as he got to his feet, pulling me up.

"I need to get closer," I shouted

"What's the plan?"

"I'm going to freeze it in ice." He frowned but didn't question me as I broke into a run, only for the ship to swing violently, throwing me off balance.

"Make sure you don't kill it," he warned, blocking a piece of ice as I deflected it with the tips of my fingers.

"Worried?" I couldn't help but ask.

"Maybe," his quiet voice answered, making my stomach do a flip.

"Don't worry, I won't kill it. I just need to somehow touch it, any part of it..."

"Well, he's fucking trying to ruin the ship. Getting close is easier said than done!" Theon called over the raging wind as I summoned lightning. The only problem was it was wrapping itself around the ship, and I didn't want to cause a fire. "I have an idea. Are you able to push him off the ship?"

"I could try," I yelled back as the winds became stronger. Focusing on my target, my eyes blazed as I summoned the power of the wind and water to me, forcing the Leviathan to loosen his hold on the ship.

"Keep going, and I'll get you closer!" His voice was emotionless yet sharp. His eyes were fixed on the dark greyish-blue monster that was trying to pull us under. The crew were trying to do their best, but we were in the hold of this monster that was so much bigger than any of us.

The ship tilted violently, and I realised I needed to shift. In my siren form, I was stronger in the sea.

"Theon, I'm going to shift!"

"Do not get in the water!" He shouted, but I pulled away.

I saw the concern and fear in his eyes as I pulled away, running to the edge of the ship. I closed my eyes, willing myself to shift. I felt an odd sensation in my legs before I transformed, jumping into the stormy sea. My eyes blazed with power as I spread my hands on the surface of the water, causing it to wrap around the Leviathan. Another terrifying roar was heard, and I saw Theon at the edge of the boat. His glowing amber aura was around him, and I heard the Leviathan hiss in pain.

This was my chance. His hold on the ship loosened thanks to Theon's attack, and I closed my eyes as I grabbed onto his tail, letting a thick layer of ice begin to spread from my finger, coating his entire body slowly and steadily.

It was a few moments later that it realised what was happening. It writhed and flailed its tentacles, but a strong swirl of water wrapped around me as I slowly let the ice encase its entire body. Our eyes met, and a final roar left its mouth before his tongue whipped out, catching me by surprise. The barbed tip sliced through my stomach, throwing me into the water. I gasped at the searing pain that tore through my stomach as the huge body of the Leviathan slowly began to sink, the ice encasing its entire body. I kept going as he struggled to crack the prison of ice.

It was my will and strength against his. Its yellow eyes burned into mine as I clutched my stomach, breathing hard. Just as the ice covered him fully, a strong arm wrapped around my chest, pulling me up. We broke the surface, and I looked into the eyes of none other than Theon.

"That was fucking reckless," he growled, his hand going to my stomach as he touched the wound.

"I'm okay," I said breathlessly. But despite that, I wrapped my arms loosely around his neck, allowing him to support me. I felt exhausted.

I was okay; the wound would heal. I let the water assist us, rising up so we were level to the deck. We tumbled backwards onto the wet floor of the deck just when the ship that had been tilted on its side was thrown into the water, knocking us both down the starboard side, rolling as we went.

I gasped when we came to a stop, and Theon's head hit my chest. The moment his lips accidentally touched my skin, I was unable to hold back the small whimper that escaped me, my nipples hardening at his touch. He tensed, lifting himself off me, his knees on either side of me, his heart thumping as he stared at my bloody stomach.

"You're injured," he said, placing a hand on my lower stomach as he tried to stem the bleeding, looking around as if for help. My core clenched as our eyes met.

"I'm okay…" I breathed.

"That was fucking crazy," he growled hoarsely, grabbing me by the back of my hair. I gasped, pleasure rushing through me. The relief and sheer reality of what we had just narrowly missed made me feel giddy.

"I am crazy," I whispered back, unable to stop myself from running my hand up his shoulder and wrapping it around the back of his neck. Just one taste.

I flipped us over, moaning when my core pressed against the hard shaft in his pants. His eyes flashed gold as his gaze dipped down, and I knew my scales had moved aside, feeling his soaking pants against my vagina. His heart thundered as he stared at my pussy, his chest heaving, and he rolled us over so he was on top. Blazing gold orbs filled with hunger and lust dipped to my lips before reality seemed to settle in, and he suddenly stood up and turned his back to me.

What was I doing?

My heart was thumping, trying to make sense of the emotions I was feeling, when Theon pulled his shirt off, tossing it at me before he walked away without even looking back. My heart pounded as I held onto the soaking shirt. I frowned, seeing the bandages wrapped around his chest. Was Theon hurt? But I didn't have the time to ask as he vanished, leaving me alone and naked, clutching his shirt, completely confused with the moment that had transpired between us.

He still made me lose my self-control. We still wanted one another even if we couldn't.

M Y R EFUSAL

HUNTER

*I*T HAD BEEN A few days since the wedding, and I knew more than ever
that my decision had been absolutely correct. Charlene was the perfect
Luna, wife, and mate. Not only was her heart beautiful, but so was she, a
perfect bonus because I craved her. One night was not enough for me. That
first night, I had made love to her twice before forcing myself to stop. It was
her first time, and I knew she would be in pain.

The very next day, I had awoken to her having run me a bath and had
my clothes out ready for me. I told her she didn't need to do that stuff for
me, I had Omegas for such tasks, but she made it clear she wanted to be
the only one taking care of me. I nearly smirked. It was almost as if she
meant something else, but I wasn't sure. I planned to tease her a little and
see if my innocent princess would indeed get jealous. I wanted her to be
possessive of me, to show me that she wanted me all for herself. Ah, it was
pleasant to have someone by my side, and although I wanted to simply bed
her day and night, duty called.

As promised, the following day, we planned and mapped our journey.
Some of my scouts had returned, and we had managed to assess what was
going on. There was something odd at work; Theoden had invited most
packs for a special event in a few weeks to show what he had to offer as their

new king. The invitation, which of course, I didn't get, looked fairly simple, but I didn't trust it, nor did I trust Theoden. There was never anything straightforward with him, and as much as my mother claimed to fall in love with him, I believed it was just the bond that had pulled her to him. The mate bond blinded you to logic. It's why I always knew I'd choose my own mate, to love her without the bond. That was true love, not a bond that makes you feel something for someone, no matter how dark or twisted they were.

We had left last night, splitting into five armies, and each was assigned a different job. The only problem was I didn't want Theoden to catch a whiff of what was going on.

I, myself, was part of the smallest group, and we were going to head to Alpha Romeo's pack. He was one of Andres' closest, and I intended to get him on board for the take-back. He didn't know we were coming, but he had expressed his concern in his letter since his pack was heavily watched. We just needed to make sure no one saw us meeting him. We had travelled all morning and set up camp for the night. I had thirty men with me, along with those from the Silver Storm Pack. It had been difficult for Raiden, but he had left his brother at my pack. I assured him he would remain safe. Charlene was, of course, with us; although I didn't want her anywhere near the battle, she had pleaded to come with me. There would be a battle, and it would inevitably take place no matter how much we didn't want war because it was already upon us...

For the sake of my mother, I avoided Theoden, but I despised him. If it hadn't been for his selfishness, she might still be alive today. For Theon as well... just how I had promised her. I needed to get him to see the truth before it was too late. I knew there was good in him because he was her son. I would hold onto that and take the role I needed to as his elder brother. If he's in the wrong, then I will show him the right way, one way or another.

I came out of my reverie, watching Ryan prodding at the rabbits we were cooking, and I glanced over at the Gamma. Charlene's father and brother... She had told me about it on the second day of our marriage, although she said he didn't know, she didn't want to keep anything from me. I loved how she trusted me, but I also worried about her trusting others far too quickly. Well, she had nothing to worry about. I was here to make sure she was safe and around those who could be trusted as much as possible.

She was currently inside our tent whilst Raiden was with the horses, checking some of the supplies. We were travelling mostly on foot or in wolf form, but we had some horses for luggage and for some of the men when they needed a break.

"So, why haven't you marked her?" Ryan asked, raising an eyebrow. I guess it was true; half-siblings were definitely not alike. This man was nothing like his sister.

"That's not really your business, now, is it, Sanchez?" I raised my eyebrow. He rolled his eyes.

"Na, it isn't, but it is weird. She isn't your fated mate, so you marking her has nothing to do with you going to war and maybe getting killed."

"I like how you don't really care if I do die… but me not marking her is something I personally do not wish to do until after the war."

"Why?" He sure didn't take a hint. He looked at me pointedly, and the urge to knock him over the head appealed greatly to me.

"She's young. If I do end up fucking dead, I don't want her to be held back by my goddamn mark," I growled lowly, trying to control my anger. I saw Raiden and Grayson turn to look at me. There, I fucking said it. Ryan looked at me in surprise before he realised what I meant.

Charlene was young, and if I died, unless her fated mate showed up, no one could remove the mark I left on her neck. I didn't want her life to end there. She had the right to choose a new mate if anything happened to me, no matter how much the thought irked me.

I stood up. I was done with this conversation and was about to storm off for a walk when I saw her standing there holding her clothes, unshed tears clear in her eyes. Fuck, now she had heard that.

I glared back at the bastard sitting there poking the fucking rabbits, entirely unbothered, before I turned back to Charlene, who had backed away, turning and hurrying towards the river.

"Charlene," I called after her. "Charlene!"

She only stopped when she reached the riverbed, her heart thumping as she clutched her clothes to her chest. I closed the gap between us and wrapped my arms around her from behind tightly, burying my head into her neck and inhaling the scent that I loved. Her heart pounded as I caressed her waist, trying to calm her anger. Ah, she was so damn cute when angry.

"I did not mean it like that," I said quietly.

"I already told you I don't like you talking about dying. This war is scary enough without me having to fear losing you." She pulled free from my hold and turned to look up at me. "Hunter... I dislike how you keep making out as if this - we - are temporary. You said that if my fated mate came, you would not let him take me... but why do I think deep down... that if he did show up, you would let me choose?" She whispered, tears in her gorgeous green eyes. My face betrayed nothing; a flashback of vague memories filled my mind. Me screaming for my mother as she walked away...

Charlene knew me... but if ever that time came, and she chose to walk away from me, and we had a child... I would make sure she took that child with her because no child deserved to be without their mother. I wouldn't do what my father did and refuse to let me go... and I wouldn't want Charlene to choose between her fated mate and our child.

The pain returned with a vengeance, accompanied by the fact that she had left me, a question I refused to dwell on. I pushed it away. I couldn't deal with this right now. I turned away from her, my emotions overwhelming me, and she grabbed hold of my arms.

"Hunter. Mark me," she whispered.

Do I deserve to do so? If she is ever marked over mine... the pain that came with it... almost like a punishment from the goddess for refusing your fated mate... I didn't want to put her through that.

She said she wasn't ready when I first proposed to her, how could she suddenly be ready in a mere few days? I pulled her into my arms, weaving my hand into her gorgeous locks, tugging her head upwards.

"Are you sure?" I asked quietly.

"Yes. When I promised myself to you, I meant it."

Our eyes met before I pulled her firmly against me and kissed her deeply. I didn't know what the future held but imagining a life with Charlene... it sounded like a goddamn dream.

"On one condition," I whispered, pulling away from those plump lips of hers.

"Which condition?" She asked innocently. I smirked as I jerked my head toward the water.

"Bathe with me, and I will mark you on the seventh day of our marriage." Her eyes widened as she looked through the trees back towards the faint fire that could be seen.

"H-here?" She whispered, her face changing to a pretty hue of red. My smirk only grew as I let go of her and pulled my top off.

"Here. What's wrong? I'm sure no one can see any wrong in it, even if they realise you bathed with your husband. Unless, of course, you are unable to keep those moans down." Her eyes widened, and I chuckled as she stared at me.

"Wh-what moans? You said a bath!" She yelped, her heart thudding.

"Do you expect me to bathe with you and not fuck you?"

I tilted my head as she dropped her clothes in alarm, running her fingers through her hair, her other hand clutched to her chest. Teasing her was indeed incredibly fun…

"I…"

I want no one to come anywhere near the water for the next half an hour, I commanded my men through the link.

Yes, Alpha, The replies came from all of them, but I didn't miss the amusement in a few of their replies. Well, I was newly mated.

"It's up to you. I don't need to mark you, I guess." I winked at her, removing my pants and making her blush as she looked at the ground. I closed the gap between us, hearing her heart pounding loudly as she quickly looked away from my crotch. Placing two fingers under her chin, I tilted it up. "Now, tell me, how much do you want me to mark you? Enough to get down and dirty with me… or… shall we wait?"

A frown crossed her face, and I smirked as she stepped back. She really was too innocent. It was a shame since I actually wanted to fuck her right then. I was about to speak when she suddenly went down on her knees, pulling my boxers down.

"I truly want you to mark me, and I plan to show you exactly how much," she whispered; her heart was thumping as she wrapped her hand around my cock that hardened in her hold, sending a dangerous wave of pleasure through me. I frowned, all amusement vanishing.

"Hey, you don't need to do that. Come, let's bathe," I said, leaning down to get a hold of her elbows.

She was my Luna, not a whore. I didn't need her to do anything of the sort, the only one who needed to be worshipped was her. She pouted, refusing to stand up, and looked away from my intense gaze.

"I… want to do this," she whispered, taking me by surprise.

So, my Luna wasn't exactly as innocent as I presumed. Reaching down, I tilted her chin up and looked into her vibrant eyes for any sign of hesitation as she ran her hand along my shaft, making me throb. Fuck, she was making this harder for me, the moment her tongue ran over her lips and she flicked the tip of my cock with it, my eyes flashed, and any hesitation I had vanished.

"Fuck, Princess."

A soft smile crossed her lips as her gaze dipped to my hardened cock. She tilted her head, running her tongue from the base of the shaft all the way to the tip, making a burst of pleasure rush through me and a low groan escape my lips.

Oh, fuck... now, this is fucking good...

"That's it."

"I think I can make you lose enough control that you end up marking me tonight," she whispered with confidence I never knew she had, her fingers fondling my balls as she looked up at me deviously. I throbbed hard as I looked down at her challengingly. Now, this was a different side to her.

"So, you plan to challenge me?" I growled, wanting her mouth back on my cock.

"Of course, and I'm certain I will win," she replied seductively, wrapping her lips around my cock and began sucking on it, sending a rush of explosive desire through me.

I had excellent self-control, but something told me she may just win...

A Prince

CHARLENE

T**HE MOMENT HE WAS** about to come, he pulled me back, releasing his load over my neck and chest. I gasped. My entire body was craving him, and my heart was thumping. I had never expected that I would enjoy that as much as I did…

He pulled me up, and I locked my arms around his neck as we kissed hungrily. Even when he tore my clothes off like a beast starved for more, I didn't care. My only desire was to feel his body against mine. The moment my clothes were cast aside, he carried me into the water, pressing me up against the cliff-side as he kissed me like there was no tomorrow.

There was something different about tonight; his touch was rougher, his hunger more obvious, and his emotions were so intense. I refused to hold back too, wanting him to lose control and mark me. He had excellent self-control; I could feel it. When he did his best not to be rough, I ground against him, whimpering softly.

"Oh, that's it, Hunter," I moaned, reaching between us and pumping his manhood with my hand as I kissed and nibbled his neck. He tugged my head back, kissing my neck hungrily, and I knew this was my chance. Locking my legs around his waist, I lowered myself onto his cock, making him swear. "Fuck me, Alpha," I moaned coquettishly as I looked at him

His eyes darkened as he cupped my bottom and thrust into me completely. I gasped, my back arching as I felt him stretch me out. I gripped his shoulders as he began pounding me hard and fast. My breasts bounced, and I felt my cheeks heat up at his gaze that was on them. I met his thrusts, sighing softly as I controlled myself from crying out loud, knowing that we weren't so far away from the rest. Oh, fuck, this was so good…

I closed my eyes, losing myself in pleasure, each thrust making me want to scream in pure ecstasy. I buried my head in his neck to muffle the sounds that were escaping me.

"Fuck, you feel so good," he growled.

"Do you like fucking me, Alpha?" I whispered, running my hands through his hair before I kissed him sensually. The pressure was heightening, the pleasure rising, and I slipped my tongue into his mouth, moaning against him as he began fucking me harder and faster. "Make me yours fully, Alpha. Mark me," I murmured in his ear, rolling my hips and burying his cock deep within me. He swore as I arched my neck in submission to him. "Mark me." I could hear his heart thumping as he fought against himself. I twisted my hand into his hair. I planned to win this.

I sucked on his neck, moaning against him, waiting for his release to be near. I could feel my own nearing and knew this was my only chance. I ran my tongue up his neck and nibbled on his ear lobe just as my orgasm hit me. I cried out, twisting my hand into his hair and pulling him to my neck as I moaned loudly, my entire body convulsing with my orgasm.

I love you, I whimpered through the bond, saying the words I wanted to sing out loud for the world to hear.

"Fuck!" I heard him growl. His teeth grazed my neck, making me sigh.

Fuck, that's it… I breathed, the aftermath of my orgasm rushing through me. I looked into his eyes, seeing him fighting for control. My eyes softened, and I was unable to hide the hurt from them.

"Do you really not want to mark me?" Those words were enough to make him frown, tugging my head to the side and sinking his teeth into my neck, the sharp pain accompanied by another jarring orgasm that rushed through me as he released his load into me.

"Fuck," he growled the moment he retracted his canines before pressing his lips against my neck. Our hearts were thumping as I felt the strengthening of the bond that we had now completed. I couldn't help but smile, hugging him tightly.

"I got my way," I whispered, feeling rather smug.

"You're a little minx." He chuckled hoarsely. He moved back slightly and stared at my neck, a deep calculating expression on his face. "I won't be able to let you go. I've fallen deeply for you."

A flicker of pain crossed his face, and I cupped it, kissing his lips softly, my heart clenching. He feared being left, no matter how much he denied it or didn't voice it, it was the fear that was birthed from his mother's abandonment.

"You won't need to let me go because I will stay with you as promised. Forever," I whispered, taking an oath on Yileyna in my mind. She was the one person that meant the most to me, and I would never take an oath upon her without meaning it. No matter what true mate showed up before me, I would not abandon Hunter. Come whatever.

The following morning, although Raiden kept winking and teasing me about my mark, I was on cloud nine! I felt happy and complete. Gamma Grayson seemed happy about it too. I wondered if he'd still smile at me like that if he knew I was his daughter, but I didn't want to ruin anything for him and Gamma female Zoe.

I was riding on a horse as Hunter walked in front, reins in hand, when we suddenly came to a stop, and he raised his hands, giving his men a signal.

Stay here, he commanded me, a deep frown on his face before he slipped away with some of his men and Raiden.

Silence ensued until I heard some shouts. A surge of power followed by a violent wind ripped through the air, making the tree branches whip around us, and hundreds of leaves swirl. My heart thudded with fear. I jumped off my horse, ready to go after Hunter, when Ryan pulled me back.

"He is going to be seriously pissed if you go," he warned. I frowned at him.

"I am not just going to stay here! That wind wasn't normal!"

"Of course it wasn't, but you will just be a distraction… women…"

I was about to argue when I heard footsteps, and to my relief, Hunter appeared from between the trees unharmed. I let out a breath of relief, placing a hand to my chest, about to relax when I saw the silver glow of his aura swirling around him and then right next to him was… Zarian?

It took me a moment to recognise the fae man. His hair was braided and put in a high ponytail. He was wearing black with dark silver armour. My eyes widened when I saw several knives to his back.

"What is going on…" I murmured, confused at the look in Hunter's eyes as he watched Zarian, almost as if not trusting the man who walked with a small smile on his face.

"Alpha Hunter seems to not trust me," Zarian stated calmly, but I didn't miss the sharp glint in his eyes.

"Do you wish to fill the princess in on the truth, or shall I?" Hunter growled, glaring at him. I wanted to move closer to him, but the moment I thought it, two of Hunter's men stepped in front of me, almost as if shielding me from Zarian. This was crazy, I knew Zarian.

"I know Zarian! We used to be regulars at the tea house he worked at!" I exclaimed, trying to move past them.

"He had his motives," Hunter's dangerous voice came, making me pause.

"Alpha Yileyna trusts him. She wanted us to seek him out," Raiden explained as he stepped out of the trees last, walking around to the front.

"Then she is far more naive than I thought. Speak or I will carve your tongue out," Hunter threatened. Zarian frowned, glaring back at him.

"I have done nothing wrong."

"Then tell them who you are. I recognised you at the engagement that day, so before you lie, think wisely. I already know your truth even if no one else does."

"Who would have thought the isolated Alpha was so efficient…" Zarian scoffed, making my eyes widen in surprise. "Fine. My name is Anzaria Zenadayn, Crown Prince of the Kingdom of Aerean." I stared at him in shock. Crown prince?

"What… what were you doing in Westerwell?" I asked quietly, staring at him as I stepped forward. This time Hunter's men allowed me to do so. He seemed to be conflicted by my question before he looked away.

"Oi! You were asked a question," Ryan growled.

"I was there to attain the heart." His words were like a slap in the face. Was that all everyone wanted?

"You… agreed to help Yileyna because you knew what she was?" I asked feeling upset. Oh, how I missed her. He frowned slightly and nodded.

"I realised she was the heart, but I helped her out of genuine goodwill."

"To get close to her you mean," Raiden added icily. I glanced at him. Never had I seen him so angry.

"I did nothing wrong. I never hurt her, nor did I try to kill her." His eyes flashed, and I ran my hand through my hair. How could we trust anyone when everyone had ulterior motives?

"But you tried to get close to her," I repeated, feeling hurt. He shook his head, sighing.

"See it as you will. Everyone wants the heart, there is no shame in it. The Fae Kingdoms are suffering because of the restrictions at the borders between Astalion and Aerean, as well as the other kingdoms. Astalion holds the most crops in abundance, yet the rulers are entitled and hold most of those crops, crops that we need as well."

"We are on good terms with Aerean, trade is always open. How can you…" I trailed off when I noticed Gamma Grayson look down guiltily, and the look on Hunter's face. "What am I missing?" I asked, hating how Dad never told me anything. No one answered, and when I looked at Gamma Grayson he simply refused to meet my gaze.

"Hunter?" Despite the seriousness of the situation, a sexy smirk crossed his lips.

I love how you just called me that openly. Call me again. I stared at him.

This is not the time! He simply looked at me, and I found myself pouting as I frowned at him.

"Hunter."

Perfect. He became serious once more.

"You may not know, but the trade is bare minimum. The amount of produce that is allowed to cross the border is a bare minimum that would not even make a dent in how much we are able to offer and how much Aerean needs. Trust me, I may be of Astalion, but the injustice done to our neighbours is far greater than you may think. But it does not mean I trust you."

"I'm glad you are not blinded from the truth, at the very least," Zarian said, looking at Hunter, who simply shrugged.

"I didn't plan to get involved, but since it's the true ruler of this kingdom who needs our assistance, what kind of brother-in-law would I be if I refused?" He asked, giving me a wink before a frown appeared on his handsome face. "Join us, and let's extend the hand of help to our Queen, the very heart of this world." Zarian seemed to hesitate.

"I do not trust your kind," he said quietly. Hunter motioned for the men to lower their weapons as he massaged his jaw.

"Don't trust us, trust her, the Heart of Kaeladia. You must know what the prophecy says, or do you not?"

"Of course, I know of it," Zarian countered.

"Then you must know that the heart belongs to all."

A Burning Regret

THEON

THE WEATHER WAS PLEASANT, and the sea was calm. It was the following day after the attack, and night had fallen. Everyone was sitting on the deck enjoying the music Leto was playing. Tankards of hot mead sat on the tables in front of us, with platters of snacks as we enjoyed the calm.

Two Sirens had approached hours after that attack, but after a word with Yileyna, they had swum away. I still didn't know how to feel about them. For them not to attack us was… strange. Her words and concern when she had turned back to us were still fresh in my mind.

"We should be safe from here. The sirens and my guards will keep an eye beneath the surface, but… even they don't know why the Leviathan was after us. It is not meant to be anywhere near here."

The Leviathan… something about it niggled at my mind. When she had encased it in ice, the darkness I had felt from it… it felt oddly familiar to the darkness I felt around Arabella… but how was that even possible? A witch, even a dark one, couldn't control a monster created by a god, especially to make it come after us…

The Leviathan was meant to stay in the depths of the ocean. Why would it attack Yileyna, someone who was tied to the sea?

Everyone knew what Yileyna was, and to my surprise, they accepted her, seeing her for who she was and not her being a Siren, but it wasn't so surprising. The crew of The Siren Killer were quite diverse, and they didn't see others for their race but for who they were. Although it had been pretty surprising to them that they had accepted it. It was impressive how she was able to win everyone over.

As for me… I was unable to forget about what happened between us, the way she had moaned… the way she had obviously wanted me. Fuck, just the thought made me hard. Even now, she was dancing with Cleo whilst Leto strummed his guitar as he sang his sea shanties.

I listened to the words, my eyes on Yileyna. She was far more beautiful than I could put into words. The changes in her appearance only made her sexier, and it was fucking hard being around her. Her eyes remained in that multitude of iridescent colours, and even just looking into them made me lose myself.

Right then, she was wearing a white dress that just about covered her ass, her corset accentuating her curves. Her sensual laugh reached my ears as Cleo spun her around, giving me the perfect view of her. Damn, her breasts were fucking fine…

Remembering the feel of her body against mine, I forced myself to look away, feeling pleasure rush south. I picked up my tankard, downing it. I looked back at her, only for our eyes to meet. Her heart skipped a beat, but I refused to look away, or I just wasn't able to…

There was no way that we could be together, not after everything I had done, but why did the urge to pull her close, apologise, and fuck her sense-less consume my mind? Regardless… I still needed to apologise properly for actions that I truly regretted.

I stood up, shooting pain rushing through my chest as I did, but I didn't let it show on my face. I had become accustomed to it. I walked to the edge of the boat just as the sound of footsteps approached. I frowned, knowing who it was before they even spoke.

"Can I get you anything, Commander?" Barbara asked.

"No," I replied curtly, not sparing her a glance.

I knew exactly what she wanted, and if I wasn't so fucking hung up over Yileyna, I would have taken her offer. But the only woman I wanted was her, and I knew none other would cut it for me. The moment Barbara put her hand on my arm, my eyes snapped to her, flashing dangerously.

"Do not touch me," I almost growled, trying my fucking best to keep my voice down.

"Are you sure? You seem tense." She squeezed my shoulder, and I clenched my jaw, knowing my muscles were all knotted up.

"One hundred fucking percent sure," I shot back, moving away from her and walking away towards the back of the ship, away from them all. I could feel Yileyna's eyes on me, but I didn't turn back.

I once said we were heaven and hell... but now we were further apart. We were still the opposites of one another, only now the distance between us was far bigger. The sound of light footsteps on the wood reached my ears, and her intoxicating scent filled my nose. I clenched my jaw. Not now, Yileyna...

Not when the urge to devour her was fucking strong.

"Here, I got you another one." She held out a tankard to me, and I was forced to look at her, taking it. She smiled slightly, raising hers, and we knocked them together before taking a gulp.

"Thanks," I said after a moment, not looking at her. She leaned her back against the rail next to me, tilting her head as she observed me. "Something on my face?" I asked, cocking my brow as I glanced down at her. She pursed her plump lips, a slight frown on her face.

"Theon, are you injured?"

"No."

"You're lying," she murmured, stepping closer and sniffing me. "I can smell blood. It's faint but it's there... besides, your eyes look duller."

"No, they don't, actually. Just because you became somewhat... dazzling, everything else probably just looks washed out to you." She frowned, staring into my eyes.

"No. Your eyes have always been vibrant, Theon. You don't look okay."

"Thanks. Like I said, your view on things has changed," I retorted coldly, downing the drink and placing the tankard down with a thud before turning away.

"Theon." Her irritation was clear, but I ignored her, walking away when she grabbed hold of my arm and blocked my view, glaring up at me.

"Don't block my path, little storm, or I will throw you overboard," I threatened, a threat with no force behind it. A small smile curled her lips, and she smirked.

"The water welcomes me," she reminded me smugly.

"How nice," I replied in the same tone, with added mockery. She frowned, looking me over. I didn't miss how her eyes lingered on the front of my pants, her heart thumping. Interesting.

"Theon, if you're injured, why don't you just tell me? Did the Leviathan hurt you?" She asked sharply.

"Doesn't really matter. Now, unless you want me to push you up against the beam behind you and fuck you until you scream, move," I whispered dangerously. Her heart was pounding, and I didn't miss the way she swallowed. Taking her silence as obedience, I stepped around her, continuing on my way down.

"Then why did you refuse her?" She asked quietly. I didn't need to ask who she meant.

"What do you want to hear, little storm? Because I don't think anything I say will help in any fucking way," I replied quietly as I glanced at her over my shoulder.

"I don't know either, I just… ignore me." She frowned, running her fingers through her hair. She was frustrated, agitated even, and I could see her nails were growing.

"Are you alright?" I asked sharply. I didn't need her going crazy Siren mode on us. She nodded, her cheeks flushing and confusing me as she quickly backed away.

"Yes, I am." She shook her head, and I noticed the tips of her hair that had begun to change returned to normal.

"That didn't look normal to me." I frowned, turning and walking back towards her. "If there's something you are hiding from me, then it's better you tell me now." Was she unable to control herself? She frowned, crossing her arms under her breasts, and it took my fucking all not to admire them.

"I have hidden nothing of importance from you," she retorted, her gaze dipping over me before she looked back into my eyes defiantly. "You're the one who refused to tell me what's wrong with you." Her gaze became suspicious, and I wondered what she'd think if I told her it was her attack that had left this injury on me.

"I don't need to share it with a dumb little blonde." She blinked, not expecting that, before her eyes narrowed.

"Well, you found this blonde appealing."

"Doesn't mean you're any less dumb," I retorted, almost smirking at the fact I had managed to deviate the conversation. She glowered up at me.

"Well, you are no smarter than I am. You have done some pretty foolish things too."

"Yeah, although I don't think they were as foolish as they were terrible…"
This was my chance. I frowned as I looked into her eyes. "I know my words
alone will never be enough, nor will they change the past, but if I could do it
all over again then I would make sure they were safe. In all of this, I would
have done my best to keep them away from any harm." I looked into her
eyes, which were filled with pain and vulnerability, her heart beating wildly
as my words sank in. "It will never be enough, but it's one of my greatest
regrets, one that I know I can never be forgiven for and one that I can never
fix. I am sorry, Yileyna, and I really mean it." My voice was quiet, blending
in with the hum of Leto's singing and the crashing waves of the ocean.

Our eyes were locked, hers pooled with tears that spilt silently down her
cheeks. The sky darkened as rain began to fall gently. The sky was crying
with her.

"I'm sorry," I repeated softly as her lips quivered, and for a moment, I
remembered the young girl who had been vulnerable and alone as she ran
to give me the key to our cabin that snowy day… "I'm fucking sorry for
everything."

I wasn't meant to let my emotions take over, and I didn't want a simple
apology to weaken her resolve, but she deserved to hear it, especially if I was
killed before I got the chance again. I looked at her, and although I wanted
to pull her into my arms and comfort her, I wouldn't because this wasn't an
act to make her heart soften to me.

"I'm sorry." With those final words, I turned and left her just as a small
sob left her lips. It tore me up, leaving her like that, but I didn't deserve
her. I stopped on the stairs, looking at Ailema, the hybrid woman. I had a
feeling she heard everything. "Comfort her," I commanded before I made
my way to my cabin.

Entering, I closed the door behind me and sat on the small bed, running
a hand through my hair. I loved her, but I had lost her, and it was indeed
too late. This was the most I could do.

I tried to distract myself, thinking of anything but the woman I had
left in tears… once more. Tomorrow morning, we would find ourselves in
Eastcourt, and from there, I would head to Lochfox. It should take no more
than two days, and by the following night, we would be back on board.

I was looking forward to seeing Thea. It had been two years since I last
saw her, and, in all of this, it would be nice to see someone who didn't

think of me as anything more than just her brother. I would say someone who loved me for me, but I don't think even she knew what I had done…

I looked at the door, the temptation to go see if Yileyna was okay nearly overcoming me, but I stayed put. Deep down, my wolf's restlessness gave me a clear message, one I was trying to deny:

Yileyna still loved me.

But even if she did, those feelings would soon fade away, too, because no one could love a killer.

A Coward's Words

YILEYNA

His apology had shaken me, but it wasn't the words he spoke that had gotten to me, it was the emotion in them, the pain in his eyes, and the obvious regret. It gave me some clarity. Even when Ailema had comforted me, I realised Theon was also suffering, far more than he showed. I had wanted to go to him, but my own emotions had overwhelmed me. The pain I felt… how could I still care for him despite what he had done? Even if he regretted it and was misguided, it confused me. There was pain and love within me, paired with the intense desire to pounce upon him.

I needed to control myself. This hunger for his physical touch was beginning to scare me, and although I wondered if another man's touch would help, I couldn't do it. He consumed my heart and mind.

The following day, the mention of that apology was not brought up again, but I felt a bit lighter. I just wished I had Mom's or Dad's view on things. What would they advise me? Deep down, I knew the answer to that. My parents had raised me well, but I just wished they were here.

We had arrived at Eastcourt, and, despite it being a big city, it was not as welcoming or busy as Westerwell. We split from the crew, and Theon and I made our way towards Lochfox. We had cloaks on and had our hoods up. Thanks to Flynn's distraction, we were able to sneak away with the help of heavy fog. We had travelled by foot and were away from the city. I glanced over at Theon, frowning. I had suggested shifting twice, but he had refused.

"I don't think a bright white wolf with a fluffy tail is going to blend in," he remarked after the third time I suggested it.

"Oh really? Or are you just afraid that I'll be faster?" I challenged. "The fog will hide us."

"We travel by foot." I frowned and came to a stop.

"We are wasting time, Theon."

"Then shall we take horses?" He shot back, his irritation rising. I was about to argue when I frowned, turning and looking up at him sharply.

"Is it because you are unable to shift?" I asked, stopping in my tracks. His heart skipped a beat. It was slight, and his face remained almost the same, but I had caught it.

"I just don't want to -" I cut him off, placing a finger to his lips as my gaze dipped to his chest.

"Theon... how are you not healing?" I asked, frowning as I grabbed his shirt, ready to push it up, only for him to stop me. His grip on my wrist was tight but not painful.

"I'm fine, it's just a small injury. We carry on, on foot," he growled.

"I want to see it. How did it happen?" Our eyes met, and I could see he was mulling it over.

"As I said, let it go. We are wasting time."

"No. We are wasting time because you are behaving stubbornly. Stop being so childish, Theon!" I snapped, my frustration growing. His eyes flashed gold as he glared at me.

"Fine. It happened when you rejected me."

My eyes flew open in shock as I stared at him in sheer surprise. I felt as if someone had just slapped me across the face. The memory of that moment returned to me, finding out the truth about my parents and then losing it. I had dug my nails into him and ripped through his chest, with the aim to kill... So all this time, he hadn't healed?

My stomach lurched as I pulled free from his hold, lifting his shirt up to reveal the bandages that were wrapped around his entire torso. The faint pink that was already staining the bandages told me he wasn't healing. My heart thumped as I looked him over.

"I'm fine. It's healing, just a bit fucking slower." He tried to move away, but I didn't let go.

"Why… why didn't you heal already?" I muttered, worry and fear filling me. He pulled away forcefully, yanking his top down. "Theon, tell me." Our eyes met, and he clenched his jaw. He knew we were wasting time.

"A Siren's touch in rage is -"

"Death," I whispered, my heart thudding as I stared at the man before me.

Death. He was dying slowly.

Now the dullness in his eyes made sense. Gawking up at him beyond those sexy looks, I realised he looked pretty pale too…

"I deserved it. Now, shall we carry on walking?" He asked me pointedly. I frowned, wanting to see the wounds, but I didn't push it.

"How about I shift, and you can ride on my back?" I suggested. He stared at me as if I had just grown another head.

"Not happening."

"What's wrong with that?" I huffed, falling into step by his side. The guilt I felt was still eating up at me. "Put your ego aside."

"No."

"Theon. Please. We'll be faster. We need to head to Naran…" I trailed off, realising what was in Naran… something that could heal all illnesses and injuries.

"What is it?" He asked, noticing the change in my beating heart. I shook my head, trying to hide the ray of hope that ignited within me.

"Nothing. Nothing at all. Let's hurry."

We finally arrived at Lochfox, but I could tell something wasn't right. Theon was frowning deeply as he looked around at the rundown buildings. Some looked charred by fire, and others were extremely ill-kept. The further into the small village we went, the worse it got, but there were still no signs of his pack or much life save the few lone wolves or humans.

"Have you ever been here before?" I asked quietly.

"A few times, we once had some of our people here. There was also another pack that resided here. Seems they left…"

"Then where do you think they have gone?" I asked.

"I don't know, but I intend to find out." His reply was cold, and I could sense the anger in it. We carried on in silence, the roads becoming rockier. It was obvious no one had been here in a while.

"I don't think anyone has lived here recently," I murmured, my foot slipping on some rubble. Theon's arm shot out, and he grabbed my wrist, steadying me.

"Careful."

My heart skipped a beat when he pulled me close, his arm snaking around my waist as our eyes met. My core clenched as I felt his entire body against mine. I slowly tugged away, trying not to focus on how good his body felt, and looked away as we continued, but his hand didn't leave my waist.

Theon led the way further in; he clearly had a goal in mind. With each passing minute, my worry for his sister was growing. I just hoped she was okay, wherever she was.

A short while later, we finally saw a small home standing alone. It wasn't in much better condition than the rest of the town, but the puffs of smoke from the window and the glow of a fire from inside beckoned us. Theon knocked on the door, and it wasn't long before it was pulled open by a middle-aged man. His smile vanished upon seeing Theon, who pushed his way inside.

"May I come in?" I asked, smiling warmly. The man looked me over, his gaze lingering on my eyes before he nodded, but I didn't miss the fear in him.

"Welcome to my humble abode, A-Alpha Theon." Theon frowned as he turned to the man. I shut the door behind me.

"No need for formalities. I came here to find my sister, only to find that there's no sign of any of the pack in Lochfox, yet you are still here."

"Why would you come to find your sister? Did your father not tell you where she is?" He asked keenly, almost curiously. I frowned as Theon looked at him sharply.

"He told me she's in Lochfox."

"Then does he know you have come here?" The man asked, wiping the bead of sweat from his forehead. I watched him sharply, seeing the slight tremble in his hand as he looked at Theon. Why was he so afraid?

"What has that got to do with anything, Cadoran?" Theon asked sharply.

"We won't hurt you," I promised, giving him a gentle smile. "We are only here for answers." The man gave me a small grimace that I was certain was meant to be a smile. The suspicion didn't vanish from his eyes, although he let out a deep breath.

"W-well, I mean no wrong. After all, you are my alpha." Cadoran bowed to Theon, making me frown. "But I didn't think Alpha Theoden would send you on a wild goose chase when he knows she isn't here."

Theon's heart was pounding as he stared at the man, about to walk over to him, when I stepped in front of him, placing a hand on Theon's chest, shaking my head slightly. Our eyes met, and he frowned, despite obeying me and staying in his spot. I didn't move away, turning to Cadoran once more.

"Will you tell us everything that happened here?"

"Wh-who are you, my lady?" He asked, taking out a handkerchief. Fear filled the room as the terrified man looked at me and wiped his forehead. There was nothing to hide.

"I am Yileyna De'Lacor, daughter of this kingdom and the Heart of Kaeladia. We have come for answers, Cadoran, to fix the wrongs of the kings before us, and we need to know anything you can tell us. It is obvious you are scared, but why? What happened?"

"The heart... then you should-should not be here..." he mumbled, looking at Theon with fear.

"It's okay. Theon can be trusted," I said, looking up at the man I loved and thought I hated. Somehow that hatred was fading...

"I wouldn't trust him, My Queen," he whispered. The bravest attempt he had made.

"I assure you I'm questioning my father's actions. So, if you can tell me what has happened here for the last two years, I would appreciate it." Cadoran sighed before he motioned to the worn-out sofa in front of the hearth.

"Then I suggest you sit down; it is a long story," he said quietly, his eyes shadowed.

I looked up at Theon, only to realise I still had my hand on his chest and was right up against him. My heart skipped a beat, and I slowly moved away. I thought I saw a small smirk on his lips as we took a seat.

"Would you like tea?"

"No, thank you," I declined politely, giving him a smile.

He took a deep breath, putting distance between himself and Theon as he sat on a stool near the hearth, placing his hands on his knees and taking another shuddering breath.

"I have always been a lone wolf living on the edge of the territory, not wanting trouble, you know that, Alpha Theon. After all, the pack's ways were not for me…" He cast a furtive look at Theon, who remained silent. "After you left… your father's ways became more obvious. With you gone, there was no front to put up. He pulled back the search parties for that wretched Siren who killed our Luna. He said our focus was on getting stronger…. even though we were growing, we weren't enough. He wanted an army, one that would be far more powerful than any other, and so… he started selling them…" His eyes became haunted, and sadness filled them, making the man look older than he probably was.

"Them?" Theon asked sharply.

"Our women."

I stared at him, stunned, as silence fell in the room, but Theon's heart was thundering louder than ever. I took his hand in mine, trying to calm the raging aura that now erupted around him.

"Explain," his hoarse command came. His chest was heaving, fighting his emotions.

"The Beta argued, but he killed him, telling us that anyone who disobeyed him would end up the same. For each young woman, depending on her beauty and her status, not to mention if she was a virgin… he sold them to other Alphas or anyone willing to trade for men."

"No… Dad couldn't… what about Thea?" Theon asked, his voice cracking as he stared at the man intensely. Cadoran looked at him with sympathy, now clearly realising Theon knew nothing.

"She was an Alpha's daughter. At first, he didn't even consider selling her, knowing what she meant to you, but when the Alpha of the Dark Moon Pack came, offering him two thousand men for her, the Alpha agreed…. She screamed and shouted, saying she wouldn't forgive him; the entire pack heard it… but he simply said she should be grateful that an Alpha was taking her, and she should be proud to do this for her kingdom." Cadoran's eyes filled with sadness before he looked up at Theon. I, too, turned to look at Theon, who was trying to hide his pain, his grip on my hand tight as his entire body shook with the revelation.

"Did no one else try to stop him?" Theon asked quietly, his voice shaking with anger.

"Those who did were killed. Before he left, he killed anyone he didn't trust. That's when I ran… like the coward I am. With the help of a serum from a witch, I staged my death. The serum stopped my heart from beating for a few minutes. I wasn't a concern for them, and they didn't do a thorough check on the small folk. When they destroyed the town, I lay there waiting for them all to leave… and now, here I am, in my home that they forgot to destroy as it's so far out. Alone."

Theon pulled his hand free as he stood up, turning his back on me and running his fingers through his hair.

"When was she sold?" He asked.

"Six months back, Alpha."

"Fuck!" Theon growled, punching the wall. Cadoran flinched, and I stood up, my heart breaking for all those women who were sold. We had to find them all… but how?

"Theon…"

"I won't forgive him. How could he do that to her… to any of them? This isn't right."

"I know it's not," I whispered softly, placing my hand on his back.

"I can't believe I listened to him like a fucking fool," he whispered, his voice barely audible.

"Theon, you didn't know. Don't blame yourself. Everything that's happened has been staged by Theoden. We need to defeat him. I know he's your father, but you need to take over and become the Alpha of your pack and -"

"My pack? He killed my pack! Those men are mere soldiers whom he has purchased! I'm going to fucking destroy him."

"Theon!" I shouted, placing my hand on his chest as he tried to push past. "Calm down! We will do this together." Theon ran a hand through his hair, looking back at Cadoran, who was watching us curiously.

"What else has my father done? Tell me the truth. Everything you know, I want you to tell me now!" Theon commanded. Cadoran lowered his head before he looked up at Theon.

"If I speak, and I will, what guarantee will you give that my safety will remain?"

"I give you my word. Nothing will happen to you," I spoke before Theon could, knowing in his anger he may not be so pleasant. Cadoran looked towards the window, fear once again settling into him.

"Alpha Theoden has dark allies, My Queen, and I fear for us all, but I am a coward, and I don't wish to die."

"You fucking won't, now spit it out," Theon growled.

"Theon, please, give him time," I whispered. I could feel the bandages under my fingertips, smell the faint smell of blood, and I knew we didn't have much time. "Please tell us. The more we know, the better."

"Then we go back, back to the time I first realised he was up to no good... a time when he killed someone very dear to you, Alpha Theon. Perhaps you have forgotten her... but she became a distraction to you, and although she was the daughter of his good friend, he didn't care. He had her killed in such a horrible way by our own men. I was there... but my job was to cry for help." I could feel Theon's heart pounding violently, but my curiosity heightened. What girl?

"Her name." Theon's asked dangerously, but something told me he already knew the name.

"None other than your first love, Alpha Theon. Iyara. Your father had her killed when she became a distraction for you."

IYARA

YILEYNA

My heart squeezed at those words. Mixed with the sadness I felt for the young woman who had been murdered for loving him, I felt something else.

Theon closed his eyes, and I could almost see him shattering. My own eyes stung with tears. I didn't like seeing him in pain. It was obvious he had been through a lot. Cadoran continued as if he had wanted to spill the burden that weighed upon him.

"It was one of the final steps to shape you into the man you would become. Your father wanted you to become his mirror, his shadow, his -"

"I will never be him," Theon cut off, his eyes blazing. "What else has he done? Tell me!"

"Aside from selling the women and killing those who disobeyed him, I know not what is true or not, but there were rumours that he had a dark power in his grasp. Something that -"

"Arabella. We know. Anything else?" Theon's anger was at breaking point, and he was fuelling his pain into rage, worrying me.

"Nothing, I'm sorry." Cadoran's fear had returned, and he cowered away. It was obvious he would do anything to survive, and deep down, I knew if someone came here asking about us, he would also out us.

"Thank you for your information. If anyone passes here asking for us, no matter who, you will not tell anyone," I commanded, my alpha aura rolling off me. My eyes blazed as Cadoran paled, my order absolute.

"I-I would ne-never."

"Good," I said quietly. "Come, Theon."

He didn't reply as we both left the small cabin. Cadoran was a man who wanted to live but cared for nothing more than himself. I wondered what kind of person could be happy like that, but at least he had told us something. Even if it was just to survive, we still got some answers. I was grateful for his answers, despite the dark revelations. It was helping in opening Theon's eyes.

Iyara. His first love. I wondered what she was like. The fact that his father had killed her had shaken him.

"Let's shift. We will go to the Dark Moon Pack," he said, pulling his shirt off. I frowned, knowing he would rip open his wounds if he did so.

"Theon, you yourself said -"

"She's been sold, Yileyna! I need to find her." Desperation and agony were in his voice. I couldn't refuse him, so I nodded.

The moment he unbuckled his pants, I turned away, taking my clothes off and placing the necklace given to me by Lavina safely inside them. Gathering them up, I shifted into my wolf. I felt her excitement when she turned towards Theon, her elation rushing through me. Although we had rejected one another, her feelings for him were there, just like mine. The moment he shifted, I flinched as his wounds stretched and tore, fresh blood dripping onto the floor.

He jerked his head to the left, picking up his bundle of clothing before breaking into a run. His frustration and rage were a storm around him, and he ran fast, that amber aura glowing around him, fuelling his speed. I noticed every time his paws hit the floor, scorch marks or little embers of fire flickered for a moment. What exactly was his power?

I wasn't able to ask in wolf form and now wasn't the time. We just needed to get to the Dark Moon Pack, and I hoped we could get out of there discreetly because we didn't need Theoden alerted to Theon learning his truth.

A few hours later, we had finally slowed when we reached a small river in the woods. Night was falling, and the glow of the setting sun was shining through the trees. We drank some water, and I realised I hadn't even noticed that I was parched. The moment Theon had his fill, he shifted. My core clenched at the sight of him in his naked glory, but those thoughts vanished when I saw the huge gashes across his chest. My stomach twisted sickeningly. They were far worse than I thought, and the fact that I had done that...

He turned away from me, pulling on his pants. My heart thumped as I shifted back and put my own clothes on. Theon opened his bag and took out a roll of gauze.

"Let me do it," I said quietly, approaching him. He didn't respond, allowing me to take the roll from him as he sat down. His breathing was shallow and laboured. I knew he had exerted himself. "You pushed yourself too far," I murmured, looking at the deep gashes. Was there nothing I could do to help him?

"Oh yeah? Or did you just find it a struggle to keep up?"

"Oh please, I was completely fine. I probably could have been faster," I replied haughtily, sending a cooling breeze over his burning injuries. I wasn't so sure; he had been extremely fast. He hissed, and I tensed, looking up at him. "Sorry."

"It's fine," he replied, looking into my eyes. I nodded before I slowly began wrapping the bandage around him.

"Iyara... what was she like?" I asked softly. The fear of him getting angry flitted through my mind, but I no longer feared his reaction or planned to walk on eggshells like I once did long ago. We were not a couple, and if I pushed him, I had nothing to lose.

He stayed silent, and I thought he wasn't going to reply. My fingers grazed his skin here and there, and often our eyes met, that intense connection swirling around us and only when I was able to move back did I feel I could breathe once again.

"She was the first who was special to me. We were friends before those feelings became more... she hoped we'd be mates, but we weren't, yet we still thought we could be. I treated her the way I did you... I left her after she gave me her all because I knew my life was meant for revenge. I couldn't have her caught up in it all." His voice was emotionless, but I knew him better than that.

"I'm sorry," I whispered. "What was she like?"

"The opposite of you in most ways. She was innocent, cherished things like the sunset or sunrise… carefree and gentle." Was it wrong to feel a pang of jealousy for a woman I didn't know? But I couldn't deny it. I should have known Theon possibly had someone else, but it never crossed my mind…

"I was innocent until you corrupted me," I mumbled. He raised his eyebrow.

"The girl who used to go perv at the White Dove?" I frowned at him, and he looked at the sky. "You were innocent too, but you two were different… I was able to walk away from her." His voice became quieter before he looked over at me.

Our eyes met, and when his gaze dipped to my lips, my heart pounded, and I knew he could hear it. I knew what he was saying. He hadn't been able to walk away from me… that's why everything got worse. We became embroiled in something far greater than ourselves, and it was our feelings for one another that suffered. He looked at the river as he continued,

"He told me it was an attack from Andres that killed her, only fuelling my hatred for him. I'm beginning to question even the smallest things…"

I wanted to move closer, but I didn't trust myself. He was still sitting there shirtless. His defined abs, those muscular biceps… his chiselled cuts and grooves of his body. A work of art that I was hungry to devour, and so I stayed put.

"You aren't him. Like I said the other day, you have good in you. You have been fed lies from a young age, and our parents' influence plays a huge part in our upbringing."

"It's not an excuse. Come on, we should head out; I don't plan to cause a scene, but I am going to find her, and I will kill anyone who has hurt her." He stood up, his eyes filled with a burning hatred. I couldn't argue with him. Just the thought of what may have happened to her made me sick with worry.

"Let's go," I said, picking up the rest of our belongings…

Fire.

The Dark Moon Pack was one huge bonfire, but I couldn't fault Theon. Women in barely any clothing were chained and treated like slaves, along with a few men who were of a more slender build and had prettier features.

When we had finally gotten close enough, we realised the Dark Moon Pack was a horrible place. Drunk men lazed around whilst the women served them, doing their bidding, whether that was feeding them, massaging them, or taking care of their sexual needs. To the side, two women had been whipped for disobeying, their bodies a bloody mess.

It was one horrifying scene that I knew I'd never be able to forget. The only words I remembered Theon whisper were,

"Those are my people."

And then he had unleashed his wrath upon them all.

Theoden had done one thing, and that was create a killing machine. His amber eyes blazed gold as he dealt the hand of judgement upon them all, slaying any who he had witnessed committing a crime. Only the abused remained, along with the women and children and a handful of men, but none were warriors. Two hours later, the remnants of the warriors of the pack were rounded up, whilst the dead were burned.

I had commanded the pack women to give the women and men who had been chained clothing. From their state, it was obvious they were only for breeding, beaten, with most pregnant and clearly exhausted.

"She isn't here," Theon said quietly as I helped one of the women, who had been beaten, drink some water. My heart sank as I looked around. Thea.

"Have you asked anyone if there's a dungeon or anything?" I asked, standing up, seeing the desperation and fear in his eyes.

"No one is speaking; they have all been through too much and aren't in their right minds. We have over a hundred men and women who are beaten and abused here. No one knows anything, and there's no order." He ran a hand through his hair, and I placed my hand on his arm.

"The Alpha, did you ask him before you killed him?" He shook his head.

"He didn't say anything, even when I asked."

"We will find her. She's your sister, Theon, there is no way that anything could have happened to her," I reassured him, hoping that we found her.

He nodded, and I took a few steps away from him, trying to clear my mind, wondering if becoming one with the earth would help. It was worth a try. It was similar to how I could sense people from the air and the ice. Finding a place free from fire and ash, I knelt and placed my hands on the ground, trying to look for life that perhaps we had not noticed...

Something slithered beneath the earth, two feet deep.... Insects... hundreds of them... the injured.... Theon... I went farther out, and it was then that I sensed two living beings. My heart skipped a beat, and I looked up at Theon, who was watching me.

"To the northwest, there's rockier terrain, there are two people there!"

He gave me a small nod before jogging off, I wanted to follow him, but there were people here who needed me. I just prayed it was her.

This Fire

THEON.

YILEYNA BEING THERE HAD been enough to control me from unleashing hell worse than I did. The moment she told me she sensed some life force, I left. I needed to find Thea. If she died… once again, I'd have failed. I was meant to protect her, but I didn't. I only ever made matters worse.

I wouldn't forgive Dad, and when we came face to face, I was going to kill him. Iyara… Thea… Yileyna… every single person that he had hurt. He would pay for those fucking crimes. I recognised some of the women he had sold, girls of our pack… we were meant to protect them, and instead, he sold them for power.

I had been around Andres for two years, and he had come to trust me, but although he was a fool, he was nowhere near as twisted as Dad is, a man who I no longer wanted to refer to as my father.

I reached the rocky terrain, and it took me a while to locate the narrow entrance. The moment I managed to squeeze in, my heart thudded as a familiar scent hit me.

"Thea!" I shouted, my voice ringing off the cavern.

"Theon?" A hoarse whisper came.

I looked around the dark cavern as I went further in, only to see two women bound in silver as they lay on the floor, beaten and bruised. One woman I didn't recognise… but the other, even bloody and older than how I last remembered her, was none other than my sister.

"Thea…" I rushed to her side, summoning all my strength and tearing the chains from her. I felt blood seep down my chest from my wound, but I didn't care. The physical pain was nothing compared to the pain inside of me. "Thea, thank the goddess," I whispered, pulling her into my arms. She was skinny, beaten, and bloody, but she was alive.

"Theon!" She gasped, clinging to me tightly as she kissed my shoulder and cheek. "Theon you're here… you came for me." I looked into her bloodshot amber eyes and saw the tears she refused to shed. Her black hair was a matted mess. I knew without her having to say anything, she had been through hell.

"I should have come sooner," I whispered before pulling her close once again. She clung to me, her entire body shaking from emotions, emotions far too strong to put into words. All that mattered was that she was alive. Fuck, she was alive. With the relief came the cold reminder that she could have been killed. "Come on, let's get you out of here," I said, looking at the other woman who lay unmoving.

"It's the previous Luna. She has a heart of gold," she explained quietly.

I frowned as I broke her free and stood up. Thea got to her feet, and I lifted the woman, who was in a far worse state than Thea, placing my free arm around my sister's waist to support her. Theoden was fucking dead.

Three hours had passed, and the fire had been doused. Everyone had been tended to and was resting. Thea had fainted halfway out of the cavern, and I had carried her back to Yileyna. When I had told her it was indeed Thea, the happiness on her face made something inside of me stir. I wanted to yank her close and tell her how fucking thankful I was for her. She had grown. She truly was no longer the girl she once was, but a strong woman, who was facing the fucking world.

We were in one of the houses that the Luna had offered us. She was still weak, yet she had submitted her allegiance to Yileyna. I was sitting on the bed where Thea was sleeping, stroking her matted hair, wondering what she had been through, when the bathroom door opened, and a thick wave of steam escaped, but it was the woman who stepped out that made my breath hitch.

Yileyna stood there, towelling her hair, dressed in red panties, which I could see through the oversized white cotton shirt, which outlined her breasts, her stiff nipples clear against the cotton of her shirt, making me throb... Fuck...

Her gorgeous eyes flicked up to me, and our eyes met.

"Want to take a shower? I'll watch over her," she offered, placing the towel down. I stood up, walking over to her, only for her heart to begin racing.

"Why so nervous, little storm?" I asked huskily, taking hold of her chin. I had washed up and bandaged myself earlier, but I still had stains of blood and ash on me.

"I'm not..." She denied, with a roll of her eyes, but her heart still raced.

My gaze went to her gorgeous neck. That long chain she had been wearing was around her once more. I swallowed hard and the urge to wrap my hand around her slender, smooth, creamy neck overtook me. I grabbed hold of it, making her heart pound.

"No matter how much time goes by... you still can't resist my touch," I whispered. I don't know why I said it, but with everything that had happened, I didn't want to lose her...

I was waiting for her rebuttal, but it never came as she simply stared at me through those gorgeous eyes. Although I missed the soft grey they once used to be, I realised neither of us was who we once were...

We had changed. Everything that happened had changed us. Where she was becoming the queen she was destined to be, finding and creating her path, I was walking away from mine; from here on, my path was to walk by her side, to make sure she was safe... to deal the hand of punishment upon those who deserved it because I didn't want her hands to be tainted with the blood of many.

As for my punishment... with time... when this was all over... it would come.

"Theon..." she whispered, her hands going to my waist as she stepped closer. Her breasts grazed against me and my eyes blazed gold.

I can't hurt you again.

Our hearts were thundering, and when she tiptoed, closing the gap between us, I found myself pulling her closer. I shouldn't be doing this...

Her scent was fucking driving me nuts.

Just one taste…

"Wow… this is not what I was expecting to wake up to." We both froze, turning sharply to see Thea sitting up, a smile on her lips as she blinked her amber eyes. "Carry on. I don't mind the show if the couple is appealing. Just keep Theon covered, I don't want to see anything of his." She shuddered. "But you are a beauty, and look at Theon's goo-goo eyes." I frowned, letting go of Yileyna who moved back swiftly, blushing lightly.

"Thea. It's nice to meet you, I'm Yileyna, Theon's… comrade." Thea frowned slightly, confusion flickering in her eyes as she looked at me and back at Yileyna.

"Oh. I thought you two were mates… the way you were looking at one another…"

Neither of us spoke, a tense silence falling between us. We may have destroyed our mate bond, but the feelings between us remained… feelings created before a bond…

I walked over to her and sat down on the bed, brushing her hair away from her face.

"What happened?" I asked.

"Or would you like some food first?" Yileyna offered.

"I think I want a bath first." She looked down at herself with an expression of disgust on her face.

"I'll run you one." Yileyna made to turn away, but Thea waved her hand.

"I'll manage, you two can carry on. I'll just shout when I'm ready to step out," she added slyly before she got off the bed with a smirk.

Yileyna glanced at me as if expecting me to deny it, but I remained silent as Thea chuckled, going into the bathroom. I didn't know what she'd been through, but at least she was still herself. Somewhat. Or at least she was trying.

The moment the bathroom door shut, Yileyna tucked a strand of her long blonde hair behind her ear and turned her back on me. Wrong move. From the low bed, I could see the curve of her ass sticking out from under her shirt, her tiny panties covering nothing…

"Theon…" Her voice was breathless and when she pressed her thighs together my eyes flashed, the faint scent of her arousal reaching me. My dick hardened, and when she spun back to me, her breasts were heaving. We were fighting for control…

I stood up, knowing I couldn't be alone with her, or I'd lose it.

"I'll go get food."

Twenty minutes later I returned to the hut with food, Thea was still in the bathroom and Yileyna must have gone to the other bedroom.

"How long?"

"I'll be a little while… my hair is knotted…" her unhappy reply came.

"Got it… I brought food."

I placed the cloth bundle of food that the pack cook had given me on the table and left the room. Although I wanted to avoid Yileyna, I just needed to make sure she was okay. The door to the room was open, and Yileyna was sitting on the small bed, her head resting against the wall as she gazed out of the window.

"There's food," I stated emotionlessly. To my surprise, she rolled her eyes, giving me a dirty look before she fixed her gaze out the window once again.

"I don't want food," she almost growled, shocking me even more. This was not what I was expecting.

"Wow… okay. Do you want a drink?" I asked. Her gorgeous eyes turned back to me, and she glared at me once more. But it was her next words that rendered me speechless.

"No, I want you to find me a handsome man to satiate my desires."

We stared at each other. There was no embarrassment in her expression, just irritation and the subtle hint of hunger. Although her words sent a flare of jealousy through me, I kept it masked. I frowned ever so slightly, wondering what had made her say that. Was it her Siren side? Their hunger for sex was something that was rumoured about, it was said to be the reason they lured men to their doom…

"I'm afraid this place lacks handsome men," I remarked, trying to keep the irritation and jealousy from my voice. I didn't deserve her, remember? Yet just thinking of another man with her was fucking pissing me off. She raised an eyebrow and stood up.

"Fine, I'll find myself one," she said, and to my surprise, she slid her shirt off and dropped it onto the floor. Her eyes fixed on me.

"Yileyna…"

She stood there in nothing but those tiny red panties, her breasts fucking begging to be worshipped and played with. Her entire body was a fucking dream and just the thought of fucking her made me throb hard. She advanced on me, every sensual sway of her hips, the way her smooth, creamy breasts moved with those gorgeous pink nipples... although I knew I could fucking leave, I didn't want to. My own body was going fucking crazy.

"Oh look, I found one," she whispered seductively when she reached me. The moment her hands touched my chest, sending off those delicious sparks, I lost all control. She wanted me.

Fuck everything.

I wanted her.

"You asked for it," I growled, grabbing her throat and pushing her up against the wall, kicking the door shut. A moan left her lips, her heart pounding as she grabbed my hips, yanking me closer.

"Oh, fuck, Theon," she whimpered, making my own pleasure rush through me. Our eyes met, and I wondered if this was a fucking dream.

No matter what was happening in our lives... the pain, the regret, the guilt... this moment... this moment was ours... even if it was the last time...

A part of me told me I shouldn't do this because it would only make it harder for her, but I was still human, and I was fucking selfish when it came to her touch. I looked into those vibrant eyes, tightening my grip around her waist.

"Are you sure about this?" I asked huskily.

"Yes," she replied, her hands grazing my hips.

I leaned in. Despite the urge to ravage her, I wanted to cherish the moment. I never thought I'd ever have the chance to kiss her again...

Our noses brushed against one another, her scent clouding my senses. Our hearts pounded, and for a moment, I almost felt afraid to kiss her. It seemed too fucking good to be true. She tilted her head up slightly, her grip on me tightening, her lips so close....

The emotions that coursed through me were intense... so many things... was it possible to feel so strongly for another? I loved everything about her. Her strength... her kindness... her selflessness... her love... her beauty... her smile... the way her presence kept me sane, the way she felt against me, the way she made me feel, the way she touched me, the way she tasted...

I had hurt her, yet she still showed me compassion...

I knew that she had become my priority. She was the one thing that mattered the most. I'll kill for her... I'll fucking fight for her... and without a fucking doubt, I will die for her...

Our lips met softly, so tenderly, as if we might break this if we moved faster. Pure heavenly euphoria combusted within me, and thousands of tingles ran through me as our lips moved against one another in the slowest, most sensual dance of all times...

I let go of her neck, admiring her face for a second; her parted lips, her eyes that were shut, her lashes brushing her cheeks... cupping her face with both hands, my own eyes closed, savouring this precious moment. One sentence burned in my mind as I kissed her deeply and slowly.

I fucking love her.

Silent Wishes

THEON

A TEAR TRICKLED DOWN HER cheeks and I moved back, concern flooding me. Did she regret it?

Her eyes opened, glistening with unshed tears. I brushed them away with my thumbs as fresh ones fell.

"Hey… what's wrong?"

"You've never kissed me like that."

"Never realised it was so bad that it made you cry," I whispered, making her let out a weak laugh as she shook her head. No. It wasn't bad… it was her realising how I truly felt. There was no hatred or rage fuelling me tonight. Just her…

"No. Far from it," she whispered, pressing herself against me.

"Let's try again then."

With those words, I threaded my hand into her hair and claimed her lips in a deep, passionate kiss. This time I let my hunger lead, mixed with everything I felt. I kissed her harder, yet slow enough that she could still keep up and savour it. This wasn't about me; it was about us.

Her arms locked around my neck, and I lifted her up, my hands on her ass as she moaned against me. We kissed each other as if we could never get enough, and my hands ran over her, feeling every part of her smooth skin that I could reach. I broke away from those plush lips, our tongues playing with each other's for a moment before I began placing hot, sensual kisses down her jaw and neck. I wish I could keep her forever…

I kissed her neck, sucking teasingly on the spot where her mate mark would sit if ever she was claimed, and she whimpered, arching her back, pressing her stomach and breasts against me. Goddess, she was fucking perfect.

I carried her to the bed, placing her down. I began kissing her down her collar bones and over her breasts. I grabbed her breasts, almost growling. Fuck, they were lush. She cried out, biting her lips as her body reacted to my touch. She unwrapped her legs from around me, parting them, begging for more…

I flicked, sucked, and nibbled on her nipples, making her shudder and whimper with every touch, my hand running down her stomach and massaging her smooth pussy. She moaned, her entire body shivering with pleasure.

"Theon…"

"Hush." Reaching up, I kissed her once more before I continued my slow assault down her stomach. I could see her body beginning to almost shimmer, the ends of her hair turning blue and purple as she moaned in pure contentment.

I ran my tongue down her stomach, making her suck it in. I peeled her tiny panties off and stared at her smooth pussy. My dick throbbed, wanting to be buried in her, but not yet. I kissed her inner thighs and over her smooth lips, making her whimper as she twisted her hand into my hair.

"Oh, fuck, Theon!" She cried out, grinding her body against my face. "Don't tease." I pinned her thighs down, slipping my tongue between her soaking core.

I missed her. I missed this… her scent, her taste, her moans.

I tantalisingly ran my tongue along her slit slowly, knowing her body begged for more, savouring the way she tasted. The moment I found her clit and swirled my tongue around it, she gasped, a satisfied moan falling from her lips as her head dropped back onto the bed.

"Theon…" she whimpered.

I sped up, flicking my tongue over her clit faster and harder as she did her best to muffle her moans. It was time to turn up the heat. I moved back, my eyes blazing. I flipped her over, raising her onto her knees as I dropped onto the floor beside the bed on my knees.

"Part these legs for me, baby girl."

"Fuck, Theon," she whimpered before I bent down once again, running my tongue down her ass, rimming her back entrance before plunging my tongue into her pussy. She cried out as I delivered a sharp tap to her ass, making her back arch as I fucked her with my tongue, burying it further into her. Reaching between her legs, I rubbed her clit with my thumb, heightening her pleasure.

"Oh, fuck, that's it," she moaned.

I delivered another sharp slap to her ass, making her groan, and felt her nearing. I pulled back, got onto the bed, and grabbed her by the hips. Her heart pounded as she looked at me.

"Up on my face, little storm. Let me eat that pussy out properly." She blushed, yet she didn't argue, straddling my face as she looked down at me.

Fuck, this angle was perfection. I buried my tongue into her, eating her out as she began riding my face. I reached up, grabbing her breast with one hand, and delivered another hard tap to her ass before grabbing her ass roughly. She whimpered, her juices trickling into my mouth. She arched backwards, her hand massaging my cock that was straining in my pants. She unzipped them, freeing it as she ran her hand over it, making me throb hard.

I slipped my tongue out of her, instead flicking her clit and slipping two fingers into her pussy. She cried out as I began fucking her with them faster, each thrust curling up against her g-spot, making her tighten. She was near…

I kept going, even when her hand returned to my hair, the other on the wall behind the bed. I didn't stop. Her juices squirted out of her, making her cheeks flush as they drenched my face and neck, despite the pleasure she was experiencing.

"Theon, I…" she moaned.

"Don't hold back. Come for me, beautiful," I murmured, refusing to let her move. Her orgasm ripped through her like a tidal wave of pure ecstasy, letting the rest of her juices coat me. Fuck. Her body shuddered from her release, and I slipped my fingers out, licking her clean.

Only when I was done did I lift her down and, yanking her head close, kissed her, letting her taste herself.

"You taste fucking good, don't you agree, little storm?"

"Theon…" she whimpered.

"Taste yourself," I commanded, quietly running my tongue along her lips.

She parted them, letting me slip my tongue into her mouth as I reached between us, slamming my fingers back into her. She cried out as she sucked my tongue before pulling away and running her tongue down my neck, tasting herself.

"Oh fuck, Theon," she whimpered.

Such a good fucking girl.

I brushed my thumb over her clit, making her gasp as she struggled to free herself. I sat up, grabbing her throat and kissing her roughly.

"Fuck me, Theon." I yanked her back by her lush locks, looking into those blazing eyes that were filled with lust and hunger.

"With fucking pleasure. Now, be a good little girl, and ride my cock," I commanded.

She bit her lip and nodded as she moved down, making me hiss as pleasure rocked me the moment her wet pussy rubbed against my stomach. Oh, she was such a fucking tease. She wrapped her hand around my cock and lowered herself onto it. She winced and took a deep breath, allowing herself a moment.

Now, this was where she belonged…

I looked down at her pussy, loving the way it looked with my cock inside of her. Reaching over, I grabbed her neck, and with my other hand, I gripped her hip tightly.

"Now, let's fuck you until you pass out," I murmured huskily.

"Fuck yes." She placed her hands on my shoulder. For a second, her hand went to my bandaged torso before she leaned down, kissing my lips softly once before I sped up and tightened my hold on her neck. She gasped, gripping my wrist as I fucked her hard and rough.

The pleasure was intense, and all I could think about was how fucking good it felt. It was just her and me.

Her tits were bouncing, and the sound of her skin slapping against mine mixed with the smell of sex was fucking heaven. With each thrust, I was getting closer. The pressure was heightening, my release was near, and the pleasure was only growing. I could hear my own groans of pleasure, but I didn't really care. I was in fucking euphoria, and I didn't fucking care to hold back how good this felt.

"Theon," she whimpered, her head tilted back as I sped up.

Sitting up, I flipped us over. Her back hit the bed, and I pressed her knees open as I rammed into her harder. I was close, and it was taking my all not to come. She cried out, one hand in her hair, the other cupping the back of my neck, and just when her walls crashed down on her and her orgasm rushed through her, squeezing around my cock, I delivered three hard thrusts before pulling out and coming over her thigh.

We were both breathing hard, and when I released my hold on her neck, I saw the imprint my hand left. Several hickeys covered her skin, and many more on her inner thighs.

"Theon..." she murmured as she looked up at me with half-hooded eyes.

I reached down, running my fingers through her hair. I knew it was just a one-night thing... but... I combed my fingers through her hair slowly, bending down and claiming her lips in a deep soft kiss, both of our hearts thumping as one...

When I moved back, she brushed her fingers over her thigh, covering the tips with my cum before she slowly raised them to her mouth and teasingly licked them clean, her eyes fixed on mine as she did so. Oh, fuck, she sure knew how to make me fucking hard again...

The sound of something in the other room made reality settle back in, and I got off the bed slowly. No matter how much I wanted to stay there and fuck her night and day, there were things we needed to do...

Our eyes met. Neither of us spoke, our eyes speaking volumes in our stead.

Fifteen minutes later, I had just finished showering and was wrapping new bandages around myself once again. The memories of what had just happened were still fresh in my mind. She was so fucking hot...

I tried to squash the thoughts before I got turned on again. When I had stepped out of the bedroom, Thea had been sitting on the bed, devouring the food I had brought, and she had smirked deviously, watching me make my way to the bathroom. I could hear them now.

"Definitely not just comrades," Thea was teasing her. She was still a devil, and I was relieved they hadn't broken her to a point of no return.

"Well, he is hard to resist," Yileyna's reply came.

I smirked slightly, trying not to focus on the way my heart reacted to her. I stepped out of the bathroom to see Yileyna and Thea sitting on the bed. Thea was smiling, and Yileyna was blushing faintly.

"Food?" Yileyna asked me, holding out the bread and cheese. I just had fucking dessert and it satisfied me enough...

Our eyes met, and her heart skipped a beat before I sat down on the floor facing the bed and took it from her.

"So, start from the beginning," I said quietly, looking at Thea. The mood in the room darkened as the seriousness of the situation settled in. Thea's eyes shadowed, and she looked at me.

"That man is not human, Theon... Theoden is a monster far worse than any he controls. We need to stop him before he brings this world to an end."

TERRIFYING TRUTHS

YILEYNA

*H*ER OMINOUS WORDS MADE my stomach twist, and Theon looked over at me. My heart skipped a beat as my cheeks heated up, and I looked away. I had no idea what we were… but… those emotions… those feelings…

Now that my cravings were satiated, my mind was clear, and although looking at Theon didn't make me want to scream and shout, I was still confused. I loved him, I still loved him, and it made me feel guilty. He was the one who sent my parents to their deaths. Was I an awful daughter for somehow still loving him? I had almost killed him too… in fact, he was dying with each passing day. I knew what a Siren's touch of death was… I needed to ask Lavina if there was anything to help, but for that, I needed to be close to water.

I forced my attention back to Thea, who was lost in thought.

"Theon, do you remember that witch, Arabella?"

"Obviously, she's in Westerwell with him."

"Do you know what the rumours are? Do you know what she is?" Theon and I both exchanged looks once again.

"What is she?" He asked.

"She is a Dark One. When Theoden and Andres conquered Westerwell, I heard they killed them all, but one. The rumours are that Andres didn't trust Theoden after that fight because of the darkness within him, because he had bound himself to a Dark One, and so he refused to allow him to lead, feeling something odd about him… but it's just rumours. Anyone who may know the truth was killed or were dead… Beta, Mother… anyone who questioned him is killed."

"A Dark One…" Theon mused.

"The Dark Ones were born from the darkness within the people, entities who fed off anything good. They were not beings, but entities of discord and evil… the rumours… there's worse, Theon." Thea seemed to hesitate; her heart began thumping.

"What is it, Thea?" Theon asked warningly.

"They said those who wish to attain control over a Dark One must fulfil some tasks… dark tasks," she whispered. My heart thundered as I looked at her sharply. Theon was watching her sharply, his entire body tense.

"What are you saying?" Thea shook her head.

"I don't know but I've heard dark, dark things, Theon. I heard that they included the death of six of your beloved, bathing in the blood of six children you are to sacrifice, and having sex with six menstruating virgins before killing them." She shuddered and curled up, wrapping her arms around her legs.

"That's… so messed up," I murmured, feeling sick. My own body shuddered with the chill that crept up my spine.

"That doesn't even fucking cover it." Theon stood up, running his hands through his hair.

"Once upon a time I wouldn't have believed it, but, Theon, when he started selling our women, I questioned him but he simply beat me and told me I'd be next. Do you know what he did to the women who no one wanted?" Thea was fighting her tears, her eyes blazing green with disgust and hatred.

"Do I even want to know?" Theon murmured, his eyes flashing.

"He-he humiliated them publicly, made them serve his men and say they were better for nothing more than to be slaves. Even those of our ranked wolves. The Obsidian Shadow Pack is gone, Theon, dead, sold, or those few who were smart enough ran. We are finished."

Theon's heart was thundering as he stared unseeing at the ground. I could only imagine the turmoil that was going through him. That was his pack.

"He didn't spare anyone, Theon. The children… he sold them, too… even… even me, he didn't care. When the Alpha tried to rape me, I bit his cock off and killed him. The Alpha out there was his brother, and he locked us away. He came to beat us daily but after he didn't go as far… but I guess I was one of the luckier ones. He came to abuse the Luna every day, then allowed others to do so before they laughed and left. He told me when I was a bit older it would be my turn and to consider it gratitude for killing his brother."

I wrapped my arms around her, my heart beating with anger at her father. How could he be so cruel? The haunted look in her eyes showed that she had been through a lot. She witnessed things she never should have.

"Theoden didn't care, and the new Alpha enjoyed the women even more, even the young ones. He was happy to take them and groom them, saying they would help grow the pack when they became women. It was a nightmare; day and night, they assaulted them all, even some of the men. Some killed themselves because of it… I heard them laugh and joke about it… hearing their cries and pleas through the bond for mercy and help, but no one came…" Her voice broke as she tried to contain the pain. Theon's aura blazed around him, and the anger in his eyes was clear. The weight of his wrath weighed down on us.

"Then, one thing is clear. We need to make Theoden pay for the crimes he has committed, not only to those in Westerwell, but for the atrocities he has committed upon his pack and upon Astalion," I said quietly, standing up and crossing my arms. Never had I felt this much hatred towards someone. "Andres may have been a bad person, but he was nowhere as bad as Theoden. I will kill him myself."

"I will be the one to kill him," Theon said, his eyes meeting mine. "I will kill him and make him pay for it all." He left the room without even casting a glance back, and I knew he just needed some space to clear the raging storm within his mind. I knew he didn't want to let his sister see his pain…

"He'll be okay," I said to Thea, who gave me a half-smile. She was so brave despite how much she had suffered.

"It's going to affect him because he has always obeyed Theoden. He's always treated that man as the person he wanted to be when he was older. Theon always had a good heart… he… there was this… friend of his -"

"His first love, Iyara?" I offered, and she looked at me in surprise.

"Y-you know of her?" She looked surprised.

"Yeah."

"He even walked away from her so she wasn't hurt in his conquest of revenge. Theoden, that man who doesn't deserve the title of father, abused that. He changed Theon, teaching him to be heartless, telling him that showing emotion and caring would make him weak. I didn't want Theon to leave because he was stronger than our father... Theoden feared no one, but deep down, I feel he feared Theon... Theon holds the special ability of our mother's heritage, the Moon Flame."

"Moon Flame?" I had never heard of it... She nodded.

"Mother was from the Della Luna Pack... a pack that is said to be direct descendants of the Moon Goddess herself." I stared at her in surprise.

"I've never heard of it..." She shook her head.

"No, they were massacred years ago, but my mother was from the Alpha line... and Theon holds the Moon Flame, something Theoden could only wish to attain. He used Theon as a tool, and the saddest part is... Theon will never be able to forgive himself for everything he has ever had to do thanks to Theoden's web of lies."

An hour had passed, and Thea had fallen asleep. Looking closer, there were still many bruises on her. She would heal, but if it wasn't for her fighter's spirit, I feared what may have happened to her. I just prayed that, in time, those internal scars healed too...

I stroked her hair until her breathing became calm and rhythmic. Theon hadn't returned, and I was beginning to worry

Where was he?

I stood up and walked out into the night. Theon's scent reached me, and I saw him sitting on the low wall, one leg up propped up on it with his arm resting on it. A piece of straw sat between his teeth as he stared at the sky. He was so handsome...

My heart thundered, and for a moment, I remembered the time when all I saw was the sexy man that I had always been so infatuated with... but he was so much more... far more complex than I could ever imagine, carrying the burden of sins that he had been manipulated to hold.

He turned his gaze upon me, and it took me a moment to clear my head. I crossed the rocky, uneven ground, wishing I had put my shoes on when I felt a few sharp pieces of slate and rock cutting into me. I finally reached him and looked up at the sky. The stars were twinkling in the deep midnight blue sky. It was a beautiful night...

"What's on your mind?" I asked softly, looking at him.

"Everything," he replied after a few moments. My heart clenched and I sighed.

"The past is behind us. One should be recognised for who they are today, not yesterday. You are on the path of redemption... Theon, you regret your actions, and the veil of lies has been lifted from your eyes. What you did was in the hands of a puppet master, but you are no longer under his control, so come on... we can do this. Let's fix his wrongs." He looked down at his hand, flicking out the piece of straw as he frowned.

"These hands have taken the lives of far too many... there may be no redemption for me, but I am ready to deal the hand of retribution upon all those who have done wrong. We head to the Iron Claw Pack tomorrow. We get that pearl, return it to the imperial ruler of the seven seas, and then we take that bastard down." His eyes were cold and dangerous when they met mine. His powers rolled off him in waves, and for a second, even I felt breathless at the sheer power of it. I nodded, and Theon stood up.

"Let's get to bed." He bent down and lifted me bridal style, and I yelped in surprise.

"You're injured! You shouldn't be carrying me," I scolded. He raised an eyebrow.

"You didn't seem bothered when I carried you to bed earlier," he remarked, making my stomach flutter. I pouted, embarrassed.

"I can walk..."

"You will get hurt," he replied without even looking at me and carried me inside.

My heart thundered, and I didn't know what to do. A part of me was ready to tell him I would sleep with Thea, and another part of me felt he needed the comfort he would never ask for... then there was the deep, dark part that somehow wanted him close... but when he laid me on the small bed we had made love on earlier, he simply bid me goodnight and left the room.

What are we?

The following day, after we had restored some order and made sure the people were safe and had some care and someone to guide them, we left on our journey. Thea kept us occupied, and things were a bit tense between Theon and I once more, with the weight of the world weighing on us. Yesterday was a moment of weakness... but... it was a moment I couldn't get out of my mind either.

We returned to the ship and sailed towards the border of Astalion. It only took us halfway, and the rest we would go on foot.

I had contacted Lavina, but the truth was that nothing but the pearl could heal Theon, and only when it was set in the trident of the imperial emperor of the seven seas. Would he agree to heal Theon? I wasn't sure, but I would try with everything I had to make sure he didn't die. He couldn't. He deserved a chance at a normal life...

We bid the crew of the Siren Killer farewell, where Captain Flynn said he might consider changing the name of his ship and hoped the Sirens would let him travel the seas in peace. The journey had taken us two days on board the ship, and then we travelled on foot or in wolf form, although Theon always shifted out of sight and I was certain it was because he didn't want his sister to see his wounds. It was the second day of us travelling by foot, with Theon hoping we'd get there by tomorrow.

"The Iron Claw Pack..." Thea mused. "Isn't that the pack Theoden hated with a vengeance?"

"Yeah," Theon replied curtly. Thea frowned as if she was thinking something over.

"Theon, is it true that's the pack Mom came from?" Theon tensed, and I looked at him sharply.

"Yes," he replied curtly. "She had a chosen mate there."

"Wow," Thea murmured.

"It's where you will remain until this issue is solved."

"What? Why? Do you think the pack where Theoden practically stole Mom from would even consider accepting me?"

"They will," Theon replied, frowning at his sister. I almost smiled. They argued like a normal pair of siblings. I missed Charlene, and I hoped wherever she was, she was safe... my beautiful queen...

"How can you be so sure?" Thea protested.

"Because the current Alpha is Mom's first son," Theon responded. Both Thea and I took a second to understand what he had just said, and we both stopped in our tracks, staring at him.

"Alpha Hunter is your brother?" I asked, stunned.

"I have another brother?" Thea added at the same time, completely shocked.

"Yes. You and Thalia were younger, and Da-Theoden didn't want you two knowing about him, or me for that matter…" Theon replied, his voice cold. Now that odd exchange at the engagement made sense.

"Wow…" I murmured.

"So I have another brother… ooh, Theon, tell me, is he nicer than you? Is he sweet? Wait, does he even know we exist?"

"Yes, he does, and he will take care of you because he loves Mom," Theon answered quietly. There was something more to it, but I didn't push it because suddenly I sensed a large number of people approaching. They were far but they were gaining on us fast. I looked at Theon, my heart skipping a beat, and I realised he had already picked it up. My eyes blazed as I created a heavy fog around us…

"We got company," I said quietly, turning towards the trees and readying myself for whatever was approaching…

REUNITING

YILEYNA.

THE LEGION APPROACHING BURST from the trees, and it was an impressive sight, one of unity and strength. Werewolves in human and wolf forms, fae knights on horses, all wielding weapons and ready to attack. They stopped upon seeing us, but it was the woman on the black horse in the centre that made my heart skip a beat and tears of happiness fill my eyes.

I was unable to say anything, my emotions overwhelming me. I took a shuddering breath as our eyes met. It took her a moment to look me over, noticing the change in my appearance, but not once did she not recognise me or hesitate. Her beautiful green eyes glistened with tears as she slid off her horse and ran towards me. My queen.

I stepped forward. Never had I been apart from her for so long and I had truly missed her.

"My angel," she sobbed the moment she flung her arms around my neck tightly. I embraced her tightly, burying my nose in her shoulder. She smelt slightly different, but it was still her, still my Charlene. I was so relieved to see she looked healthy and well.

"Thank the gods," I whispered, stroking her hair.

"Well, well, well. A traitor is in our midst. Should we cut his throat?" Ryan's harsh voice made me pull away and look at the others, many of whom were pointing their swords at Theon. Raiden, Ryan, Gamma Grayson, and many Fae all had their eyes on him, hostility and rage clear in them all.

Theon stood as arrogantly and emotionlessly as ever, as if he could take them all if the need arose. Deep down, I knew he could do a lot of damage

"No one will be cutting any throats," I declared loudly, looking up at Ryan warningly before turning and casting my gaze across the legion of men and a few women. "Lower your weapons." Fae? What were they doing here?

"It is a pleasure to see you have stepped into your powers, Queen Yileyna of Astalion." My heart thundered as I looked sharply at one of the men who had stepped forward in armour that was made of the finest designs. He removed his helmet and our eyes met.

"Zarian?" I stared at him. In his armour, with his hair braided up, he looked different…

"At your service, My Queen. You look far more beautiful than before, if that is even possible. The only thing missing is a crown adorning your head," he said, taking my hand and kissing it. I could feel many eyes upon me, but I ignored them, simply smiling at the man before me. I still didn't know what he was doing there… dressed like that.

"Thank you, however, I am missing something, am I not, Zarian?"

"All in good time; we have just reunited with one another," he smirked and moved back as Raiden stepped forward.

"Yileyna…" I turned to him, seeing the emotions in his eyes. I smiled, swallowing hard as I looked at the men gathered before walking over to him and cupping his face in my hands. The fact that this army was here meant he had done his best. A true loyal warrior.

"I did the right thing to make you my Beta. These men gathered here prove your loyalty and effort. Thank you, Beta Raiden." I pulled his head down, kissing his forehead gently. He gripped my elbows, looking into my eyes. His heart thundered, and his eyes spoke a thousand words as he looked me over.

"It was my honour," he said simply. Something had changed. Somehow… we had evolved. I knew I would never be able to return the feelings he had for me. "But nothing would have been possible without Alpha Hunter and Luna Charlene." My heart skipped a beat as I turned sharply towards her. Please tell me she didn't agree to this for help!

When I saw the blush coating her cheeks, I knew she was happy. I closed my eyes in relief as Hunter stepped forward. I saw his gaze flicker to Thea, who was staring at him with wide eyes. His gaze returned to me, and he smirked.

"My Luna considers you her sister, which then makes us family through marriage… my army and sword are yours to command, Alpha Queen." A wind rippled through the trees, and I looked at those before me. The Sirens, the Fae, and werewolves… we will be united…

"Let us set up camp, shall we? There is much to share," Gamma Grayson suggested.

I nodded and glanced over at Theon, who simply stood there, his expression unreadable as Thea clung to his cloak. I realised that despite her still being strong and brave, the glimmer in her eyes as they darted around was of fear. Fear of what these men may be capable of. It only fuelled my anger towards Theoden, a man who was meant to be her father…

It was evening, and Theon, Hunter, Charlene, Thea, Ryan, Gamma Grayson, Raiden, Zarian, a few higher officials belonging to both Hunter's Pack and Zarian's army, and I had just gone through everything we had learned and picked up on the way. The meeting that Theoden was organising was not far off, and, like Hunter said, something about it felt odd. Now more than ever, the severity of the situation was getting to me.

Zarian explained their dilemma, and although he had hidden his identity, I did not hold it against him, nor did I blame him. Their situation was unfair, and there was a lot of work to do to unite the kingdoms on this side of the great oceans. I had just told them of the emperor's wish without disclosing what the pearl could achieve.

"That is risky. Going to Naran is…"

"A death wish," Hunter said, sitting forward. "But I understand it's needed. A small team will be far more efficient, an army would be intercepted and attacked." Although he had given Thea a smile here and there, they hadn't talked. Neither had he and Theon, but I knew that was a conversation simply waiting to happen.

"I don't mind going alone if I have to. Any guidance would be welcome," I replied.

"You aren't going alone," Theon added firmly.

"If you are planning on going, I would argue against that. I don't trust you," Ryan sneered coldly. His anger was justifiable.

"I will come with you," Raiden said, his eyes flashing.

"I'll decide... Alpha Hunter, what can you tell me about the difficulties of entering Naran?" Hunter sighed, his arm wrapping around Charlene's shoulders.

"It's not going to be easy. The forestry is very dense, at some points, it's physically hard for most to even pass through the trees. Humid, suffocating, and full of deadly creatures. Getting in means they'll know from the starting point. Nagas are dangerous things, but they do fear Sirens, you will have that one up on them as you know the way they have their lands protected..."

"Makes it hard for Sirens to even venture to their territory..."

"Yes, their poison won't kill Sirens as it would werewolves or Fae. Mages are also at an advantage with their magic," Hunter continued. I almost smiled as he looked down at Charlene, giving her a special smile. My queen was in love, and it made me happy. She deserved the best, and it was clear Hunter treated her well.

I returned my attention to the topic at hand when Theon spoke. He had been silent for the most part, indifferent to the hatred and comments he received.

"So then only Yileyna, a selected few others, and I will go."

"I will be going. I am not leaving her with you," Raiden added icily.

"Theon has done nothing but take care of her," Thea added defensively, although she had remained silent for the most part. Their eyes met, and she glared at him.

"You know nothing of your brother's crimes," Raiden said, his voice softer despite the firmness of his words.

"I know because I know exactly how Theoden treated him. He hasn't only made Theon hurt others but himself. You know nothing about my brother, so at least trust the Alpha Queen's verdict. If she trusts Theon -"

"Stop it, Thea," Theon said quietly.

"We all know that the Queen's judgement may be a little... clouded," Ryan added, making my own eyes flash until Gamma Grayson growled.

"Cut it out, Ryan! Look, Yileyna has come this far, and Theon being by her side is proof enough! We abide by the Alpha's command."

I exhaled, resisting the urge to pinch the bridge of my nose. Goddess, this was stressful!

"I don't want to be an Alpha whose command is absolute. That is why we have a council, for advice... Theon will accompany me, however, if Alpha Hunter can give me any advice, maps, directions, anything, I will be truly grateful. The rest will continue as you had planned. Gathering our allies is a must for the battle we will have to fight." I looked at Hunter, who nodded.

"I will go with you. No one knows Naran better than I do." He looked at Charlene, and I felt guilty seeing the worry on her face, but I needed his help too. Any help I could get...

Charlene looked at me and smiled. I realised now I didn't have the mind link with her any longer. Oh, how short those moments were. We once used to joke about how we'd talk day and night when we attained our mind links. Life truly was different from how we pictured it.

"Who else?" Gamma Grayson asked.

"The less, the better," Hunter replied, frowning.

"Theon..." Thea murmured, and I knew she wanted to go.

"You will be safe here, little one, don't worry," Hunter told her, giving her a small smile. "You can keep Charlene company." Thea looked at her, then at Theon and me, and I gave her a comforting smile.

"I trust her with my life," I told her before looking over at Raiden. "My Beta will make sure you are safe too."

"I don't really want to stay here..." she trailed off, frustrated, and Theon pulled her close.

"You will be safe. I can't take you to Naran when I am uncertain of what will happen," he said quietly. She nodded in defeat, frowning slightly.

"Theon... for someone who saw Westerwell from the other side, what is the state of our people?" Gamma Grayson asked him.

Theon frowned, and I realised it was a question I had never asked him myself. Yes, I knew the warriors were all locked up, yet I saw many of our wolves carrying on as normal.

"The warriors who stayed true to the Silver Storm Pack were in the cells. Some who were vocal... were beaten or killed."

"So then, we have no men who will be inside those walls to side with us..."

"No. There are warriors who were released, those who submitted and vowed their allegiance to Theoden. Most were from the higher noble families," Theon said coldly, his eyes flashing.

"The likes of Gale Howden and Nikolai Levin?" Ryan asked with a disgusted look.

"Yeah, exactly like those…" His eyes flashed, and I felt a flare of anger radiating off him.

"I'm certain we can bribe them to return to our side," Raiden added, frowning. "I know many of the nobles who were ranked Zeta or Epsilon guards and warriors."

"Maybe, but some were just scum and are no longer alive."

"What do you mean?" I asked. If they had sworn allegiance to Theoden, then why?

Everyone looked at Theon, waiting for an explanation, but he simply raised a brow, his eyes meeting mine. My heart pounded under the intensity of his gaze, but it was his words that surprised me.

"I wanted a few dead, so I killed them."

HIS INTENTIONS

THEON

*I*T WAS AMUSING HOW uneasy they were around me, but I didn't plan to explain why I killed those who had hurt her. The guards who had beaten her from the Obsidian Shadow Pack were still on my list, and when the time was right, I planned to kill them too. She wanted an explanation, but I didn't bother giving her one.

Night had fallen, and we were all set for camp. I knew Hunter wanted to speak to me, but I wasn't so sure I was ready, not to mention, I was rather surprised he had chosen Charlene as his mate and Luna. Well, whatever works for him.

I had just bathed in the river and was re-bandaging my chest when I heard him approach. I grabbed my top, yanking it on just as he stepped out from the trees.

"When will you officially introduce us?" He asked. I knew who he meant, and I raised an eyebrow.

"Why do you care? It's not like you have ever known her," I replied.

"She's still my sister, Theon, and from what I deduced, she knows who I am."

"Yeah, I may have mentioned it because I wanted her to stay at your pack. I need her safe."

"I understand, and that can be arranged," he replied, crossing his arms. "So, does your woman know who I am?"

"I don't appreciate the dig. We both know I betrayed her." He nodded, smirking arrogantly.

"My mistake. I only determined that assumption due to the fact you two seem to still have an obvious connection." I refused to reply, wanting the conversation over with.

"Last time you said you had learned things, questionable things about Theoden. Is there more than what was mentioned out there?" I asked.

"I'm afraid there is, even more than what I knew at the engagement, where you actually seemed happy." I clenched my jaw, my eyes flashing as I turned to look at him directly.

"Don't push me, Hunter. Don't you think I've caused enough damage already? I'm here because I will see this through, and I will be the one to kill him." His smile faded, and he frowned, stepping forward.

"Theon... you were fed lies and raised by a tyrant. You are only twenty-four, you have your life before you. What are you planning?" His eyes were sharp as he looked at me intently, and it was a struggle to hold his gaze, our auras clashing. To my surprise, he placed his hand on my head and shook his head. "Foolish boy." I knocked his hand away and glared at him.

"You aren't that much older than me," I growled. "Stop treating me like a kid."

"I'm still older, whether that be by two years or ten. Theon, everyone deserves forgiveness, and for the Queen to trust you is the first sign that you deserve it. You are on the path to redemption. It won't be easy, but you will get there."

"No. I'm not on that path to redemption, for my crimes are beyond the point of redemption... but I am walking my path... the one I need to," I replied quietly, turning and looking at the flowing river.

"And what path is that?" He asked quietly.

"Retribution. All who have lied, committed sin, and hurt her, I will be the one to deal out their punishment."

"You do not need to take that burden upon yourself, Theon. Leave judgement to the gods."

"I am only doing the gods a favour," I replied. "Besides.... I want to see them all burn..."

"You love her."

His words made my heart race, and it took me a second to steady it, but he had already heard it. My unspoken answer.

"There's nothing wrong with loving, Theon… win her over. Earn her forgiveness, bow down to her if need be, and tell her you are ready to be the man she needs."

"I don't need advice from you on love. I've broken her far too many times to make promises that I may not be able to keep. I don't have time to waste, and I'm sure neither do you. You have a mate to return to, do you not? Tell me what you know."

"I'm afraid she has abandoned me for the night to spend time with her sister."

"Shame you can't even keep a woman, and they are not sisters." He looked at me sharply, all humour gone.

"Blood alone does not make one family, Theon. Their bond is one of the strongest I have ever seen. In my eyes, they are sisters. You think whatever you want, although I'm assuming you are simply jealous of my Luna for having a special place in Yileyna's heart." I frowned. Was it just me, or was he refusing to tell me what he knew?

"What do you know, Hunter?" I growled murderously. He looked at me and frowned before exhaling sharply.

"It's about our mother," he said quietly, his voice tense. The sound of footsteps made him stop, and we both turned as Thea stepped out from the trees. Looking between us, she hesitated.

"Am I intruding?"

"Not at all," Hunter reassured her, giving her a smile.

She nodded, looking between us, and I knew she wouldn't leave until she had officially spoken to Hunter. Why did I need to introduce her? They both knew who the other was…

"I think Thea wants to have a word with you," I said, frowning. I felt on edge. What did Hunter know?

"That would be an honour. It's nice to meet you, Thea," he said, holding his hand out to her. She looked at me before she approached him warily. She was still edgy around men… I was a fool to think she'd be fine. This was all his fault, and he would pay…

She slowly accepted his offered hand, and he gave her a small smile, raising her hand to his lips and kissing it before enclosing her hand in both of his.

"I still remember the day our mother told me you were born. I was happy to have a little sister, too," he said quietly. "Tell me, do you still have your addiction to seedless grapes?"

I looked at him sharply and realised I had forgotten... Thea loved grapes to the point she would eat any that were at home. I had forgotten, but he hadn't...

She looked surprised, too, before she let out a chuckle.

"So, she told you that?"

"Yes, as well as how you threatened to kill Theon for stealing the last grapes with a -"

"Spoon!" Thea let out a weak laugh as Hunter hugged her, giving her a squeeze.

"Yes, exactly so. You were always the most entertaining to hear about." A silence fell, and I knew we were all thinking about Thalia.

"I hope from here on we can spend more time together," Thea said, looking at me.

"I won't stop you," I remarked.

"Will you not join our hug?" I raised an eyebrow.

"I don't do group hugs."

"Oh, please, at least as compensation for the fact I had to hear you have sex?"

"Sex? Dare I ask with who?" Hunter asked, smirking. I glared at them both. Maybe introducing them was a bad fucking idea.

"Yileyna," Thea said in a singsong voice.

"Oh, and here he was acting all noble, that they just couldn't be," Hunter mocked.

"Are you two done?" I growled.

"Pretty much," Hunter smirked as Thea chuckled, not minding his arm around her shoulder. At least if I was no longer around, I knew she'd have a brother to watch and take care of her.

"Yes, so what were you going to say about Mom?" Thea asked. Hunter looked conflicted, but I gave a small nod. "She isn't a child. Say what you need to."

"It's about the ship you all boarded to escape Andres' apparent attack," Hunter began. The struggle on his face was clear.

"What of it?" I still remembered that day. The rain was pouring down as Mom begged Dad not to send us away.

"The ship was not in any shape to sail. Your father knew that."

His words rang in my mind as Thea's heart thumped. I said nothing, trying to calm myself and listen to what Hunter had to say. I wouldn't forgive him for all he's done. Some of his most trusted men were on that ship. The sacrifice he needed to control Arabella came to my mind, but would he really sacrifice his loved ones and, above all, his mate and children?

"The crystal... he gave us a crystal that would teleport us to safety if we met any danger, but it was risky," I said, frowning. Hunter nodded.

"He knew the ship wouldn't make it far, yet he sent you. If that Siren didn't kill Mom and Thalia, then that crystal would have."

"But he warned us it was risky and should only be used as a last resort," I replied, frowning.

"Of course, because when you came back via the crystal, and if anyone who was with you died on the way, he would have you thinking exactly what you are right now. Tell me, Theon... if the ship was damaged, it meant you had no other option but to use that crystal. Only those who were strong enough would have survived it, correct?" Hunter said, turning away and staring up at the sky. "A way for him to weed out the weak ones from his family and keep the stronger ones."

"I... I don't think he could have done that to Mom," Thea said quietly, her face ashen.

"He didn't mark her, though, correct? Why not? If he truly loved her, then why didn't he mark her? From her notes, she often sounded like something was troubling her... I don't think your father treated her as well as it may have appeared." Hunter frowned before he turned back to me, his eyes filled with burning anger. "I found one of the very men your father hired to damage the ship. Your father staged it all, but I couldn't find any reason he would do this. I only had assumptions but now..."

"Now?" I pushed. I had my own assumptions, and I felt sick, anger and fury bubbling inside of me. Our eyes met, and I knew for a fact Hunter was equally angry. The clear pain and rage in his eyes proved that.

"There was no attack from Andres. He set it all up to push you onto that ship. I never understood why he would do that, but he was really only expecting you to make it back, knowing you were an Alpha... tell me, Theon, weren't his most trusted men on that ship?"

I could hear the blood rushing through my veins and feel the rage bleeding into the aura that now glowed around me. Six... aside from his men and

Mom, Thalia, and Thea, there had also been three of Dad's closest friends and allies. I remembered Mom arguing that he shouldn't send them all with us, but he had been adamant that they should be with us… he planned to sacrifice them all.

Fuck.

The burden of his lies and sins was growing. Was death enough for someone like him?

No. It wasn't.

TROUBLES OF THE HEART

CHARLENE

TWO NIGHTS LATER, WE were splitting into two groups the next day. At dawn, Yileyna, Hunter, and Theon would head to Naran, and I would travel forward with the rest. I was terrified of what may happen to them, but I had to remind myself that Hunter knew the Naga better than anyone and had spent his life fighting them, and Yileyna and Theon were powerful, too.

I gazed up at the full moon as I sat beside Yileyna and Thea. I had gotten to know Thea a little better; Hunter and Theon's sister was lovely. Despite everything she had gone through, she had the will of fire flowing within her veins. Last night she had awoken screaming. It had taken Theon and Yileyna both to snap her out of it. She was taking it worse, not wanting Theon to leave her again, and I didn't blame her. Hunter's words from earlier when she wanted to go with them to Naran now returned to my mind, as another thought came to me…

"Please, Theon, let me come with you. I don't want to lose you again," Thea begged. It was just the five of us, but Theon was beginning to hesitate, and I was certain he would give in.

"Thea, it's dangerous."

"I'm strong, Theon! I can do this. I don't want to be left alone." I exchanged looks with Yileyna, feeling sorry for her.

"Thea… look -"

"She can't come," Hunter cut in, his expression hard.

"What? Why not? I'm strong, I have learned to fight!"

"You're my blood, and Naga do not forget. The fact that the same blood runs through our veins is enough for them to want to shred you apart," Hunter's serious reply came. "Yileyna is the only one of the three of us that will be safe, due to their fear of Sirens. We cannot risk your life, Thea."

"But you and Theon will be there… I don't need saving, but if -"

"He's right, Thea, you're not going. End of discussion," Theon said coldly.

"Yileyna… do you think the Naga that attacked Theon when we found him was because of their grudge against Hunter?" She looked at me sharply, and her beautiful multi-coloured eyes widened, before she nodded.

"That makes sense…"

"And then… the fact that you injured it, and it backed away… could it have sensed your Siren side?" I exclaimed.

"Wow, I never even thought of it… but I think you could be right."

"I think I probably am, for once."

"Not for once, you often are." Yileyna smiled as she leaned her head against my shoulder. She held Thea's hand, and I smiled, loving how she was making her feel involved. I could see us having an excellent bond, Thea, her two brothers, Yileyna, and I…

"I feel… agitated," Thea sighed, "I can't believe it's the full moon tonight…"

"Same…" I replied softly. Yileyna looked at us and tilted her head.

"Hmm. I feel at peace…" she whispered softly. "It's almost like the calm before the storm…"

The feeling in the air was odd, and I felt restless. Maybe with everything that was to come, I felt like this…

"Mates… so, do you think you and Theon could be mates? Wouldn't it be nice, just like Charlene and Hunter?" Thea asked her. My heart skipped a beat, and I looked down. Mates… we weren't fated.

"Theon… we were mates… but we rejected one another," Yileyna said softly. I saw the pain in her eyes, and I realised that even though they had rejected one another, she was still hurting…

"You love him, he loves you… why? Is it because of Theoden?" Her eyes flashed, and Yileyna looked down.

I knew why… because he was responsible for her parents' deaths…

"It's quite complicated, but if they are to be, I'm sure they'll figure it out. Hunter and I are not fated," I told her, trying to change the subject.

"You're not? Wow, I would never have guessed." She smiled.

"Because they are so in love. Who needs the bond?" Yileyna chuckled. I couldn't help but smile as they teased me, and for a moment, I forgot all my worries.

"Well, you are right! The fact that they are marked and are always looking at each other…" Thea teased.

"Oh, not to mention the love bites I saw on my queen's neck this morning." Yileyna smiled, nudging me as both girls started laughing.

I was about to reply when we heard footsteps and Thea tensed, her eyes blazing a bright green. Her heart began beating violently, and I turned, frowning as I saw none other than Raiden come into view holding some mugs. His eyes were glowing green, his gaze on Thea.

Their hearts were thumping, and I realised what was happening. Yileyna looked at me, and I knew she was thinking the same thing.

Mates.

RAIDEN

We had just finished the last of our planning. Yileyna had been there all afternoon but had decided to spend the evening with Charlene before they headed on their own path tomorrow.

Seeing her was as if she was someone else. I could see how the time apart had changed her. She didn't laugh as much, her smiles were smaller, and in her eyes, I could see the weight she carried…

I didn't want to see her hurt or in pain, but the moment she kissed my forehead, I realised she was someone else. She had become the queen she was born to be… someone who did not need my love, but my loyalty…

"Will you go give these to our ladies?" Hunter asked me quietly, holding out three mugs of coffee.

"You haven't seen your woman all day, do you not wish to see her before you leave?" I asked him. He gave me a small smirk.

"If I go now, I will take her from her friend and then she will not forgive me. They haven't seen each other in ages, and this meeting was fleeting. The Alpha Queen has been too busy with plans, so let them have this time."

"They will have more time," I replied quietly, taking the drinks from him. He nodded, giving me a small smile, and I wondered if it was something else that was on his mind.

I carried them through the trees, and suddenly the most intoxicating scent hit me. My heart thundered as the scent consumed me and the laughter of the women reached me.

Yileyna... She had shifted! Was it her?

My heart was racing as I rushed through the trees when I spotted the three of them laughing. Yileyna... even in the middle of the clearing, she shone like a diamond under the moonlight, but it was then that I realised it wasn't her, and my gaze snapped to the slender she-wolf by her side. Theon's sister.

Thea was my mate.

Our eyes met, and the howl of my wolf in my head echoed as he yearned to claim her, my mind shattering me. How could I have even thought Yileyna could be mine?

Thea's heart was beating fast, and I remembered what she had been through...

Her plump lips, her slender nose, and those eyes that had seen far too much looked at me with curiosity and uncertainty, and I couldn't help but look at Yileyna. She was looking at Charlene, and when she turned to look at me, she gave me the smallest shake of her head.

Do not hurt her. Her voice was firm and powerful through the mind link. I...

Look at her, not me, Raiden.

I looked back at the she-wolf, who was looking at Yileyna and me, before she quickly got up and ran. She realised. I let out a breath that I didn't even know I was holding.

"Thea!" Charlene stood up and ran after her. I saw Yileyna's eyes glow brighter as she stood up. Even in her simple grey pants and that leather corset, she looked like a goddess.

Don't do this to her, Raiden.

We do not control our hearts Yileyna... you know how I feel about you, I replied through the link.

Her eyes softened, and she walked towards me, but even her walk was different. Her shoulders back, chin up, the power that radiated off her was stronger than ever. She was not the girl I had fallen in love with, but I still loved her, loved the woman who did not need a man.

"Raiden… Thea is an amazing girl, one who has been through hell… give her a chance." I looked into those beautiful eyes that pulled you in, the urge to simply want to gaze into them forever.

"I'm not… I just, I don't want a mate."

"Wrong. You just don't want to accept anyone else, but life is short, Raiden. Don't ruin the one chance of having a true mate's love," she whispered softly, placing a hand on my arm. I looked down at it, slender and perfect…

"Am I foolish to want something else?" I asked her. Someone else?

The memory of her kiss on my forehead lingered in my mind. I loved her. I truly loved her.

"Not in this life," she replied softly, her eyes full of sadness and sympathy. Those four words broke my heart. The pain was excruciating. If this was how I felt now, then what was the pain of a rejection?

"I know I'm crossing the line… you are my queen, but can I ask a question?" She looked into my eyes and nodded.

"Is he… is he your mate?" I asked quietly. She smiled slightly, but there was only sadness in it.

"He was," she responded, making me frown. "Raiden, let me go. Move on and one day you will laugh at the fact that you actually ever had feelings for me."

"Is that a suggestion, or an order, My Queen?" I asked quietly.

I loved this woman, and I wanted her, no one else but her…. Why did she think my feelings could be cast aside?

She frowned silently at my words, but, sighing, she looked at the moon. She looked breathtaking, gazing up at the moon like that, her hair almost glowing…

Don't do that… you are consuming me already…

"It is advice from the heart. I cannot force you or change your emotions, but as a friend, I would advise you to get to know her. At least give her a chance."

With those words leaving her lips, I knew she meant it. I was nothing more to her than a friend…

I stepped back and went down on one knee, my eyes stinging as I refused to let my heartbreak show. My heart was thumping as I rested my forearm on my raised knee and placed my other hand on her feet.

"Forgive me for my rudeness and my emotions. From this day forth, I will not cross the line. I will always love you because you are my queen and Alpha. I won't cross my boundaries again. I apologise," I promised quietly, doing my best to control my emotions. She bent down and cupped my face.

"I am blessed to have you by my side." As her Beta, but at least I will get to see her and serve her until the day I die.

I stood up, taking her hands and helping her to her feet before I bowed my head to my Queen.

"It is my greatest honour. Good night."

Our eyes met, and I didn't want the moment to end.

I will miss you… I love you…

"Good night," she whispered, and I was forced to turn and walk away…

Perhaps one day I would be able to approach my fated mate, but tonight my heart was bleeding…

CHARLENE

"Thea!" I called, my tears streaming down my cheeks. Her pain was clear, and it broke my heart. Goddess, why? "Thea!" I stopped when I saw her curled up against a tree.

"I'm fine," she whispered, her head buried in her arms.

"Oh, my sweet." I knelt down next to her, stroking her hair.

"I'm fine, really." She looked up at me and gave me a defiant smile. I tilted my head and pulled her tightly against my chest. Oh, Raiden…

"Should I just reject him?" She asked me quietly, making me freeze. My heart thumped, and I looked down at her.

"Are you… do you want to?"

"Mm… he doesn't want me, so I'll reject him," she said, her eyes flashing as she took a deep breath. "Yeah, I'll do it." She stood up, and that vulnerability I had seen within her eyes was gone.

"I would say sleep on it. Come, let's head back," I replied gently as we walked through to the open area where we had set up camp

The smell of the fresh dirt and the trees around us was soothing. I knew the area was safe and guarded, but we needed to return to camp. I was expecting Hunter to come... after all, tomorrow we would be separated... but... he hadn't even approached me. The moon was up in the sky but still, he hadn't come...

Was he worried I would make it harder for him to leave? Or was he avoiding me for some other reason?

I pushed the thought away, taking Thea's hand as I guided her through the trees. She was lost in thought, and I knew no matter how she was acting, her mind was in turmoil.

Yileyna was waiting near the tent, concern clear on her face. Thea forced a smile before looking at both of us.

"I'm... going to go to bed." She waved at us both, and Yileyna nodded. The moment she disappeared inside the tent, Yileyna came over to me, and I hugged her, knowing she must be feeling awful.

"You should get to bed. We are leaving early," she said to me.

"Where are you going?" I asked her.

"For a walk," she replied.

I nodded and headed towards Hunter's and my tent. I will ask him to come watch over Thea with me. We could talk from nearby, but make sure she's okay too. I knew she probably wouldn't want Yileyna near her. It hurt knowing that Yileyna was being put into this situation when it was not her fault.

I suddenly froze. A delicious scent wafted into my nose, and with a terrifying realisation, it hit me that one of the men present was my mate. I needed to hide or get far away where he couldn't smell me!

I turned, my heart thumping, about to run, when a hand wrapped around my upper arm, stopping me in my tracks as intense sparks rushed through me like a current of electricity.

"Not so fast, Princess..."

My eyes flew open when I recognised the voice, my heart pounding violently...

In the Comfort of Another

HUNTER

ALL EVENING THE UNEASE within me was growing. The full moon was glaring at me, mocking and taunting me.

No, I didn't want a fated mate… but deep down, a part of me selfishly thought of the possibility of a dream coming true… a dream where I was mated to none other than Charlene…

I was avoiding facing her under the full moon, but it didn't matter. She was mine. She always would be, but the fear of the slight chance of someone stealing her from me would remain.

I had sent Raiden to deliver them some drinks, but it was high time I went to find her and bring her to bed. I was about to mind-link her when I saw her flaming hair as she walked towards our tent.

My heart thundered as an intense scent filled my nose, and my wolf howled. The urge to rush to Charlene's side consumed me, and she suddenly froze, sniffing the air before all colour left her face. She turned, about to rush away when I ran over and grabbed hold of her arm. Blinding sparks coursed through me as I tried to focus.

"Not so fast, Princess…" I whispered huskily, spinning her around towards me. One truth was crystal clear. Even in the eyes of Selene, she

"Hunter..." she breathed, and I realised what she had been trying to do, run from her mate. She gripped my arms, resting her head against my chest.

"Thank you, Goddess," she whispered. I let go of her arm and, cupping her face, forced her to look up at me.

"You're mine, and no one can steal you from me," I said quietly. The bond was complete, and the rush of it strengthening jarred me. I never thought our love and connection could get stronger. She shook her head.

"No one could steal me from you, even before this bond. I would never have left you, and I never will, bond or not. I love you, Hunter." My Luna...

I love you far more than I can ever express through words, Princess, I replied through the bond as my lips captured hers in a deep kiss. This was a kiss I would always remember, deep, intense, yet full of love.

There was a time I didn't want my fated mate because I didn't want it to be the reason to love someone... but I was blessed to have fallen in love with my fated mate before she was even shown to be mine. My true mate, my Luna, my love, my intoxication...

We broke apart, and for a while, I simply held her until she moved back and smiled softly.

"I don't want to ruin this moment, but..."

"What's wrong?"

Thea's mate is here, and he... hesitated, she whispered, making anger rush through me. The urge to protect my sister from anything made my eyes blaze.

"Name?" I growled menacingly.

"Hunter, calm down... he just needs time."

"So, you know him well? Is he one of your previous pack members?" She cupped my face, tilting her head.

"Calm down, my love," she whispered, tugging me closer and kissing my lips. "Shall we go watch over Thea? I'm worried."

"She shares a tent with the Queen, does she not?"

"She isn't there," she replied, but she was worried. I could see that in her eyes. I frowned but nodded, and we walked towards the tent. Thea was awake, so I sat outside the tent, pulling Charlene down in front of me.

"Let me tell you a story about the first time I fought a Naga...." I suggested clearly, knowing Thea would not be able to ignore us even if she wanted.

Wrapping my arms around her shoulders and kissing Charlene's neck, I settled back. As much as I wanted to fuck her all night, I knew neither of us would be able to focus, knowing what Thea was going through.

"Oh, I'd love to hear that!" Charlene replied, looking up at me with those beautiful eyes of hers.

I love and adore you, I said through the link. She simply smiled, clutching my shirt, and curled into me as I began telling the tale of my first endeavour…

YILEYNA

I felt terrible. Thea had been through so much, and to find her mate, who was an incredible man, and one who I knew could heal her, look away from her? I closed my eyes, feeling awful. I didn't mean for this to happen…

I leaned against a tree and stared at the moon.

Please help Raiden to move on and accept her. She deserves nothing more than to be loved wholeheartedly.

"Why do you look so upset?" His husky voice came, and I turned to see none other than Theon standing there. My heart clenched when I noticed his eyes were red and his hair was a mess. Still as handsome as ever, but there was something that had caused him pain.

"Why do you?" I asked softly.

"I don't look upset." I shook my head, smiling slightly.

"You would never admit it, would you? Then tell me, what's on your mind?" He leaned against the tree opposite and crossed his arms.

"You." I raised an eyebrow. "I asked you why you looked so upset. Surely it can't be because your precious friend will be gone tomorrow?" I rolled my eyes.

"Always jealous of her, are you not?"

"You wish." I smiled, but it didn't reach my eyes. My heart hurt…

"Didn't the days back at the cabin feel so calm? Although… I guess not for you, since you were there with an aim… but you know, back then, all I wanted was to live happily and play house," I whispered, feeling my emotions intensify.

"You're a good cook, but you're made for far more than playing house." I looked up at him, my vision blurring with tears that I refused to let fall.

"But all I wanted was to be with you, be the perfect woman for you… I wanted to cook for you, take care of you… just spend the cold nights before that hearth with you. I was a fool, wasn't I?" I whispered. He frowned, looking down for a moment before his gaze snapped up to me once more. He pushed himself away from the tree, approaching me.

"No, you weren't. You were just naïve… innocent and full of love… I'm sorry," he murmured, cupping my face. I took hold of his wrists.

My heart yearned for more. The pain within me was suffocating me. All I wanted was to crumble in his arms and cry, but I couldn't. I knew he wouldn't leave me, but I couldn't show him my weakness…

I was made for so much more…

"I was a fool, is all…" I turned my gaze away from those amber orbs of his and stared up at the moon. "They say the gods test those whom they love… this pain, this burden, it is nothing but a trial…"

"You think so? I doubt it… Selene has done nothing but destroy it all…"

"But did she? It wasn't her doing. She created us, but it is up to us to do the right thing," I responded, looking back into his eyes.

His touch still sent those beautiful tingles through me. His fingers brushing my cheeks made me feel light-headed. This closeness, this feeling… it was breaking me. I wanted to scream how I was feeling, my confusion, my pain, all of it… but I couldn't.

"What has triggered these thoughts tonight?" He asked quietly. "Is it the full moon?"

"Kind of… I just feel as if all I do is ruin things for others."

"Where is this coming from?" He frowned, forcing my face up to look at him. Would he hate me when he learned I had ruined his sister's happiness?

"Thea found her mate tonight, but he… he may have feelings for me," I whispered, unable to tell him the name. Theon's eyes flashed, and I looked down. "He's a good person, but… she's been through a lot. They are perfect for one anoth-"

"Enough." His voice was cold, making my heart squeeze in pain.

He let go of my face and pulled me tightly against his chest. One arm wrapped around my shoulders, and his other hand cupped the back of my head as he held me close. I could hear the rhythm of his heart, smell his intoxicating scent, feel his warmth and the cold reminder from the faint smell of blood...

"That is not on you," he said softly. "Raiden can make his choice, and as much as I feel for Thea, she'll be fine. Perhaps it's too soon for her to take a mate anyway. Don't hold yourself accountable, Yileyna. You don't control the people who fall in love with you."

I couldn't stop the tears from falling. His words comforted me, and I gripped his shirt gently. I wanted this. I wanted him to hold me and shield me from the world, but I couldn't ask for such. My path was to the throne, to rule the kingdom and be strong for its people.... but still, was it so wrong that I wanted to be loved and cherished?

He stroked my hair, and I didn't move, leaning into him. I loved the feel of his body. Not only did it drive me crazy, but it felt like... home. I wanted to stay there forever.

"I think Selene is really trying to fuck with me," he mused after a while when my tears had dried.

"Hmm, how?" I asked, knowing I should move away, but I didn't.

"Hunter chose Charlene. I know you love her, but she always annoyed me, and now Raiden... so fucking perfect. Can't stand the both of them." I smiled at the sarcasm dripping from his voice, but I didn't blame him for thinking that.

"Well, Hunter is lucky to have Charlene, and she is lucky to have him. They are perfect together, in love, happy... and united."

Something we could never have...

I slowly moved away.

"What is on your mind, Theon? I shared mine." I asked softly. He frowned and looked into my eyes.

"I learned from Hunter that my father had the ship damaged to make sure not many of us made it back alive. He killed her, Yileyna, and he most likely wanted Thea and Thalia dead, too... remember the sacrifices needed to control a Dark One?" My stomach dropped as I stared at him.

"Killed his own mate and child..." My heart was thumping as I ran my fingers through my hair. "He's... pure evil. How can he do that? I wish there was more on the Dark Ones... the previous king never said anything either. I can only imagine how you must be feeling. I'm sorry."

I reached up, uncertain of my actions, but no matter how strong he acted, surely he needed some comfort. Would he pull away?

Our eyes met and I slowly wrapped my arms around his neck, hugging him tightly. He only hesitated for a moment before his arms tightened around me, making my breath hitch as he buried his head into the corner of my neck.

Our hearts thumped, and I closed my eyes, caressing his back. I couldn't fathom the extent of his pain, but Theon had been through far too much, manipulated and blinded by a monster. I just hoped he found peace someday…

The following day, we bid farewell to the rest. Thea acted normal as she stuck by Charlene's side. Seeing Charlene say goodbye to Hunter and Thea hug her brothers goodbye was a dark reminder of how dangerous our mission was, but one we inevitably had to embark upon.

Everyone knew Theon and Hunter were brothers, and it had caused people to trust Theon a little more, despite the initial shock.

When I had found out Charlene and Hunter were fated mates, I had been over the moon for them. I was delighted. We were soul sisters, and we had ended up mated to two brothers. Even if our love stories were so different, we were still destined for the two. I wished her all the happiness and love in the world.

We had arranged a meeting point for our return, and if Hunter was correct, we shouldn't be gone more than two weeks max.

"My Queen, I will await your return," Zarian said with a charming smile. "Might I add, you look beautiful in your armour?" I gave a small smile as he kissed my hand. He had given me the armour I wore, one that was lightweight and beautiful.

"I will look forward to the day that we are once again all united. With this journey to Naran, I hope that we become one step closer to victory."

"I have no doubt."

"In my stead, Beta Raiden will be my voice and command. Obey and respect him," I spoke clearly one final time. A murmur of 'yes, My Queen' followed before I took a deep breath, ready for this journey.

"Then to Naran we go," Hunter added as he sheathed his sword, looking at the distant hills covered with dense forest. The borders of their kingdom…

I had already bid farewell to all, and I cast a final glance at Charlene, who gave me an encouraging smile. I waved at her and Thea, giving Raiden a curt nod before turning away and falling in step between the two brothers.

My eyes met Theon's for a moment before I looked ahead. My stomach was a flurry of nerves, but I was prepared for whatever came our way.

To Naran.

INTO NARAN

YILEYNA

FOUR DAYS HAD PASSED since we ventured into the Nara Empire. The tightness of the trees and the humidity were suffocating, and, worse, there was no water, nothing to drink. What we carried was almost finished, but we still continued.

Theon was injured, but still, he was far more bothered about me. Goddess, it hurt.

I didn't understand what we were, but I decided there was no point in labelling us. We had somehow become one another's confidants… I felt like I was seeing the real Theon and it was only making me admire him.

Sometimes it was hard to tell what time of day it was, and although I was tempted to summon my powers, Hunter warned me not to.

I looked at the huge snakeskin that dangled from a tree and shuddered as Hunter pushed it aside as we walked through.

"Is that a Naga skin?" I asked, disgusted. Sure we had seen other snake skins, but this was the largest I had seen.

"Most likely…" Hunter murmured. "We are getting closer to the other side." I could tell. The trees weren't as thick, and the dark, dreary feeling was growing.

"Drink." Theon held out his water bottle, and I frowned as Hunter

"Ah, sweet," he taunted.

"Theon," I growled. I had snapped at Theon twice already for trying to save his water and give it to me, which he denied, saying he simply wasn't thirsty. "I don't want your water." He cocked a brow.

"Why not? Only my lips have been on this. You've tasted everyth-"

I slapped my hand over his mouth, but Hunter was already smirking, as if this was amusing.

"I said I don't want it," I growled.

"Seriously, do you two need to fuck it out of your system? Because if that's the case, I could give you two some space and go keep watch?"

"Eww, no! Have you seen where we are?" I asked shuddering.

"Ah yeah, not the ideal location… but you didn't oppose the idea of fucking." I didn't miss the small smirk that crossed Theon's face as I gave both men a cold glare.

"No one is fucking, and no one is going anywhere," I retorted.

"Well, my girl's not here anyway," Hunter said, making me smile.

"Missing your beautiful Luna?"

"Of course, but I'm happy she's not here," he replied, serious once more. "I know you want to protect Yileyna, Theon, but from the three of us, she's the safest here. Naga fear Sirens and Yileyna's blood won't be affected by their poison as fast. Keep your energy up and drink. She's smaller than us and needs less."

"I don't need anyone's advice," Theon replied icily. It was obvious he didn't want to talk about it.

We continued in silence until we stopped, reaching a dangerously steep cliff edge.

"Down there?" I asked.

Hunter nodded, and my heart skipped a beat when Theon took hold of my hand. Our eyes met before Hunter led the way. We had our cloaks on that blended in with our surroundings a little, so I put my hood up, too, following Theon down the narrow edge. The view was dizzying. Down below, it was far too dark to even see what was there. The sky looked murky and dark, and there was just no wind. Strange…

"Be careful of your footing," Hunter said quietly as we began making our way down…

A few hours had passed, and there had been a few dangerous slippery moments. I did end up using the wind to stop Hunter from going tumbling down the side when the rock gave way beneath his feet. Even summoning my abilities felt harder here. Something about the entire place gave me a bad feeling.

"The path is narrower ahead," Hunter murmured, coming to a stop.

"Shall we try climbing down?" I asked. "We have daggers?"

"We may have to," Hunter replied, frowning.

"Then let's get going whilst it's still daylight," Theon said, letting go of my wrist. Naga eyesight was better in the dark. I looked at Theon, knowing it would strain his injuries.

"I could create a ledge of ice, maybe…" I suggested looking down at the narrow paths.

"We don't want anyone to notice us. Climbing makes more sense," Theon said. "Be careful."

I nodded, and our eyes met. He raised his hand, and for a moment, I thought he was going to touch me, but instead, he dropped it again and turned away. I could feel Hunter's eyes on us, but I was grateful that he didn't speak as we continued our descent.

Two hours later, we reached the bottom, and my heart was thumping. The strong smell of blood filled my nose, overriding Theon's own intoxicating scent. The moment he grabbed me by my waist and lifted me down into the murky swamp, I turned to him sharply, not caring that we were ankle-deep in the gunk beneath our feet.

"Your injuries," I stated, reaching for his shirt, only for him to move back. "They're fine."

"Theon, are you hurt?" Hunter asked, his eyes sharp.

"Not really," Theon denied coldly.

"He is," I refuted. Stepping closer, I pulled Theon's shirt up.

"Yileyna," he growled, grabbing my arms and pushing me up against the rocky mountain. He pinned my arms by the side of my head.

"Theon, let me see," I commanded, ignoring the jolt of pleasure that rushed to my core. I wasn't the only one who was getting side-tracked as Theon's gaze dropped to my breasts.

"No. I'm the one who gives orders," he growled quietly, his eyes flashing.

"Only in the bedroom," I whispered murderously, grabbing hold of his shirt once again. Hunter cleared his throat, but I ignored him as I pulled his shirt up.

Hunter swore as I stared at Theon's chest, lost for words. His bandages were soaked in blood. The blood didn't look as red either; it was dark, and the skin around the bandages was dark and discoloured. My heart pounded as Theon pulled away.

"I said I'm fine," he growled, opening his sack, and taking out some fresh bandages. His anger was clear as he ripped the soaked bandages off. He hadn't wanted us to see them.

"Let me do it," I said, trying to take the bandage from him. He glared at me, not letting go of it.

"I can manage."

"How the hell did that happen? You're fucking injured, and you didn't think to tell me before coming here?" Hunter hissed, his voice full of anger.

"I don't need your shit, I'm not a fucking kid," Theon shot back as he began wrapping the bandage around himself.

"I don't care if you are or not. You being injured could slow us down, or worse, you could be fucking killed." My heart thumped, and I felt guilt wash over me.

"I knew, too, I should have said something too. I didn't -"

"I would have come regardless of what the fuck you two thought, and Hunter, don't forget that I'm fucking stronger than you," Theon interrupted me, his eyes hard as he glared at his brother.

"You don't hold the Alpha position yet. I think we are pretty much on par," Hunter shot back, his eyes on Theon's wound.

"Even injured, I'm stronger, so fuck this and let's move. I don't need anyone to fucking save me, nor am I here to slow anyone down." His eyes were blazing, but I took the chance to take the bandage from him and finish wrapping it. This time he didn't argue, holding his shirt up for me.

"Theon…" I whispered, looking up at him. His blazing eyes met mine, and I felt his aura ease up. "Both of you, calm down, please. I think we are all nervous about being here, but if we argue amongst ourselves, it will only impact us negatively. We are a team. Let's act like it," I added, glancing at Hunter before tying the end of the bandage and brushing my hand down his chest slowly. His skin was burning hot, and his chest was heaving. Our eyes met, and my fingers lingered on his abs.

"Are you done?" He asked, raising an eyebrow. I tilted my head, pursing my lips.

"Does it burn?" I asked. He clenched his jaw, and I knew he was struggling to reply before he looked at me as if he wasn't bothered.

"Not much."

That was a yes.

My brow creased in concentration, and I sent a gentle wave of cold through the bandage, frowning as I tried to make it hold like the way the ice on the castle remained...

He sucked in a breath, and I looked at him.

"Feel better?" I asked softly.

"Thanks," he said curtly, swallowing and dropping his top as he moved away from my touch. I ignored Hunter's smirk, thinking he was enjoying this immensely.

"So, shall we continue?" He asked as Theon had already begun leading the way. He ignored him, and I instead raised an eyebrow at Hunter.

"I hope you don't tease my queen as much as you do us?" I asked.

"I do... she can get quite feisty. She's a minx, and she's mine..." I smiled at the look on his face, feeling happy for them.

"She is a gem," I agreed.

"Quit talking," Theon said quietly.

"Is there an issue with talking about my Luna?"

"Theon is just jeal-"

"Cut it out, I thought I heard something," Theon muttered. We both froze, but I didn't hear anything.

"I didn't," Hunter replied quietly.

We remained still for a few moments. The men had their hands on their weapons, and I was ready to create a shield if need be. Theon frowned before we carried on trudging through the marshes. We all remained silent just in case there was something out there...

"This smells," I murmured. The smell of something coppery and rotten filled my nose.

"It means we are making progress..." Hunter murmured.

"There's nothing here... not even the sound of an insect. Something is really wrong," Theon said quietly, his voice barely audible, and that's when I heard it, the faint eerie hiss of something snake-like, yet not a snake...

My heart thumped as I took a deep breath. I wasn't the only one who had heard it. As both men stopped, Theon's eyes flashed, and he was beside me just as Hunter unsheathed his sword.

A sinister hiss filled the air, and then I saw it slithering down the rocky wall of the mountain. He was huge, his tail a good twenty feet long, and his scales were a mix of grey and green. His hair was to his shoulders, and his reptile-like eyes were upon us as he hissed, bearing his poisonous fangs. His torso was muscular with abs, his skin tinged green, and he had a dark green tattoo-like scar on his neck. To my horror, he launched himself in the air, coming right towards us. His yellow-green eyes were full of hatred as they locked with mine. Another loud hiss left his mouth as he came ever closer.

I raised my hand. It felt slow. I felt slow...

He was fast... too fast....

A Futile Attempt

YILEYNA

MY EYES FLASHED AND it was almost as if we moved as one. Both Theon and I raised our hands, Theon's glow swirling around his sword as I raised a wall of ice. The Naga slammed into it before the ice was cracked by Theon's sword slamming through and into the Naga's stomach.

My heart thumped. His move shocked me. Sure, the barrier was not the same ice that I encased the castle with, but for him to break it so easily… he was strong, and it confirmed that he held back during our training…

I shook my head, looking for a way to get closer. If I could encase his body in ice…

"Yileyna!" Hunter shouted just as the Naga's tail slammed into me. I went flying as Theon sliced its tail off, and I flipped in the air, landing on my feet. I touched the sludgy water with my hand, sending ice through it and letting it wrap around the Naga's tail. He hissed, shoving Theon off him. He was injured, but it wasn't fatal.

"Stop," I commanded, raising my hand and creating a shield of ice. "We are not here to kill." I wasn't sure it'd work. Hunter and Theon were both holding their swords ready, their eyes flaming as their auras blazed around them.

"You do not venture into the lands of Naran where you are not welcome," the Naga hissed.

It was the first time I had heard one speak. His voice was deep and raspy, and his cold, sinister glare was trained upon me as he struggled against the ice that encased the tip of his tail and spread upwards.

"We would not have if we had any other choice," I replied firmly. His lips curled maliciously.

"Then you will die here!"

"They hold no compassion; they are more monster than human," Hunter warned coldly. The Naga smiled and turned his attention to him.

"We like the kill…" His voice was darker and more sinister, and then he suddenly lunged at me.

"Don't!" I said to the men, raising a barrier that the Naga smashed into.

"You will die!" He hissed, slithering around the barrier. I stepped back as he stretched to his limits, his lower body frozen in the ice as he thrashed around. He roared, venom dripping from his fangs as he lunged at me once more, not caring about the damage to his tail.

I was ready for him. He ripped free from the ice, his body bloodied, but before he even reached me, Hunter and Theon attacked, decapitating his head and piercing his heart. I closed my eyes as his deep greenish blood splashed across my face.

"Do you men think killing is the only option? I was trying to talk to him!" I said as the Naga's body dropped into the sludge with a thick splash.

"He isn't one we could have talked to. Look at the mark on his neck. He has been deemed a criminal by the empire itself," Hunter said quietly.

I sighed, wiping my face and staring at the green blood. I was trying… I exhaled but said nothing. Was killing the answer to everyone's issues?

"You don't plan to ask the Naga emperor for this pearl, do you, Yileyna? It won't work," Theon asked sharply.

"Yeah, the plan was to sneak in and simply search for it, right?" Hunter added.

I frowned. I was planning on trying to negotiate with them… I wanted them to know that we were not all enemies. Was I so wrong to wish for that? I looked at the body of the Naga on the floor, wondering if he had family…

"Yileyna," Theon's voice came, bringing me from my thoughts. He walked towards me. Raising his hand, he brushed my cheek with his forearm, removing some more blood. "Come on, let's go." I looked into his eyes, unable to hide the pain I was feeling.

"Theon, killing isn't the answer," I whispered. "I don't want the deaths of so many on my hands, even if refusing to kill makes me seem weak."

I was ready for him to tell me it was the duty of an Alpha to bear the burden, but it didn't come. He cupped my face, forcing me to look up at him.

"You won't have to. I'm here to do the killing and carry that burden, which really isn't so hard for me." His voice was quiet, his eyes emotionless as they stared into mine intensely. Although I knew I should argue I didn't want him to kill anyone either, I couldn't respond. His words had made my heart soar, my chest pounding as I leaned into his touch.

When the hope of ever being together was gone… why were you making it harder? Why are you showing me the you that I always wanted to see?

"It's only one Naga, don't feel bad," he said quietly.

Staring down at me, his fingers gently caressed my cheeks. Did he not realise it was his actions that were getting to me? His handsome face, even dirty, was incredibly sexy. A few strands of his coppery brown hair flicked in front of his forehead. I nodded slowly, forcing myself away from him and looking at the dead Naga.

"I still don't think killing is the answer," I insisted. Hunter sighed.

"I understand what you mean, but Naga are a cursed species, one that is more beast than human."

We carried on walking, and I didn't know how to reply, instead remaining silent. How did I argue with that when I knew that already? But then, why did it still feel so wrong?

Hours passed, and darkness was nearing. Hunter's tension was clear, and I knew that he knew far more than I about the dangers that lingered there. He had made it clear we were not to travel at night, no matter what happened. We were currently looking for a place to stay, and although we hadn't come across any more Nagas, we had seen two feasting on an alligator. Watching them from afar as they devoured the raw meat of the alligator made me shudder inwardly. We had slowly edged away, lucky that they had been far too engrossed to even notice us. The little water that the land contained did not look pleasant, and I wondered how the land and its inhabitants survived.

Theon signalled us to stop and we all froze, making sure to keep our heartbeats calm. The sound of laughter reached me, and I peered out through the trees, only to spot two young Naga females giggling and chattering as they talked in snake tongue. They were barely older than twelve. From the waist up, they looked entirely human, save for their green-hued skin. They wore black shirts. One had long hair, and the other had short hair, but it was their laughter that made me think that they were not entirely monsters, not yet.

It is the way one starts to think that makes one a killer. We can still teach love and compassion. Nagas didn't need to become the hostile monsters they were. Was it fear of the enemy? Was it the hatred for werewolves? Why were they as they were? I couldn't help but wonder.

The innocence of the girls as they chased each other unknowingly, the way they chattered and tumbled onto the ground, it reminded me of Charlene and me from long ago…

Everyone deserved a chance.

There was no way for us to move on unless they left, but they didn't seem to plan on going anywhere and instead settled down to eat some fruit. Hunter was right; often, Naga slept during the day and awakened at night, which meant the moment darkness fell, this place would be crawling with them. Their senses were keen, their poison fatal, and their strength far greater than that of a werewolf.

Hunter motioned us to follow, spotting a narrow path around the denser trees, and we did, slipping through the trees only to hear sounds from the other side. We needed to rest and find a place to lay low for the night. There were far too many things in the forest now.

"Shall I create a fog?" I murmured. Hunter frowned, glancing through the trees at the darkening sky.

"It may help a little but do it gradually," he replied quietly.

"I don't think we'll be resting tonight…" Theon added. Both Hunter and I looked at him sharply, but he wasn't looking at us. His eyes were glowing gold as he stared far beyond. We both turned, spotting the silent pair of gleaming red eyes that were watching us through the trees metres away…

"Allow me," I warned. Focusing on my Siren side, I called upon my powers, just enough to show him who I was. I saw the tips of my hair change, the shimmery hue that my skin took up, and the air suddenly felt dryer.

"You looking prettier isn't going to get him to go away or not try to kill us," Theon murmured, making Hunter snicker despite the situation. I wanted to glare at him, but I stayed staring ahead.

"Who are you, and what do you want here?" His dangerous voice came. I couldn't see him; apart from his red eyes, there was nothing more, just… darkness. Even with my fog lifted, I couldn't see him.

"I am from Astalion, and I wish for an audience with your emperor," I stated, holding his gaze. He tilted his head.

"And why do you think you are worthy of his company?" He hissed. "No Siren has ever managed to last in these lands."

"I am not simply a siren. Tell me, will an heir to a kingdom be enough for an audience?"

He stepped forward, slithering between the trees before he raised his head, and I saw myself staring at a powerful Naga with red eyes and long black hair. If it wasn't for the scales that covered his neck, one would almost forget what he was. He had plump lips and a sharp, strong nose, and he held an arrogance and power around him.

"An heir? To what throne?" He asked, crossing his muscular arms over his chest.

"The rightful heir to the middle kingdom. The Alpha of the Silver Storm Pack and the future queen of the Aethirian Ocean." He raised his eyebrows, and I could feel the hostility and dominance growing from him and the two Alphas by my side. I raised my finger slightly by my side, hoping they heeded my warning and stayed put.

"Does royal blood run in your veins, or do you just think you are entitled to those lands and the sea?" He spat venomously, his fangs glinting dangerously, but I held his gaze.

"I am the daughter of the late King Andres Aphelion of Astalion, the granddaughter of the Imperial Emperor Queseidon of the Seven Seas, as well as the Heart of Kaeladia itself, as mentioned in the prophecy of old. I have come here for a purpose, one that no one will stand in my way to stop me from achieving."

"Then you will kill me?" I raised my eyebrow.

"I do not want to leave a trail of bodies in my wake. Many have died and were killed for no reason. I am not threatening you, I am declaring my reason for being here," I replied coldly. He smirked, his gaze running over me.

"Yileyna…" Theon muttered.

I knew it was risky, but I needed to give this a chance.

"You are indeed something we have not come across before, but the emperor sees no one, not even his own kind."

"Then, who can I speak to?"

"What is it regarding? You can tell me. I am one of the emperor's grandsons," he said, crossing his arms. That made sense… I could feel his power.

"Don't do it," Hunter murmured. I ignored him; I had to try.

"It is regarding a pearl that the Naga emperor stole from the sea. A pearl that belongs in the trident of Emperor Queseidon." He looked at me coldly, his fangs flashing when he spoke,

"So he sent you? Without an army? Are you insulting our power?"

"You may have your people already gathering around us, but I assure you, you will not win this. Let it not come to that," I warned.

"Ah, but no Sirens can come here," he sneered.

"Emperor Queseidon has an army of Imperials ready to walk this land and reclaim that pearl. If it is handed to me, I will make sure that this kingdom is safe."

It was a little lie… they couldn't come here…

He let out a contemptuous scoff.

"Do you really think the words of a mere shifter will do anything? You are in Naran, and you will not be making it out of here alive." His voice changed, becoming something entirely different as he spoke in Snake Tongue.

"Not everyone is good," Theon said quietly.

"And not everyone wants to change," Hunter added.

"I know," I whispered softly.

We all formed a circle, back to back, readying ourselves as our auras swirled around us. There was no longer any need to hold back. They knew we were here, but deep down, I knew if I didn't at least try that I was no better. I had no chance to explain as the emperor's grandson lunged at us. A terrifying unearthly hiss left his mouth as Theon raised his sword, which was glowing with his amber-coloured fire, ready to meet him head-on.

From all sides, I sensed the power of many more Nagas approaching. We were completely surrounded.

Nagas

YILEYNA

OUR ENTRY WAS NO longer a secret. We fought the Nagas. They were relentless, powerful, and violent. The worst part was that we had to be careful not to be poisoned by their fangs. The two brothers had their auras wrapped around themselves. I think it was the first time they had fought side by side, and despite the severity of the situation, they were competing against each other and seemed to be enjoying themselves.

"I think that's eight," Hunter smirked, yanking his sword from yet another dead Naga.

"Nine…oh, wait, make it ten," Theon's deep, husky voice called out as he decapitated another Naga.

I would have said something if I wasn't busy making sure the Nagas didn't get too close. The emperor's grandson was obviously trying to kill us, yet he was still smart enough to keep his distance and send his men after us.

Ice may be my go-to power, but I was channelling my connection to the earth, making the roots of the trees weave through the air like tentacles. They wrapped around the bodies of the Nagas and pinned them to the ground. I was trying not to kill anyone, but I had killed two when they got too close, and I was unable to do anything but protect myself.

I gasped when the tail of a Naga wrapped around my ankle, dragging me down.

"Yileyna!" Theon shouted. He turned instantly, his hair flicking across his forehead.

"I'm fine! Be careful!" I shouted back as he narrowly missed an attack.

My sword slipped from my hands when the Naga violently slammed me against a nearby tree, the taste of dirt and blood filling my mouth as I tried to focus. I raised my hand, ready to kill, when a menacing growl filled the air, and I saw Theon's huge wolf bite into the Naga.

"No!" I shouted as the Naga fell to the ground.

Theon's body slid under me as he caught me, dropping to the ground and taking the brunt of the fall. I wasn't bothered about the Naga, but my heart was thudding in fear for Theon. The blood of a Naga was not something a werewolf should ever digest.

"Theon!" He shifted, and I felt my heart squeeze painfully as he spat the blood out. He was in a terrible state. Even if he still looked godlike, his wounds had once again been torn open when he had shifted. I created a barrier, grabbing his duffle bag and the water bottle and holding it to him with shaking fingers.

"Gargle and spit it out!" I shouted, my attention flickering to Hunter.

"I'm fine," Theon murmured after taking a gulp and spitting the water out. "Let's kill these bastards."

I was angry. He shouldn't have saved me, but now wasn't the time to argue. Our eyes met, eyes filled with so much emotion...

I saw the tiniest hint of a smile on his face, and it made my heart soar. I took a deep breath, summoning every ounce of power I could. The Heart of Kaeladia belongs to all. I belonged to this world... and the world was a part of me... right?

I stilled, focusing... feeling the power spread through me and into the grounds.

"We are not here to fight, but if it is what you want, we will not hesitate to raise our swords in defence." My eyes snapped open, looking at the emperor's Grandson, the most powerful Naga there. What was he worth? He was far off, watching and commanding his men. "I want to know what the emperor's own blood means to him. Stand down, or your prince dies!" I shouted, and with those words, the sky flashed with lightning. The tree behind the Naga prince wrapped around his powerful body as the bolt of lightning simply skimmed past him, making him roar in pain.

"Stand down!" I shouted as I blasted several of the Nagas away, my heart thundering as I saw Theon slice through two of them right down the middle. "If I want, that lightning will kill you. Call your men off, or the next will not simply skim past you."

My heart was thundering as I glared at the Naga. My mind was screaming to run to Theon's side and stop him from losing any more blood, but I remained put, channelling my frustration towards the Naga in the grasp of the tree. His eyes blazed with hatred and pure fury. His eyes flicked as he hissed at his people to back away. I picked up my sword from the floor and walked over to him, placing it against his neck and looking around at the Naga, who seemed to be ready to attack.

"I will only repeat myself once. We are not here to kill but try to attack us once more, and we will not hesitate," I growled, taking a few steps back.

I knelt down, placing my hands on the ground, and closed my eyes, allowing myself to draw from the earth. The roaring shrieks and hisses of the Naga filled the air as every single one of them was trapped by the roots of the trees. Naran may not have much water, but it had plenty of trees…

I felt my heart palpating, and fatigue washed over me. Goddess, I think I overexerted myself…

"Come on, let's keep moving," Theon said, coming over. Despite everything, my heart still fluttered as I tried not to look at his abs. He was shirtless, but he had pulled on a pair of pants.

He helped me to my feet, and as much as I wanted to collapse into his arms, I had to remind myself that he was injured far worse than any of us. How was he still fighting on? What kind of willpower did he hold? Sure, he was powerful, and his aura was magnificent, but it was his determination and stubbornness that kept him going.

"I'm angry at you," I said quietly, glaring at him. He raised an eyebrow, his hand gripping my waist firmly.

"I can tell without you having to state it." Hunter chuckled as he grabbed my sword and bags.

"Let's keep moving. They will all know we are here; we have no choice but to keep going," he said quietly as we walked through the trees, heading towards the other side. The moment we were a good distance from Naga, Hunter paused, his face becoming far more serious. "You're in bad shape, Theon," he said quietly.

"I'm fine. Tell me, even once, have I slowed anyone down?" Theon retorted icily, his voice tinged with a dangerous edge.

"No, but I'm worried you're pushing yourself too far."

"I don't fucking care," Theon shot back. "I'm done with this conversation."

"Theon, he isn't wrong. You attacked a Naga, knowing even a drop of their blood could make you ill," I whispered softly, stepping closer to him as he unwrapped a new roll of bandage. I could tell he only had a few left...

"I'm fine, and I knew what I was doing. I don't need anyone to tell me what I should or shouldn't do."

"You risked yourself to protect me. I would have been fine," I protested in frustration, snatching the bandage from him.

"Oh, yeah? From where I stood, all I saw was you being thrown around by that bastard," Theon growled, refusing to let go of the bandage.

"I can take care of myself, Theon. I don't want you to keep on risking yourself for me," I explained desperately, trying to keep calm as I glared at him and yanked the bandage free from his hold.

"I'm going to do whatever the fuck I want. I'm done listening to others. Besides, it was on reflex. I didn't think before acting."

"I need you to think. I need you alive, Theon," I said as I began wrapping the bandage around him, despite his irritation. Hunter sighed as he took out a map.

"I'll give you two a minute. I don't want to witness anything that may traumatise me for the rest of my years," he murmured. Neither of us bothered to look at him, glaring at one another. The moment he left, I sighed, staring at the painful wounds that I had created. "I'm sorry for this injury..."

"Don't be. I deserved far more," he replied in a clipped tone.

Our eyes met, and I realised his had dulled even more. They no longer looked amber but a washed-out brown. The wounds I had inflicted upon him were killing him...

"Dad always said to treat everyone with kindness. If we raise the sword to our enemies in anger or to settle a dispute, then there is no hope for our world. He told me forgiveness was the greatest strength one could have... and I failed him..." I found myself whispering, my eyes blurring with tears as I wrapped the gauze around him.

"Don't feel guilty, I'm fine." I shook my head.

"No... your father manipulated you and let the hatred and bitterness you felt at life cloud your vision, but by attacking you, I proved I was no different. I didn't realise the pain you were in, what you were going through... I'm not saying what you did was okay, but hatred and revenge do not get us anywhere. It only hurts us further," I whispered, resting my head against his arm. I was exhausted. Life was complicated. His hands gripped my elbows and his lips pressed against the top of my head.

"You don't need to forgive me, little storm," he whispered, one hand stroking my back.

"I know... and at times I feel..." I whispered, looking up at him, my heart thundering. I needed to tell him. "I feel... like I've already forgiven you... I won't ever forget what happened, and although I sometimes think I shouldn't forgive you, I'm unable to stop myself from feeling like this. My father told me never to hold on to things that will only make bitterness and vengeance grow, and I know if they were... or if I had a chance to talk to them... I know they'd want me to forgive you and to follow my heart -"

"Stop," he cut me off, cupping my face. I looked into his eyes, my heart aching at the conflict in his eyes.

"Theon, I need to say it. I don't want -"

"I don't deserve your forgiveness... nor do I deserve you. Even if it's the only fucking thing I want in this life, it's far too late. I love you, little storm, or at least I think that's what this is, but you are a queen, and I'm just the villain in your story, one who has committed far too many crimes. I'll be by your side until this is over, but there is no future for us together."

I love you. Theon had just confessed.

I gazed up at him, unable to comprehend what else he was saying as I stared at those plump, sexy lips that had just told me he loved me and also that he could not be with me in one sentence.

"You love me?" I asked hoarsely.

I was a fool. Of course he did. Every single act of kindness and concern he had ever shown me returned with full force. His anger when I had been tied up and beaten, his warning to not anger his father, holding back during training, there was so much more. He was always constantly trying to protect me, and the way he couldn't keep his eyes off me...

I smiled softly, feeling my cheeks heat up slightly. But still. He just confessed he loved me.

"Did you hear anything else I just said?" He asked, grazing his thumb across my cheek.

"Nothing else was important," I whispered, my gaze flickering to his lips, but his face didn't hold the happiness that mine held…

"Yileyna… you are worth far more than I can ever match up to, and as much as I want to never let you go… Heaven and Hell are never meant to be."

Aren't they? Then why are they often put together?

Down Dark Tunnels

YILEYNA

MY HEART CRUMBLED, EVEN when he had placed a tender kiss on my forehead before taking my hand and leading me towards Hunter. I had been unable to think of anything else but what he had said. I never knew what I wanted, but when he told me we were not meant to be, I wanted to shout and ask why? Somehow we could work, right?

A part of me told me he was right, that the kingdom would never accept a traitor as their king, but was he a traitor? No. He had been misguided and manipulated, just like many. Sure, it did not make everything he had done go away, but even people like Nikolai Levin were allowed to walk amongst us, despite their sins. Why not someone who was on the path to redemption? Fighting alongside me, ready to face his father and kill him for all he has done?

It was clear Theon loved his pack, his family, and his people, but it was his father who had manipulated him. I understood Theon wouldn't be able to simply forgive himself, but that in itself showed he was worthy of forgiveness.

We continued travelling, and we remained silent as we got closer and closer to the castle that came into view. It wasn't exactly how I had pictured it. The entrances were simply gaping tunnels with barred gates. Naga soldiers guarded them, and although I could see the black stone structure of the ominous fortress, it was half built underground. The green lights from the windows cast an eerie light on the land around it.

Dried, cracked earth spread around for miles, and the closer we got to the castle of the Naga emperor, the dryer and darker it all felt. These lands were screaming for water… if it continued like this, no life would be able to survive living here. Was their fear of Sirens so strong that they had blocked off all sources of water? It just felt wrong.

"The land is dying," I whispered quietly as we continued silently.

I had made a heavy fog fall over the area, however, we were sure they would be on high alert regardless, but even some coverage was better than none. I had felt them cutting into the trees to help those we had trapped, but it would take them time because I had made sure the trees held.

We paused when we heard a shout in snake tongue before a group of Nagas came out from the castle. The middle one reeked of power and dominance. His tail was the exact colour of a python, and his muscular body looked almost human in colour, save for the scales on his neck and shoulders. His black hair was braided from the top, the rest tied back in a ponytail. He was different. I could feel it, and when he tilted his head, baring his teeth in a cruel sneer, his eyes glinting, Hunter closed his eyes, exhaling.

"We're going to split up," he breathed.

"What?" I hissed.

"That's Xenara Khasorin, the third prince of the empire. We've met before, and he's fucking lethal," Hunter explained quietly, frowning deeply.

"Why am I not fucking surprised?" Theon murmured.

"You two carry on, tonight it's just him and I…" I knew splitting up wasn't a good idea, but if Hunter was saying to do so…

"The cave of treasures that belongs to the emperor is rumoured to be down south from here. It's beyond the castle, and I'm sure it will be guarded heavily. Theon may need to be the decoy whilst Yileyna goes in and grabs the pearl. I don't know how fast you'll find it, it's said to contain many things, but I pray that the pearl calls to you. Plus, since we mentioned the pearl to the Naga, they may have hidden it. I just hope that isn't the case. If we end up splitting, we meet by the dead oak tree we saw a while back, but we try not to, he's found us! Run!" Hunter growled lowly. His eyes blazed as he stared far ahead.

Theon didn't wait for an answer, grabbing my wrist and breaking into a run.

"Well, if it isn't the Naga killing Alpha in our midst!" The deep, dark voice that reminded me of a stormy night came.

My heart was pounding with fear. If Hunter died... so did Charlene. Neither was a death I wanted, and the very thought of Charlene dying terrified me.

Stay safe, Hunter.

I don't know how long we had carried on. The sounds of the fight behind us had long vanished as we moved fast. When we had finally reached the cave entrance that was in the shape of a cobra's mouth, Theon had pointed out the Nagas guarding it.

"Alright... Hunter may have been right. From here on, you're going in alone. I'll keep the entrance clear and kill them all. You go in and get the pearl. I'll join you the moment I'm done with them. There are chances there may be some more inside," he murmured, turning and looking at me. Even with the layers of dirt, grime, and blood covering him, he still looked like a God. "Go when I signal, alright?"

I know he said we weren't meant to be... but...

Our eyes met, and I wasn't able to say it. My heart was hurting, but the words refused to leave my lips. I love you, I still love you.

"Stay alert," he murmured, brushing my dirty hair off my face. "Stay safe."

I nodded, our eyes meeting, and that intense pull between us made my heart pound. He swallowed, forcing his gaze away, and just when he was about to turn, I grabbed hold of his shoulder, yanking him around and gripping his face. I pulled him down, pressing my lips against his.

Delicious, soft sparks of pleasure coursed through me, and it only took him a fraction of a second before he kissed me back with passion. A soft whimper left my lips. His heart was thundering, and his grip on my hips was firm, pressing me against himself completely. Oh fuck, he felt so good.

I broke away with a shaky gasp and looked into his glowing gold eyes.

"That was for luck," I whispered before I turned and slipped down the slope, not waiting for an answer.

I was ready to await the first chance I got to sneak in. My heart was soaring. The feel of his lips lingered on mine, and I slowly licked my lips. Although he consumed my mind, I needed to focus.

When Theon threw something against the tree, making the Nagas turn, I saw the signal he gave me, and I hurried towards the cave entrance. Slipping inside, I remembered what Hunter had said, that they may know we were there for the pearl. I'd be careful.

I scanned the darkness. There didn't seem to be any life… I kept walking down the tunnel, which was long and circular, almost like the body of a snake. It was cold and dark, and the sounds from outside seemed to have vanished. Was Theon alright?

I could only hear my own heart beating. I decided to try to sense if the pearl was even here. Crouching down silently, I placed my hands on the floor and closed my eyes, sensing everything through the ground. Theon and several other Nagas were far above, rodents… the insects in the ground crawling around...

The whispering coolness of something deep beneath me called to me. The sound of the ocean and the smell of it invaded my senses. My heart skipped a beat when I realised what it must be. The pearl!

I stood up, knowing I still needed to tread carefully as I hurried down, letting the pearl guide me to it. The path became darker until even I was unable to see. It was strange, almost as if there was nothing at all to see.

I felt the walls to help guide me as I continued, feeling the circular wall become tighter, and the sense of being suffocated grew. I could feel spiders and other insects crawling over my hands and the squeaking of rats as they rushed over my feet. I shuddered as I kept going. Soon the entrance became wider, and I was in a small opening area. I closed my eyes, trying to feel for life through the ground.

I was extremely far down. It was odd that no one had followed, and my worry for Theon only grew. I could sense life, but none was anywhere near, so I kept going blindly.

I could feel that I was getting closer to the pearl, and it was the only thing fuelling me to keep going. I had no idea how far or deep down I was, and soon I was on all fours, crawling through the tunnel that was becoming tighter until I was on my elbows and stomach, crawling through the shrinking tunnel. Breathing was becoming harder, and I shuddered when

I felt something crawl down my neck. I didn't mind insects, but not to see exactly what it was… I kept going, bit by bit…

I paused when I saw a faint ray of light up ahead, encouraging me to continue going. I peered out from the tunnel, my eyes widening at the sight before me. I was in some sort of stone chamber. I could tell from the well-rounded ceiling and the stone pillars that it was a room of some sort. I looked around, spotting the jewels and gold that lay in a mountain to one side, but it was what was on the left that made my stomach sink. I clamped a hand over my mouth, praying it didn't see me. There, coiled up on the dark stone floor, was a huge Naga.

His body was larger than any I had seen. Scales of pure black covered his full body, and his torso skin was dark with hints of green. He was curled up and looked to be sleeping, but I couldn't be sure. I wasn't about to risk it, but I needed to get down there.

I was about to close my eyes to feel for the pearl when I froze. My heart thudded as my eyes flew open, and I stared at the Naga. I hadn't sensed him down here… I closed my eyes, trying to focus on everything around me, and I realised I couldn't even sense him, nor could I hear a heartbeat. Was he dead? As much as that's how it looked, I wasn't going to trust it…

I felt for the pearl, feeling the pull, but I couldn't pinpoint it. Slowly I slipped out of the tunnel. If he was awake, he'd hear me. There was no way he wouldn't…

Should I freeze his body? It was already getting harder to use my powers. Maybe I should just try to look for the pearl… I silently crept over toward the mountain of treasure, doing my best not to make a sound. It was too silent, so silent I could hear my own heartbeat. It was too loud for the stillness of this cave…

Get the pearl and run back to that tunnel… I glanced towards the coiled body of the Naga, only for my heart to thump in fear. Where the body had been moments earlier, was now a huge vast empty space.

I spun around, letting my aura radiate off me just as I saw him with his mouth wide open, ready to bite down on me. A blast of wind pushed him back, and he hissed venomously, his snake-like gold eyes glowing.

"You're fast, Siren," he hissed, showing his forked tongue.

"I come only for what you have stolen," I said, trying to hide the fear that had encased me.

I hadn't heard him, nor had I sensed his heartbeat. This Naga was beyond powerful, and as he loomed above me, I saw the rustic crown that sat upon his head of pure black hair that fell to his waist. A wave of power rolled off him, and I was thrown to the ground. I raised my hand, using wind to push him back. His tail thrashed against the pillars before he was in front of me once again and began to coil his body around me. I pushed it aside and jumped up, landing on the pile of gold and jewels. Pieces of treasure tumbled down from beneath my feet, sending items scattering in all directions.

"Do you know who I am, little one?" He hissed, his voice so deep and cold that I felt as if it was resonating from within me, just as his tail knocked into my back, sending me flying to the ground once again.

I don't know why my body felt heavy, why were my reactions so slow?

"I'm sure you are about to tell me exactly who you are," I replied, looking up at him defiantly.

"I am Kshuryaron, the Emperor of Naran, and you, you are my next feast."

ICE & FIRE

YILEYNA

*H*IS WORDS ECHOED OMINOUSLY in the dark chambers as his tail hit the back of my head. This time, I raised my hand, creating a shard of ice, and slammed it into his tail. He let go, but only for a second before he was coming for me once more. I sent several shards flying at him, but he deflected them with ease. We were a blur of attacks, but he had size and strength on his side, while I had my elemental power and speed, speed that I felt was somehow being suppressed.

"No Siren or wolf is welcome here," he spat. "Your dead body will be an example for all!

"You're wrong," I said coldly as his tail wrapped around me. This time, I was ready. Placing my hands on his scales, I let ice spread from my palms. He instantly realised what I was doing and dropped me, his claws ripping into my back as he sent me flying into one of the stone pillars.

"Fuck," I growled, sliding to the ground as pain jarred through my back.

"You bitch!" He hissed as his tail thrashed around, but it was futile. The ice that I had managed to wrap around a small portion of his body was unmoving and weighed him down. Perfect.

I frowned, kneeling down and touching the ground. I channelled my all into it and let ice spread from my hands across the stone floor. His eyes flashed as he roared, coming for me, but the moment he touched the ice, I let it ensnare him, unmoving as I focused on freezing his body.

"You will pay!"

"I'm afraid not," I whispered, feeling the strain as he fought against the ice. Deep down within this cave, pulling on nature to help me was difficult, and I knew earth would do no good. I was strongest when it came to ice. I gasped when his hand narrowly missed me, clawing into my arm before the ice that wrapped around the lower half of his body stopped him from coming any closer.

"You are starting a war! I will never forget this insult!" He hissed. I stood up slowly, gripping my bleeding arm. My entire body was aching.

"I do not wish to kill you. If I wanted, I could have killed your grandson." I looked at the Naga before me, he didn't look much older than his grandson, but they aged slowly and could live up to five hundred years. They were the species with the second longest life span, after the Fae. His eyes narrowed, and I tried to calm my heart, not wanting him to know the extent of how exhausted I was.

"Lies."

"I am not lying. Don't you think we knew of the risk of letting them live? They would alert the entire kingdom, and we knew that, yet we didn't want to kill unnecessarily. I'm sure your grandson must have told you who we are and why we're here?" His eyes narrowed, and he looked at me sharply.

"I was told nothing," he spat. I frowned, looking at him sharply.

"You didn't know I was coming?" That didn't seem believable.

"No. If you didn't realise, this place is encased with powers and seals. I am kept in here. How would I know what is going on up there?" Confusion flitted through me as his words sank in.

"You are the emperor."

"By name. I haven't come across any life source for nearly a century. My eldest son rules whilst I suffer in isolation in this tomb as they wait for my death."

"Your grandson said you don't meet anyone."

"Of course, how can I down here?" He hissed. I took a step back, wondering if he was telling the truth or not…

"I don't believe you." He simply raised an eyebrow.

"You are just a child, but did you not feel the power in the air? The spells that are keeping me down here?" I looked into his eyes. No, I hadn't, or was the heaviness in the air what he meant? Perhaps they were spells meant for a Naga… there was no hint that he was lying…

"Then, how are you alive if you have been down here for so long?" I asked. His lips curled into a malicious smile.

"I hold something that keeps me alive. Even when those traitors send poisoned food, I will not die. If a Naga kills me, they would be cursed for life, and none of my sons are ready to face that. They are all cowards, but it's clear they knew you held the power to destroy me, and so they let you come here."

So he acknowledged I was strong? I didn't have time for my smug thoughts as I pondered on his words.

"I was wondering why there was no security outside. They let me in… wanting you dead… or me. Either way, it's a win for them…"

"Indeed." I had to try…

"Then allow me to start over, Your Majesty," I said, bowing my head to Emperor Kshuryaron. He tensed as I offered a small smile. "I am Yileyna De'Lacor from the Kingdom of Astalion, heir to the throne of the middle kingdom and the future queen of the Aethirian Ocean, the daughter of land and sea, and the Heart of Kaeladia."

"The Heart of Kaeladia…" His eyes seemed to deepen as they stared at me intensely. "From the prophecy of old…"

"Yes, and I wish to see a united world. I have travelled your lands, seen and felt the lack of nourishment that the earth yearns for. I have noticed the innocence of children playing and witnessed the hatred in others. Death after death and hunger for power are all everyone wants. I have come here on a quest from the Imperial Emperor of the Seven Seas, Queseidon himself, for he wants the pearl that was taken from his trident."

"He will never get it back! I need it!" He hissed.

"Is it the pearl that is granting you life and healing you?" He bristled, his eyes darkening.

"It may not do what it can in the trident, but it holds certain… abilities…"

"Do you know why I came for it?" I asked calmly. I was feeling so exhausted…

"For power! Everyone wants power!"

"For all species! We are all against one another, only caring for what we want for ourselves. Emperor Queseidon said if the pearl is not bought back to him within two moons, then he will march the lands and start a war. I am here trying to protect the people of the land -"

"Your people!"

"The people of Kaeladia! I tried to talk to your grandson, but it's clear they do not want peace. I know that the werewolves and Naga are constantly at war -"

"We are not... or a century ago we were not..." he said, his face darkening. Oh?

I knew Hunter and Theon didn't think there was hope... but I wanted to believe there was.

"Then you need to return to the throne where you belong."

"I am trapped here, little one."

"What if I can break you out?" He tilted his head, his eyes peering at me with such intensity that I could feel his power.

"Why?"

"Because I want peace."

"As the prophecy proclaimed..." he hissed, more to himself than at me.

"I will make sure the land is given the water it needs.... The rivers that have been barred will flow and this land will live. Right now, I am in a position where I can kill you, and you know that. You are the king this kingdom needs," I said clearly, looking him square in the eye.

"But are you ready to make the first move?" He asked challengingly.

I knew it was a risk; I could free him, and he could kill me. Or I could free him, and he could give me the pearl and accept my offer of peace. There is nothing without risk.

"Of course, I am because I have faith in you. I will free you first, then if the emperor deems fit, you could lift me to the ceiling of this cave, and I will try to break through from there," I stated without an ounce of hesitation in my voice.

"You will not succeed. I have tried for years and failed."

"Until I have tried and succeeded, I will not stop. If not, then I will leave this place and try from outside." He looked at me intently, before coming as close as he could with his lower half frozen in ice.

"And if after all of that, I don't give you the pearl?" I smiled slightly.

"We are rulers. We make peace and treaties in the favour of our kingdoms and in goodwill. I have faith that the true ruler of Naran will not disappoint."

"You are an interesting one," he murmured.

"I just want the best for us all."

I knew if Hunter and Theon were there, they would not be happy with this decision, but I was an Alpha and queen who needed to make my own decisions. Bravely, and risking it all, I stepped closer to him, knowing he could slice my head off if he wanted. I stayed alert, placing my hand on his tail, I heard a low chuckle from him as the ice vanished, and instantly, he spun and grabbed me by the waist. I was ready to encase my own body in ice if I needed to, but all he did was rise to the ceiling of the cave.

"I do not know if you are foolish or wise," he hissed.

"I may be both, but I know a true king when I see one."

I wasn't sure if he was the most trustworthy, but deep down, I felt he was better than those who I had previously seen. He could have killed me by now, and I hoped my compliments at least won me some favour. I took a deep breath, letting a layer of ice cover my body for protection as I placed my hands on the roof of the dome. I closed my eyes, hoping I could do this and not black out...

Please let this act of kindness be the peace offering he needs.

"You were right... there is something in the walls of this place, but I think I can break through."

"You were able to come in when none of my loyal servants were able to."

"The path was tight... maybe that's how."

"Or you are immune to the magic that is weighing me down."

Maybe... especially if this was made to keep him in... I frowned in concentration, but it didn't budge. I frowned, trying again, but I felt like I was hitting a barrier. I moved back and frowned.

"So you can't do it."

"Maybe not from in here, but I might be able to from outside," I said, looking at the narrow entrance I had crawled in to get here. He nodded slowly, placing me down. He watched me sharply before he smirked coldly.

"Then I guess I will await my freedom," he stated, placing me down. I looked up at him and nodded. From the slight glimmer in his eyes, I had a feeling he didn't think I would return. "Here is the pearl you seek. Perhaps one kingdom can walk free." My heart skipped a beat when he removed the black chain that hung around his neck with a small velvet pouch at the end.

"Thank you," I said, accepting it.

I felt a wave of coolness wash through me as the power of the pearl hummed in my grasp. My eyes blazed brightly, and I slipped it on over my neck, sliding it into my cloak before I turned, rushing to the small entrance. He didn't think I'd return or help him, but I planned to. I don't know how, but I will break this barrier and free him, so help me.

It took a while to make my way back out of that tight tunnel, but soon the scurrying of rats and the movement of the spiders became prominent, and I knew I was close to the surface. I reached the entrance to the cave and stepped out into the night, my heart skipping a beat when I spotted Theon still fighting the Naga. He was still holding up relentlessly, blood dripping down his torso as the flame-like amber aura of his powers wrapped around him. He attacked ceaselessly.

I wanted to help him, but something told me if I got the emperor out, I would have a better chance at helping him anyway. There were far too many... and they were all currently being occupied by Theon.

Keeping my hood up and crouching low, I climbed up the side of the cave, breaking into a run. I had no idea where the centre was but... I had to roughly try to pinpoint the location. I hurried along, stopping when I noticed the ground ahead was dead of any life. Here. It had to be here! I crouched down and placed my hands on the ground, closing my eyes.

I can do this... I have to do this.

Frowning in concentration, I used all my power, pushing it into the ground. It shook violently, and for a moment, I feared it caving in on Kshuryaron, but it held. I heard the sound of someone approaching and the hissing of the Nagas shouting in snake-tongue, but they wouldn't be able to get close. My power was surging, my cloak and hair floating around me violently as I fuelled every emotion I had into the ground. Without anything weighing down on me as it did within the cave, I felt stronger.

My powers slammed into something, and then I felt something push against me. The entire ground erupted beneath me, sending dirt and stone in every direction as a blinding green light erupted from the earth. A tidal wave ricocheted across the ground, knocking me back. I tried to grab onto the earth, but it was futile as the sheer force of the power rolled out in waves.

"Got you." I heard a low growl as a strong pair of arms wrapped around me. Theon. I closed my eyes, inhaling his scent that was tainted with the smell of blood. It still calmed me, and for a moment, I let it before I looked at the violent storm in the middle.

"I need to get back there."

"What are you doing?" He asked. I looked into his eyes, seeing the blood that dripped from his hairline.

"The right thing," I whispered before I pulled free from his hold, and taking a deep breath, I walked into the violent wind. It didn't affect me at all. Closing my eyes, I knelt down, ready to try this again.

"I'm going to do this…"

"Yileyna!" I turned as Theon reached my side, the wind cutting into his skin as he knelt beside me.

"Theon! It's dangerous in here!"

"I don't care. Let's do this together." I looked at him and gave a small nod. He was right; we were stronger together.

"Let's try," I whispered. "We need to break the barrier upon this cave…"

"Understood. Let's do this with fire and ice," he said in a husky whisper. Fire and Ice. That was exactly what we were…

I was unable to stop the small smile that graced my lips, or the flutter that settled into my stomach. He didn't question me, he didn't ask me anything, he simply decided to help me…

"On three," I murmured. "One… two… three!"

With those words, we both gave it our all. Our eyes blazed as an immense amount of power wrapped around us, merging together rather than repelling one another, becoming far stronger.

Fire and Ice moulding together as if they were always meant to be.

Combined as one.

Upon Dying Lands

YILEYNA

ANOTHER POWERFUL GREEN WAVE of energy erupted from the earth, and the sound of something cracking filled the air.

"Stop!" I heard a distant roar of rage. The sound of cracking became almost deafening, and I knew we had succeeded.

"We did it," I murmured in relief as I felt a surge of energy from below.

Then, the Naga emperor rose from within the ground. His power swirled around him as debris flew in all directions. Theon tensed, his hand going to his sword, but I placed my hand on top of his as I stood up slowly.

"I did not expect this from you since I had given you what you were seeking," Emperor Kshuryaron said in his deep, sinister voice as his attention flickered to someone far behind us.

"Your Majesty…" Someone murmured. The emperor said something in snake tongue, and I turned to see the Naga bow down to him.

"Queen Yileyna of Astalion… your hand."

Theon frowned as I held out my hand to the emperor. He raised it to his mouth, but where I was expecting him to kiss it, he sank his fangs into my finger, making Theon growl as he jumped forward, but I grabbed hold of him. Save the sharp sting it didn't hurt, and something told me it wasn't poisoned.

I looked at my small finger that now bore the two pinpricks of blood, watching as black symbols spread from the blood, and then I was healed. The emperor took hold of my wrist, raising my hand.

"She bears the mark of the emperor, an insignia of one from Naran. From this day forth, she will pass freely within our empire." His voice was loud, powerful, and commanding.

I wasn't the only one who looked shocked as I saw Hunter coming into view. He was shirtless, only in a pair of pants. His bloody sword was in his hand as he assessed the situation quickly.

"I do ask for forgiveness, but I may have killed one of your sons in self-defence," he said quietly. The emperor simply smiled coldly.

"Death awaited them anyway. You may leave Naran, and from this day forth, we will stay on our side of the borders." Hunter looked surprised, as both he and Theon watched me intensely.

"And the Naga may hunt for food on the border. We will work towards a better future," I added.

"By freeing me, you have already done your part, Queen of the Middle Kingdom. Naran will always be behind you." I bowed my head to Kshuryaron, who to my surprise bowed his back.

"Thank you, Your Majesty. We will head out, however, I will be in touch. Break the dams upon your rivers, and I will make sure the Sirens do not attack. You have my word, just give me a little time."

"Very well. I do not understand your kindness, but a Naga never forgets a foe or friend."

"Yeah, trust me, I know," Hunter muttered.

I smiled and thanked Emperor Kshuryaron, before I turned towards the two Alphas who were watching me with almost matching unreadable expressions. I paused and looked back at the king.

"There is one more thing I need to do before I go."

"What is it? You have the pearl," The emperor's reply came, but I didn't look at him. Instead, I took a deep breath and closed my eyes…

A few moments later, the night skies were thick with clouds as a heavy shower of rain poured down upon the dying lands of Naran. I could feel it, the life that stirred from within the parched earth as I did my best to spread the rain as far as I could…

My vision darkened, and I felt my legs give way. A strong pair of arms caught me, and I smiled softly, knowing I was safe in the arms of my love…

When I awoke, we were no longer in Naran. I could hear the men talking, and I could feel the warmth of a fire crackling nearby.

"... east from here."

"I don't know, there was meant to be a mark left for us but there's nothing." That was Hunter.

"Do you think they were ambushed?" Theon's voice was closer, and his scent filled my nose.

"I hope not. They can't be... if Charlene was in pain, I would have felt it." Hunter's voice was strained.

I forced my eyelids opened and stared at the star-studded sky. It was night and the weather was cool. Where were we?

"Yileyna." Theon's voice was filled with relief. Before I could even reply, his face came into view as he cupped my chin and caressed my cheek. "You're fucking awake. You pushed yourself too fucking far," he growled, reaching for something behind him before he held a water bottle to my lips as he lifted my head up.

"Yeah, Theon's been fucking stressed. I had to practically drag you from his clutches half the fucking time so he could get a break," Hunter growled as he came over, looking down at me like I was something intriguing.

"How -" I croaked before I wrapped my hand over Theon's and gulped some water down. Allowing him to help me sit up, his fingers grazed the side of my breast, making my heart flutter as I leaned against his arm. "How long have I been out?"

"Four days," Hunter replied, frowning slightly.

"You made it rain for two days straight. Although the emperor was grateful and made sure we got out of Naran safely, the rain was pretty wild," Theon explained, his eyes meeting mine.

"A bit of an understatement, but it works," Hunter added with a smirk.

Something the emperor said came to my mind, and I looked down, gripping onto the chain of the pearl. He said it kept him alive despite everything. What if Theon wore it and it somewhat healed him?

"Wear this," I said, ignoring them both.

"Is she alright? Maybe she hit her head," Hunter murmured as I took the pearl off and forced it over Theon's lush copper head. His hair had grown, he had stubble, and, Goddess... did the rugged look suit him.

"She's fine. Typical behaviour from this blonde beauty," Theon responded, smirking slightly as he allowed me to adjust the chain. Blonde beauty. My cheeks flushed as Hunter smirked.

"Ah, want me to give you two some privacy?" He mocked.

"How about you do just that without asking?" Theon raised an eyebrow pointedly. Hunter chuckled and walked off, leaving us both alone.

The sexual tension between us suddenly settled around us, and I wasn't sure what to do with myself. His fingers were still pressing against the side of my breast, my heart was still thumping, and my core was throbbing.

"You are the craziest woman I have ever come across, but it only makes you way more fucking incredible," he said quietly, his gaze flicking down to my lips for a second. "I didn't think I'd ever see the day we'd walk out of Naran without any issues," he added with a small sexy smirk that made my heart pound.

"Well, the world is full of surprises. What were you and Hunter talking about?" I croaked out. He frowned.

"We were meant to meet the others, but so far they've left none of the markings that they should have. Nothing to tell us where they have gone." My heart plummeted with worry.

"Do you think something happened to them?" I asked worriedly.

"Hopefully not. Hunter didn't feel Charlene in pain."

"Thank the Goddess…" I murmured.

"There's more… we've come across many dead animals in the forest, and there's a darkness approaching."

"Arabella? Or something else?" I asked.

"I'm not sure, it's not potent enough for me to pinpoint if it's her, but it feels darker. We need to carry on moving fast," he said quietly.

"And I'm slowing you all down."

"No, you aren't. We will head to Alpha Romeo's pack and see from there what's happening. You just woke up. Relax a little, we have this covered."

"I'm not stressing," I pouted, trying not to focus on how close he was. My core clenched when he took hold of my hand with his free hand and looked at my little finger, frowning deeply at the black snake symbol that wrapped around it, hints of gold shimmering in it.

"He marked you." His voice was dangerous and low, and although a part of me wanted to comfort him and tell him it was a symbol of loyalty and friendship, I decided to push his buttons instead.

"And? It's not like you were ever going to mark me," I said airily, tugging my hand free from his hold, almost smiling when I saw his eyes flash gold. "We can't be, remember?"

"Yileyna, don't push me," he growled, tangling his hand in my hair.

"Maybe I want to see you lose control," I whispered, looking into those gorgeous eyes of his.

A rustle in the bushes and footsteps made us both turn sharply. My eyes widened as Hunter fell to his knees the moment he burst from the bushes.

"Hunter!" I exclaimed as we both turned. The smell of blood filled the air as his eyes flashed. My eyes widened in horror as I saw the blade buried in his hip.

"Run," he growled as the fire was suddenly snuffed out, and I felt a thick layer of darkness fall over us.

"Yileyna. Run," Theon breathed, his eyes fixed on the direction Hunter had just come from.

I couldn't think. Something was numbing my body, and even when I opened my mouth to speak, I couldn't. Just then, before my very eyes, the trees and bushes began to die as a vast darkness enveloped us. Deep down, in my hazy state, as Theon dragged me to my feet, I knew I needed to protect them.

I pulled free from Theon's hold, seeing the blood trickle from his nose as his heart raced, whatever this was… it was killing all it touched. I needed to get away… lead it away from them…

"Yileyna, don't." His eyes were full of fear, an emotion I never saw in Theon. Fear for my life… "Don't be the hero… run."

I love you.

I couldn't speak as I dragged my feet towards the dying forest, pushing through the bushes Hunter had appeared out of. I needed to meet the enemy before it got to Theon and Hunter. The moment I stepped onto the blackened earth, it felt like a part of me was mortally injured. I gasped as I stumbled, running blindly towards the darkness.

"Found you." The voice was familiar, and when a hand reached out to grab me by the neck, I found myself staring into Arabella's hung eyes. "You are mine."

"I'm…no…"

I couldn't breathe. How was she so strong? I closed my eyes, focusing on whatever power I could muster. I needed to create something around Theon and Hunter… I knew Theon could break my ice…

"You will not succeed; we poisoned the air," she whispered.

"Yeah?" I whispered, closing my eyes. Even when I felt the shackles of silver touch me, I poured every ounce of my power into the earth beneath my bare feet.

"Find the others that were with her," Arabella commanded.

You wish.

A strangled scream left my lips as a wave of power erupted from within me, and I saw a huge wall of ice tear through the trees reaching the sky.

"Stop it!" Arabella shrieked.

I crumbled, all strength leaving me as I hit the ground, my eyes on the huge wall that split the forest. Arabella and I were on one side, and Theon and Hunter were on the other. They would be safe.

"We will return to Westerwell before she awakens." Arabella's command was chilling.

Was this... this wasn't what was meant to happen...

What happened to Raiden, Zarian, and the others? I hadn't felt any bond snap, or did it happen in my sleep? These questions swarmed my mind before I succumbed to the darkness...

In His Grasp

YILEYNA

"WELL, WELL, WELL... WE meet again."

I tried to control my anger as I stared at the man before me. I was chained to the wall, the taste of blood in my mouth almost making me sick. Once again, I was in the cells of the castle of Westerwell.

"Inevitably, we were going to," I spat, looking at none other than the monster Theoden himself.

I had been dragged back there several days ago, and every day they tried to break me or demand to know who was with me out there. Arabella was no werewolf, and she had not smelt Theon from me, but even when I had been beaten, I refused to speak. They could whip me and beat me, but nothing could break me, or so I thought.

That was when they stooped lower and threatened to kill children from the Silver Storm. I knew they would follow through on their threat, so I said it was Hunter and one of his men because I had a feeling Arabella had seen Hunter since he had been stabbed. It was safer to give them a partial truth than a complete lie. They had bought it, and I was relieved. I couldn't let them know that Theon was out there and that he knew the truth.

"Ah, well, what a shame that fool was unable to protect you. I'm sure this wasn't the way you thought it would be," Theoden sneered as he stepped

I smirked bitterly, "Well, I outsmarted your son, I will outsmart you, too," I spat. He looked at me sharply. I kept a look of pure hatred and contempt on my face, praying he bought it.

"Theon found you?"

"Almost, but he wasn't fast enough, now, was he?" Theoden slapped me across the face hard, and I clenched my jaw. I hadn't been given anything to eat or drink since I came here, and I was greatly weakened. "What's wrong, Theoden? Angry that you and your son have nothing on me?"

"I have the kingdom and your people before me. You are the one with nothing. So, I have a proposal for you. Marry me and be my Luna or the consequences will be great." His words made my stomach twist sickeningly and my heart plummet.

No. Goddess, no.

"Never," I hissed, my eyes flashing despite the silver and poison running through my veins.

"Oh? I will give you one day. One day for you to change your mind, or the streets of Westerwell will run with the blood of the children of the Silver Storm Pack."

"No king treats his subjects like this! Those children are yours to protect! You are already king, Theoden, aren't you enough without me? Why do you need me by your side?"

His fist met my face, and I felt something crack, excruciating pain rushing through me. I wished I had been able to contact the Sirens... we were right on the coast... I had seen what Theoden had done to his own pack, not to mention his wife and daughters. No one was safe from his barbaric ways.

"Do not speak back to me! If you hadn't been the heart, I would have killed you the first time you started to seduce my son," he hissed, grabbing my face. I gritted my teeth, refusing to give him any satisfaction that he was hurting me, and glared coldly at the man before me.

"Killing everyone who may pose a threat to your plan is your go-to option, is it not, Theoden?" I asked icily.

"Not you... you will be by my side whether you want to or not," he growled harshly. For a moment, his gaze raked over me, lingering on my breasts, making my skin crawl. "I cannot blame Theon for being tempted."

"Fuck off," I spat. His eyes blazed, and his grip on my face tightened. Painfully tight.

"Heed my words; you have until dawn to change your mind. Oh, and if you don't obey, I assure you I have other methods. Did I mention that I found a rather pretty orange rose? One that I'm sure you won't want me to kill."

With those words, he slammed my head back against the wall, and my vision darkened. Orange rose… Charlene… Did he have her?

My heart squeezed with anger and helplessness. The fear for my people's lives hung in my answer. What do I do? If I agreed, what did it mean? What would he try to use my powers for?

Darkness enveloped me, and I fell unconscious once more…

The sound of crying reached my ears, and a bucket of scalding hot water was thrown over me, making me scream as my eyes flew open. The sound of my voice rang in the cell as I looked around, the boiling water burning my skin. The pain enveloped me like a blanket I could not get away from. My heart thundered as I looked at the two young children that stood there, holding hands as Theoden and three of his men watched with eyes that were emotionless and hard. I smiled gently at the kids, trying to ease their fear.

"Your time is up. Now, do you agree? Or shall these two mutts be the first of many?" Theoden was not a man who cared for anyone but himself. I couldn't risk the life of anyone else.

"I agree," I said emotionlessly. My heart was hurting, but more than my own wellbeing, I wanted these kids far away from Theoden.

It's going to be okay. I said the words silently, knowing they couldn't hear me as they stood there trembling, their large blue eyes staring at me, almost begging me to save them.

Theoden let out a raucous laugh as he came towards me, grabbing hold of my hair and yanking my head back.

"I have a queen!" He roared as his men smirked, men he had purchased…. These men were trained monsters, not beings with compassion.

I will destroy you all… for the crimes you have committed. I vowed this to myself.

I looked at Theoden, but I didn't speak. For now, I would submit, because the lives of those children were far more important. He simply smirked, letting his gaze fall to my neck. He leaned in, and I clenched my jaw, trying not to recoil as I swallowed hard.

"I will look forward to marking you," he whispered menacingly before he looked at his men and gave a nod. One man stepped forward, unsheathing his sword.

Was he going to break my chains? If so, they would regret it; I could take them all. But to my horror, I was so very wrong. Without even a flicker of hesitation, the man swung his sword. I screamed in agony as I stared helplessly at the scene before me. He cut off the heads of the two children in a blink of an eye. I felt the snapping of the link that tied them to me break as burning fury enveloped me.

"You will pay!" I hissed, my voice a Siren's shriek as I glared at the man who had killed them. "How dare you! I agreed, Theoden!" My powers fought against the bindings, but despite the ice that spread across the ground of the cell, it did nothing to affect the men. Theoden grabbed me by the hair once again, smashing it into the stone behind me.

"You agreed now, but you disrespected me yesterday! Take this as a warning, never disobey me! Among the next victims, there will be Raiden Bolton and Charlene Aphelion," Theoden spat before he walked out of the cell, leaving me seething and heartbroken for the two children who lay on the ground. Their heads lay far from their bodies as blood seeped across the floor.

I'm sorry… I'm so sorry…

Tears stung my eyes as I stared at their lifeless bodies. The pain and anguish I felt were so intense. Theoden deserved the worst kind of punishment, and I promised I would make sure it came to him.

Hours passed, yet no one came for the children, and their bodies no longer bled. Their bodiless heads lay to the side with expressions of shock frozen on their faces. It was a memory that would always remain in my mind. I was meant to protect them, yet right before my eyes, that bastard beheaded them.

He will pay.

The sound of heels echoing on the stone floor made my head whip towards the bars. The rancid darkness that accompanied her told me who it was, and moments later when she came into view, our eyes met. Arabella.

"The King sent a ring for his bride," she said in her voice devoid of life. Was it me, or did she seem even weirder lately…

"Oh, does he know? What is it? A slave's collar or a ring to suppress my powers?" I asked coldly.

Our eyes met, and she lifted her hand that had been hidden under her black cloak. There it was. A black collar with symbols I did not understand marked along the entire band. As I thought, a collar to suppress my powers. But how good was it? Maybe they'd underestimate my abilities… I could hope, and I was surely going to try.

She came over to me and whispered a spell. I suddenly felt a sharp pain within me.

"I know how your mind works, Heart of Kaeladia. This collar… do you see the blood?"

I looked at her, trying to stay conscious, as she removed the silver collar that had been coated in poison and replaced it with the black one. It was thicker, heavier, and wider, restricting my movements, and I could feel the darkness embedded in it.

"What blood?" I growled as searing pain spread through me from the collar. I looked down, seeing symbols similar to those that covered the collar beginning to spread over my body in what smelled like blood. What was this?

"Blood of your people bound to their Alpha. Now, let us have you washed and bathed for the king," Arabella said as she unlocked the rest of the chains, and I fell to the ground. So, they had thought it all out. I got up onto all fours, coming level to the headless bodies of the children.

"Can I… can I place their heads by their body?" I whispered, trying to hide the pain inside.

"No," she said. Raising her hand, a black flame enveloped the bodies.

"Stop it!" I shouted, about to summon my powers when Arabella snapped her fingers, and the bodies disintegrated. My heart pounded as I let out a cry of frustration. She crouched beside me and caressed my hair.

"I wouldn't use my abilities if I were you. Those runes are tied to your people. Remember, if you try to fight the seal, they pay."

"Meaning?" I asked, feeling my stomach twist with dread. I looked at the charred floor where the bodies once lay, feeling devastated, but it was her next words that chilled me to the core, a dark reminder that I truly was powerless.

"Meaning every time you use your powers, your people will die, from the weakest to the strongest…."

HELPLESSNESS

THEON

$\mathcal{S}$HE PROTECTED US AND let them take her.

She risked herself for us.

Leaving me fucking ruined.

Two days had passed. Hunter and I were at Alpha Romeo's pack. We had snuck in last night, only to find that Raiden, Zarian, and Hunter's men had never arrived. I was fucking sick with worry for Yileyna, Thea, and, some-how, for the rest. Knowing what Theoden was capable of only made things worse. What had they told him? If any of them were smart enough, they would have made sure not to mention me because right then, I was the only one who would be able to get into Westerwell, and I was ready to kill him.

We were having dinner with Alpha Romeo, although all I wanted was to shift and go find Yileyna. Each passing second felt like an hour, and with each moment, a thousand thoughts crossed my mind. I hadn't slept nor rested, and no matter how many times Hunter told me I needed to, I couldn't. I was going insane waiting.

I forced myself to eat, but I couldn't taste anything. The memory of her soft lips and the way she tasted lingered in my mind. I wanted to hold her again, fucking kiss her, and tell her that, yeah, maybe we could be something. I was just too fucking late to even tell her that.

Romeo sighed deeply, pouring us some more wine.

"I never thought the day would come…" he murmured gravely.

Hunter, with a little input from me, had filled him in on everything. He was the strongest of the Alphas who was loyal to Andres and someone who would become a source of power.

"Why were you so loyal to Andres? He was not a great king," I asked after a moment, drinking some of the wine.

"He had his faults, but Andres was not a bad man. He conquered the middle kingdom for the benefit of us all. He was young, and I remember him fighting for not only his pack but others. That is why we supported him. When we were too afraid to fight the Dark Ones, Andres was not. He and Theoden… they were the ones brave enough to venture out, but Andres was a people's person, whilst Theoden… something about him just wasn't right…" His words hung in the air ominously.

Yeah… even I could see Andres was just a fool in some ways, but Theoden was pure evil. The lights from the lanterns flickered as Romeo sighed again.

"My army is yours, but Theoden has the entire territory surrounded."

"I have a plan, don't worry about that, but it will take a little time," Hunter replied with a frown, running his fingers through his beard. I knew he was worried about Charlene. His only reassurance was that he didn't feel any pain, meaning Charlene was safe. I just hoped I could say the same for my little storm.

"I leave at first light. Theoden's gathering is soon. Something big is about to go down, and I need to get there first," I said firmly.

"Theoden may be suspicious that you have strayed from his side. Are you sure venturing in there alone is wise?" Hunter asked quietly. I frowned. My mind was made up. I was going to face him…

He had taught me to hide all emotions, but even then, I wasn't sure I'd be able to fool him, although I would still try.

I held onto the necklace with the small pouch at the end. The pearl of the sea emperor… somehow wearing it gave me strength, and I was healing. My wounds no longer bled, and the area around them was mending.

"It may not be wise, but even if he doesn't trust me, he won't try to get rid of me up front. I'm stronger than he is."

"Theon, it's still a risk," Hunter said firmly. I looked him square in the eye, placing my empty glass down.

"Our women, sister, and our people are in his clutches. After what Thea has been through, I'm fucking going crazy not knowing what's happening. Charlene may be safe, but what is the guarantee that the others are? I'm leaving at dawn, end of discussion."

"I understand that, but if anyone mentioned you were there with them -"

"Then he knows. I don't really care. I'm going to Westerwell. Alone," I said, standing up and storming out of the room.

My heart was conflicted. Despite how much I wanted to simply shift and reach Westerwell, I knew I needed to at least get a little rest before I made the journey. I stared at the moon. The Alpha gathering he had prepared was so close; surely, he was planning something big... but what was it?

Then there was his plan for the Sirens. I didn't like them... but they had protected Yileyna and were trying to change... just like I was...

Everyone deserves a second chance.

Did I deserve a second chance? Could I be selfish enough to dream of a world where she was by my side? No, I didn't.

I rested my arms on the stone wall of Romeo's home and sighed. I didn't... but she was still willing to give me one.

I will save her, even if I die in the process. She will be freed.

I looked to the moon once more, wondering if the gods were simply watching to see how this shit played out; or did they know what was to happen? Well, I would show them. Not only them but everyone. No one fucking messes with Theon Alexander Hale or those whom he cares for and loves.

I pushed myself away from the wall and walked down the side of the house towards our quarters. I once told Yileyna I was Hell, and I stand by it. I would unleash hell upon all those who deserve it, starting with Theoden Hale. I would show him how far this monster he created would go. I would avenge them all; Mom, Thalia, Iyara, Thea, Yileyna, and all our people. He would pay. The day for his fall was coming ever closer... I knew Hunter was planning a smart attack, and I'd let him because my only goal was to kill the king who sat upon a throne that did not belong to him.

Your days are numbered, Theoden...

THEA

It was happening again; the beating, the torture, and the pain. The smell of blood, sweat, and fear filled the air as we lay there, bound in silver.

I didn't know how they had found us. Not all of us were captured, some got away. I hoped they found Theon and Hunter, but I wasn't sure if they made it away alive or if they had been killed.

My father saw me when he came to see who was there, but he didn't even spare me a second glance. That monster cared for only himself.

I wanted to be strong and brave, but the fear that consumed me seeing the barbaric guards terrified me, bringing back memories of everything I had suffered. We had been thrown into tiny cells, and somehow by fate, I was in the same cell as the mate who didn't want me but wanted my brother's woman.

It had killed me, seeing his gaze go to her that night, but maybe it was for the better. I didn't want a man, did I? But then, why was he the one who awoke me from my nightmare with concern in those gorgeous blue eyes of his? He was so handsome that sometimes I was tempted to ask him to give me a chance, but I am Thea Hale, and I beg no one.

I mean, would we even make it out of here alive? I wasn't so sure.

Night had fallen, something that the tiny window in the far cell showed, the only source of light that we had. Silence had fallen over the dungeons. Everyone was quiet or asleep. I could hear a few sobbing silently and a couple of people snoring, somehow able to sleep despite the fear of the unknown looming above us. Charlene was in the same cell as the two of us, and she was fast asleep.

The sound of crickets and the squeaking of rats seemed to be far too loud, and I sighed, rolling onto my other side, flinching when the chains screeched.

"Are you all right?" Raiden, my mate's beautiful, sexy voice came, sending my heart into a frenzy. I nodded, refusing to look at him.

I was sure my nightmares and my panic attacks had already told him how weak I was. It wasn't like he had been harsh to me. Even when we were travelling before the ambush, I often found him looking at me. He may not have directly helped, but he always made sure one of the female warriors asked me if I wanted water or anything to eat.

"Thea?"

"I'm fine," I said quietly, my heart pounding when he moved closer to me. He was shirtless, and I was doing my best not to stare at his sexy body.

I gasped when his hand touched my bare arm. He was warmer than I was, but it was the sparks that rushed through me that made me jerk up, my chains clanging.

"Shit," I muttered as Charlene stirred. She was tied on the opposite side, and even if we wanted, we were not able to reach her, the chains restraining us

"You're shivering," he murmured.

"I'm fine. The last dose of wolfsbane hurt like a bitch," I muttered, making him smirk. Our eyes met, and my heart skipped a beat.

"It's weird…" he sighed.

"Huh?" I asked as he sat against the wall next to me. I wanted to curl into him, not only for the sparks, but for the emotions that he awoke within me, and, of course, for the heat his body offered. "What's weird?"

"Well… you look a lot like your brother, but not entirely… it's just, never mind." He chuckled hoarsely, resting his head against the wall, and stared out of the small window.

"What? Is it weird that you find someone who looks like Theon pretty?" I teased before I realised what I had accidentally said. Raiden didn't find me pretty. Yileyna, the beauty of a Siren, shamed us all… oh, why was I so stupid to have said that?

"Pretty much," Raiden replied, glancing down at me. My heart skipped a beat as our eyes met, and he gave me a small, wry smile. I didn't know what to say as I slowly eased myself up against the wall, making sure not to make too much noise.

"I was kidding," I murmured, wrapping my arms around my knees for warmth.

"I wasn't," he replied quietly.

My heart soared, and with it, my confusion increased tenfold. I didn't understand it, the way the pull of the mate bond wanted me to forget everything and become his. I looked at him. He was handsome. Even with the bruises and cuts that littered his body, he was still incredibly beautiful…

The guards had taken him several times. He came back bloody and bleeding every single time, and although Theoden knew that some of Hunter's people were with us, none of us mentioned Theon. That had been Ryan's idea, something he had suggested on one of the nights when we had almost been caught…

"If we're caught, keep the fact that Zarian is a prince a secret, and do not mention Theon at all, no matter what. Pin it on Hunter because Theoden will know Hunter will have a hand in this, but Theon, he may just be the hidden trump card we may need. Play smart, assholes."

He was an annoying ass himself, but he made a fair point, and that was the story we were sticking with. Although Hunter's men had not been too keen on their Alpha taking the fall, Hunter's Beta had said it might be for the best, and in Hunter's absence, he was in charge.

They had already sent word back to the Iron Claw Pack to go into hiding. Hunter was incredible. He had thought several steps ahead and was smart enough to have planned a secret passage of safety for his pack. My only regret is he didn't get to meet Thalia. She would have loved him. I still missed her…

"I'm sorry." Raiden's voice was quiet as he turned to look at me.

"Sorry?"

"For that night… I didn't mean to hurt you," he explained, his eyes filled with guilt and sadness. "I'm not saying this to get back into your good graces, but I owe you an apology…"

"It's fine. I am just not up to par," I murmured, staring at the cold stone floor.

"It's not that. I have loved Yileyna for a while. Those feelings don't just vanish… You didn't deserve that, and neither did she… what I did hurt her too…"

It hurt knowing he was thinking of Yileyna. He still loved her… and he felt guilty for hurting her… I didn't reply. There was just nothing for me to say.

"If you wish to reject me, Thea, you may, but I'm hoping we can get to know one another." Our eyes met, and I knew what he was asking for. Asking for time to get over Yileyna, and if I would wait.

It was my choice now… life was short… and good men were like a needle in a haystack.

"You may not like me, but I guess we can be friends," I replied nonchalantly as I tossed my hair over my shoulder.

"Sounds good, but I never said I don't like you." He grinned, giving me a sexy wink that made my heart skip a beat.

Did I want him? I was certain if I did, I could win him over. The bond was on my side... but I didn't want to push him. He needed time, and indirectly, it was what he was asking of me.

"Then, as a friend, allow me to hold you. It's cold, and you will fall ill," he said, his face serious as I shivered once more. In the arms of my mate...

"Or do you just need an excuse to get close?" I frowned. "Was that why you were trying to sweet talk me?" He looked surprised and shook his head, his black locks flopping over his forehead sexily.

"No. I honestly had no bad intentions."

"So, you didn't think about feeling me against you?" I narrowed my eyes, glaring at him suspiciously. To my surprise, I heard the slight racing of his heartbeat before he looked away.

"It was not my intention," he said quietly. But he had thought about me in that way... My heart leapt, and although I wouldn't dare show him that, it made me see some hope in this darkness.

"Really?" I asked tauntingly instead, leaning closer.

"Really, really," he replied challengingly.

Our eyes met as we both tried to hide our smiles. Something told me we were going to be okay. Even in those dark, cold cells, we were finding a glimmer of happiness. Perhaps it was fate that placed me in a cell with Raiden...

"Fine then, you can hold me to keep me warm," I declared before I scooted closer, closing the gap between us.

"Understood," he replied, his voice sounding thicker than usual as he slowly placed his arm around me gently, almost as if I might break.

My heart thudded as his strong arms wrapped around me. I shivered, welcoming the warmth and the sparks that rippled through me. He sat there leaning against the wall, pulling me between his legs as he held me in his arms, and I felt safe, as safe as I felt in Theon's arms... but how when he was not someone I knew? Was this the power of the mate bond, or could I follow my intuition? The voice within me told me he could be trusted.

I discreetly took a whiff. His scent was intoxicating. Even with the blood and other smells down here, he smelt divine. Please, Goddess, I don't ask for much, just please let my mate be mine one day...

My gaze went to Charlene, who lay just out of reach, her face pale, her breathing shallow as she lay there shivering so close, yet so far. Raiden had given up his shirt and torn cloak, which were on top of her, but it still wasn't enough. Charlene wasn't well, and none of us knew what was going on… I just prayed we were found soon because I didn't know how much longer she would last down here. Her life was also tied to my brother's, and I needed them both safe.

I didn't want to keep on expecting others to save me, but somehow, I always ended up in such situations…

My Fear & Surrender

YILEYNA

I LOOKED IN THE MIRROR at the gown that I wore, trying to calm the storm that bubbled beneath the surface. It was the following day, and after being given food and allowed to bathe, two Omegas had come to help me get ready. Save for the thick black collar around my neck that was cutting into my skin, I looked like a queen, but it was not the queen I wanted to be.

I was wearing an off-shoulder amber gown that was cinched in from the waist with a jewelled corset and skirts that flowed to the floor with two slits down the sides. My hair was up in a coiled bun and adorned with a gold tiara. My arms and hands were covered with jewellery, and my make-up was dark. Theoden's queen, that was what I had become. I didn't recognise the woman staring back at me.

I wish I had some way to contact Deliana, but Goddess knows where my necklace was. I had tried to reach out to Raiden since he was meant to be in Theoden's hold, but it was clear they were bound in silver or given wolfsbane. I would need to tread carefully.

I was in the Alpha's quarters, in the room that had once belonged to the previous king and queen, and although Theoden didn't come last night, I wasn't so sure that would last forever. I had seen the way his eyes ran over me, and it made me shudder.

The doors opened, and the monster himself stepped inside. He looked me over and gave me a small nod.

"You now look befitting of being my queen... Don't you agree?"

I didn't reply as he came over, my chest heaving with unspoken rage that I was trying to hide. He grabbed hold of my jaw, squeezing it painfully. I could feel the darkness around him that I hadn't noticed or felt last night. It was more than his own evil; this darkness felt like Arabella's. It encased him like an armour.

"You will answer when I ask you a question. Understood?" He hissed.

"Understood," I replied icily. He let go of me, but he didn't get angry as I expected. Instead, he looked at me again.

"You've changed since you escaped. You no longer look like the girl who left from here."

"It's only been several weeks. I am still the girl I was."

No I wasn't, not in mind or body, but I didn't like the way he was looking at me, as if he had not seen me properly before. He let out a sinister chuckle as he stood behind me.

"Lies," he whispered in my ear.

I wanted him away from me, but I was not ready to anger him when he had so much that he could use against me. The image of the two children came to my mind, and I closed my eyes, wondering about their parents. Did they know their children are dead?

"Do you know what day it is today?" Theoden asked, his fingers ghosting down my back. I pulled away and turned to face him, my stomach twisting.

"No, I don't, but I am sure you are about to tell me."

"Today is the day I have announced to the entire city that we will officially unite in matrimony very soon and become the king and queen of this kingdom. The entire city will see that you have consented to this marriage. Isn't that what you wanted? To be queen?"

No, but for some reason you want me to be your queen.

"No, but I have no choice. Tell me, Theoden, why do you want me as your queen when the kingdom is yours?" I asked, trying to remain as calm and respectful as I could. His eyes darkened with fury as they blazed orange.

"You will not question me. Your only duty is to stand by my side, understood?" He hissed, grabbing the back of my hair and yanking me closer. "I said do you understand?"

I flinched, before clenching my jaw, feeling the pull on my powers. The red symbols began spreading from the collar, and I took a calming breath. Was I harming my people? But I was right, there was definitely a reason behind him wanting me as queen.

"I understand," I almost spat.

"Good, then soon we will be married."

With those words he strode to the door. I watched him leave, my heart thumping. I could almost see the darkness around him, just the way it surrounded Arabella…

The door shut with a resounding slam, and I let out a shaky breath. I looked at the windows. They had been barred… Theoden was not going to take any risks…

I didn't expect the wedding to be so soon. Married to Theoden… would he mark me? I thought I'd have time… I needed to think of a plan, fast. I closed my eyes, placing my hand on my forehead as I began pacing the room.

Think, Yileyna, think…

Hours had passed and night had fallen, yet I still had no plan. I had been dragged from my quarters to appear on the balcony of the castle, and I had seen many people gathered below, many of whom I recognised were of the Silver Storm Pack. I had been made to wrap a scarf around my neck to hide the collar that was sealed around it. For obvious reasons, Theoden didn't want to let the people know about it. A ruler is nothing without his subjects. No matter how much power he had, he needed the people on his side. His words replayed in my mind, and I frowned.

"Together, the Heart of Kaeladia and myself will be bonded in matrimony! We will rule this world side by side!"

Not rule the kingdom, but rule the world? Was it a mistake on his part, or did he literally mean that?

"Goddess, what do I do?" I muttered in irritation.

The only thing I could think of was Arabella. She was the one who had created the collar, meaning she was the one I needed to kill first… plus I knew Theoden would be on full alert around me. I could try to kill him, but I had to make sure my plan was fool-proof, otherwise, he would kill many more of my people to punish me. I sighed as I leaned my head against the wall of the bedroom.

I wish I had an answer…

I heard footsteps approach and swiftly moved to the bed and lay down on it, steadying my breathing as I pretended to sleep. The key turned in the lock, and the door opened, but still, I focused on my breathing. It was Theoden and a scent I didn't recognise, along with the delicious taste of roast chicken and potatoes, but even if I was hungry, I continued to pretend to sleep. My chest rose and fell steadily.

"Place the food down. If she awakes, she will eat it," Theoden said coldly. "Leave! And close the door behind you!" Why was he staying?

Despite the fear beginning to gather in my stomach, I continued to breathe steadily. The door shut quietly, and I heard his heavy footsteps approaching. I was ready for his touch, and I didn't react, although I wanted to recoil. His fingers ran down my shoulder slowly, the touch of a man with evil intentions.

"Beautiful, indeed…" he murmured before his hand brushed over my breast.

My eyes snapped open, and I grabbed his wrist, stopping his advancing hand. My hand felt like it was on fire, the darkness biting into me so much I hissed in pain. He smirked coldly.

"Do you think I would be around you without any protection? I know what you are capable of, wench," he growled before shoving me back onto the bed. "I thought you were asleep?"

"I was. But I am not a fool to not sense someone touching me," I hissed. So I was right, there was some sort of protection around him.

"You are mine to do as I please with, and if I say you will spread those legs, you will."

This man was a monster. The hatred within me was bubbling, and I was unable to control my anger as I felt my teeth sharpen.

"You will not touch me," I warned menacingly, trying to reign my powers back. His eyes flashed as he slapped me across the face. That was clearly this bastard's favourite move.

"You will be marrying me, and I will be fucking you, whether you want it or not. You are nothing more than a whore!" Over my dead body.

"Then your men will be ready to die," I hissed. I was unable to control the rising anger, but when he let out a dark chuckle of amusement, I felt uneasy.

"What a disobedient one you are. I like it... keep going. I will bring those who have died because of you losing control to you."

Those words made my anger vanish, replacing it with fear. I could tell he was telling the truth...

Calm yourself, Yileyna.

It was hard. The Siren side within me wanted to lash out and attack. Did I kill someone? I needed to control myself, but it was getting harder.

"Ah, how I wish I kept Andres alive... at least long enough to fuck his daughter in front of him, and then let him watch as I passed you onto my men when I was done." He chuckled darkly, and I had to fight myself not to react.

Breathe...

My people will die...

Calm down...

His words had created a storm of anger within me, and not only was I fighting the urge to unleash hell, but I was trying to reign my emotions in so no one else suffered. I could feel the sharp pain around my neck, almost as if the collar wanted to react.

"Seems like you have learned your lesson. Ah, look, a present for your loss of control. Come in!" Theoden commanded.

The door opened to reveal one of Theoden's men, holding a bundle which he tossed onto the bed. What was it... A chilling thought came to me, and I prayed it was not so.

"Do open it." Theoden laughed raucously.

My heart thundered as I reached over, opening the blanket to see the lifeless body of a baby, but what made my blood run cold was the red engravings that covered his entire skin. Engravings just like the ones on my collar.

"It's one of the Omega's. I heard her screaming that her child had simply died," the man said in a gruff voice.

I did this. Goddess...

"Ah, I see... oh dear, what have you done? And how many more lives will you take because of your anger?" Theoden taunted. "Now, see, the thing is, every time you act selfishly, you will only be killing the innocent. The weakest will go first."

My eyes stung with tears of anguish and pain. I had killed another child.

The door shut behind the man, leaving the lifeless baby on the bed. With shaking hands, I reached over, wanting to fix the odd angle his head sat at, only for Theoden to let out a menacing roar.

"Leave it!" He grabbed the bundle and threw it across the room.

I screamed as I jumped off the bed. In a flash, I was across the room, but I was too slow as it hit the wall and dropped to the floor. I picked the baby up from the floor, cradling the lifeless body to my chest. I was unable to stop the tears that fell down my cheeks.

"I'll do what you want, just stop hurting them! Stop this!" I screamed, pressing my lips to the baby's forehead.

I'm so sorry. What have I done…

"Good. So how about you throw that thing out and strip."

My head snapped up to the monster before me. I looked at the baby in my arms, a child whose life was stolen from them before even having had a chance to live…

I stood up and placed the bundle safely on the dresser. I will somehow try to get you back to your parents. I promise.

"Now undress," Theoden commanded as he began to undo the buttons of his shirt.

Fear enveloped me, and, when I reached for my corset, I realised I was shaking. I was scared, so scared… I looked at him with blurred vision as he advanced toward me.

"Good… now… show me how well you pleased my son in bed."

He was disgusting. I flinched when his hand grabbed my sleeve.

Suddenly, Theoden froze, his head snapping towards the door just as it opened to reveal Arabella. Never had I been happier to see her. She bowed her head, but I could sense her panic as she breathed heavily, a clear sign she had run fast.

"Your son is back, Master."

I fell to my knees. A shuddering whimper left me as Theoden strode to the door.

"Lock her in," he commanded, but I could hear the tension in his voice.

The moment the door slammed shut, I covered my mouth with my hands to muffle the sob of relief that left me.

Theon. Theon was here.

HIS LIES

THEON

THE DOORS TO THE castle were opened for me, and, although I could sense the tension and uncertainty from the guards, it was obvious that despite the fact that they may be suspicious or cautious of me, they were unable to refuse me entry. All eyes were on me as I walked through the courtyard, illuminated by a few dim lanterns.

"The king's son is back!"

"Alpha Theon is here!"

"Alpha, come, I will have a room ready for you immediately," one of the castle servants offered.

"I wish to see my father immediately," I replied coldly.

Despite the calmness I was portraying, I was a mess inside. I wanted to see Yileyna, wanted to make sure she was okay. It was plaguing my mind not to know what she was going through. I had travelled for hours straight, and I made the journey that should have taken much longer in a day. Just the thought of Yileyna was enough to keep pushing me to carry on. My muscles were screaming in exhaustion, but I didn't let it show.

"The Alpha is ready to see you in the throne room," one of Theoden's men said, making me turn my head to him sharply.

"I don't need an appointment to see my own father," I said before pushing past him and heading for the throne room.

I walked through the castle, paying attention to the changes. There was no hustle and bustle around here like there once used to be. Sure, it was night, but there was always someone walking around the castle when Andres was in power. There was no odd cry of a child of one of the families residing here nor the smell of something pleasant from the kitchens. I didn't realise it when Theoden had taken over as much as I did now, as I looked at the world around me with a new outlook, one where the haze of lies had been removed from my eyes.

The Obsidian Shadow Pack insignia had replaced the ones of the Silver Storm, and they glared down at me. A pack I was once proud of… I realised that this would be the end of the Obsidian Shadow Pack. When the war was over, and victory was ours, I would ask Yileyna to accept the people who were innocent into her pack. I couldn't ask Thea and Raiden to head the pack either because Yileyna needed Raiden. There was too much darkness and too many sins tied to the name of the Obsidian Shadow Pack, sins that could not be wiped away or forgotten.

The passageways were lit dimly, and there were far more guards scattered throughout, guards that he had purchased at the expense of our people. That knowledge sent a flare of rage through me. The urge to draw my sword and slay them was tempting, but I held back. I needed to find Yileyna first.

I entered the throne room to find it empty. It had changed, with the banners and colours now of the Obsidian Shadow Pack adorning the entire room. Colours I was once proud of…

This belonged to Yileyna, and I knew she would be the queen that everyone would love when the time came.

"Theon!" His merry voice was a front, and when I turned to see the smile on his face, I noticed it didn't quite reach his eyes, even as he rushed towards me, arms spread. I smiled slightly and closed the gap between us, knowing I was far better at hiding my emotions.

There was a powerful darkness encasing him, almost like a layer. What was that? It felt like Arabella's darkness…

"Dad, I'm finally back," I said as we embraced. The urge to rip his heart out right then overcame me, but I could feel the darkness pushing against me, and I stepped back, trying not to be repulsed or to let my anger show. My stomach twisted as I smelt Yileyna's scent lingering on him.

He had her.

I didn't know how to feel. It meant she was safe, but it also fucking terrified me, not knowing if she was okay.

"That you are, that you are, and in good time! I was wondering where you might be," Theoden exclaimed, striding over to his throne and sitting down. I looked at him emotionlessly, crossing my arms.

"I was tracking the heart, however, she kept on slipping through my grasp. I'm sorry, but these injuries slowed me down." I frowned icily as I glared at the floor. I was getting better but I didn't plan on telling him that.

"Oh, I see. Well, good news! I found her." I nodded.

"I know. I tracked her close to here and had a feeling you succeeded. I'm glad to hear it," I replied smoothly. He ran his fingers through his beard, watching me intently,

"You know we need the heart on our side for the betterment of the future, Theon," Theoden said, lacing his fingers together as he sat on his throne arrogantly.

"Of course."

"Well then, it was a hard decision to make, but I think it's the right one… I am afraid I have decided I will marry her myself."

My heart thundered; thousands of emotions flashed through me as my eyes flickered. I wanted him dead. He watched me keenly, and never had I ever had to try harder to keep control of myself as I lowered my head to him.

"I am truly relieved. I am sorry, Father, I know you wanted me to marry her at one point, but despite wanting to please you, marrying someone who is part Siren… it would have been hard. You are far stronger than I am, mentally and physically." I looked up at him, wanting to rip his head off.

Our eyes met, and I made sure to keep my emotions in check, looking at him with fake approval and relief. His eyes flickered before he let out a small chuckle and sat back, clearly much more at ease.

"Ah, you always understand, and fear not, the poison for the Sirens is prepared. When the time is right, I will release it into the ocean, and we will kill them all. We will get our revenge," he said darkly.

"I can't wait. They deserve all that is coming to them. Tell me, what do you want me to do? I'm back, and I'm ready to assist you, with this plan or anything else. We need to kill them all." He was nodding slowly, looking at me with pride, yet his orange eyes held a manic light as if he was lost in envisioning what the future would hold.

"For now, I want you to tighten security. We will soon have the Alpha gathering, and there… there I will become stronger. You have always been a good son, and when this is over, I will give you land and a pack of your own." So, he would try to keep me far away.

"Thank you, but more than an Alpha position, I just want revenge on all those who have hurt those whom I love. I will find contentment the day they are all slain. Only then will I be at peace," I said murderously, fuelling all the hatred and rage for him into my words. My eyes blazed venomously, and I felt satisfied when he looked a little unnerved.

"Ah, of course, I want only the same. Now, tell me, Theon, have you heard anything of Hunter? Rumours are he is standing against us," he declared, clearly changing the subject.

"Hunter?" I asked sharply.

When I was let into Westerwell, I knew even if he had Thea, Raiden, and the others, it meant he didn't know of my involvement, or they were playing smart. But now, seeing him, I had a feeling he really didn't know what I had been up to, and that was exactly what I wanted. I still wouldn't trust him, and I wasn't so sure he'd trust me entirely, however, I knew I was and always had been just a pawn to use in his game. At least I'd play along, act like I respected him and wanted to serve him when all I fucking wanted was to kill him. Until I found out what that darkness encasing him was, I had to be careful. I couldn't attempt to kill him, only to be thwarted. There had to be a plan in place.

"Yes, Hunter. He was creating a resistance, gathering those loyal to Yileyna De'Lacor. I want him dead, and perhaps you are the person who is best suited to find him." His eyes were on me keenly and I was sure this was another test…

If he was trying to outwit me, then he could carry on trying. I was not a fool.

"I'm afraid Hunter is not someone I will touch. We promised Mom… yet I understand that he is trying to thwart your plans, and if that is the case, then I will not protest if you have someone kill him. I just apologise that I cannot be part of it," I replied quietly. Our eyes met and he nodded slowly.

"I understand. Your love for your mother holds no bounds." He nodded curtly, and I knew he had bought it when he began talking about his plans.

Now all I needed to do was assess the numbers and prepare for a takeover but before that… I needed to see her…

I left the throne room after telling Theoden I would turn in for the night. I was glad my room hadn't been stripped bare, although I knew someone had been in there. If they had been looking for anything, then they had probably been met with disappointment. I was not someone to keep anything materialistic, nothing that could be held against me and nothing personal.

I showered quickly. My chest no longer needed bandaging. Although I was still wounded, they were getting better with the help of the pearl that I knew possessed exceptional powers. Whatever this thing was, it was powerful. I had tried to open the small pouch, but the intensity of the light from it burned, and so I had quickly closed it again. After getting dressed, I had taken a charm to hide my scent before I set out to find her.

It hadn't been as simple as that. I learned she was in the Alpha quarters, but the entrance was guarded and the windows were barred, so I had to wait for the guards to move. However, even when the guards changed shifts, I didn't manage to slip inside. I had gotten to the door, but it was locked. I had heard the guards approaching, chatting quietly, and so I had slipped away before I was caught.

The only other way I could think of was through the window in the guest room that looked out to the courtyard. I wasn't sure if that one was unguarded, as it was a difficult place to get to, but I planned to find out.

It took me a while to sneak past all the guards, and, looking up at the window, the memory of that night returned to me, and my heart thudded. Memories that were so much lighter than the ones surrounding us now.

I climbed up swiftly, knowing I was going to have to pry the window open. To my dismay, it was barred too. Frowning, I glanced down before getting to work swiftly. I began work on loosening the bars with the sharp point of my dagger. One bar almost slipped from my hand, but I caught it just as two guards passed by far below.

"Did you hear that?"

"No, what is it?"

"Never mind."

I closed my eyes, exhaling softly before getting back to work. It took a while, and balancing dangerously on that ledge as I worked wasn't easy. A few times, more guards passed by, and I had to do my fucking best not to make any sound. When I had finally managed to take a few bars off, I pried the window open and squeezed inside, shutting the window behind me and silently made my way out of the room.

Silence filled the main hall, and Theoden's smell was faint, meaning he hadn't come back after our meeting, but there was one scent that was stronger. A scent that made a wave of relief flood me: Yileyna's. My heart was racing as I followed it to the old Alpha's bedroom. I saw the key in the lock and turned it slowly before opening the door, trying to control my raging heart.

There she was, dressed in an extravagant dress. The first thing I noticed was the large black collar that oozed darkness wrapped around her neck as she hugged a bundle to her chest from where she sat on the floor. Her head snapped up to me, and our eyes met. Pain and anguish filled her red eyes, and tears streaked her face. She was in pain.

"Theon," she whispered.

My heart squeezed and white-hot anger raged through me as recognition filled her eyes. She had been so shaken she hadn't even been able to recognise me. I did my best to keep my voice level, but even then I was unable to hide the pain from it.

"Hey, little storm. I'm here."

I Promise You

THEON

She stood up, still clutching the bundle in her arms as I entered and swiftly shut the door behind me. Closing the gap between us, I pulled her into my arms. Our hearts hammered as I held her tightly.

"Theon," she whispered. My hand weaved into her hair. I tugged her head up, pressing my lips to her forehead as I closed my eyes, inhaling her scent. Fuck, she was here... alive...

"Hush, I got you," I murmured.

She clung to me with one hand, the other clutching the bundle that she was treasuring, and I forced myself back to see what she was holding.

"It's a baby," she whispered, fresh tears spilling down her cheeks. There was no heartbeat. My heart sank as a thousand thoughts ran through my mind. "The baby died because I lost control of my powers," she whimpered, staring at the dead baby in her arms.

How could he? I tried to control my emotions as I slowly took the body of the baby from her. She let go reluctantly and I placed him down on the bed. Theoden was beyond fucking messed up. The first rule of war... the children, women, and elderly must not be harmed.

A stifled sob made me turn back to her, and I pulled her into my arms, embracing her tightly. There was nothing to say that would ease her pain and so I just held her, rubbing her back and arms as she clutched my shirt tightly, sobbing to her heart's content into my chest. I placed soft kisses on her shoulders, head, and cheeks, trying to comfort her, wanting to ease the pain that was tormenting her.

I was seething with rage. Every time the collar touched me, it reminded me of its presence. How dare he fucking collar her like she was his belonging! His words from a short while earlier rang in my head,

"I will marry her..."

That's never fucking happening...

"I love you. I love you, Theon," she was whispering. I moved back reluctantly, cupping her face and tilting it up as I looked down at her.

"And I, you, little storm, beyond anything else." I brushed her tears away, kissing her forehead once again.

I did this. I let that monster into this kingdom... that child's death was on my hands.

Her gorgeous eyes pooled with tears as she slowly ran her hands up my chest and cupped my neck, pulling me closer. Our eyes met, and despite the emotions she awoke within me, the pain she was in was fucking killing me.

"What did they do to you?" I asked hoarsely, trying to fight my emotions as I pressed my lips to hers softly.

The tingles of pleasure danced through me, and the emotions that were attached to them were far more than words could ever speak. I was so fucking sorry for everything I had ever done. I made the vow to be here for her, and this time I wouldn't let her be taken from me.

She sobbed as she kissed me back tenderly, her plump soft lips caressing mine in an agonisingly yet beautiful movement. I fucking love you.

I broke away after a few moments, both of us breathing hard despite the slow kiss. Our emotions whirled around us.

"Tell me, little storm," I whispered, wiping a fresh wave of tears from her face. I had not seen her so broken in a while...

"He tried to rape me, Theon."

My heart stilled, shock hitting me hard as I looked at her. I felt numb, and my head began pounding, but I couldn't comprehend anything.

"But Arabella came and said you were back... he stopped before... before..." Her voice broke as she clamped her hands over her mouth to silence her cry of pain. I pulled her back into my arms, hugging her tightly.

"No one is going to fucking touch you again." A promise to myself more than to her. Theoden's death was going to be painful. So fucking painful. I would be the one to rip him apart, inch by fucking inch.

"Yileyna, mark me," I said the words quietly, yet she stiffened, looking up at me in fear as she shook her head.

"No, not when there's a chance I might die. I don't want you to die -" You're not ever fucking dying.

"Hey... look, we need a means of communication, and this will give us the link. It's not like I can mark you with that collar." She didn't buy it, looking at me with hurt in her eyes.

"You wouldn't mark me, though, because you would risk your own life but not let harm come to me," she said, her eyes flashing. Oh, my beautiful little storm. Of course, I wouldn't let any harm come to her. "We may have rejected one another, but that bond will come to life once more if we mark one another."

"Look, we need the mind link," I said, caressing her cheek. It wasn't only the mind link. I also wanted to have that connection to her so I knew if she was ever in pain.

"Theon, if I die -" I placed a finger to her lips, cutting her off.

"You won't die. Our people and your kingdom await. We will make it through, and we will defeat them. Arabella is the one we need to get rid of first. Look, Raiden, Charlene, and the others are here in Westerwell some-where. I will make sure they're safe, and we will work on a plan. You are not alone, and we will come out of this victorious, but you need to mark me, beautiful."

"I dreamed of us marking one another so many times... but none was in this scenario," she whispered, kissing my finger.

"I'm sorry." I wished I could make it better for her. As much as I wanted to fuck her whilst she marked me, it was far too risky. I lifted her collar, feeling the burning darkness from it, and saw it was burning her neck, too. Angry red marks ran along her skin where the collar touched her.

"It's tied to the lives of my pack. It's how the baby died," she said, her eyes full of anguish.

"We are going to get through this," I promised. "The baby's death is not on you. It's on Theoden, and he will fucking pay." I pulled her against me, kissing her jaw. The very urge to rip this collar off her was difficult to contain.

I threaded my hand into her hair. "Mark me. I have to leave before Theoden notices, but with the link, I will be able to know if you're in trouble."

She hesitated as our eyes remained locked before she nodded reluctantly. She tilted her head up, her gaze flickering to my lips. I leaned down and kissed her deeply and passionately. She moaned softly, and the scent of her arousal reached my nose, making me throb. Fuck.

I slipped my tongue into her mouth, deepening the kiss. I pulled her dress up, slipping my hand through the slit and cupping her ass as I pulled her against my hardened dick. She sighed as she pressed herself against me, kissing me back with equal passion. I forced myself away after a few seconds, my eyes blazing as I grabbed her waist and lifted her up, arching my head to the right, allowing her full access to mark me.

Our eyes met, and a thousand emotions rushed through me. I never thought I'd ever let anyone mark me... I never thought the day would come when I'd be full of so many fucking emotions that it would be fucking hard to breathe, but even then, I wouldn't change this.

"Are you sure?" I smiled faintly.

"The entire kingdom wants Yileyna De'Lacor on their arms, but she belongs to me, and I will wear this mark proudly. Maybe when things settle, I'll even flaunt it to let a few jealous men, like a certain Fae, for example, know that you are mine."

"Of course. I've always been yours. I fell in love with you, Theon, from the very start, and nothing changed that," she whispered, caressing my face.

"I couldn't walk away from you even when I wanted to," I replied, combing my fingers through her hair.

"Your eyes look alive again."

"Because they are gazing upon you." She smiled, rolling her eyes despite the faint blush that coated her cheeks.

"Who knew Theon Hale could be so charming?"

"Trust me, even I didn't. However, it's the doing of the pearl."

"I hoped it would work." So she made me wear it for a reason...

She chuckled weakly before we became serious once more. Our eyes met, and she took a deep breath, extracting her canines as she leaned in. My heart thudded as I waited for her fangs to sink into me, and when they did, I closed my eyes, intense sparks rushing through me. I felt the magical pull of the bond strengthen, a bond that we had destroyed. It was strong, and her scent heightened, as seductive as ever, just ten thousand times more. Fuck...

A part of me began to wonder how it would feel if I ever got the chance to mark her too…

Pleasure rushed to my cock as she moaned against my neck. I never fucking wanted her to move. She slowly extracted her teeth and teasingly ran her tongue along my neck, making my breath hitch.

"You're mine." Her voice was seductive and possessive, and when our eyes met, hers were glowing vibrantly.

"Always," I replied with a smirk before claiming her lips once more in an electrifying kiss that made me fucking see stars.

When we broke apart, we were both breathless, her more than me, which satisfied me. She could be the queen, but I was the one who could sweep her off her feet. I kissed her forehead once more before I slowly placed her down.

"I need to leave now. I was wondering what you wanted to do with the pearl?" I asked quietly. She looked down at my chest, frowning slightly.

"The Sirens gave me a necklace so that I could contact them. Theoden or Arabella took it. If you can find it and then go to the coast…."

"Continue," I urged, seeing her hesitate. I was beyond the point of hate. This was all a game orchestrated by the biggest villain of all time, the rest were simple victims of his evil plans. She nodded.

"Call them. Deliana… give her the pearl, and then tell her what is happening. Ask her for help. I'm sure she will assist us, Theon."

"Understood," I said, cupping her face. I kissed her lips once more. "We are going to fucking win this, come whatever."

With those parting words, I left the room with an aim in mind. Theoden's end was near, and it was time to get the ball rolling…

A Precious Surprise

CHARLENE

*I*T WAS LATE WHEN Theoden had entered the cells with a few men, pointing at a few of us and talking through the mind link. I wasn't sure what they were saying. My heart filled with fear as Raiden, Thea, and I were dragged from the cells, bound and blindfolded. Where were they taking us? Gamma Grayson had been taken not long ago, and I was terrified to think where he may be.

The beatings I had seen others go through terrified me, and just the memory of Raiden being tortured again made it hard to breathe. Luckily, Theoden hadn't seen my mark, the high-neck dress I had been wearing had hidden it, and when the guards had seen it afterwards, none cared about it. I was not a threat, but I knew if they even got wind of the fact that I was Hunter's mate, the consequences would be horrifying. Chosen or fated, they would not let me go. It was Hunter's name that was plastered across the resistance, and they hadn't hidden the fact they wanted him dead.

Now more than ever, I needed to be safe because I knew I was with child. I had missed my periods, but the slight nausea I had been feeling was the first sign. Although I had not thought much of it, it all fell into place when I felt the faint butterfly sensation in my stomach. I only wished that this had happened when I was with Hunter. We were going to become parents, yet there I was, terrified, not knowing if my baby would survive or not. The wolfsbane and silver we were being injected with were of a high level, and although I prayed that our baby was okay, I was scared for its safety.

"Where are you taking us?" Thea hissed. She was the only one brave enough to argue with her father, and when I heard the sound of a resounding smack, I knew he had hit her. What a monster he was.

"Thea," Raiden warned. I could hear the anger in his voice. I had seen them become closer over the last few days, and I hoped when things were better that he would accept her.

We were led out into the open, but I couldn't make out where we were being taken. The path was confusing, and I held no sense of direction, far too weak to focus on anything. In my delirious state, I wondered why he was moving us personally. I could sense Arabella's darkness, too, as it surrounded us and made me feel even more nauseous. We continued to walk for Goddess knows how long until I felt we were going downwards. Perhaps it was a slope... I wasn't so sure. I remained silent, not wanting to anger them.

"Get in," someone hissed before I was shoved forward, feeling the temperature drop.

I didn't let a sound escape me, and I shuffled forward until I knocked into someone. Ryan. He nudged me behind him, and although I couldn't see him, I felt safer. I wanted to hide away to protect my baby.

"Let them rot in here. No one will find them," Theoden growled.

When the door slammed shut, I breathed a sigh of relief, paying attention to who was there.

"Why not just kill us now? Dumb fools," Ryan remarked. "We've been through too much shit to die so easily, though." I smiled despite his words. Regardless of what he said, it was nice to hear another familiar voice.

"Dad, Mom?" Raiden's voice called.

"Raiden," Andrea's voice answered.

I felt someone pull the blindfold from my eyes, and my heart skipped a beat when I looked into the eyes of none other than Zoe, once again feeling the guilt of my birth flit through me.

"Thank you," I said softly.

I looked around, trying to see where we were. It was some sort of stone room. We were not in the vicinity of the castle; I could see that from the colour of the stone. Embedded in the stone were odd engravings. There was something wrong with this place. There was darkness here, and the markings that covered the walls gave me an ominous feeling.

Ryan went and rammed his shoulder against the stone entrance. I wasn't the only one who flinched at the sickening crunch of his bones, but it did nothing more than cause him pain. Both Thea and I shook our heads at his antics.

"That sure didn't work," Ryan muttered, making Raiden sigh before turning to his parents.

Andrea let out a sob as she walked over to him. With his arms bound behind him, there was little he could do, save lean his forehead against his mother and tell her he was fine. Both Andrea and Zoe were far too skinny, and I could tell they had seen many trials. They were covered in many scars and bruises that marred their bodies, yet they lived up to the titles of Gamma females, for the fire still burned in their eyes. Gamma Henry was in a worse state, but even he was still smiling.

"Rhys. Where is he?" Andrea whispered.

"Safe," Raiden reassured her gently.

Zoe was kissing Ryan as he kept telling her he was fine. Seeing their happiness made me feel happier; it gave me hope that not all was lost. They had been apart for so long, yet there they were, united once more. I hoped soon I would be reunited with Hunter, too.

"Where is your father?" Zoe whispered. Ryan shook his head and became serious.

"I don't know. When we were ambushed, I think he may have gotten away."

I hoped he was okay. Lately, I considered telling Gamma Grayson the truth, and I promised if I saw him again, I would, but seeing Zoe made me hesitate. I watched Thea observing the Boltons curiously. Her intense stare made Andrea notice her.

"This is…" Raiden smiled slightly as he motioned with his head for Thea to step forward. "Thea."

"Thea Hale," Thea added, not ashamed of her name as Zoe and Andrea tensed, but Gamma Henry sighed heavily.

"And yet he has you imprisoned. You are not one of his, but one of us," he said with a small smile. She smiled back as she stepped up close to Raiden, her cheeks heating up as she poked her eyes out at him. If it wasn't for the bruises on them or the fact that they were collared and cuffed in silver, one would think they were just a young couple, shy and in love.

"What?" Raiden whispered, but we all heard.

"Won't you introduce who I am?" She asked, stressing on the 'who'.

"You want me to?" Raiden asked quietly. I smiled, watching them as Ryan scoffed.

"Seriously, we might die any minute, and you two are taking forever to make one damn announcement? They fell in love, I guess." He shrugged, and I shook my head. That man was so infuriating at times.

"Wrong actually, I mean... we... we're fated mates," Raiden announced proudly, smiling down at her as she smiled, equally proud. Yes, they were going to be okay. Andrea gasped before she congratulated them both and kissed Thea's cheek.

Smiling, I slowly slid down the wall, feeling exhausted as I tried to control my laboured breathing.

"Are you okay?" Ryan asked, looking down at me sharply. I forced a smile and nodded.

"Yes."

"You don't look it," Raiden added, coming over as he crouched down next to me. All eyes were on me, and I felt my heart thud nervously. I didn't like all attention on me...

"I... I might be pregnant," I shared, making Raiden's eyes fly open before concern settled into them.

"Fuck," Ryan added as Thea hurried to my side. Her eyes sparkled.

"I'm going to be an aunt?" She whispered.

"Theon is the father?" Gamma Henry asked shocked.

"No!" I exclaimed, appalled at the very thought. "He is Yileyna's!"

Goddess, how had I ever liked him? Will I have to share that fact with Hunter? Oh, Goddess!

"It's a long story, so how about we all settle down in this stone tomb where we may actually die and let's fill you in shall we?" Ryan suggested. Actually, I think we needed him there because he was that annoying companion that you just couldn't help but love.

It was dark, with no light, yet the company that surrounded me filled my heart with a glimmer of hope and warmth. Hunter, Yileyna and Theon... they will save us.

SOMETHING PURE

CHARLENE

WE TALKED HOURS INTO the night, filling each other in on everything that had happened. Listening to the things Thea had been subjected to at the hands of her father shocked me, and I realised how lucky I was to grow up with a father who sheltered me. Even if I never saw eye-to-eye with my mother, it was still nothing compared to what she had been through.

We all had slowly drifted off, but my sleep was plagued with nightmares of burning bodies, Hunter dying… Yileyna dying, and the world being conquered by evil. The following day, no one came, and we simply sat there; starving, thirsty, and tired. I felt too exhausted to talk much, and the day passed painstakingly slowly. I was unsure when sleep kept pulling me into its folds, and I had come down with a high temperature. I knew they were talking to me, but nothing made much sense anymore…

I awoke with a jolt and sat up, my heart pounding as I scanned the area, trying to figure out why I had awoken when I saw the entrance scrape open. I wasn't the only one to get up, not knowing what was to come. My heart was in my throat as I looked at the tall, hooded figure that stood there. His glowing eyes were something I had never seen before. They were a variety of golds and oranges, so similar to Yileyna's yet so different… it was only

Who is that?

Everyone was tense, wondering what was to come, but when he spoke, he took us all by surprise.

"I never thought I'd say this, but it's good to see you all alive," the deep voice said. My heart skipped a beat.

"Theon!" I exclaimed weakly. He removed his hood and came over to Gamma Henry, breaking his silver collar and cuffs off.

"We need to move fast," he said quietly as he began breaking the chains on everyone with ease, completely barehanded. His aura felt different, too. It was stronger...

My heart thumped as he approached me. Why wasn't Hunter there?

"Are they alright?" I asked softly. His eyes met mine as he broke my collar. His eyes were multi-coloured, just as I had thought I had seen from afar.

"They are," he said, breaking my hands free, and I felt as if a weight had been lifted from me. The pain that the silver was causing vanished.

"Theon, what's going on?" Raiden asked as Thea kissed her brother, hugging him tightly.

"We don't have time, I'll explain on the way. I arrived here yesterday, but it took me a while to find you. Tomorrow is the Alpha Gathering. I still don't know exactly what he's planning, but I have my theories, and if I am correct, then we need to fucking stop him. I will take you all to safety; Grayson and Zarian are not far outside of Westerwell. I'll take you there. I don't think anyone will come for you today..." He scanned the cave.

"Sounds good to me. Why the fuck have your eyes changed?" Ryan asked as everyone was finally free.

"He's marked," Thea said smugly. "Don't you think the eyes look familiar? Almost like Yil..." she trailed off, her heart thudding as she looked at Raiden. I didn't miss the look of sadness in his eyes, but he said nothing, holding his hand out to her.

"Congratulations," he said after a moment, giving Thea a small smile before he turned to Theon. Their eyes met, and tension filled the room.

"Do not hurt my sister," Theon said dangerously to him.

"I won't," Raiden replied, his blue eyes sharp. "Don't hurt our queen."

"I don't need to be told. I won't hurt her." A silence followed before Ryan cleared his throat.

"Wow, the ten-"

"Ryan! Do you need to always comment?" I exclaimed, taking everyone by surprise, and, for once, I rendered him speechless...

We began to head to the exit.

"What is this place anyway?" Thea asked as she looked at the engravings.

"I can't be certain, but those engravings look just like the ones Arabella works with. I think this place belonged to the Dark Ones," Theon replied as he led the way out. A shiver ran down my spine, but I had a feeling he was right...

"Won't they find out we escaped?" Gamma Henry asked as I stepped out to see dusk had fallen.

"No. Theoden is too busy preparing for the event tomorrow. Hunter should be here by nightfall. Tomorrow night when this gathering takes place, we attack," Theon explained.

Hunter....

I knew the upcoming war was scary, but the fact that it was here meant we would lose many... I was to meet Gamma Grayson, and I knew before this war I needed to tell him. As for Hunter, I would have to tell him about our baby, too.

"Theon, Theon," Thea was whispering.

"Hmm?"

"Hunter's going to be a daddy." Theon looked at her sharply, before glancing at me.

"He will be happy," he said simply, and I smiled weakly.

It may not be a direct compliment, but from Theon, it was a great thing to hear. The closest thing to a compliment or a congratulations I would ever get, and it was enough

"Come on, you little pipsqueak. I'm still shocked you shouted at me," Ryan said, taking hold of my arm and slinging it around his neck as he supported my waist.

That's what sisters are for.

The words were on the tip of my tongue, but I held them back. I needed Gamma Grayson's blessing before I told anyone else, and if he did not want me to ever tell Ryan, then I wouldn't.

We managed to leave Westerwell undetected, and sure enough, it was clear the city was preparing for a grand festival or something, but I had a feeling the meaning behind it was going to be a lot darker than that.

Theoden was up to something, and Theon's words echoed in my mind repeatedly as I tried to make sense of them.

I felt my vision darkening, and then I lost consciousness...

I could feel the intense tingles wash through me, and I wondered if I was dreaming. That felt like Hunter's touch... If it was a dream, then I never wanted to wake up. This scent... it was his, too...

My eyes fluttered open, and I realised I was lying on a bed in a cosy room, bathed in a warm glow, but it was the handsome man gazing down at me that made my heart skip a beat.

"Hunter!" I cried, flinging my arms around his neck. He caught me, pulling me into his lap as he hugged me tightly.

"My Luna," he murmured huskily as he began kissing my neck, making my core clench.

"I missed you," I whispered, kissing his lips deeply.

He didn't reply, simply kissing me back hard. We didn't speak for several moments, simply kissing one another like there was no tomorrow. When we finally broke apart, breathing heavily, I buried my nose in his neck. It felt like a dream come true to see him here.

"How long was I out?" I asked softly.

"A few hours; the doctor checked you over, she said you were weak but well."

"I'm glad," I whispered. "Did she say -"

A knock on the door interrupted us, and we turned to see none other than Ailema standing there with a knowing smile on her face.

"Ah, I see I'm just on time to check on my patient," she stated.

"You're a doctor, too?" I asked surprised.

"I am many things," she replied secretively, her eyes sparkling. "I am uncertain if you know, but you are -"

"I know," I interrupted, giving her an apologetic smile as Hunter frowned, looking between us both sharply.

I guess no one had told him anything. My thoughts were confirmed when Thea appeared at the door. She had showered and her hair was in a ponytail. Despite the fading marks of the collars, she looked much better.

"Go on," she urged as Ryan and Raiden appeared behind her. I turned to look at Hunter, who was looking between us.

"So, what am I missing?" He asked.

"Give them some privacy. Come now," Ailema said as I turned to Hunter, hearing Thea's protest.

"You are going to have to make sure you come back to me safe and sound because it's not only my life that is now tied to yours... so is our pup's," I said, gently placing his hand on my stomach. His eyes widened slightly, his heart racing before he looked down at my stomach. My stomach was a mess of nerves, my heart thundering as I watched his reaction.

"I put a pup in you..." he murmured. I smiled at his shock before a smirk crossed his lips, and he tugged me closer, kissing me hard.

I will definitely return to you both because I have so much to live for...

Yes, yes, we do.

I heard the door shut, but I didn't care, allowing my Alpha to pin me to the bed. He kissed me as if it was the first and last time.

An hour later, although I had wanted Hunter to make love to me, he refused, saying I was far too weak yet. I guess I was...

I had showered before going outside to see exactly where we were. We were far enough from Westerwell not to be discovered. The trees were an excellent cover for us, and magic was masking where our armies were gathering. To my happiness, Madelia and several other mages and Fae were willing to help us, some of whom had fled when Dad had died. Men were readying for war; Fae, Mages, and Werewolves all united.

Thea told me that the warriors had been working on the battle plans, and Theon had said he and Yileyna would lead the resistance from within. The plan was to trap Theoden in the middle and kill him, but Theon's first aim was Arabella. He had left earlier, not being able to be away from the castle for long, but Thea was still part of his pack. Even if her father had sold her, she had never been initiated into the pack of her abusers. She would keep him filled in, being the link between him and us.

I was mustering the courage to speak to Gamma Grayson, and when I saw him walk away from the crowds, I looked at Hunter, who gave me a nod. I didn't need to give him an explanation for him to understand. I just hoped Gamma Grayson wouldn't shun me…

"Gamma," I called when I caught up.

"Princess, you need to be careful, what with the good news," he said, and I smiled.

"I will be careful," I promised, fidgeting with the hem of the tunic I had been given to wear. "There is something I wanted to share with you, Gamma Grayson… if I offend you in any way, please don't hesitate to admonish me."

"Speak your mind, you need not hesitate," he encouraged, looking at me with concern.

"I will understand if you don't want me to ever repeat this again, but with the war looming above our heads, I wanted to tell you… King Andres was not my biological father," I whispered, looking at him with fear in my eyes. Did he understand?

My heart thundered as he stared at me. His expression betrayed nothing, and those few seconds felt like years. I didn't speak, waiting for him to make an excuse to leave, but he didn't. He stepped closer, cupping my face.

"You're mine," he said quietly. Tears stung my eyes.

"I know the way mother tricked you was wrong… she admitted to using magic, but she was your fated mate. She spelled Dad because she wanted to be Luna…" I mumbled.

"None of those things matter," he said before he welcomed me into his embrace. "I always held a special spot for you when you were a child, yet I thought it was because you were my Alpha's daughter, not knowing it is because you are mine." I closed my eyes in relief as I hugged him back.

"So, that was some interesting shit."

I froze when Ryan's voice came. I pulled away quickly, only to realise he wasn't alone. Zoe was standing right beside him. No, I wasn't meant to ruin this. My heart was thumping as Zoe came towards me, and where I was ready for her wrath, she simply took my hands, smiling softly.

"Grayson told me of what occurred between himself and Soleil, and when you told him just now that she used magic against him… I understood how lucky I am to have him in my life. If she had claimed him as her mate, I would not have found such a perfect husband. I will never forgive Soleil, but Grayson's daughter is my own." Her words made me overwhelmed, and I couldn't stop the tears that fell from my eyes as I hugged her tightly.

"I'm so sorry for all the pain this may have caused you."

"Do not apologise for something you had no say in. The goddess bestowed you in Soleil's womb, but if you were mine -"

"Then you wouldn't be so pale, and you sure as heck wouldn't be ginger," Ryan added. Both Zoe and I turned to look at him, before looking at one another.

Then, we all burst into laughter.

"This boy is a fool," Zoe scolded, smacking her son lightly over the head.

"I agree, and the queen made him Gamma," Gamma Grayson chuckled, pulling Zoe into his arms and planting a tender kiss on her forehead. I smiled as Ryan simply smirked at me.

"Even if we are siblings, you don't get to tell me what to do," he stated.

"We shall see," I replied, smiling sweetly, making the elders smile. Suddenly, I felt like I had a perfect, beautiful family once again, but this time, it just felt so much purer.

Thank you, Goddess.

The Final Sunset

YILEYNA

THE DAY OF THE gathering had come, and I was lucky that I hadn't seen Theoden again. The memory of what almost happened still placed a sliver of fear within me. What could have happened if Theon didn't arrive?

A guard would come to give me food a few times and had taken the baby. Although I had asked if he would return the baby to the parents, I wasn't sure he would, as he had simply slammed the door behind him.

Theon had slipped inside yesterday, leaving a dagger and a few charms with me, telling me that today was the day of the attack. Theoden was planning something tonight. I had to stay alert. As for the necklace given to me by Lavine, he had said he had a good idea where it might be, and if he didn't manage to find it, then he would go to the coast and try to contact someone by other means. I was certain the Sirens would be on alert, waiting.

I was pacing the room, feeling suffocated and useless, when suddenly the door opened, and Arabella entered, along with two Omegas who were holding bundles of items and what looked to be an extravagant gown.

"Alpha King Theoden sends a wedding dress for his bride," she declared, motioning for the omegas to step forward. Her words sent a sliver of hatred through me, but I kept my face passive. I had no interest in seeing it at all. "You should take a look because you will wear it soon," she announced emotionlessly. Soon?

"Care to elaborate?" I asked coldly, observing her intently.

"Tonight, when the Alpha King takes the hearts of the Alphas and paints the streets of Westerwell in crimson, becoming the supreme Alpha of Alphas, he will marry and mark you."

Tonight.

But more than that word, it was the rest of her sentence that struck me hard. Was he planning to kill the Alphas so he could take over their packs? What else could she mean by 'takes the hearts of the Alphas'? How would that even work? One man alone could not rule the entire kingdom. Nobles of ranked houses and Alphas were needed for each region to maintain peace.

If Theoden was thinking he would kill the Alphas and claim their packs... this was something he couldn't do unless it was a challenged duel or if he was planning to force their hand and make them hand it over. Either way, it would be horrifying and a total massacre, for although many respected their sovereign, Alphas were born to be possessive and dominant of their packs. Besides, from what I learned, not everyone trusted or liked Theoden.

I felt sick at the very thought of his plans, but in all of this, I at least had a means to talk to Theon, something that had helped so much, knowing he wasn't far, and every half an hour, he would check in on me... even through the night. Sometimes when I stirred or could not sleep, he would be there for me, making sure I was fine. In a way, I felt he was near, and I was beginning to await the day when he would mark me. There was a time that I did not think Theon and I could ever be, but why else was fate forcing us together time and time again? No matter what or where life took us, we were still drawn to one another, and above all, I had marked him. I made him mine, and he would surely make me his. We were meant to be one.

"Get her ready," Arabella commanded icily as she stood to the side, watching me sharply. I stared at the beautiful dress that brought me no joy. A marriage to my lover's father? The very thought of the man made my skin crawl.

Theon? I wondered if he was within range.

Hey, beautiful. My heart skipped a beat, and I couldn't deny that hearing his voice in my head was a pleasant sensation.

Arabella just told me that the wedding is tonight, I said quietly.

Silence. I wish he was here so I could see his expression.

Play along, and keep the dagger close. We attack tonight. His words made my stomach flutter with nerves. He didn't say anything about the marriage...

Okay, I replied softly.

He will not marry you, little storm, I won't fucking allow it. Ever. Wait for me, and we will take back your kingdom together. I smiled softly. I looked in the mirror as the Omega began working on my hair.

I will always wait for you.

I remember the moments in the cabin from long ago when I would wait for him. Will we ever have that again?

I look forward to it. I do have some good news; I found the necklace, and I plan to go down to the coast as soon as I can. I will be back in time.

Theon, I think your assumption was correct; he wants to be the ultimate Alpha.

I'm not surprised. We will make it on time. I promise you.

I have faith in you.

Arabella approached, her heels echoing on the hard floors.

"Why are you smiling?" She asked me, crouching down as she stared into my eyes.

"I just... never realised becoming queen would be so easy. The king himself chose me."

"You do not love the king," she declared, sounding almost bitter. I looked her in the eyes, keeping my emotions in check as I observed her intently.

"But you do," I murmured quietly. Lately, I realised despite her emotionless exterior, she was displaying slivers of emotions, especially around me.

"He is my master, nothing more. Do not disrespect him," she hissed, her eyes flashing as her dark energy filled the room.

"You are bound to him, correct? By fulfilling the conditions, you are entirely at his will," I replied, picking up the jewelled earrings from the velvet case that the Omega had placed down.

"Even without it, I would serve him." She stood up, turning away as she pulled her aura in.

"Hmm. Of course, I wonder if he just didn't trust you?" I mused. "Why else did he make sure you were entirely under his control?" She turned, her eyes filled with rage, making the Omegas flinch and move away.

"It gave him power, too! He trusts me, it was not because he didn't want me to go against him!" She hissed, grabbing hold of my arm. I clenched my jaw, feeling her touch burn me. I pulled free and stood up.

"Watch yourself! I am positive the king would not be happy if he saw his bride with burns. Especially with the entire kingdom here to witness this wedding," I growled.

"You will heal," she said, dangerously clenching her hands. I raised an eyebrow.

"With the silver in my system, I doubt I will heal so fast. Now, leave me be. I need to prepare for my wedding." I smiled mockingly, knowing she was somewhat jealous.

In truth, I pitied her. She had been taken as a child, and she was born with evil within her. Theon had done some research, and although he didn't find much, in some old archives, Andres had left some diary entries about killing the Dark Ones. A dagger through the forehead was the only way, for they had no real hearts. He also said they thrived on darkness and discord. So, the closer she was around someone like Theoden, the better and stronger she'd feel in comparison to if she was in the same room as me.

"She will be weaker around you than me because you don't have darkness in you."

Theon's words played in my mind, and I realised why my smile had angered her; I was happy, and that weakened her. I tried not to think of the worries or the fight ahead, and focused on the good in my life: Theon, Charlene, her happiness, everyone I loved. My people. The future I wanted for us all.

Even when the veil was arranged in such a manner to hide my collar, I didn't let it dull my positivity.

"You are ready, My Queen," the Omega whispered, lifting the veil from my face. I looked at her. She was one of my pack members. I smiled at her, seeing the fear in her eyes.

Fear not, all hope is not lost.

I turned to the mirror and gazed at my reflection. This colour wasn't for me… the only warm colour that looked good on me was Theon. Oh, how I yearned for the moment I could take his hand and be free. The day I could tangle my fingers into his dark coppery locks and feel his lips on mine…

"Remain ready. When the time comes to call you, I will come to get you myself," Arabella said before motioning for the omegas to leave before her.

Once they left and the key scraped in the lock, I waited for a few moments before I went to my hiding spot. I took out the charms Theon had given me and slipped them down the side of my dress. Then, sliding my skirts up, I slipped on some pants; I would rip the skirts off when the time came. Strapping my dagger to my thigh, I realised it wouldn't be the fastest place to access, but I had no other choice.

Theon?

No reply, which meant he was out of range, perhaps down by the coast. So now I must wait. I hoped everything went well.

A few hours had passed, and I was still in my room, simply waiting and feeling restless.

Yileyna? I tilted my head as Raiden's voice came into my head. Theon had found them, and a few of them were in hiding within the city.

Raiden.

We will be here, keeping an eye, don't worry about anything. We are going to win this... as for your request, it has been passed on. My heart skipped a beat and I smiled softly.

Thank you. I appreciate it.

I want to tell you one more thing...

Of course.

You were right. Thea is incredible, and once this is over, I will be asking her to marry me. My heart leapt with joy as I fought my emotions of happiness. He had felt he needed to tell me, and I hoped this was the beginning of his true happiness.

I'm so happy for the both of you. She will make the perfect mate and Beta female.

That she will; she is brave, strong, and beautiful.

She is. Congratulations to you both.

Thank you.

We ended the link, and I turned to the barred window.

Let's see what you have planned, for I will be looking forward to seeing the look of defeat upon your face when we overthrow you. Every action has consequences, Theoden, and the time has come for you to pay for every crime that you have ever committed.

I gazed at the setting sun, the colours bathing the room in hues of blood red and deep simmering oranges. The sun must always set, and today, not only will it set on a day gone by, but upon the reign of a tyrant king. For tomorrow before sunrise, I will be queen.

ANOTHER STEP CLOSER

THEON

"THEON... ARE YOU CONTENT with what I am doing?" Theoden asked as he patted my shoulder.

I had just talked to Yileyna through the link and was planning on leaving soon. Most of yesterday had passed looking for the necklace and to see if I could find anything on the Dark Ones. Theoden was far too busy to do much, and he kept giving me jobs away from the castle, not that I minded since I needed an excuse to leave at times.

"Of course," I replied.

I was wearing a high-neck top to cover my mark, and it was taking me immense restraint to keep my powers in check, powers that had strengthened since she marked me, the mark upon my neck which I did not deserve. I was lucky that I trained for years to gain self-control and pull back my aura.

"Then trust in me. No matter what happens, remember your father is only doing what the gods would approve of. It is time for all those who have hurt us to pay, the beginning of the end for the Sirens will happen, as I promised!"

"I can't wait," I replied coldly. He nodded as he gazed out of the window, watching the Alphas of the kingdom pour into the courtyards far below.

"They come as if they have never turned against me... bearing gifts and offerings. Tell me, Theon, do we accept them?"

Yes, because everyone deserves a chance, but I know the answer a monster like you wants.

"I don't think they deserve our forgiveness," I replied icily, fuelling hatred into my voice. He chuckled as he slapped my back. I clenched my teeth, feigning a flinch of pain.

"Ah, I forgot you are not well," he said with a glimmer of something in his eyes. I couldn't read it… but I was sure he would happily kill me now that my part in this was done.

"I'll be okay… it's just not healing," I lied, frowning. Although the pain remained, the wounds were healing far better than Theoden knew.

The Alphas were pouring in, a mix of expressions on their faces; some intrigued, others excited, and many were on edge, unknowing of what was to come, yet unable to refuse the calling of their king. Who could blame them? Only the foolish would think there was nothing more to this than the king's invitation to get to know his subjects. This was a planned takeover on Theoden's part and one we needed to put a stop to. Theoden's plans were sickening.

I left when he dismissed me. Blending in with the shadows, I cloaked myself and left the castle through a rather deserted narrow servant entrance, making my way towards the outer wall of the city. I paused when I heard two men walk by, dragging some crates, dressed in armour bearing the crest of the Obsidian Shadow Pack. They were clearly my father's men. What was in those crates? I was questioning everything, on edge, and I wouldn't rest until Theoden was dead.

Once I had passed the wall of the city, I first made my way to the camp where Romeo's and Hunter's armies had arrived, as well as Zarian's Fae army, their assistance in return for crops and food. I was shocked that such a large number had gotten passed the border without Theoden finding out. It was thanks to a few packs Hunter knew they were able to enter with ease. I understood now why Mom always said that he would be there for us. He was powerful and not blinded by greed or lies…

They had kept their presence masked with mages standing at every corner of the forest, blanketing us in an illusion. Everyone was already ready, or almost ready, decked up in armour and sharpening their weapons. I had just gone to one of the tents to put on my armour, not wanting to be away from the city for long, considering Yileyna may need me, although Raiden, Ryan, and Thea were already in Westerwell, posing as Omegas.

We were lucky that Theoden hadn't bothered to check on them. He had placed them in that cave that had been difficult to access to make sure I didn't find Thea. I was certain of it. And with Yileyna being injected with silver, they didn't realise she would still be able to mind link her people. Fools for underestimating one of the most powerful beings on the planet.

I looked at the armour Hunter had just presented me, not knowing what to think. It was made of dark silver and black with a crest that almost mirrored the mark upon my neck – a mark that stood for Yileyna. A full moon with a howling wolf, the sea, and a crown circling it. It was beautiful. However, it was the insignia on the shoulder pad that caught my attention. Supreme Commander of the armies. The mark of the Champion.

They wanted me to lead…

"So, what do you think of it?" He was smirking. He was proud of the armour he had prepared for me.

"Why does it hold the crest of the Champion? I don't deserve to lead." He sighed as he patted my shoulder.

"The queen commanded it. She chose you to be her Champion," he said seriously before that smirk returned. "I'm sure you are a lot more than just her Champion, but…" He cleared his throat and I cast him a cold glare.

"Focus on your unborn pup and woman," I remarked.

"Ah, your sister-in-law?" I narrowed my eyes but said nothing as I looked at the black cloak that also held the silver symbol. Her Champion. After everything… why me? "You will not fail her, nor any of us. You have come a long way, Theon. The only thing left is for you to forgive yourself. Tomorrow is a new day, a new start, and a new dawn. So why not let your past remain behind?" He asked seriously. "Carry your sword in the name of your people and your queen. Let's move on from our past." I sighed as I ran my fingers across the armour.

"You know… if I were in your place, I would have let the bitterness of the fact she abandoned me get the better of me," I said quietly.

I didn't know if tomorrow we would see one another again, if we would survive the war… but I needed to tell him. Our eyes met, and although he tried to hide his pain, he was failing.

"I wouldn't have done what you did. I wouldn't have been able to love her for leaving me when I was a child. You deserved better, Hunter, far better, but I do want to tell you… although we will never learn of exactly what went through her mind, I can at least say that she always cried whilst penning those letters…" He knew who I meant; I didn't need to clarify it. "She was not complete without you, and there were countless days that her mind was elsewhere. Thea often asked her who her favourite child was, and she would say all of us. Thalia would be adamant it must be me, but I already knew that position was taken."

Fuck, it was hard putting this into words. It brought back memories of her anguish and pain. It fucking hurt. Looking back, I was sure Theoden had kept her from Hunter, probably even blackmailed her… was she ever really happy?

"Thank you for telling me that," he said quietly, turning his back on me, and I knew he was trying to hide the tears in his eyes. I smiled slightly. He had deserved better. He deserved his happily ever after more than I did…

I wouldn't be able to tell him that I'd be there, watching his back. He had a child on the way, and no child deserved to grow up without the love of their father, so I'd be there to make sure he made it back alive. I had once orphaned a young girl, tore her world apart and broke her. Now… now I will try my best to make sure no more children are orphaned because of me.

"Hunter. If anything happens to me, be there for her," I said quietly, my voice thick as I was unable to hide the pain from it. He turned to me sharply, his eyes blazing. "Please."

"Theon. For her, you are going to fucking survive. She's been through too much for you to even think -"

A commotion outside made us turn, and although he wanted to say much more, he didn't, as I knew someone had mind-linked him. We both ran out.

"Alpha! Commander! There are Nagas outside asking for an audience!" The warrior who had come running exclaimed, his face pale. I exchanged looks with Hunter.

"Let them in," we said at the same time, exchanging a look as many of the men looked between us hesitantly.

"There are at least 500 Nagas…" one of the men said, getting clarification from the scouts.

"Let them in," Hunter commanded.

The men simply nodded, despite the tension and fear that had fallen over them all. Even Romeo looked worried. It wasn't long before three Nagas entered, their upper bodies clad in armour. The one in the middle held a scroll out to me. He was powerful, and he reminded me a little of the third prince, but far younger. Perhaps his son... I wasn't sure.

"I am Prince Darshian of Naran. Our Emperor sends his assistance to the Queen of Astalion," he hissed, his green eyes fixed on me as I opened the letter. I skimmed through it and passed it to Hunter.

This was her true power. To earn alliances and victory with compassion and love, not with fear or weapons. My beautiful storm truly was incredible. I still remember her sneaking off to the coast or the White Dove... I almost smiled at the memory but kept my face smooth.

"Welcome, and thank you. The queen will be truly grateful. Would you like food from your journey? And may I ask how you crossed the border?" Hunter asked with a smirk. The Naga grinned, his sharp eyes on Hunter.

"As a matter of fact, it was your pack that saw this letter and granted us entry."

"Alpha." I turned to see the young boy who stepped forward, seemingly having accompanied the Naga.

"Kasien?" Hunter asked frowning.

"The Obsidian Pack was sent to attack us, and although we all went into hiding, the Naga pack killed the attackers." He smiled at the Naga. It was strange to see but I was glad they were safe.

"I see... I am glad. Thank you." Hunter lowered his head to the Naga.

Setting aside differences for the greater good... it was high time I set aside mine...

I had put my armour on before I left the camp, telling Hunter I would meet them at the gates. I looked at the amulet that the Sirens had given Yileyna, not knowing how it worked, but as I stood on the coast, the water washing over my boots, I held it up to my lips.

"I am here with the pearl of the emperor, on command of Queen Yileyna."
Nothing.

"Can anyone hear me?" I looked at it and frowned.

There was no such thing as a speaking device...

This was fucking dumb. I crouched down, tilting my head thoughtfully before I lowered the amulet into the water. A soft light spread from it before the water began rippling. I let go of it, stepping back. Suddenly the water began swirling, and a powerful surge made me step back before three Sirens appeared, two I recognised: Deliana, the blonde who looked a lot like Yileyna, the redhead who I had injured on the Siren Killer, and the third looked older, but she held power.

I removed the chain containing the pearl from around my neck and held it out to Deliana as per Yileyna's request.

"Yileyna wanted me to return this to you. As promised, she has fulfilled this condition," I said, waiting for her to take it. It was hard being in her presence. The memory of her killing Mom and Thalia returned. She took it slowly and I turned my back to her. "Theoden, the current king, will try to poison the oceans tonight or before dawn. Although we plan to stop him, place your own measures in place," I said coldly.

"Where is Yileyna?" She asked sharply, ignoring my comment. I swallowed, trying to calm my emotions.

"He bears her mark," the elder siren murmured.

"So handsome, obviously she couldn't resist," the redhead added. Had she fucking forgotten I almost killed her?

"So you are hers... Theon," Deliana said, making me tense. "Look at me, child."

I clenched my jaw, trying to fight my pain and anger as I turned to her. The water swirled around her tail, lifting her up and bringing her closer to me. She knew who I was. I could see it in her eyes, the guilt and the shock. She recognised me, and she knew I recognised her.

"You accepted her despite the fact you knew she was my daughter..." Her eyes were softer than I had ever seen Sirens' eyes, aside from Yileyna's.

"She is not like you," I replied emotionlessly. She nodded. Her eyes seemed to sparkle with tears, and as much as I wanted to think Sirens didn't cry, I could feel her pain.

"No, she isn't, for I let my anger and hatred get the better of me."

Like me.

"I am sorry. I know it will never bring your family back... but I am truly sorry that the vengeance I felt towards Andres got the better of me. I was angry at all Alphas for the sins of one."

Just like me... I hated Andres, yet I took it out on Yileyna. What difference was there between the two of us? None.

"It is in the past. Let's leave it there." I said quietly, and I meant it. She smiled faintly and nodded. "Yileyna is currently held captive, but we plan to take back the kingdom tonight. She wondered if the emperor would grant his assistance?" I asked.

"With this pearl returned? Oh, he certainly would," the elder siren replied with complete confidence.

"Oh, Lavina, we don't need Father. Yileyna is heir to the Aethirian Ocean itself," the redhead declared. "I will go on land right now."

"Father will want to know... he will grant us more power. A werewolf was able to bear the pearl, that in itself would impress him. Perhaps it's her marking him."

I didn't care to tell her I had the pearl before she marked me. It was none of their concern, nor did I care about their conversation between themselves.

"How long will it take?" I asked.

"Oh, not long. This pearl will be enough to bring him here... I will ask to be permitted to walk on land once more. We will come and assist you, fear not. Within the hour, the Imperials will walk on land for our princess," Deliana said confidently. "We will await your command once we are upon land."

"I will see you at the wall of Westerwell," I said, about to walk away when Lavina, the elder siren, spoke.

"Wait... you are injured..."

"I'm fine," I growled, hating how she had even found out.

"When the pearl returns to the sea emperor's trident, it will heal you," Lavina said quietly.

"I'm sure Father will grant our Yileyna that wish. She wouldn't want her plaything injured," the redhead chipped in.

"I don't need it," I replied icily. Not waiting for a reply, I walked off.

Theoden may control a Dark One and may have rallied most packs underneath him, yet the true queen had not only a few powerful werewolf packs but Fae, Naga, and Sirens behind her.

The throne was hers for the taking.

The Start of a Dark Night

YILEYNA

THE LAUGHTER AND THE music felt distant. The largest courtyard was transformed beautifully, decorated with lanterns, flowers, and vines. They ran across the tables, the pillars, and the furniture. Two thrones sat upon a dais, where Theoden and I now sat. I still wore my veil to disguise the collar. The moment for our wedding to take place was coming ever closer…

The long tables were full of meat and wine, although I could tell that not everyone was enjoying themselves. What had started off with the Alphas offering their gifts to Theoden with fear and uncertainty was now a place of false merriment. A few looked at me guiltily for betraying me for their own well-being and safety, but most were far too cowardly to care. Yet I was proud to see that many were not impressed with Theoden.

With each passing moment, I could feel the darkness becoming far more potent. I could sense it in the air, feeding on the Alphas' restlessness and the fear that they were trying to hide. They were far drunker than they should have been, yet many didn't seem to even notice as they ate and chattered, making jokes or discussing their achievements. I could tell which were good and which were full of greed.

Only a few ate little and politely joined in on the conversations taking place, very aware, like myself, of the extreme level of guards all around.

Those who had brought their own men had been forced to leave them in the warriors' hall, where they would drink and dine with the other warriors of the Obsidian Shadow Pack, an excuse to separate them. The few alphas who had refused to enter the gathering without their warriors had been denied entry, but I feared for their safety.

It was a shame that neither Raiden nor Ryan had been able to get in here. However, they had accessed the warriors' hall and said, like the Alphas, they were all extremely drunk.

I had heard Theoden ask for a list of Alphas who hadn't shown up, and I knew he was seething. Although I hadn't heard the orders, his expressions and the look on the face of his men who he commanded gave me enough of an idea. He would punish those who did not come.

I was glad the family of the Alphas who had come were not here in the courtyard, fearing for their safety. If Theoden wanted to blackmail these Alphas... he would target their families.

Only Theoden and I had not touched the food. Even when Theoden had announced our marriage would take place tonight under the moonlight, I had only pretended to drink, letting the liquid spill down the side of my face and neck. With my veil, no one could tell, and I was not going to be so foolish as to drink anything he offered me.

"Now that we are all fed and full, may I have your attention?" Theoden commanded suddenly. The chatter died down as everyone looked at us. "Tonight is a very important night. Tonight, not only will I take the Heart of Kaeladia as mine, but I will also become the king of kings, the one that will hold the most power in the entire world, and you, you will all help me."

His words held power and greed. The dark manic glint in his eyes said enough, and although most Alphas were too delirious to focus, some looked unnerved. He turned to me and took hold of my hand, gripping it painfully tight.

"You will do everything that I say," he commanded darkly, "or your entire pack dies."

"Understood," I said coldly as Theoden stood up and Arabella motioned for me to stand.

"Everyone present will hand over their title to me, forfeiting their position as Alpha to their pack!" Theoden's voice rang in the air. Several Alphas jumped to their feet.

"What is the meaning of this?" One Alpha roared, his eyes blazing blue.

Theoden's eyes flashed, and the next thing I saw was the spray of blood as he was decapitated where he stood. A few shocked curses or gasps filled the air. My own heart was thundering. These were my people. I had to wait for the signal, but I knew there was about to be a blood bath here.

"Who else will defy me?"

"We all do respect our Alpha King, but please spare us," another Alpha said, bending his knee to Theoden, despite the fact that I could see how hard it was for him. He was an Alpha-blooded wolf; bowing to others was not easy.

"Hand it over or die," Theoden challenged.

"Then I would rather die," the man replied quietly.

"Your wish is my command. However, although I know you did not bring your family here, we made sure they came." Theoden chuckled as if he was stating the weather. The Alpha's face filled with fear as Theoden snapped his fingers, and two men brought in a young man who looked around seventeen or eighteen and a girl about eight. I looked at the Alpha who had spoken and shook my head slowly, trying to warn him. His gaze flickered to me, and I stood up, not wanting those children to suffer.

"Hand him the title," I commanded softly.

"No need to plead, My Queen," Theoden hissed, grabbing my arm in a death grip and pulling me back.

The man hesitated, yet, looking at his children, he was faltering. The boy had his chin up, defiant and hiding his fear, yet the girl was shaking, and silent tears were falling down her face. Theoden must have had their packs watched. He didn't have enough manpower to have an entire squad watching those packs, but as king, he held power, and with the Alphas not there, there was nothing the men of the packs could have done, even if a small group came in and took the Alpha's families. This man was sick.

"Very well. I will hand over my title." The Alpha lowered his head, then his son turned sharply.

"No, Father! Do not bow down to a monster! I knew he never should have -"

"Stop!" I shouted, but it was futile as Arabella yanked me back. Theoden was before him in a flash, yet before he could even kill him, the Alpha stepped in front of his son and Theoden's hand went right through him, ripping out his heart.

"You're next," Theoden growled as he attacked the boy.

I couldn't wait any longer.

Theon. Now! We cannot waste time! I shouted through the link, hoping he would hear me.

Understood. A single world that held power, comfort, and strength.

I ripped my veil off and pulled a charm from my top. Whispering the release incantation, I tossed it in the air. A thick mist fell upon the entire area and Theoden roared in rage.

"We shall take back what is ours. We will not bend to a monster," I shouted clearly, letting power ooze into my voice and letting my words travel to my own pack members too. I know most of the Alpha's were weakened, but if they had any will, they would still fight.

"You wench!" Theoden growled as I ripped off the skirt of my so-called wedding dress.

"It's high time I showed you who I am," I growled, stepping out of the layers.

I couldn't use my powers, but I didn't need them for now. I just needed to buy us some time...

"Your powers are sealed, you can do nothing," Arabella hissed as she lunged at me. The darkness that surrounded her made it easier for me to pinpoint her.

Commotion ensued as many Alphas started shouting about why they couldn't link their soldiers. The food must have contained silver. How had they not noticed it? Because they were already drunk.

I spun, aiming a kick at Arabella, but once again I missed. She was backing away, but why wasn't she defending herself? She was humming something, but nothing was happening. Then that heaviness that I felt in the forest began growing and spreading through the courtyard. I couldn't... move... Fuck...

I fell to my knees as Theoden's cold laugh came, and I was yanked to my feet by my hair.

"I think it's time I marked you and made you mine," he spat.

No.

Theon... I groaned.

"Remove her collar," Theoden commanded.

Hold on, little storm. I'm coming.

A sharp blade pressed to my stomach as Arabella began chanting something, and the very life seemed to be sucked from me. Once it was off, I'd shift. How strong was she?

The collar was removed, and I tried to focus on my abilities, but I couldn't. The darkness was eating me up...

Theoden leaned in, readying to mark me, when suddenly the sound of several horns blowing and a bell ringing made Theoden tense just as a huge explosion filled the air.

"We are under attack!"

"Alpha! The city wall!" Someone shouted.

The sky erupted with fire as another violent explosion shook the grounds beneath my feet. Lightning flashed in the air, and it was not my doing.

"This can't be true..."

"We're done for..." The distant shouts of the people intrigued me as hope filled my heart.

"Arabella!"

Theoden's heart was thundering as Arabella's darkness wrapped around me tightly. Lifting the three of us into the air, Theoden's hand tightened in my hair as we stared at the scene far, far away from us, but with our sharp vision, we could see clearly. Hundreds of thousands of soldiers were teeming into the city, surrounded by shifted wolves, magic, fire, air, and water, full of extreme power and strength.

Fae, werewolves, mages, and sirens.

Together.

For one cause.

"What is this...?" Theoden growled. Despite his rage, there was a glimmer of fear and shock in his voice.

"This is the true power of a united world, Theoden," I said calmly.

His eyes were trained at the man at the front, a far more powerful glow around him than I had ever seen. He was one of the strongest there as he slayed the warriors of the Obsidian Shadow Pack with ease.

"That is..."

"The true king," I said quietly. The shock and betrayal in his eyes were satisfactory. "How does it feel Theoden, being betrayed by your own? Theon is no fool."

Pulling free from his hold, my eyes blazed, and I spread my hands, unleashing a violent wind with every part of me that I could muster and sending them both careening away from me. With her power gone, I fell. Flipping in the air, I landed on my feet, breathing hard and shakily. It took me a moment to regain myself.

I'll handle Arabella, I said quietly through the link.

I will meet you soon. Take care of yourself.

My heart skipped a beat, and as much as I wanted to look down below at the walls of the city in the distance, I had to focus on Theoden's main source of power. It was time to wipe evil from this city, forever.

STRONGER TOGETHER

THEON

THE MAGES CONTINUED TO hold the illusion as we made our way closer to the outer wall. I could see the warriors on the watchtowers seem to hesitate, scanning the grounds. We stopped far behind. The battle plans were in place, and when I was about to give the final command to march onwards, everyone seemed to be distracted. I sensed them before I even turned to confirm it.

The Imperial Sirens. Even with legs, they still didn't pass as humans; their beauty was different and seeing them in such a large number made them stand out even more than the Fae. These were the Imperial Sirens of the emperor… Yileyna's family. There were over a thousand, for sure. Their armour was a shimmery, metallic blue-silver. At the front were two men and Deliana. The three held tridents, whilst the rest behind them wielded swords or whips.

The Naga tensed, and no one spoke as the man that was beside Deliana looked at me intensely. The Imperials were watching the Nagas, but neither species said anything.

"I come to assist my granddaughter, the Heart of Kaeladia. She has proven herself efficient. Tell me, as the queen's mate and Champion, will you ride into battle with the pain that you hide?" All eyes turned on me and I looked back at him, my eyes flashing.

"It has not held me back, even when I went with Yileyna into Naran," I replied firmly.

"Strong and stubborn. Pride fit for a king, boy. However, your pride will not help you," he stated arrogantly.

He shifted his trident in his hand. The power radiating off it was obvious, and I could feel it sending waves through the crowds, but there was nothing dark in it. He raised it and pointed it at me as several of Hunter's men tensed, ready to protect me if need be. I raised a gloved hand, stopping them. It was obviously Hunter's orders.

"A small injury will not hold me back. It never has, and it never will. We must continue on," I stated clearly.

"And we shall," Queseidon said as a blast of light left his trident.

I didn't move, not that there was time. A blinding light struck me, and I felt the rush of power pour through me. Then, it felt like the pain had been lifted. Energy returned to every inch of my body, and my eyes flashed powerfully. I had almost forgotten what it felt like to be without the pain. I had grown accustomed to it, and to be honest, I didn't think I'd ever be fucking free from it.

"Thank you, Your Majesty," I replied seriously, lowering my head slightly to him. I never thought the day would come where I'd be having a civilised conversation with a species I once hated.

"Just do not hurt her again, for a Siren's attack is indeed deadly when she is scorned." I saw Hunter smirk.

"Understood," I almost growled. He gave a curt nod, gesturing to the man beside him.

"You already know the queen of the Aethirian Ocean. Allow me to introduce my son, King Earendor of the Metiolodia Sea." I stepped forward and held my hand out to him. His hair was flaming red, and his eyes a sharp aqua-green. He took my hand, and we exchanged a firm handshake.

"Thank you for coming to our assistance," I said.

"We work towards a better future," he replied in a deep voice.

"My job is done... I will return to the ocean. Happy? I healed him," he muttered, glaring at Deliana. Her smile was faint, and she lowered her head to him.

"Yes."

It was because of her that I was healed. I wasn't sure how to feel about that. Seeing her again wasn't as hard as it was down by the coast, but perhaps the fact she was in human form helped.

He gave a small nod, motioning to his army of Imperials before a large wave of water swirled around him. He turned, walking away, his cyclone of water growing larger before he disappeared into the darkness.

For a moment, I had wondered if the men would get distracted by the Sirens, but they were not there to play, their attention on their commanders. Hunter, who had just bid farewell to Charlene, looked more emotional than I had ever imagined he would, but the fear of not knowing if we'd make it back alive was inside of every man and woman, regardless of how brave they were or appeared to be...

I nodded before getting onto the black stallion that awaited me. Although many would be attacking in wolf form, there were some who would shift later, but for now would go on horseback.

As Champion, I had to give a word of comfort and confidence. I wasn't made for this... but for her, I would do it. I looked around; not everyone was in my line of sight, but I spoke loud and clear, my voice powerful and full of certainty.

"Our army is powerful, with every race on this planet ready to fight for the middle kingdom, an honour many would only wish to witness. Together we raise our swords against the enemy, but remember, we do not harm the women and children, but those who raise a weapon towards us. We fight for the betterment of our own lands, and for the queen who has shown us nothing but compassion and kindness. May this union spread past our borders to other kingdoms! Tonight, we ride for victory, for justice, and for a new dawn!"

Only the shouts of support and confidence followed. Zarian, Hunter, Earendor, Darshian, and Deliana all stepped forward. Ready to lead their ranks into war. Raiden would aim to free some of the Silver Storm on my signal, and lead them from within... We were ready.

I gave the signal before breaking into a gallop...

Yileyna's cry for help made me speed up as we broke through the defence around the wall with ease. Arabella's spells resisted, but with the combined effort, we blew up part of the wall, allowing us access. He had his men on alert, and even when the bells of war rang in the air from the tower of the temple of Selene, we didn't slow down.

I saw the blast of power fill the sky from the castle far ahead, and my heart skipped a beat. It was followed by a blinding light, one that I knew was Yileyna's.

I'll handle Arabella. Her voice came through the bond.

I will meet you soon. Take care of yourself, I replied before I rode faster. If she was using her power, it meant they had removed the collar.

I was halfway to the castle when I felt the flare of Arabella's power erupt in the air once more. The horse neighed, and I pulled its reins, trying to calm him, before I cut through two of Theoden's men, feeling the darkness spreading.

"Finally."

I turned to see Thea yielding a sword, cutting through another warrior as she burst out from the castle gates.

"Be careful, I'm going ahead. This battle ends if he dies," I replied quietly.

"Take care," she whispered as she spun around. "Go, I'll hold them off!"

I was worried for her, but I had to leave. I saw Ryan and Raiden jump from the wall, and I felt a little more at ease. Blood splashed everywhere as I slayed Theoden's men, galloping through to the courtyard. Alphas were sprawled on the floor, some bloody, some simply unconscious, whilst others engaged the enemy.

My heart raced when I spotted Yileyna, encased in a shimmering shield of what looked like ice, her power radiating off her. She looked like a goddess, and if the matter wasn't so fucking dire, I would have spent a little more time admiring her.

Parts of the castle walls were destroyed entirely. Wolves and men were fighting all around, to the point where I did not know friend from foe.

I sensed him before I heard him, and I spun around, my eyes blazing as I raised my sword that was coated in my flaming aura – an aura that had turned into a deadly fire-like energy since she marked me.

"You betrayed me," he seethed. His eyes were filled with blistering rage as our weapons met. I looked at him with unmasked hatred as our weapons clashed once more.

"You betrayed me, Mom, Thalia, Thea, our entire fucking pack! You killed them all, and you think I would stay loyal to you? That I'd never fucking find out?" His eyes blazed orange as he stared into mine, with clear confusion and anger on his face.

He killed the horse I was riding, and I jumped off, bringing my weapon down, but it was met by the barrier of darkness around him. I could see Yileyna fighting against Arabella, but I could also see that the latter was holding strong. We needed to kill her first, and together. She was fucking powerful…

"What are you?" Theoden hissed venomously as I blocked another swing of his sword.

"The Queen's Champion and the one who bears her mark," I replied coldly.

Anger flashed in his eyes, and I slammed my sword down on his shoulder. It hit the shield of darkness that was coating him, doing nothing but send shock waves of pain through my arm. He cackled manically.

"I will never die, Theon… Never!"

"We'll see," I challenged quietly.

Yileyna, encase him in ice. We deal with her first.

Got it, she replied. Raising her hand, she turned her attention to Theoden.

Arabella let out a cry of rage as she lunged at her, and a menacing growl left my lips. I was in front of Yileyna in a flash, bringing down my sword. She blocked, her eyes flitting to Theoden. Protecting him had been rooted so deeply into her.

"Arabella!" Theoden hissed.

She backed away from me, creating a shield as she whispered something, and that same darkness we felt in the forest began weighing down on us. She darted for Yileyna, but I intercepted her as Yileyna worked on the barrier of ice around Theoden, who was trying to get away. He shifted, roaring menacingly as he made to lunge at her. His powerful aura swirled around him, but I blocked him.

A Naga came into view, and I almost prepared to defend myself on reflex when he went for Theoden, but his teeth didn't penetrate the barrier.

"What on Kaeladia…?" Theoden hissed as he pushed the Naga away.

"Naga… here in Astalion…" Yileyna seemed shocked before a smile graced her face, although she was still attacking Theoden.

"We will fight by your side, Alpha Queen," the Naga said, his strength immense as he knocked Theoden to the ground. Yileyna nodded turning her gaze back to Theoden.

"We are not alone, Theoden. Truly every species is now here to defeat you," she said icily She aimed a wave of ice shards at him, but they simply deflected off the barrier. Taking the chance, the Naga and I pinned Theoden down.

"Now!" I shouted.

Two Sirens were attacking Arabella, and then I saw Zarian race towards her, a powerful blast of air pushing her back. Yileyna ran over to us, taking the chance with the distraction Zarian had created. Grabbing Theoden's head, she frowned in concentration. I could feel the darkness burn my skin as I kept him pinned down. Ice began spreading from her hands, only for Arabella to rip me away from Theoden. The Naga hissed, his tail knocking aside two of Theoden's men.

"I'm fine!" Yileyna called as Theoden's anger rose. "Evil will never conquer!"

She jumped back, avoiding his attack, but despite Theoden struggling with the ice that encased half of his body, he was no longer able to move. He tried to shift, and Yileyna tensed, ready to act, only for a roar of pain to leave him. He fell forward, breathing hard, unable to move or shift back. If he didn't change back, he wouldn't be able to command Arabella...

I saw her throw Zarian to the ground, blood pooling around him, and I wasn't sure he was alive as I fought the darkness. My aura around me seemed to be the only thing keeping it at bay.

"Zarian!" Yileyna screamed at the same time Arabella seemed to realise Theoden's situation.

"Master!" She shouted, wiping blood from her face where Zarian had managed to leave a mark. Her eyes were full of hatred as she turned towards Yileyna. "You hurt him." Her voice was sinister and full of hatred.

But with Theoden out of the way, both mine and Yileyna's attention were now upon her. We fought the darkness, giving it our all. We were a blur of attacks and defence. Attack after attack, she countered. I could see the wolves around us dropping, unable to stay upright with the darkness that had wiped out all light that once lit up the courtyard.

We were thrown back once more, but we both grabbed onto whatever we could to stop ourselves from being thrown further.

"Give me your hand!" I shouted to Yileyna as she tried to create ice to hold onto and failed. Our eyes met, her hair whipping around her. Her crown was gone, and her hair had mostly come undone.

"Ice and fire?" She said softly, holding her hand out to me.

Try what we had back in Naran? It might work...

I nodded, taking her hand and pulling her close as I got my footing. Holding her tight, she raised her arms, summoning her abilities as she pushed against the darkness that was attacking us violently. We both looked at Arabella, who was beginning to chant something. We focused all our power together and gave it our all. The blinding light of our powers combined hit her powerfully, but I could feel the barrier that was whirling around her.

It wasn't working.

Help is coming, Yileyna murmured through the link as we were both thrown back again. Flying debris filled the air, and I saw pieces of rock slicing into her bare arms.

Theoden's roar caught my attention, and I realised the Naga by his side was dead. He was beginning to break through the ice. The pillar I was braced against ripped into the air, knocking us both to the ground.

"Theon... mark me," Yileyna said suddenly.

"What?" I asked sharply.

"It will strengthen me. Complete it!" She shouted as a dome of darkness crashed down around the courtyard, just as I saw the brilliant trident with electricity wrapped around it hit the dome. Deliana's scream of frustration reached our ears before she was thrown off. Fuck, we could have used another hand.

I looked around as Theoden shifted back to his human form, his eyes burning with rage as he honed in on me.

I had to do it. Arabella rushed over to Theoden, and they said something which I couldn't hear before I looked into Yileyna's eyes. It was just us against them...

"Shield," I commanded quietly as I stood from where we had been brought to our knees.

Yileyna raised her hand, and although Arabella was fast to act, a blinding circular dome of ice encased us, and I slowly pulled her to her feet. My heart was racing as I realised if I marked her... we would be tied forever... a dream that I didn't deserve...

She reached up. The white glow of the ice dome made her skin sparkle as she cupped my face, her chest heaving.

"Theon, do it now," she whispered, looking down. I took hold of her wrists and stared into the eyes of the one woman who meant everything to me.

"Another unconventional place," I murmured, knowing I was stalling, but when Theoden began hammering on the dome, I knew we didn't have time.

"With the one I love."

"I want to let you know that I loved you long before I ever admitted... when I left you at the cabin.... it fucking hurt. That is a moment I'll never forget and always regret." A crack began appearing in the dome, but Yileyna smiled softly, her eyes glistening with unshed tears.

"Then let's go back to that cabin," she whispered, "but this time, come home. Tell me I cooked your favourite dish. Tell me that you love me every night, and when I awake, be there with me."

"Even though I don't deserve you?" I asked quietly, my voice thick with emotions I failed to hide.

"You do. You are the only man I want," she whispered,

"Then I may just be fucking selfish and take what I want," I growled huskily.

Tangling my fingers into her hair, I tugged her head to the side a little roughly, just like she liked it, making her gasp. She twisted her hand into my hair as I leaned down, sinking my teeth into her neck just as the dome above us shattered...

Under the Stormy Skies

YILEYNA

PLEASURE ERUPTED WITHIN ME, and with it, a blazing surge of power rippled through me. I gasped as the bond was finally completed, and intense sparks like lightning coursed through me.

A powerful aura swirled around us as he held me, one hand twisted in my hair, the other tight around my waist. Despite the ice dome shattering, the energy around us deflected everything, keeping them both at bay. I closed my eyes, relishing in his touch. My love…

He extracted his teeth, licking the area and sending a jolt to my core before placing a soft kiss there. Moving back, I looked into his eyes that were so much like mine… simply shades of reds, golds, and oranges. Like a burning sunset…

"It's time," he whispered, and I nodded.

"Let's do this."

"Time to send you back to hell where you belong," he growled, raising his hand as Arabella managed to destroy the dome entirely.

The power that had swirled around us vanished, but we both radiated energy. Mine was a silvery blue, whilst Theon's was an orangey amber. This time, when we both raised our hands, despite Arabella's chanting, we didn't even budge, as if the darkness itself was evading us. The air was full of broken pieces of stone, yet it did nothing to us.

"For all you have ever done," I said softly, looking into the eyes of a being who had no compassion. She was born from evil and knew only evil. I never wanted to take a life, but this was one that we had to.

"I will never die as long as evil lingers," she hissed, looking from Theoden to Theon, but it was too late.

As one, we channelled everything we could into it. The wind was whirling in the sky, lightning flashed dangerously, and the rain was poured down, but all I focused on was pushing against every limit I had. When our power surged through the air, blindingly hitting Arabella in the chest, I could feel the ground tremble with the sheer force of it. Even with her shield, there was nothing she could do. Fear and shock were clear on her face as she screamed in pain.

"Master!" She shrieked as her dome of darkness that covered the courtyard began weakening.

"Useless," Theoden spat at her as he raised his sword, striking the aura that swirled around us like a barrier, with no result. For a moment, I felt pity for the one whom I shouldn't pity, but it was only for a moment. Her master didn't care for her.

She dropped to the ground, struggling to fight against us, and even Theoden's armour of darkness was dissipating. A dagger to the forehead. I pulled the dagger I had strapped to my thigh and focused on the kneeling woman. I threw it with extreme precision, just like I had practised for years. It was a throw that Dad would have truly been proud of...

It struck her in the centre of her forehead, and her gaunt eyes widened before her skin began to turn black.

"No... Master... I failed...you..."

Her body fell forward until she became a pile of ash. The dagger fell to the ground as Theoden roared in a rage, about to attack when Theon grabbed him by the neck and threw him to the ground.

"He's mine," he said. His voice was so cold, it reminded me of the night he had turned upon us.

His vengeance.

I thought he'd pick up his sword, but he didn't. I could feel his pain through the bond, his anguish, his regret, his sadness, and above all, his rage...

"You will pay for all you have done," he hissed. His claws came out, and he dug his hand into Theoden's stomach, but instead of ripping his insides out, he twisted his hand, making Theoden roar in agony.

"Theon! I taught you… better!" He grunted.

"You destroyed it all, and I was a fool to believe it." I could feel the pain in his voice. Even when Deliana dropped down beside me as rain poured down on us, Theon didn't even spare us a glance.

"You're safe," she breathed, hugging me tightly.

I hugged her back, and for a moment, Mom and Dad came to mind. Hidden in the rain, I allowed my tears to fall. For a moment, time seemed to stand still as I rushed to Zarian's side with Deliana. Luckily, he was alive. Deliana removed her top, wrapping it around his bleeding abdomen. Zarian raised an eyebrow, a small smirk crossing his lips.

"If I'm going to die, this wouldn't be a bad way to go," he smirked, making Deliana raise an eyebrow at him.

"Have you not seen boobs before?" She asked coldly.

"None that are…" He flinched as Deliana tied his stomach painfully tight. I stepped away; he was in good hands and obviously with a good view.

I turned to see Theon breaking or crushing every bone in Theoden's body one by one, his aura swirling around him.

"For Mom… Thalia…" He kept listing them all, Iyara, Thea, me, our packs, the kingdom…

Theoden gargled blood as Theon kept plunging his hand into him and began ripping his body to pieces, limb from limb. He was leaving the torso for last to prolong his death…

The scene was horrifying, and I realised Theon was no longer aware of his surroundings. Even when shouts of victory filled my head through the mind link and from around us, he didn't stop. I saw him gouge Theoden's eye out.

I couldn't breathe. I could feel his pain. It was so intense… How had he kept all of this inside?

"For looking at her with evil thoughts in your mind," he hissed before burning the eyes in his hands. His heart was thundering, his aura swirling around him to the extent that rain was not even touching him.

"Theon…"

Deliana gave me a nod as I walked toward Theon. He had pulled his guts out. The only thing left in his body was his heart. He had tried to prolong his death… but as Theon kept attacking Theoden, his life was fading.

"And this… this is for me," Theon whispered before he ripped his heart from his chest, letting out a menacing growl of rage that rang through the air.

"Theon," I whispered, dropping to my knees behind him and wrapping my arms around his shoulders tightly. My own tears stung my eyes. I could hear his thundering heart, his pain, and his hands were shaking. I pressed my lips to his jaw, sending a rush of sparks and calmness through him. "He's gone. He won't hurt anyone anymore."

His heart continued to pound violently, but he was calming down. His aura vanished, and we stilled. The sound of the pouring rain was loud in our ears as it soaked us both. We stayed like that for several moments. I vaguely noticed Deliana moving Theoden's body pieces from in front of us, but when the sound of shouts and talking reached our ears, Theon tensed and slowly unlocked my arms from around him.

Exhaustion settled in, and I was suddenly aware of the pain in my body. We were both tired, with cuts and bruises.

He stood up, pulling me up with him, and although I didn't want him to let me go, he stepped away, looking at his hands. The rain washed the last of the blood from them. The signs were gone, but the memory wasn't.

"You did it," Hunter's voice came, and we turned. There he was, supporting a bloody Gamma Henry, with some cuts and bruises himself.

The Naga prince, Darshian, came holding the bodies of two dead men that were of Theoden's and threw them down. Earendor came next. Thea, Raiden, and several Alphas who were at the gathering all stepped forward as Zarian got to his feet, clutching his stomach.

Theon reached up, and for a second, I thought he was going to caress my cheek, but he instead pulled out the last two pins holding my hair up and let it cascade down my back.

"We have won," Deliana said with pride.

"The kingdom is yours," Zarian added, looking at me with a smirk.

"Thank you, all of you, for your help and sacrifices. I will never forget what you did for us. Astalion will always be ready if ever any of you need me," I vowed softly. They nodded as Zarian and Deliana smirked slightly.

"We're free," Thea whispered as she wrapped her arms around Raiden, who kissed her forehead. Hunter cleared his throat, making several people present chuckle. "She's marked," Thea added, pointing at me, making Raiden place a finger to her lips. She pouted, nudging him.

Oh, they truly were perfect together.

I looked at Theon, who was standing silently, staring at the dark sky that was pouring down. I knew it was washing away the blood that coated our streets...

He sensed me watching and looked into my eyes with those burning amber ones that made my heart beat a thousand miles. He stepped back and went down on one knee, taking my hand in his and raising it to his lips. My heart hammered as he didn't break eye contact and kissed it softly, making my breath hitch.

"Kneel to your sovereign," he said clearly, his voice thick yet steady, sending pleasure to my core at how sexy he sounded. My heart leapt when he lowered his head to me. A man who never bowed to anyone… a man who was dominant by nature, yet a man who loved me so deeply that nothing else could compare.

"To our queen." A murmur followed as every werewolf present kneeled before me. The royals of other species lowered their heads in respect, but I looked at the man who was leaning before me.

"Rise," I commanded softly.

He did as I said, and I almost smiled, about to comment on it, when his hand snaked around my waist, and he yanked me towards him.

I'm only obeying this time. Don't go getting ideas, he said through the link.

Our emotions were a storm, and I knew he was fighting himself, trying to hold back, but we were struggling. I leaned up and was about to kiss him when he placed a soft kiss on my forehead instead and let go of me suddenly. A flicker of confusion filled me, but when he smiled slightly, I felt at ease, pushing the doubt away.

"Yileyna!"

I turned, a smile lighting up my face as Charlene ran towards me, clearly having rushed to get there. She flung her arms around me, and I hugged her tight, fighting my own tears.

"My queen," I whispered.

"No, you are my queen," she whispered, laughing weekly. "You are going to be an aunty." My eyes flew open as she whispered the second part ever so quietly. So many emotions went through me, but I was unable to put them into words, so I simply hugged her tightly.

"Ah, she was bursting to share that with her sister," Hunter remarked.

"Not jealous, are you?" Thea teased.

"Actually, I am," Hunter said with a smirk as he walked over to us and pulled Charlene into his arms for a tight hug. The mood instantly lifted, and suddenly I felt lighter.

Everyone looked relieved, and although we had a lot of work before us, I just wanted to cherish this moment. I scanned the area, only to realise Theon was nowhere in sight.

The Truth of the Aftermath of War

YILEYNA

"WHAT DO YOU PLAN to do from here, My Queen?" Someone asked. I turned to look at the young Alpha who had asked the question.

"We fix our kingdom, make amends within, and with our neighbours. There is a lot of work to do… but for tonight, let's bury our dead, mourn our losses, and celebrate our victories," I said softly. I had felt the link break with many as we fought.

"That sounds like a plan. Spread out, separate our people from the enemy!" Hunter commanded as he kissed Charlene's forehead. "Take a moment. I'll handle this," he added to me, and I smiled gratefully at him.

He left us, and I turned to look at Theoden's remains, only to see Deliana standing over him. Her hair hid her breasts, and she looked as beautiful as ever, but to my hidden disgust, she had his heart in her hand and was devouring it. Her eyes glimmered, one foot on his bloody chest, as she ate it. I gulped as she gave me a bloody smile, showing off her sharp teeth. That only made a shiver run down my spine.

"He is okay to eat, correct?" She asked as if she was asking if she could have the last fruit in the fruit bowl.

I nodded, trying to smile, but it came out more of a grimace as Charlene gripped my hand. We both turned and left as swiftly as possible without it looking like we were running away.

"She is... beautiful," Charlene said, shuddering.

"But that was disturbing," I whispered back, chuckling softly.

She giggled as she hugged my arm, and for a moment, I forgot everything. I was pulled back to the two of us running and playing on these very grounds. Back when life was so carefree...

We stepped over rubble, and I made sure to hold her firmly, not wanting her to slip in her condition. I couldn't wait for their little bundle of joy to come into this world. Rain poured down on us, and when I reached the gates to the castle, staring down at the city, I realised it was truly over... Theoden and Arabella were dead. The kingdom was free.

Yil- My Queen, we are getting rid of the poisons Theoden had made immediately, Raiden's voice came into my head.

Yileyna is fine, Raiden, and thank you. That's a good idea. I don't want any of that left behind. Destroy it all.

Yes, Yileyna.

"It's truly over," Charlene said softly as we stared at the skies that were crying with relief before we turned our attention back to the bodies that covered the ground below. Theoden had had mages on his side, necromancers who had been powerful, and we had lost many...

My smile vanished, replaced with dread, when I saw Ryan sitting on the ground not far below. His head hung as a body lay before him. Who was dead?

"Charlene," I said, my heart thudding in fear. "That's Ryan... correct?"

Her faint smile faded as she turned in the direction I was staring. Her eyes widened, and she clamped a hand to her mouth. Not speaking, she began running, leaving me behind. Her heart was hammering and came to a sudden stop, mere feet away from Ryan, who didn't even look up. I approached slowly, worry and fear filling me, and my heart sank when my worst fear was confirmed. There on the ground, with his heart ripped out, was none other than Gamma Grayson.

A wail left Charlene's body as she fell to her knees next to the body of her father. My heart was hurting. Tears streamed down my cheek as I dropped to the ground between the siblings and wrapped my arm around them both, trying to comfort them when my own heart was shattering. Gamma

Grayson had played a vital part in this entire journey. Charlene had just found him, and he had been ripped from her...

Ryan's body was stiff. He was simply staring at the body of his father as I mind-linked someone to carry the body into the castle and to bring Zoe. It was a few moments before Zoe came running, tears streaming down her cheeks as she fell to her knees, throwing her arms around him as she cried in agony. The pain of losing your beloved was clear in her wails of anguish and pain. Just thinking of being in her place made it hard to breathe, and I looked around, moving away. Hunter, I needed Hunter here.

If anyone is close to Alpha Hunter, send him to the gates immediately, I commanded through the link. Andrea, Gamma Henry, Gamma Grayson is no more. Please, come to the palace gates.

Andrea's gasp and the strain in Gamma Henry's voice were obvious.

We will be right there.

"Your Majesty, you're needed by the city wall," someone said behind me, and I nodded at them.

"I'll be there soon," I replied quietly as they jogged off. I spotted Hunter run over. Once I knew Charlene and the family had someone to watch over them, I turned away. I had a city to erect upon its feet once more. As queen, I had to be strong.

"Could you ask Alpha Romeo if he will have a team go down to the dungeons and have them release the rest of the warriors from the cells? Feed them and get them beds to rest," I asked, spotting his son Julian, who was in his early twenties, walking over.

"My Queen, my father fell in battle." My breath hitched, and I took a few deep breaths, trying to control my emotions.

"I'm so sorry," I whispered. Alpha Julian shook his head.

"He died for his queen. He would be happy. Fear not, I will handle the cells right away. Where do we put the enemy?" He was strong, even though I could tell he was looking for a distraction from his pain.

"In the dungeons," I replied. He nodded and walked away, and I, myself, headed to the wall.

Theon had vanished, but I had heard from someone that he was burning the enemy's dead. I was tempted to call him through the link to ask if he was okay, but after what happened with Theoden, perhaps he needed some time. He had put up a wall, shutting me out from his turmoil.

Now that it was over... it felt surreal, and despite the fire that still burned in places, the bodies that littered the city grounds and the lasting effect this would leave on us were heavy in my mind. I knew that when dawn came, it would be a new start. A new reign where equality, justice, and compassion prevailed.

I reached the wall, seeing the damage and the huge fire that Ariella was trying to put out. It was beginning to spread despite the rain and her powers. Flames created by magic. I raised my own hands, my aura raging around me and readying myself to put the fire out.

"Queen Yileyna." I turned to see none other than the sea emperor standing there. His eyebrow raised as he looked at the area around him.

"Your Majesty," I bowed to him, and he raised his hand.

"A royal does not bow to a royal. I have come to heal those who are injured. Since you retrieved the pearl, it's only fair..." He frowned, looking at Ariella, who was smiling seductively at several warriors who were clearly admiring her. He sighed and looked back at me. My heart skipped a beat as I looked at his trident, wondering what the extent of its abilities was. Gamma Grayson's body flashed in my mind, and I looked up at the emperor sharply.

"Can the..." I trailed off when Queseidon shook his head slowly, a knowing look in his eyes.

"None can cure death," he said quietly.

"I understand," I whispered. I tried to smile and nodded gently, not knowing what else to say...

RAIDEN

It was almost four in the morning when things were finally in some order. I had ended up throwing some of the Silver Storm members who had succumbed to Theoden into the cells. With due trial, their fate would be decided.

The fires were put out, and the bodies moved and separated. Yileyna didn't rest; she had spent hours putting out fires and even resurrecting walls of ice to hold certain things in place. Gamma Grayson's death had shaken me, and Ryan's emotionless front still played on my mind. His body had been moved to their quarters so the family were able to mourn in privacy. Charlene was as distraught as Zoe, and Hunter's concern was valid. She was pregnant, and it was taking a toll on her. Thea and Andrea had been by their side whilst Gamma Henry and Alpha Hunter had to carry on helping around the city.

Theon had stuck to the outskirts of the wall, burning the bodies of the dead enemies whilst separating our people. I had seen him staring at his dad's remains at one point before he had shoved them in a sack, taking them to the bonfire of the dead.

We also had to house the Alphas who had been drugged at the banquet and those who simply stayed behind, wanting to know what Yileyna planned next. The entire city had come together. The people had prepared food and drinks as well as helped take care of the injured. The healers started healing those they could until Emperor Queseidon had shown up and healed those who were mortally wounded.

The Nagas and Sirens had left after a discussion with Yileyna. I couldn't help but worry about her. When I told her to rest, she would simply brush me off, saying she had a lot to do.

I sat down. An Omega had brought me coffee, and I welcomed it as I rested my head against the stone wall behind me, drinking it. The sound of footsteps made me turn to see Thea walking toward me. She looked tired, yet her eyes held the fire that they always did, showing the strength that she had.

"Hey," she murmured as she wrapped her arms around my neck. She was about to sit beside me when I placed my cup down and pulled her onto my thigh, inhaling her scent. Goddess, she smelt so good.

"Hey," I responded, my gaze falling to her lips. I hadn't kissed her yet… not on those plump lips of hers, and the very urge was threatening to take over.

She rested her head on my shoulder and sighed. I stroked her thigh, resting my head on top of hers.

"Many died, Raiden… the guards of the Silver Storm that had been let out during the fight, a few were killed as they were too weak… Alpha Romeo… he's passed, too." My eyes widened in surprise. Alpha Romeo had helped us a lot… "Hunter's Beta… Ailema died, too. She was trying to protect the orphanage from one of the necromancers who was destroying all in his wake, and she was murdered." I closed my eyes, feeling her pain as I tightened my arms around her.

"We lost many…" I murmured. She tilted her head up, her nose brushing my chin before she reached up and cupped my jaw.

"Life is so short, isn't it?" She whispered.

I swallowed, trying to control myself because with her in my lap… was it wrong that I wanted to take her away and do far more to her than I could out here?

"No one can escape death, but that's why we need to live life to the fullest." I looked into her amber orbs. Her heart was racing as she nodded slowly in agreement, but I knew there was more. She wanted to say something. "What is it?" I asked, smiling slightly.

"I just told you that life is short… yet you still make no attempt to kiss me." I let out a chuckle, wrapping my arms around her slender body tightly.

"That's one way to make me kiss you," I whispered seductively, "but I'm not sure if I start kissing you, that I will ever stop."

She sat up slowly from where she had been leaning on me and turned in my lap until her legs were on either side, straddling me. Her core was pressing right against the bulge in my pants as she locked her arms around my neck.

"Then don't stop," she whispered.

My eyes flashed, and all the self-restraint I had worked so hard on broke free. I ran my hand up her waist before letting go of it and cupping her face. Her scent and touch soothed my mind, and pleasure rushed south as I claimed her lips in a delicious kiss, one that almost felt like my body hummed along to. A soft sigh escaped her, and her arms tightened around my neck as she pressed her body firmly against mine, deepening the kiss.

It was perfect. Sweet as honey, soft as silk, and far more pleasurable than I could have imagined. This was the taste I'd never get enough of, a taste I would always relish and crave, because she was mine.

LET'S GO BACK

THEON

T HE QUEEN...

Someone who fucking deserved the best, but I had marked her. The pull towards her was a storm in my mind, and although the bond was completed, all I fucking wanted to do was fuck and claim her all over again. Seeing everyone bow to her and my mark adorning her neck had overwhelmed me with emotions that were far too many for me to process.

I was Alpha now; I felt it the moment he died, the transfer of power...

I had walked away, helping with the worst job, disposing of the dead before I had washed my hands with soap a thousand fucking times, wanting to remove the memory of Theoden from my skin. It was strange how everyone looked to me for guidance, as if they had forgotten what I had done in the past. Was it just me who couldn't forgive myself?

I was down by the coast, sitting on the edge of one of the rocky cliffs, not wanting to run into any Sirens down in the water below. I just wanted peace. I had unleashed my anger upon Theoden, but his death had taken no more than a few minutes... he deserved far worse...

Would he go to hell? Was it enough for him? Was Mom looking down on us? Did she know all he had done? Did she think I deserved forgiveness? And what of William and Hana De'Lacor? Would they have forgiven me?

In those final moments of his life, I had wanted to ask him why? Why did he fucking do this to us? We could have been a happy family. Living together and enjoying mundane things like dinner together. Thalia... she would have been on her way to becoming a woman. Meeting her mate just like Thea...

I licked my lips and hung my head, closing my eyes. Was this what revenge was meant to feel like? Once it was over, was I simply supposed to feel lost? My entire life had been a journey for vengeance...

I opened my eyes and looked up at the sky. The rain had eased up, and only a light sprinkle fell as I stared at the shining moon. What is my life's purpose now that vengeance and retribution have been dealt?

Yileyna. Live for her.

Although it's what I wanted, I didn't deserve forgiveness... I know I kept thinking about it, but it was hard not to. I needed to be punished for my crimes, too. Misguided or manipulated, it didn't matter... I committed crimes that I would never be able to ever simply wipe from my book of sins.

The sound of heels on the ground, and an intoxicating scent that belonged to none other than the one who was always on my mind, approached.

"Why are you here?" I asked as I got up and turned to look at her.

I could smell the scent of her shampoo, so subtle compared to her own scent that was already making me feel light-headed. She had showered and changed, now wearing a white shirt with several buttons opened, exposing her breasts, tucked into black pants. Her hair was open, and she had her hands in her back pockets, looking as breathtaking and sexy as always. Did she realise her top was getting wet, showing off the pink bra she wore beneath it?

"To check up on you. I'm sorry I didn't come sooner," she whispered as she closed the gap between us. She placed her hand on my chest, and even through the black tunic I wore, I felt the intense pull of the bond. I had removed my armour, but I was still wearing what I had worn in the battle. Although she looked too fucking perfect to touch, I still gripped her hips. Satisfied when her heart began racing.

"I'm sure the queen has a lot more to put her pretty blonde head to work on," I remarked teasingly.

"Mm... but you were the one filling this blonde head of mine," she replied, poking her eyes out at me. I didn't reply. Reaching up, I brushed her hair back, looking at the mark that adorned her neck. One that matched mine… "It's beautiful, isn't it?"

"Yeah, it is… but not as beautiful as you," I murmured, brushing my fingers down her neck. Her eyes fluttered shut, her breasts heaving as she reacted to my touch fucking perfectly…

I had to focus not to let the pleasure fucking get to me, and instead brushed my fingers slowly across her collarbone, down towards her breasts. She sucked in a breath as her eyes opened, filled with love and desire as she looked at me through those thick lashes.

"Theon…" She gripped my hand, stopping my fingers from skimming her breasts, and instead kissing my fingers, closing her eyes.

"Yileyna…" I teased in the same tone she had used. Her eyes looked upwards to meet mine, and she stepped closer. Oh fuck…. "Yileyna. Those who have committed crimes will be trialled, and so should I." She frowned, searching my eyes for something before she shook her head.

"You sided with me before victory was ours. Those in the cells are those who chose to follow Theoden for their selfish gain. You completed your redemption Theon, when you led this army and fought for justice and good. Let it go. You are not a villain."

"I feel it's too easy," I murmured, looking away from her, but she refused to let me go, instead forcing my face back to look at her.

"Theon, your entire life, you have been punished and groomed to become a tool for vengeance. No. You will not be punished for anything more. You are my mate and king. Plus, you have a pack that has been abused. You need to give them hope -"

"I am no king, Yileyna. As for the pack, I was going to ask if you can take the Obsidian Shadow Pack members into the Silver Storm. There are not many." Her eyes filled with hurt as she nodded.

"Of course, into our pack. Theon, to run this kingdom, I need you by my side," she whispered. She wasn't going to agree, and so I simply nodded, my gaze dipping to her pouty, sexy lips that had been taunting me ever since she had shown up. "How are your wounds? Deliana told me that the emperor healed you." Her fingers brushed my chest, and I nodded.

"He did. I'm perfectly fine once again."

"Good. Consider that injury as your punishment for your crimes, Theon. Those injuries caused you great pain. Leave it all in the past."

I didn't respond. I deserved far more of a punishment, but I couldn't ask for anything physical when I was bound to her. She ran her fingers along my jaw, and I spotted the ring on her finger. My heart skipped a beat, recognising it. I looked into her gorgeous face, which now held a soft smile.

"This is…" I took her hand, looking at the ring I had once given her before I broke her trust in me entirely…

"An Omega had found it and kept it safe. She returned it to me earlier, saying it was the king's ring for his queen… people are already considering you their king, Theon," she said softly as I kissed her knuckles.

"Doesn't it bring back memories of my betrayal?" I asked quietly.

"Hmm? No. It brings back your vulnerability as you begged for me to side with you so I would be safe. You thought Andres was the true villain, and you thought you were doing the right thing. Although… don't try to throw me off a balcony again," she frowned.

"I caught you, if that helps." She smirked, amused, before she looked into my eyes. Her smile faded away, but the love in her eyes didn't vanish.

"What are we, Theon?" She whispered, reaching up as she brushed her lips down my neck. She flicked her tongue against my mark, sending delicious rivets of pleasure through me. Her hand travelled dangerously low, lingering on my abs. She was weakening my self-control, and the urge to ravish her was fucking making me go crazy. I yanked her head back, looking into her eyes.

"Two opposites that somehow go… no matter how much I tried to stay away, you came back into my life, time and again. No matter what I say or do, I am unable to stop thinking about you to the extent that I can no longer control myself," I confessed quietly, my gaze dipping to her breasts.

"Good, because I want to be the only thing you think of," she replied, biting on her lower lips for a second as she watched me.

"Hmm… and you wore white when you know it's raining… was it your aim to seduce me?"

"That depends… is it working?" She asked as the rain began pouring harder, soaking her white shirt in seconds. I smirked slightly as my eyes flashed, my fingers tightening in her hair as I looked down at her almost exposed breasts. Her shirt was completely see-through, and I could make out her stiff nipples.

"Oh, it fucking worked."

"Good, because I got a little charm put on this ring before I came to find you," she whispered teasingly, running her finger down my chest as she looked up at me with those eyes that were going to be the fucking end of me. "So you don't need to hold back." Oh fuck.

"Fuck. You make me lose control," I growled huskily, bending down and lapping up the water from her neck right down to her cleavage. She whimpered, pressing herself against my manhood, which was already semi-hard, as she tilted her head back.

"Then lose control," she whispered softly.

And I did.

I yanked her head up as I kissed her so fucking hard. A blinding kiss that, with the bond complete, felt something between a million fireworks and pure ecstasy. I felt fucking drunk on her. Tasting her, touching her, kissing her. Passion and emotions wrapped around us in a cocoon, and nothing else mattered.

Let's go home, her seductive voice came through the mind link.

I knew what she meant. The one place we could truly be ourselves... I may have been the fucking villain, but I was already given heaven.

Hot as Hell

THEON

*I*LIFTED HER BRIDAL STYLE, carrying her back to Westerwell. Not many were around, save the guards standing on duty. Neither of us cared for our surroundings as we made our way toward our cabin, a place where we had spent time together only fleetingly, but a place that held some of the best memories we had together.

I kicked the door shut behind me, turning the lock in the key before I carried her to the bedroom. Pulling back the top layer that may have collected dust and placing her down, I turned one of the lanterns on. I wanted to see her tonight… properly…

The dim light cast a glow around the room, and she smiled softly up at me as I slowly pulled my tunic off, tossing it aside. Her eyes raked over my body, her heart thundering. I could see the love in her eyes, the desire and anticipation as she propped herself onto her elbows. Reaching up with her leg, she ran her foot over my cock, which was already semi-hard at just the fucking thought of fucking her.

Removing my shoes, I then slipped hers off, tossing them aside as I kissed her feet sensually, making my way up her leg with kisses before I climbed on top of her. For a moment, our eyes met, both blazing with intense emotion, and I kissed her deeply, letting down the walls around my emotions as I ran my hands over every part of her body. She kissed me back with equal passion, wanting this as much as I did. I tried to fucking take it slow, but my restraint was breaking. The things I wanted to do to her…

I squeezed her breasts, and she moaned sexily against my mouth. I took the chance to play with her tongue, sucking on it. Her hands were already working on the button to my pants. Fuck, I could kiss and play with her forever…

I ripped her shirt off, pulling away from her plush lips so I could get a good look at her. Her breasts were exposed in that tiny bra that she was almost spilling out from. I grabbed them, assaulting her neck with hot, rough kisses at the same time. Yanking her bra down, I ran my tongue over one of her breasts before twirling it around her nipple, making her whimper as her head dropped back on the pillows. I reached behind her, unhooking her bra and pulling it away as I squeezed both of her boobs together, licking one and twisting the other nipple between two fingers.

"Oh, fuck, Theon," she gasped, placing her hand over mine as I sucked on her nipple. She whimpered, arching her back in pleasure.

The scent of her arousal surrounded me. I switched, paying equal attention to her other breast before kissing her down her stomach. Her core brushed against my leg, and my eyes flashed as I bit into her waist, sucking hard. She sighed softly, wriggling in my hold as she pulled away, running her hands down my chest.

"Tease," I groaned huskily, wanting to devour her entirely.

I slid her pants down, pulling them off and tossing them aside, only for her to roll over onto her stomach, casting me a sexy smile over her shoulder and giving me a good view of her plump ass as she wriggled her hips. Oh yeah. I delivered a sharp tap to her ass, making her moan in pleasure. She was so fucking perfect, with a body made for sin and a personality to match. When we were in the bedroom, she was the perfect little plaything.

"Well, if we're playing…" I growled. Picking up her bra, I grabbed her wrists, tying them together behind her back with the flimsy fabric. "Make sure you do not break free," I commanded.

"Yes, Alpha," she replied, pouting as I delivered another smack to her ass. I loved when she called me that.

This, this was where I fucking wanted to be. I leaned over her, wrapping my hand around her throat as I pulled her up onto her knees. I bit down on her shoulder, sliding my hand around her front and massaging her pussy.

She whimpered, her hands that were tied behind her straining to stroke my cock. I let her, enjoying the way she tilted her head back and sighed in pleasure. I throbbed against her hands, wanting to fuck her hard and right then. She was soaking wet, her legs trembling when I rubbed against her slit. Teasingly… tauntingly…

"Please, Theon," she moaned as I tightened my hold around her neck.

"Patience, little storm. Tonight, I want to play."

She nodded, and, with my hand still around her throat, I slipped my index finger into her mouth. She sucked on it like the good girl she was.

I pushed aside her panties, hissing as my finger brushed her clit, sending pleasure through us both. I throbbed hard as I shoved two fingers into her, making her moan in pleasure, and fucked her with them. My eyes raked down over her large breasts, nibbling and sucking on her ear. I let go of her neck, grabbing one of her large breasts in my hand and bit into her throat.

"Oh, fuck… don't stop," she whimpered.

I felt her nearing, squeezing and twisting her breast just as she came. She let out a loud, sexy moan as her entire body reacted to her orgasm, a look of pure ecstasy on her flushed face. She was fucking breathtaking. Her heart pounded, and I wrapped my arm around her waist tightly. Her juices coated my fingers. I slid them out slowly, delivering a sharp slap to her pussy.

"You're so fucking perfect," I murmured whilst kissing her neck. I ripped off her lace panties before slipping my fingers into her mouth, allowing her to taste herself. Watching her run her tongue over my fingers made my dick throb hard, pleasure fucking driving me insane. "You taste so fucking good," I whispered huskily before I pushed her down onto the bed, my eyes on her ass. I delivered another sharp spank to it, satisfied when it left a mark, before I flipped her over onto her back.

She was the most beautiful and sexiest woman I had ever laid eyes on. Every curve of her body was made to be devoured, her large breasts with her pink nipples, her round, sexy hips, those thighs… and as she lay there, her arms tied behind her back, she was a fucking goddess just waiting to be worshipped.

"I want to feel you against me," she whispered seductively, her gaze dipping to my pants.

I didn't refuse her, removing my pants and allowing her to have a good look as I wrapped my hand around my shaft, stroking myself slowly. She bit her lips, her eyes darkening with desire before she licked her lips and sat up, her eyes fixed on my dick.

"I want you to fuck my mouth," she begged seductively; her eyes were coated with lust as she licked her lip with a hunger that was fucking messing me up.

"Not yet… my turn first," I growled, grabbing her throat and pinning her to the bed before kissing her roughly. She kissed me, her moans loud as I ravished her mouth, feeling my dick press against her soaking pussy. Although she spread her legs wider, arching herself up to meet my cock, I refused to fuck her yet.

Reaching between us with my free hand, I grabbed my cock and rubbed it against her clit, making her groan in pleasure. I broke away from her lips when she gasped for air, placing hungry, rough kisses down her stomach until I reached her pussy. I lifted her legs onto my shoulders, slipping my tongue into her. So fucking good…

I craved how she tasted, the way her body reacted, and the way she moaned in pleasure…

I didn't let up even as she cried out, feeling her orgasm nearing, and when she came, her juices squirting out of her, I continued eating her out until she had ridden out the aftershocks of her release. I could feel her entire body trembling and knew she was extra sensitive from it.

"Delicious," I growled as I moved back, wiping my chin as I looked into her eyes with unmasked hunger. She lay there, trying to catch her breath as her gaze dipped to my cock. "Now, you can have a taste."

"Oh, fuck, yes," she moaned.

Her eyes darkened as she got off the bed, dropping to her shaking knees, her hands still bound. I tangled my hand into her hair, yanking it back as she stuck her tongue out hungrily, raking up the drop of pre-cum that sat on the tip of my dick. She moaned in pleasure before wrapping her lips around me and beginning to suck hard.

Pure addiction. My head became fucking hazy, and all I could think of was the woman who was sucking me off and how fucking good it felt. I tightened my hold as I began thrusting into her mouth, enjoying the way she was totally at my mercy.

Do you like that, my king? She asked hornily through the link as I hit the back of her throat.

"Fuck, yes," I growled.

She was the queen of the kingdom, but in the bedroom, I was always going to be the king, the Alpha, the one in charge.

The pressure was building. I was so fucking near. Speeding up as I fucked her roughly, the pleasure consumed me. I came, shooting my load into her mouth and seeing fucking stars as the intense pleasure washed through me, wave after fucking wave. I pulled out, delivering a few quick strokes to my dick, releasing the last of my cum onto her tongue.

"I want more," she whispered, looking at me as she breathed heavily.

Oh, so do I, little storm, so do I...

Her eyes darkened with lust as I let go of her hair. I pulled her to her feet by the throat, kissing her lips, and, reaching behind her, I tore the bra off her wrists. Turning her around, I pushed her onto all fours on the bed. Just staring at her sexy ass, or imagining my white cum dripping from her pussy, was enough to turn me on all over again.

"Fuck me, baby," she moaned.

"Oh, I'm fucking going to, and I'm not stopping until you fucking collapse," I growled, grabbing her hips and positioning myself at her entrance. Then with one rough, brutal thrust, I entered her, making her cry out in pain and pleasure.

She gasped, trying to get her bearings, and I felt myself harden as her tight walls clenched around me before I began fucking her pussy hard and fast. Her moans mixed with my own. The smell of sex and her arousal were like a drug scenting the air. I tilted my head back. This was fucking heaven. Right here, with her...

A Decision at Court

THREE WEEKS HAD PASSED since that night. I took the throne and became the Alpha Queen of Astalion by default. The last few weeks had been a blur of work. Not only were there things to do within Astalion, but there was so much to work out with the other kingdoms and how we would go from there.

The foremost was the funeral of our fallen heroes, the victims of Theoden's actions. The kingdom was in mourning for three days, and until those days were up and everyone was buried with full honours, there was no merriment. The fallen Sirens, Nagas, and Fae were also engraved on the memorial stone in the courtyard of the temple of Selene, for they died for this kingdom and fought bravely alongside us for our people.

After the funerals, the next job was making peace between the Sirens and Nagas, something that went well enough. Despite the fact that the two species will never mix, they came to an agreement, and the Naran empire broke down their dams, letting the water their land so desperately needed enter. The Sirens would not attack, and they would stay away from one another.

As for the Sirens, Queseidon refused to allow Deliana to walk the land, saying the curse he had made in anger was not one he could lift entirely;

he had been able to grant her legs only for the battle. I had seen the pain in her eyes when she realised she couldn't visit me often, but I promised I'd visit her down by the coast and in the ocean, too, when I could.

Ariella was often walking through the city and had taken somewhat of a job at the White Dove. She chose whom to sleep with, and the lucky man paid the owner of the White Dove since Ariella didn't want any money, just a taste of men. They were even making a pool room where she would entertain her company in Siren form. Well, the White Dove sure became a spot where people from other cities came to visit and hope for a taste of the forbidden sin that it now offered. I had a feeling if Queseidon found out, then she'd be stripped of her legs, too, but I was a curious thing, and she was too, just far wilder than I ever was, of course. I was glad she got to enjoy her life however she deemed fit, and the Sirens were welcome in Astalion whenever they wished.

Of course, aside from Westerwell, we all knew it would take time for people to accept them completely. We needed to work on that slowly rather than overwhelm them, but I was positive about the future.

The story of the battle of Westerwell had travelled across the borders, a miraculous moment when every kind of being united to defeat a Dark One, a story those who were a part of told with extra joy. Of course, the story began to take many forms, but the truth remained in there, for now.

As for the Fae Kingdom issue, food rations were sent, and an open trade passing was set up, so they would never need to worry about this issue ever again. Astalion was bountiful in its crops and produce; it accumulated more than we could consume. Although I'd miss him, Zarian had to return and take up his duty as prince, one that he had been away from for several years.

Last of all, the crew of the Siren Killer renamed their ship The Queen's Voyage. Although they had been devastated about the loss of Ailema, as was I, she would always be remembered. She was a lovely woman, the kind that everyone needed in their lives.

My official coronation was in a week's time, and everything was hectic, with everyone expecting Theon and me to marry. It was still something that Theon was uncertain of. We were sitting around the conference table consisting of Theon, myself, four Alphas, Raiden, two Nagas, two Sirens, three Fae, and one mage. It was a council I had put together, wanting other species to live among us and a means for them to be the link to their kingdoms.

"Regarding the marriage, My Queen, perhaps we can hold it in the Temple of Selene in the morning hours before the coronation?" Raiden suggested. I glanced at Theon, who sat next to me. The very first day, he had refused to sit in the throne-like chair that matched mine; he now sat in a chair that matched the rest.

"We will not marry," he said coldly, looking around the table.

A ripple went through those at the table, but I kept my face emotionless. Theon had been by my side every morning and every night... he'd hold me in his arms as I fell asleep and kiss me awake, so his words didn't affect me. It was a different matter for those around us.

"Why not?" Hunter asked, raising an eyebrow.

"We will marry someday; I proposed after all, but I'm not marrying for the throne. I will not take the title of king. This kingdom is Yileyna's, and even if our packs are combined, I will not be king but remain Alpha alone." His eyes were cold as he looked at his brother firmly. I sighed softly. This was a conversation I had had with him several times, and he kept brushing it off.

"It's just a title. She is the heart, of course, she will remain the ultimate ruler, but you are almost equal in power, Alpha Theon," Alpha Julian added quietly. He had stepped up well into Alpha Romeo's place proudly, and I was sure if his father could see him, he would be truly proud, just like I was certain mine would be. Alpha Romeo was someone we would always be grateful for.

"I'm not going to accept it, am I speaking a foreign language?" Theon asked icily, his eyes flashing, making me reach over under the table and run my fingers down his thigh. He gave me a look.

It's so sweet of you to be so adamant that I'm the queen when you love to be the master in the bedroom, I remarked teasingly.

Precisely. That's my forte, and unless you want to be punished for being so fucking stubborn, I suggest you agree with me, or I swear, little storm, I will slip my hand under that dress and make you come right here. My cheeks burned. I knew Theon enough to know he'd follow up on his threat.

You're playing dirty, I pouted.

Don't we always? He countered arrogantly, and my heart thumped as I looked into his gorgeous amber eyes. Now be a good little girl and agree with me. My stomach knotted, and I knew he had won. Was it necessary to push him when all he wanted was to remain Alpha and not be king?

"Then, it's final," I declared, sighing. "Theon will remain Co-Alpha of the Silver Storm, and when we do marry… and we intend to… he will be known as Prince Theon. Fair?" Now that I had changed my verdict, everyone who had opposed him would now agree.

"That is an excellent idea, Queen Yileyna."

"Reasonable," Jaen, one of the Nagas, hissed.

"Fair enough. Prince Theon sounds cute," Hunter taunted his brother, smirking.

They're a bunch of fucking puppies. You were the only one pushing this argument, Theon said through the link as he looked at me questioningly. Well….

I didn't reply to him, keeping my hand on his strong thigh. Was it wrong that I wanted to get him alone and have him punish me?

What will you do? Punish me?

Oh, I plan to.

Yes, please, Alpha.

"Then I'll make sure that everything is prepared for the queen's coronation," Raiden said, bringing us out of our secret conversation.

"Perfect. Send invitations to all," I commanded. He nodded, and my attention fell to his neck. He and Thea had marked and mated, yet Thea was not living with him in the Beta quarters, much to my surprise. She was currently staying with Hunter, who would be leaving Westerwell after my coronation. I didn't want to think of them leaving… I would miss Charlene, who had remained to spend time with her brother and Zoe after the death of Gamma Grayson. Rhys had also returned from Hunter's pack, which was currently being run by his Gamma and his new Beta.

"Meeting adjourned," I declared as everyone began getting up and bowing.

Yileyna, can you ask Theon and Alpha Hunter to remain for a while? I looked at Raiden, wondering why, but gave a slight nod.

Of course.

"Alpha Hunter, Theon, Raiden, I want an additional word," I said, making the men nod. The rest took their leave after paying their respects.

Was it wrong to feel sorry for Raiden? The day after he had marked Thea, Theon had lost it, furious that she was only seventeen, until I had to remind him that he had fucked me at seventeen, too, which had stopped him in his tracks. Double standards when it came to his sister. The girl is happy; honestly, these men!

I heard footsteps as everyone left and saw Thea enter. She looked much better than she had a few weeks ago, having gained a little weight too.

"Thea, what are you doing here?" Theon asked, frowning. She simply poked her eyes out at him and walked over to Raiden, who stood to meet her, kissing her lips. Both brothers growled, and I closed my eyes.

"Seriously? You both are growling? You both have mates," I frowned.

"Exactly, tell them, Yileyna. Charlene," Thea said, turning her attention to the open doors as Charlene walked in with a bump that was noticeable. My queen was glowing and looked absolutely radiant in her pregnancy. Although many asked Theon and me when we were going to have pups, the answer was not yet. I had a lot to do yet, and I wanted to make sure that when the time came, I was there for my child. When we had the conversation, although Theon looked a little uncomfortable, he simply said he had just gotten me all to himself, and he was not ready to be a father yet. We both agreed now was not the time, and we were happy.

"Hunter, leave them alone," Charlene cajoled as she walked over to him. He stood up, kissing her forehead softly before turning her back to his chest and wrapping his arms around her firmly, placing his hand on her stomach.

I looked at Raiden, wondering what he wanted to say.

"What is it?"

"I actually wanted to tell all of you, as you are Thea's family, that we are planning to move in together, permanently," Raiden said, smiling slightly as he looked down at his mate.

"She's only seventeen," Hunter reminded us yet again, and I resisted the urge to roll my eyes.

"Yeah, agreed," Theon added, although he seemed a bit less bothered than Hunter.

"I'm only eighteen, and I remember you encouraging your brother several times," I frowned, glaring at him. "Not to mention Charlene is just nineteen, yet she's pregnant."

"A good age to be a mother." Hunter frowned as Charlene nodded, far too enraptured by her husband to disagree.

"Exactly, Yileyna is right." Thea frowned. "Raiden and I are perfect for one another, and we are moving in together regardless of if you want us to or not."

"Theon?" Hunter said, looking at Thea with concern. I don't think he realised she was a woman who was mated...

"Let them. It's true… they aren't kids. If he hurts her, I'll fucking castrate him," he said, his cold eyes turned on Raiden.

Castrate… I had heard the story of Nikolai and Kyson's deaths… and although no one had ever confirmed it, I knew it was Theon. When I asked him, he simply looked me dead in the eye and said, "What a shame they didn't die a far more painful death." That had confirmed he had been the one behind it.

"I will only request that you always keep the queen happy, too," Raiden replied challengingly, making Theon's eyes flash and his aura flare.

"Well, since that's sorted, let's end this discussion!" I declared, standing up and placing my hand on Theon's shoulder, giving him a view of my breasts, which were showing plenty of cleavage in my sage green floral corset. His hand instantly went to my ass, the other tangling in my hair as he pulled me down and kissed me, sending rivets of pleasure coursing through me.

"My threat stands. Don't hurt her," Theon said when we broke apart and gave Raiden a cold glare as he stood up. His eyes raked over me, and I knew exactly what he wanted to do.

"Well, I guess if Theon is okay with it, there's not much I can say." Hunter almost pouted, making Charlene caress his cheek.

"Of course it's fine, let them be together. You know how hard it is to be apart." She reminded him softly.

Hunter looked at Raiden and Thea, who were lost in their own world, and his face softened. Sighing, he nodded. Letting go of his Luna, he walked over to the duo and placed a hand on both of their shoulders.

"Well, since I'm outnumbered," he smirked before kissing his sister's forehead. "Welcome to the family, Raiden."

I smiled, watching them, before Theon's hand squeezed my ass, drawing my attention back to him.

"If the queen's finished with her affairs of the court, shall we head home for the night?" My heart skipped a beat as I ran my fingers through his hair. Home, a place we tried to go back to when we could, a place that now had homely touches to it and had been fixed up – our cabin.

"Let's," I whispered as he stood up, yanking me against him roughly, making me gasp.

"We're still here." Hunter reminded us, clearing his throat.

"Good, stay here. We're leaving for the night," Theon replied.

"It's not even dusk yet," Thea teased.

"Well, I have been working all morning," I remarked, letting Theon lead me out.

"And now you'll be busy with other... work," Hunter teased, earning himself a scathing glare from Theon.

I simply smiled up at the man I loved. Even then, as I looked at his side profile, admiring it, I realised how things had changed from years ago. I no longer walked behind him, rushing to keep up... I now walked beside him, hand in hand.

I was once a girl who was infatuated with the handsome, cold guard. That obsession grew into unconditional love, love that he reciprocated. Now I wasn't that little girl but a woman walking beside her man.

"What shall we eat tonight?" I asked, leaning my head against his arm.

"You."

Our eyes met, and I couldn't help but blush faintly. Oh, how life was perfect...

ABOUT THE FUTURE

YILEYNA

THREE HOURS HAD PASSED, and we had just showered after a very sizzling few rounds of sex. I had put some roast chicken and vegetables in the oven that would be done soon, and I was slipping on a black silk nightdress that reached mid-thigh. I sat in front of the vanity mirror, opening Mom's jewellery box. The few remaining items that I had managed to salvage were all there, along with the amulet that belonged to Theon's mother. I had been given it by one of the Omegas who were doing a thorough clean of the castle and had found it in his old room, but I hadn't managed to find the right time to return it to Theon. I knew it belonged to the Obsidian Shadow Pack and was a painful reminder of the wrongs that stained that pack, but it had also been his mother's.

I shut the jewellery box, clutching the necklace in my hand as I walked out into the main room. The room was glowing with the warm lights of the lanterns, and two windows were open. With summer approaching, the weather was far warmer than it was a month or so ago.

There he was… my sexy god, in nothing but a pair of grey pants that hung low upon his hips, placing dishes on the table. I licked my lips, tempted to yank them down and -

"I can hear your thoughts, little storm," he reminded me in his deep sexy voice without even turning. Smiling in amusement, I placed the amulet aside and walked over to him.

"Oh? Well, the idea was enticing," I replied, running my hands down his abs as I hugged him from behind.

"Obviously…" He gripped my wrist, turning and yanking me roughly against him. "But unless you want me to fuck you right now -"

"You had something you wanted to talk to me about, right?" I cut in as he kissed my neck. "Behave."

"I did, and you started this." I smiled teasingly before pulling away.

I walked over to the oven and took the roast tray out, carrying it to the table. The delicious fragrance made me lick my lips. Oh, I was hungry! When we were at the palace, we always had big four-or five-course meals, but here in the cabin, I liked to cook myself. I picked up the amulet, walked back to the table and took my seat. We helped ourselves to the food before I gently placed the amulet next to Theon's plate.

"I found this when the castle was being cleaned," I explained gently. He looked down at it, frowning slightly before he placed his fork down and picked it up. "It's your mother's. I thought you might want to keep it," I explained, my gaze dipping to my wrists that still held bruises from our sex session, the memory making my core throb.

"It also bears the crest of the Hale family, but she once told me that when I found my mate or took a chosen mate, she would give this to her daughter-in-law," he said, frowning as he looked at the amber jewellery. He placed it on the table and slid it back. "It's yours, although the Hale crest no longer holds any significance, and it's a name I want to bury. This was hers, and she wanted you to have it." A wave of emotions washed over me, and I looked at him.

"Theon, not everyone in the Hale family was evil… when the time comes, and we plan to have children, they will carry the Hale name, won't they?" His eyebrows shot up as he drank some juice.

"Children?"

"Well, not yet, but someday we will have children, correct?"

"Not for a very long time," he replied pointedly, reaching over and brushing my hair back. "I want to play with you how I deem fit without having to worry about a pup in you."

"Like I said, someday," I retorted.

"Yes, and they'll carry my name, Theon Alexander. Not Hale," he said quietly, making my eyes snap up to his, and I smiled faintly.

"That's perfect," I replied, kissing his lips softly before sighing as I looked at the amulet.

"It's yours." It was a gift from Theon's mother…

I took it slowly and nodded, feeling a storm of emotions within me.

"I will treasure it because of her," I promised, wishing that she was there, just like Mom, Dad, Gamma Grayson, and Theon's little sister. Wouldn't life have been so great? He said nothing as we both sat back in our seats and carried on eating.

"What did you want to talk about?" I asked, eating some chicken. He frowned slightly as he ate slowly, as if thinking about how to phrase what he had wanted to say.

"It's regarding something I want to do… I know you have forgiven me, and it's me who hasn't been able to forgive myself, but there is something I wanted to do."

"Something you want to do as punishment?" I asked sharply.

"Not exactly, but the tomb of the Dark One where Theoden had locked Thea and the others was something we didn't even know of. With the kingdom recovering from everything, and all the changes you have instilled, I want to travel the kingdom and make sure there's no trace of any of the Dark Ones left or of Dad's wrongdoings. To make sure something like this never happens again," he explained quietly. My heart was thudding as I realised what he was saying… he was leaving.

"Theon -"

"Hear me out, beautiful. Please." His voice was slightly strained, and I realised this was something that had taken him a lot to speak of. It took my all as I watched him. I could tell he had given it a lot of thought.

"On this journey, I will travel to all of the villages and cities to assess how things are and make sure that everything is in order. A visit from the queen's mate might even strengthen people's opinions and trust in us, too. I know it will take me months… but… I need to do this for myself." I looked at him, my eyes stinging with tears.

"You will leave me again?" I whispered, knowing how selfish I sounded. He stood up, shaking his head, then went down on one knee beside my chair.

"No. I will never fucking leave you… I just need to complete this journey so I can be at peace…" he whispered as he cupped my face, brushing away tears that I didn't even know had fallen. "I'll be back. It's just a trip, and the end destination is you."

"Then… I can't stop you," I whispered, flinging my arms around his neck and hugging him tightly. My heart was pounding at just the thought of him leaving. He moved closer, hugging me tightly as he rocked me gently.

No matter what my heart wanted… Theon needed this for himself.

"Thank you," came his quiet reply.

I closed my eyes, shielding the pain in my heart at the thought that he was going away, but for him, I'd hide this pain…

HUNTER

It was evening. I was with Charlene, Zoe, and Ryan, enjoying dinner at a grill house. Both had accepted Charlene with all their hearts, much to my happiness. Zoe, despite the loss of her husband, was doing better, doting over Charlene, and I knew it was a pleasant distraction for her. Ryan had a job to do here, but there was something I wanted to do for Zoe, if she agreed, of course.

"Ah, this meat is delicious," Charlene gushed as she turned the strips of sizzling beef over on the grill in front of us.

"Oi, you are eating too much," Ryan complained, swiping the next cooked piece. Charlene pouted as Zoe swatted Ryan's hand.

"She's expecting, be nice to your sister."

"Favouritism," Ryan complained.

I smirked while watching them. My Luna had gained a little weight with her pregnancy, and I loved it. She looked breathtaking, and I was glad she was keeping my pup fed. I would always remember the time she told me she was pregnant. I was so stunned but happy. I would have a family by my side forever, one I would wake up to and sleep with every day.

"At this rate, you two will eat everything," I remarked, taking the cooked pieces off and sharing them out on everyone's plates as Charlene added more to the grill, licking her lips. That tongue sure could do magical things…

Fuck don't think of that.

"She's pregnant, she has an excuse. Ryan doesn't," Zoe said, smiling up at her son.

"Hmm, I work hard for the queen," he stated. Or with a certain someone…

"That you do," I agreed with a nod. "As you know, Charlene and I must head home after the queen's coronation next week."

Zoe's smile faltered as she nodded with understanding. Charlene looked a little wistful. I knew leaving her sister and family would be something she'd feel.

"Yeah, once you go, more meat for me," Ryan added, giving Charlene a pointed look. They exchanged mock frowns, and I smirked.

"I was thinking you should come with us, Zoe. Ryan will be busy with work here, and until Charlene has the baby, perhaps you can keep her company?" I suggested as Charlene took my hand under the table, giving it a squeeze as she looked at me in surprise. Our eyes met, and I leaned over, kissing her forehead softly before turning to Zoe, who looked rather shocked.

"I… go to the Iron Claw Pack?" She looked at Ryan, who gazed down at her with a far softer expression.

"Why are you looking at me? If you want to go, go. I think it's a good idea. You women seem to bond super great anyway."

"I don't want you to be alone here either," she explained gently, looking at him with concern. He frowned slightly and sighed, looking at his plate, a thoughtful expression on his face.

"As Hunter said, I am busy with work, and I won't be alone, Mom. I have Raiden and the others here. You're the one who is home alone for a lot of the day. I think it'll do you good and keep your mind off things." He was a little unfiltered at times, but the boy had a good head on his shoulders. Zoe nodded slowly before smiling.

"I think I will. I want to be there when my grandchild comes into this world," she said, looking over at Charlene with happiness and sadness in her eyes. For Grayson. He would truly be proud of her.

Charlene reached over the table, taking her hand and giving it a gentle squeeze as they both exchanged a tender smile.

"I would love that, too," she whispered as Ryan swiped the entire grill of meat sneakily.

This was going to be good for both women. Zoe had lost her mate and needed something to fill that void, and Charlene had a father she had just found stripped from her…

"Oi! You took it all!" Charlene exclaimed, despite the smile of amusement on her face.

"He's a glutton!" Zoe added.

"You two always tag team against me," Ryan grumbled. I didn't say anything, placing a fresh round on the grill as Zoe chuckled.

"You know, Grayson was a glutton, too..."

"Really?" Charlene asked with interest clear in her beautiful eyes.

Zoe nodded before she began telling her tale. Charlene leaned forward with avid anticipation, still holding my hand. Even Ryan was paying attention, although he was pretending not to.

"Yes, in fact, he ate so much he was banned from all-you-can-eat nights down at the tavern...."

They were all going to be okay because although we never got over someone's loss, we learned to carry on without them. Death is but a part of life, one that we will always experience at some point...

The Coronation

ı

YILEYNA

HE DAY OF THE coronation had arrived. I was wearing a sequined strapless silver dress, which was fully embroidered and encrusted with pearls and jewels on the bodice. It was fitted to just above my knees before it flared out with a long trail behind it. The embroidery was lighter on the skirt, with a full border at the bottom. A matching cape stood to the side that I would wear once it was time to take my oath.

My make-up was glowing, and my hair was half pinned up with soft curls tumbling down my back. I wore silver heels, as well as a large silver necklace and earrings. Matching gloves reached my elbows, and I wore a few rings.

I was currently in the new royal quarters, a place I had chosen for Theon and myself. It was towards the back of the castle, despite it not usually being the place preferred by royals as it was smaller. However, the view was stunning. Looking out over the gardens below and the coast in the distance had tempted me to choose this part of the castle. Also… it was somewhere Dad used to come to do paperwork, and because he didn't want me disturbing the other men working, he would bring his work here so I could play.

Today was a day that would hold many memories, but it was also Theon's last day before he went on his journey of redemption. The day had come too fast, but I knew before he could let himself enjoy life in contentment that he needed to do this.

A knock on the open door made my heart skip a beat as his scent filled my nose. I turned, and the two Omegas lowered their heads to their other Alpha before they left the room, giving us some privacy. Theon's eyes ran over me as he slowly entered the room, closing the door behind him. His eyes were blazing as they drank me up slowly, and I felt my cheeks heat up, knowing exactly what he was thinking...

"Theon... your thoughts and gaze are turning me on, and I'm needed in the throne room in a few minutes," I whispered.

Oh, if we weren't werewolves with such a sensitive sense of smell, I wouldn't mind him pinning me right there and taking me hard...

He looked incredible in a black tunic, dark grey pants, and black boots. His sword was in his sheath, and, despite the fact he wore no jewellery, he still looked like the king I knew he was. He didn't need the title to be known as one.

"You look... absolutely fuckable right now," he growled, his eyes dipping to my breasts. I bit my lip, locking my arms around his neck, only for him to grab my waist and yank me against him.

"As do you," I whispered. "I know that neither of us will be sleeping tonight."

"Oh, absolutely," he murmured, squeezing my ass as our eyes met, and we kissed. I could feel his hands tightening on my waist. The urge to grab my hair was one he was resisting as he kissed me hard, sending off those euphoric sparks that always consumed me.

We broke apart, breathing heavily, and for a moment, we simply remained close, our noses brushing, our lips teasingly caressing each other, letting off volts of electricity. He reached up, removing the large necklace I was wearing and placing it down on the vanity table behind me.

"I told you, little storm, the only thing that I want around this neck of yours is my hand," he growled huskily, wrapping his hand around my neck, making me gasp.

"Understood, Alpha," I whispered.

Our eyes met once more, and at that moment, if we didn't hear footsteps, I knew we would have lost control. My heart was still thumping when one of my advisors and Raiden approached, announcing that we were to go to the throne room.

The matching lace robe was placed around my shoulders by the Omegas, and then I took a deep breath, ready to do this...

"I, Yileyna De'Lacor, vow to protect the people of Astalion with everything I have. To uphold the laws and regulations of the kingdom and its people. To carry out justice and to always rule with a pure heart," I finished as I held the staff of truth and the sword of justice in my hands.

"I give you Alpha Queen Yileyna De'Lacor, the true ruler of the middle kingdom. Rise and bow to your sovereign," the high priest proclaimed, and then everyone stood and bowed down to me.

"Long live the Queen!"

The symphony began playing as I cast a quick glance around, proud to see the Fae, Nagas, and Sirens amongst the werewolves. All my loved ones were there, too. They smiled up at me with pride and approval as I placed the staff and sword down.

I stood, bearing the huge crown upon my head, and made my way down the steps where Theon was waiting for me. A faint ghost of a smile upon his face, he held his arm out to me. I smiled, knowing this was not the kind of thing Theon enjoyed, but for me, he was playing the part so perfectly. I slid my hand around his bicep, squeezing the muscle slightly as we walked out of the throne room and onto the balcony, where our people were awaiting us. I was going to miss having Theon here for the next few months... I pushed the thought away and smiled down upon my people.

The moment they spotted me, the sound of trumpets filled the air, the gong of the bell of Selene's temple rang loudly, and everyone broke into applause.

Wave to your people, My Queen, Theon said mockingly through the link.

Oh, is Alpha Theon teaching me etiquette? I asked teasingly as I raised my gloved hand, waving to my people.

Not at all.

I smiled as I pressed myself closer to him. This was home, where Theon was beside me and my people, safe and content.

Thank you for making this possible, for helping rid this kingdom of evil, I said softly as I turned and kissed him on the lips...

It was evening, and we were all enjoying the banquet, drinking and indulging in the lavish feast that had been prepared for all.

"I'm going to miss you," I said, holding Charlene's hands tightly. I had removed my cape, along with my gloves, and replaced the huge crown with a slightly smaller one.

"I shall too..." she replied, her eyes filled with sadness. She looked breathtaking in a pale peachy nude dress. It was a sequined net dress with an open-front tulle skirt on top. They would be leaving at dawn... just like Theon. No one knew about him yet, and I decided to leave it to Theon to tell them if he wanted. Although I would feel lonely, I didn't want Hunter to delay returning any longer when he had already been here long enough, considering he had a pack to handle too.

"You know, the way they act, I wonder if they love each other more or their mates..." Ryan smirked, making both Theon and Hunter look at one another and then at us. Charlene's eyes widened, and I smiled.

"A sister's bond is far different than that of a mate's. No one can replace Theon, and no one can replace Charlene," I said, smiling as I kissed my queen's forehead. "Charlene will always be my queen, and nothing will ever change that."

"Ah, it is a bond that even I'm jealous of," Thea teased, "but I'm lucky. I have two amazing brothers..."

Thalia... I could see she was remembering her from the look in her eyes. Hunter put his arm around her, and then Theon reached over and poked her cheek.

"Well, you have both of us as your sisters now," I said with a smile, and Charlene nodded in agreement.

"Yes, you do," she said, holding her hand out to her.

"I will have to remind myself not to get jealous of my sister-in-law," Hunter joked, drinking his wine.

"I don't think you need to worry. Theon's already looking rather positively jealous," Raiden added with a small smile.

"Jokes aside, Yileyna is right; a sister's bond is not the same as a mate's, and no matter what life throws at us, we always remain strong," Charlene reminisced. It was true... so much had happened, yet we were stronger than ever.

"Yeah. Remember the days you both were so infatuated with Theon? Charlene, more so, I'd say," Ryan remarked, eating a pastry from a passing waiter's tray. Silence fell over us as Hunter and Thea both looked at Charlene, who blushed.

"It was just a crush…" she mumbled, rushing over to Hunter, who looked surprised now. They exchanged words through the bond, and he looked satisfied. Charlene looked at us, rushing to explain herself. "Once Yileyna and he went further, I instantly took him off limits. I promise -" Hunter cut her off with a finger to her lips.

"It's fine. You're mine," he stated before pulling her close and kissing her. Although he said it was fine, it was clear he was feeling possessive. Thea giggled.

"Oh damn, poor Hunter." She giggled. "They are both handsome, so I think both girls are lucky."

"Seriously, Ryan, can you stop spilling everyone's secrets?" Raiden remarked, shaking his head.

"I didn't spill the fact you and Yileyna kissed…" he trailed off when Theon's eyes flashed, cutting him off. Thea shrugged.

"I already knew that," she murmured, wrapping her arms around Raiden's neck. He bent down, kissing her lips as Ryan shrugged.

"Great," he said, unbothered.

"So how about the fact you have been meeting a certain red-headed Siren pretty often, to the point it's not even in the White Dove…" Theon remarked as he pulled me close, wrapping his arm around my waist tightly. My eyes widened in surprise as I realised who he meant. Ariella.

Ryan simply smirked, choosing not to answer.

"Ooo…" Thea giggled.

"So is a Siren fun?" Hunter teased.

"Ask Theon," Ryan shot back, and all eyes turned on us.

"Let's not discuss our sex life," I said sweetly, blushing whilst Theon simply raised an eyebrow.

"Who said they were talking about sex?" He asked, smirking mockingly, making my cheeks darken as the rest laughed.

"So tell us, do you like to do it in Siren form?" Thea asked in a loud whisper, getting a shocked look from Charlene but making Hunter and Ryan snicker.

"She'll tell us in private," she mouthed quietly to Thea, although everyone heard.

Oh, will you? Theon asked through the link, kissing my neck.

Not everything, don't worry. Some things are just for the two of us... I whispered back through the mind link. But, you know... do you want to fuck me in Siren form?

He moved back slightly, his eyes searching mine, but he didn't reply, simply kissing me hungrily. I think I just got my answer.

"So, Prince Theon -" Thea began, only for Theon to glare at her.

"I will be referred to as Alpha. Prince is merely a title I will hold but not use when I marry Yileyna, and that isn't for a while."

"Yes, don't tease, or he'll never marry me," I pouted.

"Since he's getting everything already, what incentive does he have to marry her?" Ryan asked.

"It's not that, it's the title of -" Charlene was cut off by Ryan and Thea.

"Prince Theon," they cackled, making me sigh.

"Cut it out." Theon's voice was low yet dangerous, and both fell silent. I guess some things never changed...

"Ah, the newly crowned queen." We turned as Zarian came over. In all his lavish clothing and a crown upon his head, he looked like a true prince.

"Your Highness, it's a pleasure to see you here," I replied equally formally before we both chuckled, and he met me with a kiss on the hand.

He turned to greet the rest, and I looked around the room, feeling content. We chatted for a while before I looked at Theon. I didn't say a word, simply leading him to the dance floor...

The party had died down, and Theon and I had made our way to the roof of the Moon Goddess's Temple. We simply sat there, side by side, holding hands. I looked over to the sea in the distance. The waves were crashing against the shore, and I sighed softly.

"Do you miss it?" Theon asked quietly. "Being near the sea, or onboard a ship?"

"Mm, yes. I have always been drawn to the sea, but my place is on land," I replied quietly.

"One day, let's go on a cruise and visit several kingdoms, not as Alpha Queen, but just Theon and Yileyna," he suggested, making my heart skip a beat. I looked up at him.

"Do you think we can do that?" I asked softly.

"Absolutely. When I return… we will have plenty of time. I'll make sure you enjoy life to the fullest, just like your father wanted you to," he promised quietly. My heart ached slightly, but it wasn't painful like it once used to be.

"Yes… let's do that, Theon," I whispered, looking up at him with a spark of excitement igniting within me. "Come back quick, okay?" He nodded. Bending down, he kissed my lips deeply.

"I plan to, and when I do, I won't leave you again," he whispered seriously, and I knew he would hold true to his words.

"Write to me, okay?" I whispered, trying to hide my pain at the fact that he was leaving.

"I will, at every stop, let you know where I will be next," he promised. I pouted and nodded.

"Good, because if you take too long, I will need to find other men to please me. You know my desires cannot be satiated easily." I frowned, although it was only partially the truth. I would never cheat on him, but I hoped the threat scared him a little.

He didn't reply, and I looked up at him only to be met with a dangerous look. His eyes blazed as he leaned over, grabbing my throat just the way I liked, sending an intense jolt of pleasure to my core.

"No one will ever touch you, little storm, aside from me. Do I make myself clear?"

Of course, my possessive Alpha.

"No. Maybe you need to be a little clearer, Prince Theon," I whispered teasingly, raking my claws down his shirt, tearing through the fabric as I licked my lips hungrily. His eyes flashed as he pushed me to the ground.

"You are going to get a lesson and a fucking punishment for calling me prince," he growled, making my pussy clench.

Yes, please.

Oh, I knew it was going to be one hell of a lesson…

HIS DEPARTURE

THEON

WE HADN'T SLEPT THAT night. Even after sex, we couldn't sleep, not with the fact that I would be gone in the morning…

My heart felt heavy as I picked up my coat, and my small bag was ready. She stood there dressed in one of my shirts with a corset around her waist, paired with simple grey pants. Her heart was thundering as she watched me. It fucking hurt…

She had bidden Charlene, Hunter, and Zoe goodbye just an hour ago, and now it was time for me to leave. I knew she didn't want me to go; I had seen the tears she shed when she thought I was asleep in the early hours of the morning, the front she put on to be strong… and I fucking wished I could be here, but until I felt like I had done enough to be worthy of her, I would never be at ease. Yet, once again, because of me, she was hurting.

"Hey… if you want, cry," I said quietly, pulling her into my arms and tightening my hold. Fuck, I was going to miss her. A soft, heart-breaking whimper escaped her as she bunched my shirt into her fists.

"I… I don't want to make it harder for you, but do you have to go?" She whispered, looking up at me with those beautiful iridescent eyes of hers. Fuck, if only you knew how much I didn't want to…

"I'm not a good person Yileyna, not the type of Alpha you need by your side right now. I've committed so many crimes. I need to do this, but know that this is fucking hard for me. Fuck, I wish I could get rid of these thoughts and just stay here because you know the only place I want to be is with you, or in you," I whispered, looking down at her as I cupped the side of her face with one hand. "But I also want to be the man you fucking deserve."

"You saying that already shows you are that man," she whispered.

Fuck, beautiful, don't make this harder...

I kissed her lips deeply, knowing that it was going to hurt... so fucking much. To be deprived of her... to be away from her... waking up alone... sleeping without her...

"When I return, I'm never leaving you again," I vowed before I claimed her lips in another deep, passionate kiss.

She kissed me back like there was no tomorrow, tears streaming down her cheeks. The pain was fucking unbearable. The intense sparks of the bond danced between us, swirling around us like a storm. She was my world.

When she needed air, I slowly pulled away, not wanting to ever let go. I threaded my fingers into her hair, our noses brushing against each other's.

"I will always write and look forward to hearing what you have been up to around here," I said quietly. She nodded, hugging me tightly.

"I will miss you, Theon... so much... I love you." Her emotions were intense, and I could hear them in her voice.

"I'll fucking miss you too, little storm. You will definitely be the only thing on my mind day in and day out... it will be my incentive to return as soon as my work is done." I pressed my lips against her forehead, inhaling her scent. Fuck I hated the fact that we would be apart...

She said nothing, clinging to me, and I held her as if she would fucking break if I squeezed too hard. Our hearts were racing, and even when I slowly led the way to the door of the cabin, it was hard, like I was having to drag my feet. She held onto me tightly as she walked me to the edge of the city, her heart beating fast as soft rain fell from the skies. It wasn't so cold anymore, and I knew the rain was her doing. Each step was difficult to take knowing I would be saying goodbye very soon.

I was fucking right... to be away from her was the worst fucking punishment. I was also punishing her with my punishment.

"May the gods be with you," she whispered when we stopped at the open gates to the city.

"And with you," I replied quietly.

I looked her over slowly, wanting to burn this image of her into my mind. My beautiful little storm... from her gorgeous blond hair that fell to her hips, her voluptuous breasts, narrow waist, and curvy hips. Those dainty hands and those plump lips...

"Wait for me, beautiful."

She nodded, unable to speak for a few moments as she gripped my wrists, and I cupped her face, kissing her once more. Many were gathered, and although they kept their distance, their eyes were on us, but I didn't care...

"The Alpha's leaving." The whispers had begun spreading, and I knew before noon everyone would know.

"I will. I will always be waiting," she whimpered, her voice breaking as I ran my thumb over her lips.

"Be strong."

She was fucking strong, I didn't need to tell her that.

I kissed her one final time before I slowly forced myself away from her. She tried to smile, her lips quivering as Raiden walked over with the reins of a stallion in his hands. We exchanged looks and I said nothing out loud.

Take care of her.

I will, he replied, and I knew he would. He may be Thea's mate but there was a level of love that he held for his queen.

Thea was watching me, too. She looked upset but was trying to keep strong, and I gave her a tight hug.

"Take care of yourself." She nodded.

"You too, Theon. Don't take too long. We are all waiting for you to return."

"I will try not to," I said, ruffling her hair.

"You will be missed," Raiden said quietly.

I couldn't reply as I stared at the woman I loved. She was staring back at me, trying to be strong... she really was so fucking brave.

"I love you, little storm... take care of yourself."

She nodded, and I cupped her face one final time, kissing her so deeply that I hoped she never forgot it before I pulled away and mounted my horse. I couldn't look back, her pain through the bond crushing me as I urged the horse into a gallop.

I love you more than life itself, I murmured through the bond.

Same, you have taken my sunrise and my sunset... return to me soon, my love.

I will. I will, little storm.

I kept the link open, our emotions mixing into one but neither of us could speak any longer as I nudged my horse to go faster. The sound of his hooves hitting the dirt and the wind rushing through my ears were all I could hear.

I never expected so much from life, but she had given me a taste of what I may have. I opened my heart to her, a heart I never knew I had, one that she forced me to reveal to her. I learned to feel and love; all of that was because of her. Although I hurt her countless times, she still loved me through it all. I was so focused on revenge that I was blinded to everything, and I committed crimes that I would never be able to forgive myself for, above all, her parents' death. Yet she found it within her to forgive me.

Theoden was dead, and the truth was unveiled. Now all that was left was for me to do what I could for this kingdom and for my queen, and then... then I would return to her, marry her, and spend the rest of my fucking life with her.

Wait for me, little storm, because I will be back.

ℰPILOGUE

YILEYNA
NINE MONTHS LATER...

Nine months had passed, and I lived for Theon's letters. In his absence, I put my head down, focusing on the changes I wanted to see in the kingdom. I even found time to visit Deliana down in the sea. She had been happy; I often went for a swim in Siren form with her.

A lot had changed. Hunter and Charlene had a beautiful baby boy, who they named Nathanial Gray Carson, after Nathalia and Grayson. It was the perfect name for him. He was an adorable little boy with brown hair and big, soft green eyes. To my absolute delight, Charlene spent a few weeks here when he was a month old, and I loved their company, enjoying the chance to shower my nephew with lots and lots of love and gifts. I didn't want to give him back, but I had to. Oh, he was adorable! I wrote to Charlene almost as often as Theon, although the messages were so much lighter than the longing and pain I tried to hide in the ones to my beloved.

Thea and Raiden were engaged, and they would wed in a year or so. I had a feeling they were waiting for Theon's return. Everyone tried to make me feel better. Though I hid my emotions, they knew I missed him, and in turn, they tried not to talk about him, so as not to upset me.

As for Ryan, much to everyone's surprise, he and Ariella were in a relationship. It wasn't the standard type of relationship, but they were both happy. Although she no longer worked at the White Dove, she still had her harem in the sea. Ryan made it clear he should be the only man in her life, but he didn't care for the fish in her life. It was an insult to mermen, but she had simply laughed and agreed. Lately, I saw her more and more on land, to the point that they even purchased a place together near the coast where she lived with him, with the water not so far from her. They were getting serious, and despite everyone being quite shocked, I was happy about their union. Unlike me, who was a tri-form shifter, she was a pure Siren, but they were perfect for one another despite being two entirely different species who were not mated. I just secretly prayed Ryan never made her angry with his unconventional remarks at times.

Everything with the kingdoms around Astalion was going well, and I had even received letters from beyond the neighbouring kingdoms, invitations to weddings, and gifts to congratulate me on my new position as queen.

The only thing missing was Theon, and although I visited the cabin often, keeping it clean, he was missed. The cabin on the left had been on sale, and I had purchased it for more land. I even had a wall built around the entire garden and began planting flowers in my free time. I had set up a little pond in the now much larger garden. I hoped one day we could make the cabin larger, where we could come and spend the weekends with our children someday.

I miss you, Theon. Come home soon…

It was just another day. I was currently in my office working; I had spent the morning in court handling affairs of the kingdom before I spent an hour signing documents and legislations for certain building projects that were to be started soon. Ah, I was tired!

I sat back in my chair, looking out at the leaves that were swirling around in the air. Summer had come and gone; autumn had arrived, yet there was still no sign of Theon's return. Nine months had passed since he had left. His letters still came, accompanied by gifts. There was always something different from where he had visited, from jewellery to clothes, or an ornament, things I treasured and placed in our cabin, but I still wanted him there. That would be the greatest gift I could ever ask or hope for.

I left my office and returned to my quarters, smiling politely at those who greeted or bowed to me in the halls. I went to our bedroom and, sitting on my bed, I opened my bedside drawer. I took out the pile of letters and the last gift he had sent me; a pair of earrings from the village of Frindor. I smiled faintly as I looked at the beautiful silver earrings set with an array of jewels in aqua blues and greens with some purple. They were intricate and beyond beautiful.

I often heard of Theon's endeavours from those who visited, or from other Alphas. True to his word, he helped in every village he went to, not only making sure things were in place, but physically helping around the town. He would usually send a request written personally with what he thought the village could use, alongside a private letter to me alone. I would then send my reply, the supplies, and anything he needed before he would have a final letter sent back to me, telling me where he was headed next.

Over the months, hearing him talk, I could feel it was helping him. The mentions of not deserving me, or how he must do more became lesser. I could tell his anticipation to return was growing and I, too, wished for him to be here.

I picked up his last letter, my heart clenching as I ran my hand down the paper. He had touched this...

"Dear Storm,

I love you and I miss you.

Days in Frindor went by well, and I've now moved on. To think, in nine months I have travelled the kingdom, is something that I'm proud of. At every stop, as always, people wished to know when I was to return to my queen, or when we would have heirs. It's odd, and as much as I refused to accept the title of king, it's all I'm called these days, unless I am extra firm that Alpha is fine. Being called king is a word that I only yearn to hear from your lips.

I smiled. Of course, no matter what he thought, he was already king the day he led the army into Westerwell and to victory. I placed the letter against my lips, kissing it softly as I closed my eyes, inhaling it. I miss you, my love... I fought back the tears and paid attention to the letter once more.

Hunter is demanding a playmate for Nathanial, too, last I heard from him anyway. I met him, and he was cute, I will admit that, but as I said, I want some time for just you and me...

Congratulations on the opening of your school for the kids in the orphanage in Westerwell.

And as for your question regarding how many women tried to seduce me… not many, and I assure you none got within a foot of me. Rest assured, this man belongs to you and only you.

I saw these earrings; they reminded me of you. I hope you like them; I don't really have much taste in jewellery.

I know you miss me, and I promise I will return soon, and when I do, I want to make you mine. I will marry you, little storm, I promise. Let's have a small wedding, just us, family, and friends. Maybe by the sea so your Siren family can be there, too. Will you wear a white dress or something different?

I think of you, like always, before I sleep. You fill my dreams and I often find myself imagining fucking you in every way possible. Soon.

Love – Yours forever – Theon Alexander.

I lay down slowly, clutching the letter to my chest.

I want that, I want to wear a dress you love, Theon. I want to marry you and promise myself to you forever…

I had even purchased him a ring with a chain so he could wear it around his neck, so he wouldn't lose it when he shifted. I just want you back…

I don't know when I fell asleep, the tears silently streaming down my cheeks. His letters brought happiness, yet with them came the wave of strong emptiness that he was not here with me…

"Yileyna, hurry up!" Thea scolded as she finished playing with my hair.

I looked in the mirror. I still got dressed up; as queen, I had an image to keep, but really, I did not think it was necessary. She and Raiden had invited me to dinner at a special place, and so she wanted me to dress up just as she was. I was wearing a low-cut organza embroidered dress. The net was a violet colour with the underneath layer a pretty aqua blue, giving it a two-toned effect. There was a ribbon drawstring corset around the waist and the dress fell to my knees.

My hair was up in a low bun, with two braids down the side and a few strands of my hair framing my face. The only jewellery I wore were the beautiful earrings Theon had sent this time and the engagement ring. Oh, how I missed him.

"Okay, okay, I'm coming."

I stood up, slipping on my sandals and hurrying after her. Raiden was dressed smartly, too, and he was smiling when he saw the both of us, offering Thea a hand.

"So, it's a little walk, but let's get going," he said, kissing Thea softly.

"Where's this picnic?" I asked, thinking neither was holding anything.

"The Omegas have set it up. It's a beautiful spot that Theon discovered, actually, when he did a search of the city before the coronation and thought it would make a rather beautiful haven."

"He really didn't leave even a stone unturned," I mused, looking up at the night sky as we walked through the streets of Westerwell.

"No, he didn't. We all await the return of the king," Raiden said quietly.

I nodded and Thea sighed softly as we carried on walking. People stopped to greet us, complimenting Thea and me, asking how I was and, of course, about their king.

"When is King Theon returning, My Queen?" An elderly woman asked seriously.

"I am not sure yet. We can hope soon," I replied, smiling gracefully.

"Ah yes… we want our king back so the city is complete." I nodded and I gazed at the sky.

See, Theon? This city needs you home. They acknowledge you for the king you are, not for your past deeds that feel like years ago… Come home, my love.

We kept walking, leaving the people behind.

"Those earrings are so pretty. Another gift from Theon?" Thea asked.

I nodded, feeling a bit guilty. He had sent Thea a few items alongside mine, but I felt bad that they were far less than the letters and gifts to me… he spoiled me.

"They are beautiful. Don't worry, I don't feel jealous. You are his queen, I'm just his sister who is now mated." Thea grinned as she kissed Raiden's hand, which was intertwined with hers. "Raiden gives me plenty." They exchanged a moment, and I smiled, watching them. They were perfect for each other.

The ground became rockier as we continued on foot in silence. Raiden led the way, and soon we were stumbling along steep cliffs and then going down. This was away from the coast where Charlene and I used to play. Finally, we slowed down at the rocky arch that held a pair of doors, and I could see a wall surrounding this area. Many new places had been built around Westerwell; this one was not one I had paid attention to before. Well, it's not like I come around this side often.

"What is this place?" I asked as Raiden pushed the doors open slowly. They creaked open to reveal the dim glow from ahead.

"Oh, it's pretty! Let's keep going. Is the picnic further ahead, baby?" Thea asked Raiden.

"Yeah, straight's through," he murmured, pulling her close.

They began kissing, and I walked ahead, giving them a moment alone as I looked around the empty, rocky land that was sealed away behind the doors.

I could see an archway ahead, and I carried on walking, spotting the glimmer of light from somewhere further on. I walked through the next archway, feeling compelled to keep going. Three identical archways later, I came to a halt as I gazed at the scene before me: a pool with red rose petals and candles in the water. At the edge of the water were a tray of wine, a bouquet of red roses, and a platter of chocolates and fruit. There were trees around the side of the rocky wall that surrounded the place, and with the night sky above, it was like a magical little world. My eyes snapped to the large four-poster bed that was covered with just organza curtains, right ahead past the pool. It was breathtakingly beautiful. Whichever Omegas had planned this, they had indeed outdone themselves. I spotted a table to the side with two chairs, platters of food covered, simmering on a grill in the middle.

Oh no, I think this was meant to be for Thea and Raiden. The Omegas must have misunderstood! Well, I need to somehow make an excuse and leave! I couldn't intrude on their romantic evening. I turned, ready to leave, when I thought I smelt something intoxicating… something familiar. My heart pounded as I spun around, scanning the area. Nothing.

I shook my head, turning away. How stupid. Of course, he wasn't there… I started to walk back the way I came when I heard footsteps behind me.

"Leaving so soon?" The seductive, deep voice that reminded me of a winter's night in front of the hearth came.

I froze in my tracks, my heart racing so fast I could barely breathe as I stared ahead, unable to move for a few seconds until I felt him behind me. His scent hit me like an avalanche. His arms wrapped around me from behind, sending electrifying jolts of pleasure through me, and then reality hit.

He was here. Goddess, he was here.

"I missed you, little storm."

He was home. He came back to me. His lips met my neck in a deep kiss, and I could feel every muscle in his body tense as he controlled himself from ravishing me. His kisses became hungrier as I forced myself to turn in his arms. I looked up at the man I had so dearly missed. Our eyes locked, his blazing mix of oranges and golds meeting my own. My emotions made my hands shake as I cupped his face.

"You're home."

"I'm home."

He smiled faintly before our lips met in a deep, passionate kiss, a kiss that made my knees give way, and if he wasn't holding me, I would have fallen. The prickles of his short beard tickled my chin. The minty taste of his mouth and his scent devoured me just as his lips dominated mine, kissing me hard and rough. He lifted me entirely from the ground, and I wrapped my legs around his waist as I kissed him back hungrily. He pushed me against the wall, slipping his tongue into my mouth like a man starved for far too long.

I moaned helplessly, my core clenching. The scent of my arousal hung in the air as Theon's hands ran down my back, squeezing my ass, and the moment I gasped for air, he broke away, instead kissing me down my jaw and neck. My eyes fluttered shut, and my heart filled with so many emotions as I hugged him tightly, drowning in the pleasure he was inflicting me with. I was in his arms once more…

He kissed my breasts before making his way back to my neck and then my lips. This time we kissed slower, relishing and savouring every caress. It was deep and sensual, and my heart was thumping when we finally broke away. I looked at him as I breathed hard. His hair was longer, reaching his shoulders. He had a slight beard and tan. Was it just me, or did he just look even sexier? Was that even possible?

"I missed you," I whispered, running my fingers through his hair before I hugged him tightly, not caring that I was burying his face in my breasts.

I missed you too, he replied through the link, his lips grazing against my breasts.

I slowly let my legs down, biting my lip at the large shaft that was straining against his black pants. He looked incredible in them, with a smart white shirt.

"You look breathtaking," he complimented huskily, looking at me with so many emotions in those amber eyes that I was unable to reply. The love, the adoration... the animalistic hunger that he was fighting to control...

My own desires were about to devour me, and although I had so many questions for him, I knew until we had satiated our hunger, we wouldn't be able to talk.

"Take me, Theon," I whispered.

His eyes blazed. There he was, my dominant, sexy, animalistic Alpha. He tangled his hand in my hair, yanking my head back as he ran his tongue from the tip of my ear down my neck, making me sigh softly.

"Strip," he commanded, stepping back as he slowly began to undo his buttons, his eyes upon me.

My heart thundered as I slowly began undoing the string ties on my dress before I unzipped it and slowly slipped it off my shoulders. I teasingly turned my back to him, pushing my dress down my waist sensually and shimmying it off my hips. I could feel his gaze on me and heard him swear when I revealed my ass in a tiny aqua thong to him before I kicked off my sandals. I didn't turn, my heart thundering as I reached for my hair, pulling out my pins, knowing he liked my hair down.

"Fuck."

I heard him growl. I smiled seductively as I turned back to him, covering my nipples with my hands.

"Like what you see?"

"Fuck, yes," he murmured as he pulled his shirt off, stepping closer.

Oh, Goddess...

He was divine... from his tattooed chest to those muscles.... The scars that remained from my attack only made him look even more dangerous, and that delicious Adonis belt... oh, Goddess...

He watched me, and I knew when he caught me... I'd be ravished by the beast he was. I smiled teasingly, backing away before I turned and jumped into the water. I laughed as the water splashed him, but it didn't deter him. In a flash, he was in the water, his hand wrapping around my upper arm as he pinned me against the stone wall of the pool. I gasped as I felt his manhood press against my pussy.

His mouth latched onto my nipple, and he sucked hard, making me gasp. After a moment, he bit down on it, making me cry out as pain and pleasure rushed to my core. His hand was already tearing away my thong from me as his fingers rubbed my clit. Oh, fuck, I needed this…

I missed this so much. Oh, fuck…

I swallowed hard and enjoyed the pleasure as he bit and sucked on the area around my nipple, making me whimper and moan in pleasure before he did the same to the other, leaving dark hickeys in his wake. He lifted me up and placed me on the edge of the pool, a few red petals clinging to my skin. He admired me for a moment before he pushed open my legs and plunged his tongue into me. Heaven. I was in pure bliss.

"Fuck, Theon… that's it… oh, fuck, lick my pussy just like that…" I whimpered, not caring how horny I sounded.

Wave after wave of pleasure rushed through me as he devoured me, not letting up even when I gasped for air. He thrust two fingers into me, and I felt myself nearing, my juices leaking out of me, but he still didn't move back. Our eyes met, and when he flicked my clit hard, I cried out, teetering on the edge.

"Come for me," he commanded huskily, and I let myself go, staring up at the night sky as my vision darkened. I saw stars as that immense storm of pure blistering pleasure washed through me, wave after intense wave.

"Yes, oh, fuck, Goddess!" I moaned as Theon pulled me close, licking up my juices.

"Fuck, you taste so good," he growled.

"I want to taste myself," I whispered hornily.

Moaning, Theon slammed his fingers into me, sweeping them around inside of me before he slid them out and slipped them into my mouth. I whimpered, licking them clean, but there was something else I wanted in my mouth.

When Theon ran his tongue down my pussy and between my ass, I whimpered. I locked my legs around his neck and pulled myself up onto his broad, muscular shoulders, sighing as his tongue went deeper into me, making me moan louder as he cupped my ass. Oh, fuck…

I unhooked my legs, letting them drop into the water before I went underwater, yanking his pants down and admiring his cock. Oh, I was in heaven…

His hand tangled in my hair as I wrapped my mouth around his cock. This felt good underwater. I began sucking him harder, feeling he was near, and as much as I wanted him to come in my mouth, I wanted him to fuck me, too…

"Fuck!" He growled as he began ramming into my mouth harder, hitting the back of my throat.

His moves became rougher. He reached down, grabbing my breast, squeezing it hard as I moaned against his dick. Low groans of pleasure escaped him, and I looked up at him, my heart full of so many emotions. I ran my hands up his hard, muscular thighs, moaning in approval. He was so damn sexy…

He was back… he was back home where he belonged…

When he came, releasing his load into my mouth, he yanked me up, breathing hard as he kissed me roughly on my sore lips. His hands were squeezing and raking over every inch of my body, and when he pushed me up against the stone wall, parting my legs and thrusting into me, making me cry out, I struggled to breathe. Fuck, he was so big…

I clung to him as he began fucking me so good, rough, and fast, just the way I liked it. He hardened once again, each brutal thrust hitting the perfect spot. My cries of pleasure filled the air.

A devious thought came to my mind. I shifted, exchanging my legs for a tail. Theon froze as he looked down at my pussy. His eyes darkened as he pulled out, running his finger between my slit and rubbing my clit. I whimpered as he shifted position, positioning his legs on either side of my tail and thrusting into me once more. He wrapped his hand around my neck, the other playing with my breasts as he continued to fuck me.

His eyes dipped down, watching as he fucked me before he looked into my eyes, his lips crashing against mine in a sizzling kiss once more…

An hour later, we were both still in the pool. Well, Theon was; I was sitting on the edge with my legs in the water. I had an organza sheet wrapped loosely around me, eating some of the fruit dipped in melted chocolate as he stood between my legs.

I had wanted so much more, to keep going, wanting him to take me repeatedly, but I knew if we didn't force ourselves to stop, we wouldn't be able to at all.

"Does it have a charm on it?" He murmured, looking at my ring before kissing my fingertips and licking the chocolate that coated two of my fingers.

"I didn't know you would be back," I replied, tilting my head. My heart skipped a beat, realising why he had asked. We had just had unprotected sex. He kissed my thigh.

"Hmm..."

Our eyes met, but I knew if I ended up pregnant, this child would be loved by both of us.

"It doesn't matter. So, when did you return?" I asked softly, playing with his wet hair.

"This morning. I had written to Raiden ahead and had asked for certain supplies. I had commanded this place to be created when I left. Guess they did well. Dinner is over there, although it may be a little cold now. I wanted to come to you... but then I also wanted to surprise you with a little something."

"I'm sure dinner will be perfect. I skipped to dessert, and I loved it. As for all of this... it's more than a little something. Thank you," I murmured before I ran my fingers through his hair.

"In my letter, I asked you to marry me. Will you?" My heart skipped a beat, and I nodded, not needing to think about that.

"Yes. I agreed to be yours the day you took my virginity. From that day, I only ever wanted you," I whispered, bending down and kissing him deeply. The taste of chocolate and wine lingered in his mouth. "But..."

"But?"

"Will you be my king?"

Our eyes met, and I knew he understood what I meant, to take the position of king by my side. Did he still not consider himself worthy? He raised an eyebrow, looking slightly amused.

"Fine. It sounds fucking better than prince, but you will remain the official ruler," he muttered, making me giggle as my heart leapt with joy.

He had finally forgiven himself. I didn't care if he wanted to be king consort... as long as he agreed. It meant he was finally at peace.

"Then I will marry you," I whispered.

"Perfect. Let's do it soon..." he said, his gaze trailing over my breasts.

"Mm, of course... I love you, Theon."

"And I, you, little storm, so fucking much."

I smiled, sliding into the water and kissing him once more...

We spent the night talking and making out long into the night, laughing and catching up over dinner before Theon carried me to the bed, where we would make love until sunrise...

I was once a girl who was naive, living life without worry, unaware of the darkness that poisoned the hearts of men. I was just that young girl who hoped for a day full of giggles and mischief... until my life was ripped from me, and the veil of illusion was lifted from my eyes. When everything was taken from me, I turned to the very man who would become my very rise and my downfall. He became my world. But despite it all, we were drawn together time and time again.

Our journey was full of pain, love, passion, and betrayal, but in the end, it was perfect, with all the imperfections that only made this love even more precious. We were opposites from the day we were born. Heaven and hell, ice and fire...

Born to be two very different people but with one entangled destiny. Against all odds, we survived everything we were subjected to.

My name is Yileyna De'Lacor, and this, this is just the beginning of our story...

THE END

GLOSSARY
SPECIES

WEREWOLVES

Werewolves are one of the fastest growing species on Kaeladia and, due to this, have become the ultimate species in power.

Appearance: Lean, well built, tend to be toned and muscular. Even the women will have more of an athletic build. They are usually more on the tall side. Omega-ranked she-wolves are more feminine in appearance and were originally only for mating purposes.

Abilities: They are extremely strong and fast in both human and wolf form, with heightened senses once they have shifted.

Shifting: The average age of shifting happens between 14-18, however, the earliest recorded shift was 13 years.

Lifespan: Werewolves live to about 200 years old.

Mates: They can find their mates on a full moon as long as both parties have had their shift.

Pregnancy: She-wolves can get pregnant, whether by their mates or another man, does not need to be marked to do so.

Deity: Selene – Said to reside on the moon itself, she cares greatly for her children. Known for her love and compassion.

Feared species: Sirens

NAGAS

A proud race who keeps to themselves. However, if you cross paths with them, it can be life-threatening.

Appearance: Well-built with a human upper half of the body with a scaled snake lower half, and range from anywhere between 5-8 feet when they are upright, however, depending on the actual length of their tails, from head to tip can be anywhere between 15-25 feet. They cannot gain legs on any account. There are different types of Nagas – Sea, Desert, and Forest, and this is reflected in their appearance and habitat.

Abilities: Keen senses, can also speak in snake tongue as well as the common tongue. They can see better in the dark than day. Their bite is poisonous, and they have incredible strength.

Lifespan: Live to about 500 years old.

Mates: Nagas do not have fated mates and tend to live alone, and the females are usually only used for mating purposes.

Deity: Nagina – A goddess known for her cunningness and deception. It is said whoever looks her in the eye would turn to stone.

Feared species: Mages & Sirens

SIRENS

They are not necessarily cruel, but they do have a tendency to look down upon other species, save the Fae. They are often playful with a strong sexual desire; however, if wronged, they will hold grudges.

Appearance: Extremely beautiful with full, large breasts and flawless skin. They tend to be 7-8 feet from head to fin with scales of different colours.

Abilities: The ability to enchant and control their victims through their music. They can see slightly better than humans but nowhere near as far as other species. They can, however, see perfectly underwater and in the dark, including the ability to see everything in colour. They can be of different elements. Most will be water, ice, or air; however, the imperial family often can control the weather itself.

Shifting: Members of the imperial family are the only ones who can take the form of man, however, they would be mistaken for Fae due to their extreme beauty.

Lifespan: They live around 300 years.

Mates: Sirens may often have true mates, and they can sense this by the intense bond towards their counterparts. It may not be as strong as a werewolf's bond, but it does exist.

Deity: Oshera – The sea goddess is said to be equally terrifying and beautiful, with her face of utter beauty yet her lower body a vast darkness of tentacles.

Feared species: Fae

FAE

A powerful species that is smart and powerful.

Appearance: Extremely beautiful, with a leaner and more graceful build. They tend to be tall with flawless features. Their features may often give away what element they hold.

Abilities: Elemental; they have the ability to bend their element and conjure it from thin air. However, taking from the surroundings can fuel their abilities.

Lifespan: Can live to over 1000 years.

Mates: It is rare for them to be mated, yet it has happened a rare few times in history.

Deity: Etaar - A being that was neither male nor female but held such beauty that no mortal could look them in the eye.

Feared species: Naga

MAGES

They are human in every aspect aside from having the ability to cast magic.

Appearance: Human as we are.

Abilities: Can cast spells and enchantments, may be stronger in certain elements than others. There are two types of mages, light and dark, and both follow separate gods. Dark mages are rarer.

Lifespan: Mages live slightly longer than their human counterparts and have an average life span of 150 years.

Deities: Hecate – The goddess of witchcraft (Light)

Dezeenath – The god of trickery (Dark)

Feared species: Werewolves

The eight elements
- Wind
- Water
- Fire
- Earth
- Lightning
- Shadow
- Light
- Ice

OTHER WORKS

FOLLOW ME ON:
Instagram: Author.Muse
Facebook: Author Muse
Amazon: Moonlight Muse

AUTHORS SUPPORTING AUTHORS
Check out these work from some amazing authors!
Tempting Darkness – Jessica Hall – Kindle
The Omega's Awakening – Dee Gleem – Goodnovel
Subduing the Alpha – Yukiro Fayt - Goodnovel

Made in the USA
Monee, IL
30 December 2022

24084925R00222